ALPACALYPSE

HEIDE GOODY

IAIN GRANT

Copyright © 2023 by Heide Goody and Iain Grant

All rights reserved.

No part of this book may be reproduced in any form or by any electronic or mechanical means, including information storage and retrieval systems, without written permission from the author, except for the use of brief quotations in a book review.

1

As he was lowering the shutters for the evening, Ben Kitchen noticed a wallet lying on the cracked pavement outside his shop.

Ben locked the padlock on the shutters and picked up the wallet. It was brown leather and bulged. He hesitated a moment, feeling that to open someone's wallet was to enter a private portion of someone's life, as unpleasantly intimate as sticking your hand in their pocket. Beyond mere money, what would it reveal of the person's inner personality? Would he find betting shop receipts? Condoms? A membership card for the Ku Klux Klan?

Ben wasn't exactly sure if the Ku Klux Klan issued membership cards, but the point was he didn't want to find out.

What he did find was fifty quid in cash, a Blockbuster card, a Hallowed Grounds Café loyalty card, a bus ticket, a business card for a double-glazing firm and a driving licence for one Julio Mendoza Benito Credenza. There was an address on the driver's licence and a picture of Mr Credenza.

Ben recognised both the address and, despite the huge droopy moustache, he recognised the person in the picture.

Ben wouldn't have to take it to the police. Nor would he have to put a sign up in his shop window with the words LOST WALLET FOUND. COME IN AND GIVE A GRAPHIC DESCRIPTION TO CLAIM IT. Nonetheless, the fact that he knew the owner of this wallet was somehow worse.

It was a fifteen minute walk from Ben's bookshop to the Boldmere Oak pub, past charity shops and restaurants, past tidy suburban bungalows and green spaces, past St Michael's church and posh mock Tudor houses. The evening was cool, the walk refreshing and it gave Ben time to think about what the wallet signified and what he should do about it. When he walked into the saloon of the pub, he was still none the wiser.

"Evening, Lennox," he said. "Pint of cider and black."

He took out one of the ten pounds notes from the wallet and passed it over to the barman. "Check that it's not a fake."

Lennox gave him a querying look.

"Dodgy provenance," said Ben.

The money checked out, and Ben was presented with his purple pint. It would soon be six. His friends and housemates would be along soon enough.

The door from the bar slammed opened and a hunched, bearded figure in a soiled raincoat shambled in. The man, limping like a bad actor doing Richard III, approached a group of drinkers.

"Wanna buy a baby?" he said in a throaty growl.

The men, an easy-going blokey bunch, possibly a building crew having a post work bevvy, tried to ignore him.

"Wanna buy a baby?"

Ben saw that the figure had a thickly wrapped bundle in his arm.

"Wanna buy a baby? Reasonable price," he rumbled.

"Piss off, mate," said one of the drinkers and returned to his conversation with the others, about football or sports cars or whatever it was regular blokey men talked about.

The shambling babymonger immediately moved along to the next group: a trio of seasoned all-day drinkers and made his offer again.

"What's that?" said an old boy in an open shirt and gold chain.

"Baby," growled the disgusting man. "Wanna buy it? Good prices."

"What would I want a baby for?"

"Make a nice present for the wife. Bet she'd love a baby. Yours for a thousand pounds."

"Fuck off," said the man in genial surprise at the price.

"Five hundred to you, sir." He jiggled the bundle. "It's a lively one. Nice and fresh."

The old boy pulled a sour face. The offer didn't appeal.

The baby-seller tried two more tables with no more success and then, flashing a glance at Ben, scurried out.

"You saw that?" Ben asked Lennox.

"I saw that," said the barman wearily. "Did you notice how he forgot which leg to limp with partway through and switched?"

"I did not." Ben took a sip of his drink and pulled a face at the delightfully tart flavour. "What the hell was that all about?"

"Wait a minute," said Lennox. "The other one will be here soon."

"The other—?"

The bar door slammed opened and this time, a tall leggy woman with a headscarf knotted under her chin like a Soviet era housewife came staggering in, an overwrought look of distress on her face. She went up to the blokey drinkers.

"Have any of you seen my baby?" she said in an appalled whispered.

The men weren't interested.

"My baby, my baby, she's gone!" she gasped.

"Piss off, love," said one of the blokes.

The woman moved to the next table. The old boy with the gold chain looked her up and down with lingering eyes, sucked his teeth, then seemed to forget she was even there. The woman moved on, table to table and then, momentarily locking eyes with Ben at the bar, dashed out.

Ben simply stared for a while. The little episode with both characters had lasted no more than a minute. "What the hell was that?" he said before stopping himself. "I mean, that man was Jeremy Clovenhoof."

"Yes," said Lennox.

"It looks like he stole that coat off a homeless man."

"Probably did."

"And that beard..."

"Think he just glued a cheap wig to his face."

"And then that woman was obviously Nerys Thomas. The headscarf wasn't much of a disguise."

"I don't think she was prepared to go full method like your Jeremy,"

"And where did they get the baby?"

"It's not a real baby," said Lennox.

"You saw?"

Lennox started stacking clean glasses. "It's the fourth time they've done that routine this week. Yesterday, it was kidneys."

"Kidneys?"

"Kidneys."

"As in he goes round saying 'would anyone like to buy a kidney?', and then she comes in and..."

Lennox nodded. "Looking for her lost kidneys. She'd put some make up on to make her look really pale, but I drew the line at all the fake blood she was dribbling on the floor."

"What did they use for the fake kidneys?" said Ben.

Lennox frowned thoughtfully. "Kidneys," he said. Before Ben could properly choke on his drink added, "Cow kidneys. Pig. I dunno. I'm not great at offal identification."

Ben was stunned, although it was a gentle and familiar kind of stunned. Sharing a house with Jeremy Clovenhoof meant he was so regularly stunned, shocked, astounded and bewildered that he had almost become numb to it all.

"Why do you let them do it?" he said.

"I treat it as a sort of free immersive theatre performance. As long as they don't actually upset anyone or lose me business, I let them get on with it."

Ben downed much of his pint, then showed the barman Mr Credenza's driving licence. "That's just Jeremy with a dodgy moustache," he said.

Lennox looked at it admiringly. "So it is."

"What's he up to?"

Lennox's expression became tight and serious for a moment. Lennox had been landlord of the Boldmere Oak for decades. He was a big, easy-going man who worked hard, treated everyone fairly and didn't let life faze him. He rarely assumed deadly serious expressions.

He leaned over to Ben. "You do know he's the devil, right?"

Ben blinked. "He's a bit of an arse at times."

"No. I mean, the literal devil. He's Satan."

"He's annoying rather than evil. An irritation rather than a diabolical schemer. I know he must cause you grief at times but—"

"No. I mean literally. He's a fallen angel."

"He probably did look a lot more handsome in his youth. That beer belly doesn't help."

Lennox huffed. "He's got red skin."

"Years of alcohol abuse, I guess."

"He's got hoofs, Ben."

Ben nodded. "He does have an unusual attitude to footwear. He might have been a hippy."

Lennox looked at Ben. Ben met his gaze, but only for a second because Ben had real trouble looking people in the eye for very long. It was a level of intimacy he wasn't prepared for and he worried that if he locked eyes with anyone for too long he might, in a moment of panic, kiss them or something.

"You don't know, do you?" said Lennox, sadly.

"I know he's annoying and needs to get out more," said Ben.

Lennox gave an unconvinced nod and then poured Ben another cider and black. "On the house," he said.

"Really?" said Ben, delighted.

"It's a pity pint, you understand?"

"A pint's a pint," said Ben cheerily.

2

Jeremy Clovenhoof kicked open the door to the Boldmere Oak. Every time he did it, he left a little hoofy impression in the black paintwork. He liked to think that over the years he'd eventually leave a deep clean hoof imprint in the door for future generations to marvel at. Apparently, there were dozens of places around the world where curious indents in the rocks were given names such as 'Satan's footprint' or 'Devil's hoofprints' and Jeremy didn't see why the Boldmere Oak shouldn't be given its own, genuine article.

"Stop kicking the door!" Lennox snapped.

"Lambrini me, barman!" Clovenhoof retorted.

Nerys, at the bar, waggled an already filled wine glasses at him while Lennox gave her change from the till.

"Impeccable timing," said Clovenhoof, whisking the glass of fizzy perry from her hand.

"Ben's paying," she said, and with her own large glass of Chardonnay, gestured at Ben in the corner.

Clovenhoof plonked himself on a seat in the booth. "This is unusually kind of you, Ben. You're usually such a tight-fisted miser."

"Oh, this isn't on me," said Ben and tossed a wallet into the middle of the table. "Mr Julio Credenza is paying."

Clovenhoof regarded the wallet. He could see Nerys doing the same. "Obviously, I win this one," he said, quickly.

"I think you're talking bollocks," said Nerys speedily.

"He returned the wallet."

"After taking the money."

"But only because he saw it was mine."

"It's still a selfish act."

"A biased act."

Ben waved his hands to shush them. "Would one of you please tell me what's going on?"

Jeremy opened his mouth to speak. Nerys opened hers to speak louder. Clovenhoof coughed to divert her. She shushed him. He tried to put a hand over her mouth. She kicked him under the table. He kicked back harder. A hoof to the shins made her eyes go wide and robbed her of speech. Another victory for the hoof!

Clovenhoof cleared his throat and placed both hands together on the table. "We are conducting a series of important experiments into human nature. Ms Thomas here, my darling lady wife, contends that the world is getting worse day by day, and suffering and misery are on the rise."

Nerys finished rubbing her shin. "And Mr Clovenhoof here

says that the world has always been a horrible shitty place and is no worse that it always was. Mr Clovenhoof should also remember that he and I are only married out of necessity and if he calls me his wife once more, I will sneak into his flat in the night and squish his dick in a sandwich toaster."

"I'll try anything once," said Clovenhoof, undeterred.

Ben frowned. "And that's why—?" He flipped over the wallet. "So you're dropping random wallets, with fake names for some reason, and seeing if people are good enough to return them?"

"He's in an intelligent mood tonight," said Clovenhoof.

"We're keeping track and recording the results," said Nerys. "Apparently, someone refuses to see the evidence of his own eyes, that our world is going down the toilet fast."

"*Pfff*," spat Clovenhoof dismissively. "How?"

Nerys held up her hand and ticked her fingers off. "Economic disasters. Environmental ones too. The number of people in poverty. The fact that we're living through a massive mass extinction event."

"That's not a reason to get upset," said Clovenhoof. "Thousands of years ago, the dinosaurs all went extinct. All of them. Big rock! *Paf! Boom!* You didn't start weeping over that, did you?"

"I mean, I wasn't there," said Nerys.

"Sorry, did you say thousands of years ago?" said Ben.

Clovenhoof slurped Lambrini. "Thousands. Hundreds. I wasn't paying attention. It was a Friday, if I recall. Bloody dinosaurs didn't even get to enjoy a weekend off."

"So, you're trying to test the innate goodness of people—"

"Or innate badness!"

"—by dropping wallets in the street, and seeing how people respond to being offered babies for sale?"

"It's not a real baby," said Clovenhoof.

"Obviously."

"Obviously. Real babies cost a fortune. Have you ever tried buying one? Ridiculous."

"We looked," said Nerys, draining her glass. "I really wish we hadn't."

"Anyway, we're running lots of different experiments to test morality. I've been dropping down and pretending to be dead in the street to see how long it takes anyone to come to my aid. The record's three hours and ten minutes by the way."

"Wow," said Ben.

"Just to add some razzamatazz, I've set myself on fire a couple of times and then flailed about a bit before 'dying'. People respond a lot better to fire.

"Meanwhile Nerys has been testing people's tolerance of morality. We've gone to various places and she's undressed, one item at a time, and we wait to see how far down she'd get before someone asks her to stop."

"I dread to think," said Ben.

"She got down to her bra and knickers in St Michael's church last Sunday before someone told her to stop."

"It was a beautiful service," said Nerys.

Ben flicked a finger between the two of them. "What is it with you two? Why is it that all your escapades end up with *you* on fire and *you* with no clothes on?"

"That's not true," said Clovenhoof indignantly. "Sometimes I'm naked too."

Ben sighed. "We need another drink." He got up to go to the bar.

"He's a good man in a dark world," said Clovenhoof.

"Oh, and Mr Credenza is paying for these," said Ben, waggling the wallet.

Clovenhoof held out a hand. "But that's my money. Mr Credenza, that handsome devil in a moustache. That's me."

"Oh, I know," said Ben and went to get a round of the usual.

OUTSIDE IT STARTED to rain while they were on their fifth round of drinks.

"I don't see why you two are having this argument," said Ben. "As far as I can work out, you're either just watching bad stuff happen or actively causing it. It's basically misery porn."

"I'd watch that," said Clovenhoof. "Like they're at it but they're crying at the same time."

"No, I—"

"Ooh! Ooh! Or porn set at a funeral. Sexy widows, all in black. Organ music. 'Oh, missus, let me comfort you in your hour of need—'"

Nerys slapped him down just as he was about to mime his way through act one of his new idea.

"We need to test," she explained, "so we can decide what should be done."

Ben nodded in ready agreement. Three pints in and he was well-oiled and nodding easily.

"If I can convince this numbskull that there is worsening suffering, then maybe we ought to do something about it."

Ben laughed, a blast of rude loud laughter.

"What?" said Nerys.

"You. You talk a good game but you're not going to do anything about it."

Nerys puffed herself up. "I've done lots of good works for charity. I spent all of the pandemic lockdown doing good deeds."

"To make yourself look good," said Ben. "That's the point. You only ever do good things because you think it will reflect well on you. You have never performed a selfless act in your life."

Nerys spluttered, hurt written large across her face. She could be a good actress when she chose to be one. "I am constantly selfless!"

"Constantly selfish!" Ben countered. "We're all selfish. All of us."

THE THREE NEIGHBOURS walked close together in the drizzly night as they made their way from the Boldmere Oak to four hundred-and-something Chester Road and their sub-divided house. Ben wobbled a little drunkenly. Clovenhoof did a tipsy tippy-tap tap dance in the puddles and kicked a pile of drinks cans clustered by the alley some distance from their house. Nerys exhibited perhaps her greatest skill, that of walking in high heels while quite thoroughly drunk.

"If there's a God..." slurred Ben.

"*If?*" said Clovenhoof.

"Yeah, if," said Ben. "If there's a God, why does he let all this bad stuff happen?"

Clovenhoof scoffed. "Oh, that old chestnut. Too dull to answer. Go ask Reverend Zack for the church's answer to that."

"Yeah, no, but why?" said Ben. "He's meant to, you know, love us. Why does he let bad stuff happen to us?"

"Like bad phone network coverage," said Nerys.

"Or world hunger," said Ben.

"Or mouldy bananas."

"Or childhood diseases."

"Poor Wi-Fi connections."

"You've already mentioned that," said Ben.

"I said phone network coverage. Totally different."

"It's a test!" said Clovenhoof, mostly to shut them up. "It's all a test! The world is a test."

"A test?"

"A test! The Almighty wants to see who's good and who's not. All you mortals are given—" he belched "—free will and then the Big Guy sees how you behave during your life. Good or bad. Heaven or Hell. A big test until Judgement Day."

"Sort of like a TV reality show?" said Nerys. "Everyone trying to do their best and avoid getting sent home in a public vote."

"There's no public vote. There's these two angels who write down everything you do and then the Big Guy weighs up the good against the bad on a big scale."

"Everything?"

"Everything."

"Like they follow me everywhere?"

"Yup."

"I thought," said Nerys, screwing up her face with

concentration, "that they sort of weighed your heart against a feather. Metaphorically, like."

"That's stupid," said Clovenhoof. "The heart would be heavier."

"Metaphorically," said Nerys.

"Metaphorically or not, it's the heart. It's a lump of bloody meat."

"That's what Egyptians do," said Ben.

"Weigh hearts?" said Clovenhoof.

"They have a different system to the rest of us," said Nerys. "Sounds unfair."

Ben shook his head which threw his wobbly progress off completely. "In Egyptian mythology. Anubis weighed your heart and…"

"We're not talking about Egyptian myth," said Clovenhoof. "We're talking about—" He gestured vigorously upward at the Heavens, which were currently covered in dark rain clouds.

"It's all just made up stuff, innit?" said Ben.

"Oh, be sure to tell the Big Guy that when you see him."

Ben didn't seem to be worried. "It's all stupid anyway."

"Oh, is it?" said Clovenhoof.

"It can't all be a test. If God wants to know who's good enough to go to Heaven, then he already knows. He's omnispient."

"Sorry?"

"Omnictopus. Omnibilous? You know, he knows everything. Cos he's all powerful."

"Oh, that. He is. He does."

"So, basically, he knows what we're going to do before we

do it, right?" said Ben. "He doesn't need a test. He doesn't need this suffering. If this life is a test, if all this suffering is a sort of entrance exam for Heaven, then either he doesn't know everything already or he's just being ... well, he's just being a bit of a dick."

"He says He knows everything," said Clovenhoof. He stopped by a neighbour's hedge. "Does He know I'm going to piss in this bush? Yes, He does. Does He know I'm going to do a sexy little dance to this cat when I'm done? Yes, He does. He knows everything, but His plans are ineffable so you don't get to question them."

"Is someone having a disco outside our house?" said Nerys.

"What?" said Clovenhoof and turned round to look.

There was a nimbus of lights, purple, pink and blue, just outside the front door to four hundred-and-something Chester Road.

"What the hell?" said Ben.

"I think I know what that is..." said Clovenhoof and took a step towards it.

"You want to put your penis away first?" suggested Nerys.

Clovenhoof looked down at his open fly. "Little Jeremy likes to be aired from time to time. And you shouldn't body shame me."

"Your penis is shameful and ugly, and if you don't put it away I will go and get that sandwich toaster."

Grumbling as he did up his flies, Clovenhoof led the way to the front door. There, in the yellow light coming through the frosted glass stood an angel, its halo a swirl of glittery lights.

"Eltiel. What in blue buggering fuck are you doing here?" said Clovenhoof.

The angel smiled and turned to them. The halo light shifted to become an ethereal spotlight that cast the winged figure in a most flattering light.

Clovenhoof had known Eltiel from a long time ago, a long, *long* time ago. Before he'd been fired as Lord of Hell, before he'd even been thrown down to Hell. Even before the War in Heaven, when the Archangel Michael had cheated and lanced him when the light was in Clovenhoof's eyes. Way, way back Eltiel had been a beautiful and proud angel. Although back then his halo wasn't quite so bling, and he hadn't worn robes apparently made from cheap gold lame.

"Lucifer!" cried the angel, delighted. Before Clovenhoof could do anything, the divine creature had grabbed his shoulders and given him two loud air kisses a considerable distance from his cheeks. Clovenhoof slapped his hands away.

"Why's that man all sparkly?" said Ben.

"Um," said Nerys sharply, with decisive indecisiveness. "I think you and I should go inside, Ben. Get you out of the rain."

Nerys bundled Ben past, giving Clovenhoof a fierce look that said, *Why the hell is there an angel on our doorstep, Jeremy?* Clovenhoof tried to shoot one back that hopefully said, *I don't know. I didn't invite him. Just get rid of Ben, ta. And maybe dig out a bottle of something strong for a nightcap, eh?*

Clovenhoof was perhaps optimistic about how much meaning he could imbue in a single glance, but Nerys pushed Ben inside and shut the door.

Clovenhoof turned his angry and now considerably more sober attention back to the angel. "To repeat, what the fuck, Eltiel?"

"Can I just say it's lovely to see an older gentleman feeling so comfortable in his own skin," said the angel.

Eltiel's hand didn't quite reach out to caress Clovenhoof's beer belly, but it came close. Clovenhoof gave serious thought to reaching out and breaking a few angel fingers.

"Explain yourself," he said. "I've not had an angel come to my door for bloody years. Not including that arse Michael, but he's technically human now so doesn't count."

"It has been a while," Eltiel admitted, "but I like to think we've got one of those relationships where we can meet up after simply ages and just slot back in like nothing had happened and – *aaah!*"

Clovenhoof had gone for the fingers and twisted them savagely. Eltiel sang in pain. It was a wonderful sound.

"You've been summoned!" Eltiel squeaked.

"What?"

"Summoned! It's the End Times. Your final performance."

Clovenhoof let go in surprise and stepped back. "W-what? No. What? That can't be. What?"

Eltiel shook out his hand, wiped a single glittering tear from his eye and nodded.

"It's true. The final days are upon us. Armageddon. Doomsday."

"No, that can't be. That can't be now. That's not meant to be until, you know, the end of time."

"Yes. The End Times," said Eltiel. "Now. The signs are

clear. Famine, pestilence, wars and rumours of war. Lawlessness and immorality. People losing their faith."

"No, no, no, no." Clovenhoof wasn't sure if he was just surprised or also objected to the damned inconvenience of all this. "I was just telling Nerys that—" He shook his head.

"It is the Divine Will and it is happening," said Eltiel. "Gosh, you really zinged my fingers. Lucifer, still full of surprises."

"But I'm not Lucifer anymore. Not officially. I'm just Jeremy. I'm retired or on gardening leave or whatever. You don't need me."

A little of Eltiel's sparkle was returning. "It's all in the script." There was suddenly a Bible in his hand, with gold-edged pages and a diamante-studded cover. "You get a starring role. You have a function to fulfil. It's all very cinematic big budget stuff. The horsemen. The Great Dragon. The final battle with the Archangel Michael."

Clovenhoof realised that there was someone stood at the bottom of the path, by the pavement. Michael, wearing a slimming herringbone suit, with his collar pulled up against the rain, mooched miserably up the path.

"Michael, can you believe this bollocks?" said Clovenhoof.

The look on Michael's beautifully sculpted face was one of utter bereavement. "It's all true. Apparently."

"But—"

"I know," said Michael. "Andy and I had a three-week holiday to Puerto Rico booked. All-inclusive too."

"Yes, you're probably not going to be able to do that," said

Eltiel with a minimum effort at sympathy. "Although if you've got insurance, you might get a refund."

"Armageddon insurance?" said Clovenhoof.

Eltiel gave a helpless shrug.

"So this is it?" said Clovenhoof. "We get – what? – whisked away to enact the highlights of the Apocalypse and ... and ... that's *it*? No. I know how this is meant to go. I'm meant to be released from my imprisonment and then prepare to storm the walls of the Celestial City and ... and..."

"I'm sure it will all be made clear," said Eltiel.

"No. No." Clovenhoof realised that just saying 'no' over and over again wasn't really going to work, but his brain had very little else to offer. "Please." He cast about. "Just ... just give me two minutes."

He snatched the Bible off Eltiel and ran inside.

3

Nerys was in Ben's flat. Ben was in the kitchen. He'd managed to both dig out a bottle of gin and put the kettle on. It was uncertain if he was going to make tea or gin and tonics, or indeed some horrific drunken combination of the two. Nerys stood by the living room window and tried to look down at the conversation going on outside the front door. The angle was all wrong and all she could see was the angel's sparkle and an occasional outflung hand.

Nerys had known Jeremy Clovenhoof was Satan for more than decade. It was not easy knowledge to live with. While most other humans somehow failed to see they had a red devil living among them, she was faced with the horrid truth that Satan was real, God was real, and that her neighbour wasn't just a dirty old man with a massive ego and no moral compass but the very devil himself. Such knowledge made

Nerys feel like she was a buffer between innocent humanity and the terrifying divine.

As such, when she heard the front door and the clatter of hoofs on the stairs, she turned to demand some answers. Clovenhoof came in, breathless, with a jewel-studded gold Bible in his hands.

"What in God's name was all that about?" she hissed.

"I haven't got time," said Clovenhoof. There was a note of sorrow in his voice that cut through her anger.

"What is it?"

Clovenhoof was flicking through the Bible. "Matthew twenty-four," he said, thrusting the open Bible at her. "Plus the whole of *Revelations* for background reading, I guess."

"What are you talking about?"

He pushed his rain-soaked hair away from his brow. "You were right."

"What do you mean, I was right? I mean, I'm always right. I know I am but—"

"The world," he said. "Things just generally going to hell. Ha! To hell."

"What's this all got to do with the angel? Was that Michael down there too?"

"Yes. We're being taken away, for the big dress rehearsal in the sky or something."

"What?"

"Armageddon."

Nerys looked at the Bible. The chapter heading read *The Destruction of the Temple and Signs of the End Times*.

"Wait. What? No. This can't be happening."

"That's what I said. But apparently the worldwide Shit-O-Meter has hit some sort of tipping point."

"And that's it?" she said. This was all too nonsensical to take in. "This isn't a joke, right?"

"Oh, fuck, I wish it was," he said earnestly. "I was actually enjoying life on Earth."

"How long have we got? You know, until fire from the sky, and dark riders, and all the goblins coming out to kill us and…"

"I think you've somehow confused the Biblical Apocalypse with *The Lord of the Rings* there, Nerys."

"For fuck's sake, Jeremy!" she spat. "How long?"

He shrugged with a uselessness and sad energy that made her see how dejected he'd suddenly become.

"A week? A month? A year? No one will know the day or the hour and all that ineffable bollocks. Time runs differently in the Celestial City."

"But we must be able to do something to stop it."

"Take the one ring to Mordor you mean?"

"Shut it. I mean, if it's because of evil and immorality—"

"You can't change the world, Nerys," said Clovenhoof. "Get your own soul sorted. Let that selfishness shine. Pray a lot. Sort Ben out." He looked to the kitchen door and sagged. "Fuck."

"You're never this pessimistic," said Nerys.

"I'm not usually up against the Almighty," said Clovenhoof.

"You're always up against the Almighty," she reminded him.

"He's not so bad when you get to know Him."

"Then do something. Talk to him."

He nodded but she could see the defeat in him already.

"I'm sorry. I..." He reached into his pocket, took out his wallet and solemnly presented her with a piece of paper. "Two-for-one voucher for dirty burgers at McDoner's kebab shop," he said. "I'm not going to get to use it now and I *love* dirty burgers."

"Er."

He folded her fingers gently around it. "Have a dirty burger each and think of me, eh?"

Nerys tutted. "It's not like you're dying."

He pulled a face and tapped the Bible in her hand. "Read it. It does not end well for me."

"Er, guys!" Ben called from the kitchen. "I've forgotten what I'm making. I've got tea bags and tonic water."

Through the open flat door there came a growing nimbus of pink light and footsteps on the stairs. Clovenhoof looked at the light and then at Nerys.

"Bugger," he said bitterly and left.

The kitchen door opened and, at the same moment, the light from the hallway abruptly vanished.

"How d'you make a Long Island iced tea?" asked Ben.

Nerys went out onto the landing. There was no one there. The stairwell was dark.

Ben looked out. "Where's Jeremy?"

"He—" Nerys didn't have the capacity to answer that one. "Vodka, tequila, gin, rum, er, triple sec and coke," she said. "I'll make us some."

4

Limbo was a vast spiritual plain composed of wispy mists beneath an off-white nothing sky, over a landscape that was blobby shapeless grey material and, simultaneously, nothing whatsoever. It occupied the space, or indeed the non-space, between Heaven's Celestial City and Hell's infernal pits.

Walking through Limbo was basically really boring. Clovenhoof had been to some boring places in his time – that Belgian battle fields camping trip Ben had taken them on, the week they'd been forced to spend in Kent after Ben got arrested for bringing excavated munition shells back into the UK, the three days spent at a magistrates' court hearing Ben plead for forgiveness – all very, very boring. But nothing could top the boredom of Limbo.

Eltiel's sparkly halo led the way. Michael, downcast, trudged after him. Clovenhoof sighed and sang to himself a tune of his own devising.

"Limbo. Limbo. Limbo-bo-bo. Limbo-bo-bo. Limbo-bimbo, baby, baby. Unh! Unh! Bobo-bimbo. Unh! Unh! Touch it, baby!"

"Can't you shut up?" Michael snapped.

"What?" shrugged Clovenhoof. "Just trying to entertain myself."

"You are in a sacred place."

"Not particularly sacred looking. There's nothing here."

"Exactly. This is the nothingness that existed before the Almighty formed the world. This is a raw reminder of the wonders of creation."

"Because it's not here?"

"Because it's not here."

"Making something out of nothing. Nothing special about that. You saw the bog roll mummified angel I made for the tree last Christmas."

"You have no reverence," said Michael and stalked ahead.

There had been a particularly hard and miserable edge to the usually smug angel's voice. He was evidently as unenamoured by the prospect of an imminent Apocalypse as Clovenhoof. It was quite possible that the pair of them had both been tainted by their years on earth, that both had ... well, not exactly become human, but just grown to appreciate some of the more enjoyable aspects of human life. Like alcohol and peri peri chicken, and ripping the protective plastic off a new phone. It would be a deep shame to see those things vanish in the flames of Armageddon.

"Nothing special about nothing," said Clovenhoof, and to prove a point scooped up a ball of nothing and rolled it out into a sausage shape. "Took the Big Guy six days to make animals, huh?"

He gave his lumpy creation a bunch of long legs formed from other balls of nothing and jabbed his fingers into one end to give it piss-hole eyes and a wide lippy mouth. And, because he was a considerate creator, jabbed a hole in the other end for its arse. It was far too long really, so he bent the front half up so it became a long thick neck, putting the misshapen head at the same level as his own. Floofy hair and tall ears finished off his animal creation.

He stepped back to admire it. It had a goofy mindless look about it, and if it did wobble unevenly on its four long legs then that was just part of its charm.

"Creation's easy," he said and ran off to catch up with the others. "Hey, Eltiel!" he shouted. "If Limbo is just nothing, like no space at all, why is it taking us so long to get where we're going?"

"We're here," said the angel.

In the huge whiteness, a meeting house had been constructed from glimmering, shimmering crystal. To Clovenhoof's eyes it looked like someone had carved it out of a giant hard-boiled sweet. He resisted the urge to run up and lick it to see if it tasted minty.

At a table in the open-sided hall sat delegations from Heaven and Hell.

"I think we're about to see declarations of intent," said Michael as an aside to Clovenhoof.

"Some pre-match trash talk," Clovenhoof replied, nodding.

He recognised the hellish contingent. Lord Peter, former

saint and now ruler of hell since Clovenhoof's absence, took the centre seat and tried to look noble and commanding; generally ruining it by looking round to see if anyone had noticed how noble and commanding he looked. Arrayed to either side of him were three of the dukes of hell – red-skinned Berith, the clawed crafty worm Azazel, and the wrinkled raisin in a wheelchair that was Belphegor.

Across from them was Heaven's much much larger contingent, with three archangels, Gabriel, Samael and Raphael in prime position, and a wide Who's Who of saints and lesser angels behind them. Clovenhoof threw a *Peace Out* gesture at Joan of Arc at the back of the crowd and she gave a little embarrassed wave back.

"Our two generals have arrived, at last," said the Archangel Gabriel, in the pompous and ominous voice he'd been practising since the dawn of time.

Two more chairs in prominent positions appeared from nothingness, one on each side of the table. Michael gave Clovenhoof an uncomfortable look, which Clovenhoof mirrored right back at him, and they each went to join their former colleagues.

Clovenhoof shuffled into place. "Good to see you, Azazel. Looking buff there, Berith. New set of wheels, Belphegor?" He dropped into his seat. "Wassup, Petey-boy."

The current Lord of Hell gave him a distasteful look. "Satan," said Peter begrudgingly.

"We are gathered now," said Gabriel, "as the days of Earth grow short in number and—"

"Hang on," said Clovenhoof, who wasn't prepared to sit

through one of Gabriel's grand speeches. "Is that actually happening?"

"Yes, Satan," said Gabriel coldly.

"Yeah, yeah, yeah, but is it *really* happening? I mean, really *really* happening?"

"It is happening," said Gabriel.

"I mean, not like, 'Whoa Earth, you better mend your ways or you're going to bed with no supper' kind of it's happening, but like a real 'I've paid a non-refundable deposit on this Apocalypse and the taxi's already on its way here' kind of it's happening?"

Gabriel's brow twitched in irritating confusion. "It is happening, Satan."

The inventor-demon Belphegor slid a piece of paper along the table so it rested in front of Clovenhoof. It was an agenda and including items such as:

- *Introductions*
- *Housekeeping and Ground Rules*
- *The Rapture*
- *Doomsday and the Final Battle*
- *A New Heaven and a New Earth*

THERE WAS EVEN an *Any Other Business* at the bottom.

"Fuck," said Clovenhoof. "Armageddon comes with its own agenda?"

"This stuff doesn't happen all by itself," said Belphegor. "It needs organising."

"We need to be clear who is specifically responsible for which element and the timescales they are operating to," said Gabriel. "For example, have you selected an Antichrist yet?"

"Some of us having been having a small wager as to who it might be," said Archangel Samael. "My money's on that billionaire with the space rockets."

The demons of Hell looked at one another.

Peter cleared his throat. "Lords, fellow saints, we were very much under the impression that Heaven would be responsible for the Antichrist."

"Don't be ridiculous," said Gabriel. "The Antichrist is the symbol of all evil on earth."

"Exactly. It is an earthly matter and the corporation of Hell has generally confined its activities to Hell itself."

"What nonsense!" said Gabriel. "Heaven's actions will all be responses to Hell's transgressions. Hell's Antichrist comes to power. Heaven enacts righteous judgement, the Four Horsemen, the seven seals, the trumpets."

Clovenhoof was for a moment taken by the notion that the seven seals could be seven aquatic flippers-and-fish seals rather than waxy seals and wanted to ask if they would have a trumpet each, but was pre-interrupted by the demon Berith.

"That's not how it is. The Four Horsemen of the Apocalypse are ours! We have been training them up to scourge the earth."

There was hubbub among the celestial folk and cries of horror.

"Not at all!" said Samael, Archangel of Death. "The Four Horsemen are powerful symbols of religious righteousness."

There was equal furore among the demons. Azazel clawed at his own flesh in distress. Clovenhoof threw in a cheery "Bollocks!" as a contribution.

"Stop! Stop! Cease!" said Gabriel, rapping his angelic horn on the table to regain order. "You see?" he said to Clovenhoof. "This is why we need an agenda. So much to sort out and so little time."

Clovenhoof stood up. "First of all, I can't put up with this crap without a drink. You—" he clicked his fingers imperiously "—yes, you in the halo. No, you. That's right. Get me a Lambrini. Get me two."

The angel in the middle ranks dithered, but eventually slid away, hopefully to go get some fizzy plonk.

"Secondly," said Clovenhoof, "I don't see why we have to do any of this shit. I'm not interested in it. You want us to play pantomime villain to your CGI blockbuster spectacular? Well, I'm not interested."

"Not interested?" said Raphael, surprised.

"I said you shouldn't have bothered inviting him," Lord Peter muttered.

"Why do we have to have a big war, eh?" said Clovenhoof. "I don't want to do it. I'm Switzerland as far as this is concerned. Slathered in chocolate, morally okay with hoarding Nazi gold, and not interested in fighting."

"Why fight?" said Samael. "*Why* fight? Do you not recall? You rebelled against the Throne. You challenged the

Almighty. You refused to bow before Man, His greatest creation. You thought you were equal to the Almighty – that you would be as worthy a creator as Him!"

"*Pfff*. Nah. Not me. I'm much more chilled about things. I don't want to be the Big Guy. I don't want to rule Heaven. I'm not a creator."

At that moment there came a weird kind of gasping, yapping sound, and a thing bounded and wriggled into the hall. It was long and tall and moved like no normal creature. It had four spindly legs, a curly perm for fur, and a goofy floppy mouth that was all lips. It leaped onto the table, did a number of laps that caused angels and saints to recoil, then stopped before Clovenhoof and stood to attention proudly.

"Okay," said Clovenhoof. "Apart from this thing. Yeah, I made this."

There was uproar on all sides. Gabriel battered the table with his horn to try to get everyone to calm down, but even when he'd put a dent in it, still no one was listening.

5

The twenty-four hours following Clovenhoof's departure were a drunken miserable blur for Nerys.

It went in a sort of cycle. It started with her cursing Jeremy Clovenhoof and banging on the door of his empty flat demanding answers. Then, she sat down and opened the posh Bible he'd left behind and tried reading the relevant passages. It wasn't written in proper English so it was difficult to maintain her focus and only got as far as *The sun will be darkened and the moon will not give its light; the stars will fall from the sky and the heavenly bodies will be shaken* before she felt violently ill and reached for the boxed wine on the kitchen counter, drinking until all thought and feeling were driven away. And then the cycle started again.

She woke from a stupor to bright sunlight and the ringing of the front doorbell. She stumbled down to the ground floor to open the front door to a courier from a local wine merchant. Buying in bulk had seemed like a grand idea at three in the morning when she'd come up with the idea. The courier handed over the boxes, then pulled out his phone.

"Mind if I take a picture?"

"For proof of delivery?"

"No, for our socials. I think people will love how you're using our products."

Nerys shrugged. "Sure." At some point during the last day she'd invented the boxed wine sling, a sort of papoose for alcohol. It saved time and energy she could ill afford. She'd stabbed a hole in the top of the wine box currently nestled against her breast and pushed a piece of silicone tubing through the top. She sucked at it gamely while the delivery man took his photo.

She closed the door and started the laborious task of lugging her supplies up to her flat, while slurping at the remains of the current box. She dropped her new alcoholic supplies on the kitchen counter and turned to look at the Yorkshire Terrier sitting meaningfully next to his food bowls in the corner.

"Come on Twinkle, back to Bible studies," she said, gave him a bowlful of biscuit and sat down blearily at the kitchen table. She propped up the big Bible and peered at the dense text. She realised half an hour later that she was moving her eyes over the text without really getting any further.

"I need to *read* it Twinkle, not just read it," she slurred.

She tried using a highlighter on important sounding passages, but that really didn't help – because who knew what might end up being important? It was likely to be some overlooked detail which would prove useful.

She tried using her wall to map out the various ideas using Post-It notes, like a TV detective. Numbers seemed as if they might be significant, so she had an area for numbers, with arrows leading off to the things they described, but she quickly ran out of space.

Twinkle nudged her leg, indicating that he had needs, even if the world was coming to an end. She took him for a walk, so he could have a good sniff round at all of his favourite places.

They wandered down Chester Road, past the big pile of drinking cans in the alleyway. Litter was a perennial nuisance. Nerys lost count of the Red Bull cans which littered one stretch of the road. Did they flock together because of magnetism, or was it someone's daily habit to throw a can from their car at the same spot? It would all be swept away in the fires of Apocalypse. And maybe a species which allowed such a mess to occur didn't deserve to survive.

Nerys stared at a can for a moment. A bee emerged from the opening and flew away.

"Should bees be drinking that stuff, Twinkle?" she murmured with a frown.

Poor bees, she thought. She hadn't really given much thought to bees before. Human action of some sort (she was unclear on the point) was driving them to extinction. And here was one, living like a tiny hobo, in discarded drinks cans.

She walked to Short Heath Park, becoming slightly morbid as she watched Twinkle, wondering how it would feel if she knew for certain this was his final walk, and all of his final sniffs. Should she indulge him with an enormous bone, or a tin of tuna? The big problem with the end times was that she hadn't found anything like a timetable. Did it all happen really quickly, or was it drawn out for months? If she triggered Twinkle's occasional digestive difficulties would she still be around when it needed cleaning up?

A bunch of youths had made an impromptu skate park at the end of the park, leaning boards up against railings to create ramps. One of them was repeatedly trying and failing to ride a fencing rail, much to the amusement of his friends.

When one of them loudly called the failed railslider an 'absolute cockmuppet' Nerys realised she knew some of the lads. That one was Kenzie Kelly and that one was – er – PJ something-or-other. And that lad, pootling around idly on his skateboard while working on a laptop held in his hands was the infamous Spartacus Wilson.

Nerys wasn't sure it was safe to use a skateboard while typing, but he seemed to function perfectly fine.

"What you working on Spartacus?" she asked, nodding at the laptop as she approached.

"Cougar alert!" shouted one boy.

"Bag lady alert!" threw in another to much laughter.

Nerys was about to give them a mouthful of return fire when Spartacus said, "Oi! It's Mrs Nerys. Don't be giving her cheek."

Spartacus had been the de facto leader of his little tribe all his life and the others shut up and went back to their skating immediately. Over the years, the boy Spartacus had shot up to become a gangly sixteen-year-old. He'd not yet rounded out into the man he would become, but Nerys could already see in his cocksure attitude and easy smile that he would be a heartbreaker and, if he was anything like his absent dad, would be leaving lots of little Spartacuses in his wake over the years to come.

Except there would be no years to come, she realised coldly. There would be no Spartacus the man. There probably wouldn't even be time for him to break a single heart before the end of the world came upon them.

"I'm coding," he told her. "Writing a password generator."

"Surely there are plenty of those already?" she asked.

"Not ones where you can embed swear words into the middle of them, so that they are more memorable." He typed and spun the laptop in the palm of his hand. "PandaMinge441. Tell me that doesn't stick in your mind."

Caught between the horrors of Armageddon and this boy's cheery vulgarity, Nerys could only laugh. "Nice work, Sparts," she said and turned away before the laughter turned into tears.

She returned to the flat and gave Twinkle some regular food. A hangover was trying to creep into her head, so she treated it with further heavy doses of alcohol.

She discovered, while searching for help, that the internet provided audio performances of Bible passages, where breathy voice actors would read the *Book of Revelation* as a dramatisation. Swelling strings and twinkling magical sound effects brought it to life, as though it was the build-up for some sort of fantasy series that Nerys would definitely not be watching.

Ring ring.

Nerys ignored her phone. In theory she was working as a temp at a van hire company, but she didn't feel like calling in and explaining her absence. It was unlikely they would understand, so she turned off the ringer and buckled down on trying to understand the whole end of the world thing.

She had half-believed she wouldn't make it until the morning on the first night, but when she woke up hungover for the third consecutive morning she decided she had more time to seek answers. She hadn't yet worked out how long the end times actually lasted, but it looked like weeks rather than hours. This was an unwelcome development, because it meant she would have to engage with the rest of the world as if things were normal, and she very much felt as if they were not normal.

THE NEXT DAY, she picked up a breakfast bap from the Hallowed Grounds coffee shop and headed round to Boldmere's Church of St Michael.

She found the Reverend Zack Purdey getting ready for a coffee morning. He was dressed in his usual off-duty uniform of cardigan and corduroy trousers. There was something about Zack Purdey that made Nerys feel like the man was constructed of Lego, and it wasn't just because he had a sort of square boxy head. Zack Purdey was solid and dependable; without complexity or guile. It made him the kind of man she needed at this time.

"Hello, Nerys. Do grab a cuppa and a biscuit."

"Can I eat my breakfast bap here? I have questions."

"Of course."

Nerys sat at one of the Formica-topped tables, beneath a charity thermometer measuring how close the church was to raising funds to buy a new boiler. She unwrapped her breakfast. As she hefted it in her hands she tried to decide where to start with her questions.

"Let's start with the Bible," she said.

"Oh good, there's a chance I can help with that. I tend to fall down on the sports questions, so don't ask me one of those."

Nerys chewed while she nodded acknowledgement at his attempt at humour. "All the stuff in the Bible about the end times. I need your take on it."

"My take on it in what way?"

"Like ... how do we know when we get there?"

"Heavy stuff for this early in the morning. Breakfast, Bible and the End Times."

"How long will the whole thing take?" she said. "The end of the world?"

"Ah, I think I understand what you want to talk about now. It's natural for us all to react to events taking place around us; to try and make sense of them. Anxiety about the state of the world is something I've been hearing a lot recently."

"Yes," said Nerys. "And? What do you tell people?"

"I tell them that there have always been challenges, but we can all rely on having a place in God's—"

"—No, I don't want to hear that vague stuff." She realised she'd cut him off quite angrily, her temper born from a hangover and the sheer inability to understand what the

Bible verses she'd tried and failed to understand were telling her. "Sorry, rev. I mean, I want specifics."

"Specifics?"

"The Church of England has got a lot of money, right?"

"Depends on how you measure such things."

"One of the biggest landowners in the country, right?"

"Well, that might be the case, but we don't see much—"

"So has it done any prepping for the end times?"

"Prepping?" He frowned deeply, his thick, rectangular, dependable eyebrows coming together. "You mean like making pickles and having a bag packed?"

"What? No. Not that kind of prepping."

"Prepping how then?"

"Something more like knowing when the end times are actually happening." Nerys cast around for an example. "Does the church have an early warning system? Does it monitor the news for unexplained apocalyptic trumpeting?"

Zack reached across the table and put his hand on Nerys's. "*The Book of Revelation* does have a knack of getting under people's skin, Nerys. I personally don't think we should necessarily take it quite that literally."

"Are you saying that you don't believe what's written in the Bible?"

He pulled an uncomfortable face. "Ah. Well. The Anglican Church is a very, very broad church. There are lots of opinions. As for me, I'm not saying that some of it isn't true."

"Right?"

"I'm saying that there are some parts that are a little more, um, *showbiz* than others. It's like— For example, if we were to read the Bible literally then the devil possibly doesn't even exist."

"Well, I know that's not true for a start," she scoffed.

"There are various devilish characters, but no one person encapsulating all those roles. So, should we believe in the devil or not? Perhaps the Bible wasn't given to us so we could tear it apart, piece by piece. I would consider the overall message before delving into the nitty-gritty."

Nerys chewed on her breakfast bap as she pondered his words. Reverend Zack was a lovely man, but he had none of the answers she needed. It would rock his world if he ever found out some of the things that Nerys knew. He probably thought Heaven and Hell were states of mind, not actual real places. Nerys wasn't going to ask, because she might be tempted to tell him she had been there.

"So, the church doesn't have any kind of Revelations early warning division?" she asked finally.

"I think if they did, the local vicar probably wouldn't know about it anyway," he smiled.

"Thanks for the chat, it's been very reassuring," she said as she got up.

"Wait. Can you tell me what's really bothering you, Nerys?"

"The world is going to hell," she said.

He didn't disagree; he simply nodded, slow and sad. "Things can look bleak at times, can't they?"

She opened her mouth to argue with him, but he was shaking his head now, vigorously.

"One of the foolish things about a small number of our fellow Christians – if I may be so callous and cruel – is they are so focused on the world to come in the hereafter that they do not focus on the world we have. They overlook the pain and suffering and hunger in the world we live in now, looking only towards the fierce and holy light of God's Armageddon. We should not pay heed to teachings about life after death, and remember there should also be life *before* death."

"That's all very sweet and true, rev, but—"

He held up a hand to interrupt. "Can I offer just one piece of advice, Nerys?"

She sighed. "I suspect you're gonna do that anyway."

"When things look black and dark for ourselves, one of the best ways to lift ourselves up is to reach out and help others."

She nodded only to show she had heard. At that moment she wasn't ready for such homespun wisdom.

As she neared the door, she paused. "But can you make some calls to head office anyway?"

"Calls?" said Zack.

"Maybe ask about Armageddon. See whether there's anyone who has a preparedness plan?"

"Let me think about how I would phrase the question, Nerys," he chuckled. "It's not a conversation I can picture going well, if I'm honest."

6

The Archangel Gabriel had to threaten to hose everyone with holy water before order was restored in the meeting house in Limbo. Clovenhoof's unholy creature was chased from the meeting, and the rest of the agenda was worked through with the haste of individuals trying to build a house of cards on a powder keg. When the details of the final battle were shared, Michael looked at Clovenhoof and saw equal hesitance in the old devil's eyes.

"If I may?" said Clovenhoof. "Why does the Final Battle have to involve me and Michael duking it out like prize fighters?"

"It's in all the literature," shouted a saint from behind Michael. "The Archangel Michael versus the Great Dragon."

"Yes, yes, but we already did that aeons ago. We had our fight. The War in Heaven. Done. Dusted."

"I won," Michael put in, in case anyone had forgotten.

"The sun was in my eyes," said Clovenhoof.

"Excuses."

"You had a lance. I didn't have anything." Clovenhoof shook himself. "Point is, it's done."

"I agree," said Michael. "Done and, as my esteemed colleague, the filthy Angel of the Bottomless Pit says, dusted."

"There is no distinction between past and present in the Kingdom of Heaven," argued the saint. Michael didn't want to turn round but he suspected it was that tubby philosopher St Thomas Aquinas, a medieval monk who loved arguing black was blue almost as much as he loved big bowls of oil-drenched pasta.

"But that fight *was* in the past," said Clovenhoof. "We don't need to do it again."

"Time is eternal in the Kingdom of Heaven!"

"Sounds like it's going round in bloody circles."

The disgusting Duke Belphegor leaned over and muttered something to Clovenhoof. Meanwhile, Samael turned to Michael and whispered, "Have you got a problem with fighting the Fallen One once more?"

"Me?" said Michael. "Me? No. I'm all up for it. I just don't like unnecessary redundancy. It's like Andy and I went to see *Hamilton* in the West End. Do we need to go see it again? Yes, it may have some very catchy tunes, but it's no *Les Mis* and we've done it once so, no, we don't need to repeat things."

Samael nodded but, in that nod, his eyes took in all of Michael, his slim figure, his perfectly tailored suit, his neatly manicured fingernails and … was that a note of judgement in his eyes?

The meeting moved on. Berith's request to eat 'One of the

little humans at the back' to sate his hunger hastened it all to a conclusion.

The two parties withdrew simultaneously and cautiously. Michael noted how Joan of Arc had her hand resting lightly on the pommel of her sword, a casual posture which would allow her to draw it at a moment's notice.

Michael watched as the angel Eltiel sidled up to Clovenhoof. "Um, Satan? I've been reminded. I gave you a copy of the Holy Bible. From the Celestial City's own library. I seem to recall giving it to you before we left Earth."

Clovenhoof shrugged like he really didn't care. "I gave it to Nerys."

"Nerys?" Eltiel frowned and then recalled. "Oh, the somewhat inebriated woman with the short skirt. She gave me cause to wonder – is she what they call a 'painted Jezebel'? I've never really understood the phrase until now."

"Yeah, yeah. Why don't you call her that and see what happens?"

"Actually," said the angel, looking round nervously, "I seem to have caused some annoyance by letting the Bible go and I don't think a fresh visit to Earth would be looked upon favourably. Could *you* possibly...?"

"My Lord Satan has more important things to do, you pathetic sparkler," said Belphegor, whipping across in his chair. "You think he has time for jaunts back to Earth?"

"Actually, I don't mind—"

Michael could read his old adversary like a book. Clovenhoof would jump at the chance to go home again, even if it was just to pack a suitcase with hideous smoking jackets and to delete his internet browsing history.

"I will send someone to collect it," said Belphegor. "He'll even deliver it in a gift box."

Eltiel retreated. Belphegor scooted away, beckoning for Clovenhoof to follow, but instead Clovenhoof looked across at Michael and gave the subtlest of head nods to the side. Subtlety was not Jeremy's forte and that alone made Michael respond to the gesture and come down to the end of the table to meet him.

"They think I'm going to lead Hell's forces into battle!" Clovenhoof hissed.

"Mmmm," Michael nodded neutrally. "That seems to be what's going to happen."

"I don't want to do any of this."

"Well, me neither, obviously."

"We're both very happy on earth. Spartacus Wilson was going to show me a dead badger at the weekend. You've got your holiday booked to Margate."

"Mauritius."

"Same difference. Sand, sea. Point is, I don't want it all to end and I definitely don't want to fight. I haven't been into battle since ... well, since the dawn of time."

"There was that fight you had with Animal Ed over the last packet of peanuts in the Boldmere Oak last week."

"Okay, apart from that."

"You fought off a whole bunch of angry pensioners after you doodled on the tapestries in that National Trust place."

"Okay, okay. I mean a proper fight. I certainly don't want to fight you."

Michael cleared his throat and tugged at his lapels self-importantly. "Well, obviously. And I support that opinion."

Clovenhoof's eyes narrowed and his lip curled in irritation. "Because I would absolutely twat you," he said, like it was obvious. "And that would just be embarrassing for you."

"Oh," said Michael. "I thought you didn't want to fight me because you had gone flabby and weak in your old age and feared a humiliating defeat. I was agreeing out of sympathy for your condition."

"Condition? My fucking condition is that of a devil who has far better things to do than engage in a fancy dress war with those feathery bastards. But, for the record, you have the strength and resilience of wonky deckchair, and if we ever met on the field of combat again, these hands would snap you like a bloody twig."

"Those hands?" Michael scoffed. "They haven't done anything more vigorous than open a packet of crisps in over a decade."

"For your information, buddy, these hands get lots of exercise. Especially this one. You actually want to do this?"

"What?"

"You actually want to fight me?"

Michael opened his mouth, then realised the conversation had turned a hundred and eighty degrees away from where he wanted it to be. "I... Do you?"

Clovenhoof seemed to be equally struggling. "Surely, um, the point is that I would beat you, not whether we actually want to do it."

"Your overconfidence is galling!"

"My justified confidence induces exactly the right amount of gall!"

"What does that even mean?" said Michael.

"I know what I am but what are you?" Clovenhoof retorted.

Michael made an exasperated growl. "Talking to you is pointless."

"Too stupid to see sense."

Raphael called to Michael. The Heavenly delegation were departing. Above Michael's head the meeting house was fading into grey cloud and blobs of non-stuff, coming apart now that it was no longer needed.

"I have known you since the beginning of time," Michael told Clovenhoof. "You are an arrogant moron with the imagination and self-control of a toddler. I don't think I have hated any individual as much as I've hated you."

It was odd but, in those words, Michael somehow bizarrely hoped he had managed to sum up his lifelong affection for the old goaty devil; but on reflection he wasn't sure he'd quite nailed it.

"Yeah, fuck you too," said Clovenhoof and, with a vicious fart in Michael's direction, went off to join the demons moving in the direction of Hell. The horrific long-legged mutant thing Clovenhoof had created gambolled at his feet, making sounds that were perhaps meant to be barks but sounded more like the chesty rasps of an unrepentant smoker.

Michael slouched miserably to join the celestial crowd. Raphael fell into step beside him. The archangel of healing wrapped a strong arm around Michael's shoulder.

"I know. It's a surprise to the lot of us, right? So much to take in."

"Yeah, I guess," said Michael.

"Don't worry. You'll soon get into the swing of things when you see what glorious things are to come."

"Yeah," said Samael, coming up on Michael's other side, "Earthquakes! The sun turning black! The moon becoming blood! Mountains crumbling and stars falling from the sky!" The angel of death's teeth were locked in a wide bright grin as he spoke.

"Or indeed, the nice stuff," suggested Raphael. "The holy people with their palm leaves. The mighty temple of God being revealed. The good and great people of earth being lifted up in the final rapture."

"And all the animals too," said St Francis of Assisi.

"What?" said Raphael.

"The animals. All the blessed cweatures," said the bearded saint next to them. "Lifted up into Heaven."

Samael tutted. "Don't count on it, Francis. I don't think there's any plans to save any animals. I mean, can you imagine the scale of the task of bodily lifting up millions of righteous souls before the final cataclysms? That's a tough gig as it is."

"No mention of animals in Heaven in any of the texts I've seen," agreed Raphael.

Michael had a fairly ambivalent attitude to domesticated animals. Generally, they shed too much loose fur for his liking, and they had very poor hygiene routines. Nonetheless, he couldn't help but feel a pang of sympathy when he saw the stricken look of St Francis's face.

"Wait," said the saint, "you are telling me that when the Wapture physically lifts the saved into Heaven, their favouwite cats and dogs and budgies and goldfish will be left behind?"

"That's pretty much it," said Samael.

"*Their* pets? And you think they will be *happy* about that?"

"The people are going to Heaven."

"But who will feed the adorwable animals?"

"Um, no one."

Francis quaked in horror, picked up the hem of his monk robes and ran to the head of the line, shouting, "Gabwiel! Gabwiel!"

Raphael sighed sadly.

Samael smirked. "If I get to exist for another ten billion years, I will never understand humans," he said.

7

Nerys was woken by the ringing of the doorbell.

It would have been nice if, in her sleep, she had forgotten the business with Clovenhoof and the angel and the Bible, and all that doomsday crap, but the truth of it all had just seeped through in her dreams until its stain had touched every part of her. As the doorbell rang again, she pushed herself up, tipping aside Twinkle who had been asleep on her belly. Twinkle yipped in surprise, then leapt to the floor and ran circles around Nerys's feet while she fumbled her feet into her slippers.

The doorbell rang again.

"Yes, just wait," he muttered.

A fresh hangover of boxed wine was slithering around the back of her brain. It might yet grow claws and pounce on her or it might fade and die, like so many before. Nerys ambled downstairs in her dressing gown. Daylight streamed through the door's windowpane. She licked her furred teeth and opened the door.

There was a demon on her doorstep. She assumed it was demon. It was squat, yellow, and its big round head was covered in ears. Two of its hands held a clipboard and a pencil. Another hand was busy putting pencils behind its many ears, or catching those pencils which failed to stay on their ear perches. It seemed to be an entirely unconscious act, like he was juggling in his sleep.

The demon sniffed and looked at Nerys. Nerys supposed that on any normal morning, she would probably scream. This was not a normal morning. There possibly wouldn't be any normal mornings ever again.

"Pick up for Mr Satan?" said the demon.

"Is that a question?" said Nerys.

"More a general request, luv," he said.

"I am not Satan."

"No, luv. Din't think you were," said the demon. "Is your master about?"

"Master," she said and laughed. The hangover started to flex its claws. "Jeremy – I mean Mr Satan is not here."

"I know he's not 'ere. I'm picking up for him." The demon clicked his cheek. Nerys was pretty sure it was a he. It had a blokey attitude. She wouldn't be surprised if it had a copy of the *Racing Post* and a packet of fags in its back pocket.

"What are you picking up?" she asked.

He checked his clipboard. "Bible. It says. Belonging to those hoity-toity types in Heaven."

Nerys took the proffered clipboard and inspected the documentation. Superficially the paperwork looked like an ordinary delivery form, although much of it was covered in a scrawl of letters in an alphabet that Nerys not only didn't recognise, but which also made her brain hurt more just by looking at it. There were a few bits in writing she could read, even if they made no sense.

"Hodshift?" she read. "What's that?"

"That's me," said the demon. "I'm just the courier. Lord Belphegor picked me on account of the fact that I don't explode in sunlight or go stark ravin' mad." He looked up at the sky. "Frankly, I don't see what are the fuss is, do you? Clouds and sunshine and wotnot. It's all just badly organised gas and energy. Give me a dozen boys and a full weekend on double bubble, I could have all of this sorted out with ducts and pipin'. Bish bash bosh. Much neater."

"Right," she said. "I'll go get it for you then."

She went upstairs. The Bible was open on the kitchen table. There was large wine stain running through several pages, but if Heaven wanted to complain about it then they'd have to do it in person. She took the book downstairs and offered it to the demon Hodshift.

"Woah, woah, lady. What d'ya think ya doin'? Can't just give it to me. One touch of that and – *poof*! I got exploded by holiness once before. Took me years to put myself back together, let me tell you."

He produced a sphere of metal which he unfolded, then unfolded again, until it was a box that, once fully open was as solid a construction as anything Nerys had ever seen.

"Pop it in 'ere. This is a genuine bon-a-fid-ee holiness containment trunk ya got here. Safe as houses. Like a house that's *really* safe."

She lowered the Bible into the box. Hodshift leaned as far back as his arms would allow while still holding the box.

"So, do you know when he's going to come back?" she asked.

"Who?"

"Satan. Clovenhoof. He told me the world is ending."

The demon chortled. "Tell me about it. Oh, we've never been busier down there. You'd think we'd have had all eternity to prepare but, no, suddenly it's overtime with no pay and chop-chop get that Lake of Fire up to optimum temperature, boys."

"The world is really going to shit?"

"And how," said Hodshift. He put the box down, reached into his back pocket and produced – not a packet of cigarettes, not a copy of the *Racing Post* – but a long thin device which sort of looked like the offspring of a spirit level, a tyre pressure gauge, and one of those wind measuring devices with whirling cups. He held it up and looked at the needle.

"One point two gigapeccados a second," he said. "We're well over."

"Huh?"

He pointed at the gauge. "One gigapeccado is yer basic benchmark for an Apocalypse. That's like high tide. That's like water breaching the dam. We're well over."

"This thing measures how bad the world is?"

"A sort of general Shit-O-Meter, yeah, luv."

"And if the level dropped below the one gigapiccolo—"

The demon chortled. "Gigapeccado. It's yer metricated measure of evil. No chance of it dropping below it."

"But if it did…"

He puffed out his cheeks which caused half a dozen pencils to be dislodged from behind individual ears. "Well, yer Apocalypse would be on hold, won't it?"

Nerys thought fast. "Can I have that?"

"What?"

"Your Shit-O-Meter."

He seemed affronted. "But it's mine. I don't get issued with one of these every millennium."

"I'll buy it from you."

"A deal wiv a devil?" he said, amused. "Doubt you've got anyfing I want, luv. Don't want none of yer gold and pearls and that."

"What do you want?"

He scratched his head, tucking pencils away once more as he did. And then he laughed to himself. "I tell you what, I'd swap it for a six amp fuse. Can't get them in our circle for luv nor money. Old Crudflange up in the Seventh has got a whole box of them, but will he share them? Will he buggery."

"Wait there!" she said and ran upstairs.

She hammered on Ben's door. A few moments later there was a deeply unsatisfied mumbling and groaning from within and then Ben appeared, wearing a faded heavy metal t-shirt and his boxers. His morning hair looked like it had lost a fight with a tornado.

"Fuses!" said Nerys.

"Morning?" said Ben.

She pushed in past him. "You're a man. I've bet you've got some fuses somewhere."

Ben blinked blearily and pointed at a cupboard. "Try the box of *Very Important Cables*."

Nerys opened the cupboard and saw the red plastic tub. Nerys was not a man but knew their ways. Many men kept such a tub. Or a box or a drawer. In it went all the cables, clips, connectors, and electrical oddments that they should have thrown out but simply couldn't. In a ramshackle private room in her parents' Welsh home, her dad had a simply enormous box of such things: gadgets and wires for devices that had ceased production decades before. Ben, it seemed, was a perfectly ordinary man in this regard.

Nerys grabbed the whole tub and hurried downstairs, fearful the demon had already gone.

"Look in there!" she told it. "Have what you want."

He started to rummage through and almost immediately froze with surprise. "Could it be?" he whispered.

"What?"

He pulled out a beige cable like it was a wriggling snake. "A twenty-five-Way D Male to thirty-six-Way Centronics Male parallel printer cable!"

"Is that a good thing?" she said.

"It's the unholy grail, luv. You know where you can get these nowadays? Bloody nowhere." He grabbed another. "SCART cables!" He stretched it. "One point eight metres! Perfect!"

"You like this stuff?" she said.

"You kiddin'?" he said. "This is a bloody treasure trove. The problems I could fix downstairs with this stuff! Could get the spikey endoscope working again. Restart the presses of the *Infernal Daily Mail*. With a couple of these, we might even be able to get the Fulfilment Accelerated Actuator up and running once more." He looked up expectantly at her and she realised what he was asking.

"Yeah, sure," she said. "Take it. Take it all. I'll have your Shit-O-Meter—"

"Technically it's called a peccadometer."

"Yeah, yeah, yeah. Shit-O-Meter."

"And don't forget yer receipt, sweetcheeks," he said, thrusting a carbon copy of the paperwork at her.

"No. Of course."

And with that the demon picked up the tub and the box and, chuckling to himself like he'd just got the deal of the century, scuttled down the path and away.

8

Nerys spent much of the morning just staring at the Shit-O-Meter. She made herself a strong coffee or three and thought deeply about how a measuring device such as this and the knowledge of the impending Apocalypse could be put together with the specific intent of stopping the end of the world.

The little gauge on the side of the tubular device wavered a little but not by much. In the afternoon, she decided since she had the Shit-O-Meter, she might as well put it through its paces. Her first thought had been to establish whether she could detect different readings in different places.

With Twinkle on his lead, she'd taken the device into St Michael's church, the local bookies, and the double-glazing showroom. Neither the benign comfort of St Michael's, the desperation of the bookies, or the outrageous claims of the double-glazing salespeople had made any difference to the reading.

Unimpressed, she slammed the door as she went back into the shared house and stamped up the stairs. The noise brought Ben out of his flat.

"I thought it was Jeremy coming back at last. I assumed he was kicking in his door because he forgot his key again."

"No, it's just me," said Nerys. "Come up and help me brainstorm something, will you?"

Even though Ben was oblivious to the fact that Satan was his neighbour and friend, he was adept at puzzles and logic problems.

"Busy. I'm doing a maintenance wash on my washing machine," said Ben.

"What the hell is one of those?"

"An essential routine that gets rid of harmful build-ups."

"Pretty sure my washing machine doesn't even have one," said Nerys. She carried on up the stairs, knowing she had issued a challenge that Ben would not be able to resist.

"Oh, I bet it has! Are you telling me that you've never run it? Let me come and see."

Ben was at her door before she had even unlocked it.

She put the kettle on while Ben pressed buttons on her washing machine. Nerys consulted the Shit-O-Meter while he was distracted, but the reading was still the same.

"I saw that there's a new superhero movie coming out," she lied.

"Oh?"

Inspiration came in the form of the sweetener as she popped one into her tea. "Canderella, who vows to tackle all the evil in the world."

"Well that's a bit of a wide scope," said Ben. "What kind of superpowers does he have?"

"She." Nerys had her pen ready. "Good question, though. Where do you think she should start?"

Ben turned the large dial on the washing machine with the concentration of a safe cracker. "I bet it's here, under *other programmes*. Do you have the manual?"

"Focus, Ben! What are Canderella's obvious quick wins to make the world a better place?"

"Can she fire a ray gun from space to cause people pain if they do bad stuff?" asked Ben.

"No!" said Nerys. She wished she hadn't started down the superhero route. "She hasn't got that sort of superpower, she just has a lot of, erm, energy."

"It sounds like a terrible film if I'm honest, Nerys. I don't think I want to go and see—"

"—You're not even trying, Ben," she snapped.

"She would probably need to start local, establish a kindness movement."

"A kindness movement?"

"You know, just encourage people to be nice. At the same time, she could be learning how to run social media campaigns on a huge scale and somehow leverage that to make kindness competitive."

Nerys scribbled down the word *leverage*. "This is great. Multi-tasking will be essential as she is definitely on a tight deadline."

"What sort of outfit does she wear?" asked Ben.

Nerys paused for a moment. It was always pleasing to conjure up a smoking hot outfit in her mind, but she suspected it might distract Ben if she described anything too racy. "She walks amongst us, looking just like a regular babe."

"Ha! I've got it!" said Ben suddenly.

"Yes?"

He pointed at the display screen on the washing machine. "It was here under *Settings and Troubleshooting*." He pressed the button and the machine began to fill with water. "You need to run a maintenance wash, Nerys. Clear out the clogs and the nasty build ups and then your machine will be as good as new."

Nerys sighed. "You're a very annoying man at times."

"I know," he said. "Clovenhoof put that as my description when he set me up with a Tinder account."

NERYS DIDN'T OPEN a fresh box of wine when she sat down for dinner that evening. Once she'd kicked Ben out, she spent the afternoon scribbling down notes. The appearance of the Shit-O-Meter and the chat with Ben had got the cogs turning in her brain.

She had pages from a notepad spread all over the table, with circled headings like KINDNESS CAMPAIGN and SOCIAL CHANGE and PUBLIC CONSCIOUSNESS, and all around them were dotted sub ideas. But the more she wrote, the more she came to the same conclusion.

"Money, Twinkle. I need cash. Spondoolies."

Twinkle looked up at her and licked his own nose.

"I need money to kickstart a kindness campaign," she said.

The impending Apocalypse put a new perspective on things she might otherwise have baulked at. Working a regular nine to five job was out of the question so she needed to bankroll her own expenses as well as the ones she would incur as she took on the world's problems.

She stood up. "Jeremy would want me to do this, so I'm sure he's fine with me selling his things to fund it." She moved to the door and Twinkle followed. "No, you stay here, boy. I have no idea what you might catch in there."

After spending twenty minutes with a YouTube video and a bent hairpin, trying to pick his lock, Nerys realised that Clovenhoof's door wasn't even locked, so she let herself in. She looked around for anything she might sell, but realised nearly everything he owned was irretrievably grubby or broken. There was a big television, but he'd put deep scratches in the screen with his horns, bending down to switch it on and off.

Even his porn selection had moved entirely online, so after scouring his flat, Nerys had nothing that was saleable. Maybe she would come back later for the television.

Her mind had been reaching for the next logical step while she had been searching Jeremy's flat. If the world really was going to end, then she could borrow money without any concern for how she might pay it back. If she succeeded in averting the crisis, then she would need to think of something, but right now she was desperate.

FIRST THING IN THE MORNING, she went into town, placed an order at the t-shirt printing shop, then went into the bank.

"Do you have an appointment?" asked the receptionist when she asked about loans. The name of his lapel badge didn't describe him as a receptionist but a CUSTOMER FOCUS ASSISTANT.

"No," she said.

"So sorry, you'll need to make an appointment with one of our specialists."

"Fine. Can I please make an appointment?" Nerys asked.

"Yes, I have one for eleven fifteen," he said, checking a screen.

Nerys looked up at the clock on the wall. "That's now."

"So, will that be suitable, madame?" he asked.

She sighed. "Yes. Obviously. Given that I'm here."

He led her away to a desk in an open plan cubicle. "How can I help you today?"

Nerys looked around and then back at him. "You're the specialist, then?"

He steepled his fingers and leaned forward. "I am a customer focus specialist."

"I thought you were a customer focus assistant."

"I am both," he said. "I am a specialist and I will be assisting you throughout your customer journey."

"How much money could I get as a loan? And how quickly?" asked Nerys.

"Personal or business loan?" he asked, tapping his keyboard.

"Um, it's business I guess."

"And the nature of the business?"

Nerys thought quickly. "It will be to help people. And communities. And society."

"Uh huh. A social enterprise then. Your scope sounds somewhat undefined though. Can you pin it down?"

Nerys scowled. "I'm working through that. I need money to help me figure it out."

"A test and learn approach. Got it." He wrote more notes.

Nerys was surprised to hear there was a fancy way to describe her process of winging it. "Yeah. That. So, what do you think?"

He sat back. "Of course, there will very likely be grant opportunities for an undertaking with provable social outcomes. You should look at those. Once you've got your business plan and your financial forecasts together, we could probably get you up and running inside three months, all being well."

Nerys sighed. Everything was far too slow for what she needed. She left the bank with a handful of leaflets but no actual money.

She collected her t-shirt order, walked to the park, put on some fresh lipstick and started filming.

"Hello everybody and welcome to my crowdfunding video. I want to share my vision for a world where kindness is more of a habit than an afterthought. No, scratch that, I want to make it a sport where we can have an Olympics Games of competitive kindness. I need money for that, which is why we're here. Take a look at the t-shirt I'm wearing. It's your reward if you become a tier one backer. *Honk if you're Helpful* will be a viral message very soon." She pushed her chest out to make the slogan more visible. "Even if you can't afford to back me, you can still join my kindness army and start to make a difference."

"What are you doing?"

This came Spartacus Wilson, who was scooting idly along the path on his skateboard.

"Oh, hello," said Nerys. "I'm just doing a short video for my new kindness campaign."

Spartacus read her t-shirt. "Honk if you're helpful?"

"That's right."

"Is it about helping geese?"

"What? No. It's like for car drivers. They see someone wearing a *Honk if you're Helpful!* t-shirt and they beep their hooters. Build up a sense of camaraderie."

"Right," he said slowly. "Cos that's not how I read it."

"No?"

"Particularly since you've got it across your..." He gestured generally at her chest area. "Honk sounds like an open invite."

"Spartacus Wilson!" she gasped.

"Not that I would," he added.

"I'd expect so!"

"I mean you're far too old for one thing."

She fumed noisily. "Starting up a worldwide campaign to create goodness and save the world isn't very easy, you know!"

"No, I suppose not. You know what I would do?"

"Pray tell," she said.

"I'd set up an on-line platform where people could request things they need help with and other people could volunteer. Sort of like a dating site for help people."

"A kindness exchange?"

"Yeah, that."

She tilted her head. "Not a bad idea."

"I could knock something up over the weekend, if you like."

"I do like," she said. "Thank you, Spartacus!"

He sniffed and nodded, the deal done. "All of this is on the understanding there's no *Honk me if you're helpful* stuff on the platform. You'd get the wrong sort."

He pushed away and skated out through the park gate.

ON THE SATURDAY, Nerys ate her breakfast and mused on how she might encourage punters to sign up for the platform.

"I need a role model, Twinkle. Someone amazing who will perform acts of kindness and show the world what this is all about."

Twinkle lifted a leg to lick his private parts.

"Oh, you clever dog. Yes! Of course, I could be that role model. I should be the change I want to see in the world."

After breakfast, she went to the supermarket, portable camera mounted on her head, ready to capture footage. She carried a ukulele, reasoning if there was one thing better than carrying out small acts of kindness, it would be doing them with a musical accompaniment. As she walked through the car park she strummed the ukulele and smiled at passers-by. Many of them glared at her with naked hostility and deep suspicion.

"Do you take requests?" called out a man pushing a trolley.

"Yes!" said Nerys. "What would you like?"

"Fuck off, that's my request."

Nerys was undaunted. She watched the crowd for people who might be struggling with their bags, but everyone seemed to be coping well. She saw an elderly woman waiting at the side of the store. She had picked a terrible place to cross the road as it was near to the entrance to the car park.

"Let me help!" shouted Nerys and she trotted over. "I will make it safe for you to cross. One moment."

She strode at the oncoming traffic, holding up an arm and a ukulele in an imperious manner. She made eye contact with the driver of the next car and gave him the most penetrating glare she could muster. The car slowed to a stop and Nerys stood in front of it, still holding up the ukulele to make it clear that no cars would be permitted to move until she said so. The woman seemed nervous about crossing, so Nerys went over to the side of the road, keeping her eye on the driver of the first vehicle in case he tried to make a move.

"Come on!" she said. "No need to be scared." she pulled the reluctant woman across the road and delivered her to the other side. "There you go!"

Nerys stepped back to the side of the road and waved the traffic on.

"You're welcome!" she called to the world in general. She felt good about herself, and hoped the footage would be good.

Nerys made her way back to the store entrance to look for the next person who might need help. She was slightly perplexed to see the old woman she had helped across the road making her way through the car park towards the crossing. She crossed the road back towards Nerys and seemed to be heading back to the place where she'd originally been standing.

"Are you sure you want to do that?" said Nerys.

"Yes!" snapped the woman. "It's where my son is going to pick me up."

Sure enough, as the woman approached her original spot, a car pulled over and she climbed in. Nerys could see an animated conversation between the woman and the driver before they pulled off. It looked very much as if the woman was complaining about being forcibly marched across the road.

Nerys sighed and went back to strumming the ukulele.

9

Clovenhoof took in a deep breath and savoured the stench of sulphur and soot, the stink of human filth and desperation.

"Shitting hell, you forget how thick the smell of the Old Place is."

"We pride ourselves on making Hell a flavoursome experience," said Belphegor.

It wasn't just the smell, thought Clovenhoof as they entered Hell's great reception cavern. He'd forgotten the smell, yes, but he'd forgotten the noise, the oppressive heat, the sheer scale of the place. Below the elevated path from which Clovenhoof and Belphegor watched, the newly damned shuffled along a zigzag of barriers towards the gates and what were essentially the immigration checkpoints of Hell.

"Did this place always look like JFK airport?" he said.

"We did a bit of remodelling," said Lord Peter coolly. "We had a lot to learn from US Immigration."

Demons roughly shoved new arrivals for no good reason, and one was pinned to the ground while the demon dog Cerberus treated him to a *very* intimate examination.

"We did give the security demons assault rifles and tasers at one point," said Belphegor, "But it's actually much harder to deal with damned individuals if they're already full of holes or had their brains cooked."

Clovenhoof's long-legged creature formed from Limbo-stuff strutted and swayed among the demonic procession. Peter had to lift his sandalled feet to avoid tripping over its hoofed feet.

He muttered something under his breath and turned to Clovenhoof. "Satan … Lucifer … your return to the Inferno is something of a surprise. Not that we aren't pleased to see you down here. Hell is, after all, exactly where you belong."

"Ah, tell me about it," Clovenhoof grinned. "I have missed this place so much." Although having said that, he did feel it was perhaps a little too warm for his liking; and would it hurt if the cursed souls of Hell turned down the volume of their screams just a bit?

"Things have changed," said Peter. "There is now structure. There is order."

"I kept things in order," said Clovenhoof.

Belphegor's wheelchair wheel squeaked. Berith shifted uncomfortably. Azazel seemed to take a great deal of interest in the dribbles of molten rock on the wall next to him.

"Okay," Clovenhoof admitted. "When I was in charge, it

was more like a free form jazz improv band. But I slayed it as band leader."

"Improv," said Peter thoughtfully.

"Look, if you're worried about me coming here and taking over, do not worry, baby. I have bigger fish to fry in the world above."

"Oh?"

"Oh, yeah. I organise bingo mornings at the care home. I sell rude carvings at the local farmers' market. And ... and I'm learning to play the piano. Properly. I can play *Jingle Bells* now."

There were more embarrassed shufflings, and still no one could meet his eye.

Peter cleared his throat. "Well, that's—"

"Including the chorus!" Clovenhoof added. "And that's not easy."

"Yes, Lord Satan. I see. Your mind is indeed on loftier things. Well, now that's cleared up, it seems that your return to Hell in these End Times is purely a figurative one. We all have a job to do. I am ever Heaven's servant and I will ensure that Hell continues to run smoothly under *my* effective management."

"Absolutely."

"And your role between now and the End of Days will be more symbolic. A figurehead."

"Like a king," said Clovenhoof.

"Or a mascot, perhaps."

"The poster boy of the Armageddon."

"Yes."

"Yes."

The former angel and the former saint eyeballed one another at length.

Peter gave a decisive sniff. "Very well. Belphegor, give Satan a tour of Hell's many improvements and then bring him to the Corporate Management Centre. I'm sure Berith is keen to show you the armies you will be leading into battle."

"Armies? Oh, yeah. Er, can't wait."

Peter strode away, possibly aiming to look like a very important man with important things to do, but coming across much more as a petty functionary having a sulk.

"What a dick," grinned Clovenhoof.

"He has improved Hell, sire," said Belphegor. "There can be no doubt of that. Clear management structure. Accountability at all levels. Data-led decision making."

"Yeah," said Berith. "But we preferred it when you was in charge."

"Thank you, Berith," said Clovenhoof.

"We could do whatever we wanted and you didn't have a clue."

"I shall take that as a compliment."

Azazel snagged up Clovenhoof's wobbling mutant creature in his knife-edged claws. "I can destroy this aberration if you wish, Lord."

"Don't you dare. I think it's adorable."

"It's misshapen and ungainly and does nothing but flap its ugly lips and get under people's feet."

"Adorable indeed," said Belphegor, wryly. "What is it meant to be?"

Clovenhoof looked at its long neck and goofy face. "It's a

sort of... What are those South American sheep things called?"

Azazel and Berith looked at one another, neither of them familiar with creatures of the world above.

"Sheep?" said Belphegor.

"Alpacas!" said Clovenhoof, clicking his fingers. "It's sort of like an alpaca."

"Does Earth have such misshapen creatures?" said Berith.

"Alpacas are cool," said Clovenhoof. "They spit at people when they don't like them." He swung himself onto the back of his creation. As it bucked in surprise and annoyance, he raised his phone high and took a selfie of himself.

A split second later, the alpaca had bucked and tossed Clovenhoof to the rough ground.

Azazel let out a weary sigh. "I have no time for this nonsense. I have preparation to attend to."

"And the armies await your inspection, Satan," said Berith, indicating the way.

"Oh, jolly good," said Clovenhoof, with as much enthusiasm as he could muster. He checked his selfie and, impressed with it, sent it to Michael. He had no idea what the mobile phone signal was like down here, but he guessed it would get through somehow.

He looked at Belphegor. "So, the, er, Corporate Management Centre?"

"Corporate Management Centre of Nameless Dread," Belphegor nodded as he pushed the lever to drive his steam-powered wheelchair onward. "Repairs to the Fortress of Nameless Dread proved too onerous, so Lord Peter had chief architect Mulciber design a much more ergonomic base of operations."

"But the fortress ... I really liked it. It was huge and thrusting and ... Mulciber loved it."

Belphegor chuckled drily. "I know Mulciber felt that the tower was nothing but a vulgar phallic insult aimed at the Almighty who cast you down here."

"I know!" said Clovenhoof. "It was brilliant."

They moved down the path to cross by the queue of souls waiting to enter Hell. It never ceased to amaze Clovenhoof that given a choice between queuing patiently to enter Hell and fighting and screaming to get away, most people seemed unable to avoid the lure of a big long queue.

To Clovenhoof's eye, half the demons who caught sight of him were awestruck, some even throwing themselves on the ground in prostration. The other half seemed to turn to their colleagues and ask: "Who's that wanker in the ugly shirt?"

Such was the fleeting nature of fame, Clovenhoof supposed. As the reappointed figurehead for Hell, he guessed he ought to show an interest in what the demons were doing. He addressed two lowly scab-faced demons.

"Hello, who are you?"

One snorted back a dribble of snot. "Pisskettle, your worship."

"I ain't tellin' you nuffin," said the other, gripping his pitchfork tightly.

"Ignore Lynchgill," said Pisskettle. "He's just had a tough few centuries."

"Oh, really? And what is it you do?" said Clovenhoof,

who felt it was the sort of thing Hell's symbolic leader should ask to put the workers at ease.

"The damned come through here to processing and we pokes 'em in the bum," said Pisskettle, with a demonstrative stab at a passing soul. The damned human yelped, sobbed, and moved on.

"And then?"

"We pokes the next one, your worship."

Clovenhoof nodded. "Important work. Very, very important work."

"It is. Thank you, sir." Pisskettle gave an especially vigorous pitchfork poke at the next soul to show his gratitude.

"Yeah, but it's just Pisskettle and me doin' it," said Lynchgill bitterly. "Poke, poke, poke. What management don't recognise is that not only are more and more damned coming through 'ere, but the bums is getting bigger."

"Oh?" said Clovenhoof.

"Thirty percent increase in average bum size in the last sixty years," said the unhappy demon. "That's a lot of bummage for two demons to cover."

"I suppose it is," said Clovenhoof. He gazed around the crowd entrance and processing area. "Still, I suppose that when Armageddon comes and all the remaining humans have been judged then your job here will eventually be done."

"What?"

Clovenhoof raised a hand to the arched gate to Hell. "Everyone will be dead. Blessed and damned will either be here or in Heaven. You'll eventually get to poke your last bum."

The two demons looked at each other. "You mean ... we'd stop poking bums?" said Pisskettle.

"No more bums to poke," agreed Clovenhoof. "So, that's a cheering thought."

As Belphegor and Berith led the way onward, the two demons behind fell to a quiet intense squabbling, but were soon lost in the crowds of the damned.

Clovenhoof and the two dukes proceeded through the infernal circles. Howls of agony and the clanking of heavy chains reverberated among the gargantuan stalactites overhead. Misshapen winged horrors flapped against the dull orange firelights of Hell. It was as Clovenhoof was admiring Yan Ryuleh Sloggoth, Elder demon of the impenetrable depths playing with his food in the pool of Negligent Oil Tanker Captains, that a small yellow demon came huffing and puffing up to them with a plastic tub in his hands.

"Hodshift," said Belphegor. "A problem with the assignment?"

"Nah, chief. Bible delivered back to the stuck-up Heaven's lot wiv no trouble. Bish-bash-bosh, job's a gud un. Barely singed my feet on their doorstep."

"So what is this?"

"Is that Ben's box of Very Important Cables?" asked Clovenhoof.

"Very important and very valuable," said Hodshift. "And look – a SCART cable! I was reckoning that wiv this we could get the Fulfilment Accelerated Actuator up and running again."

Belphegor hissed and drew back. "Really? Last time we tested that, we nearly demolished the Seventh Circle."

"Yeah, but it was only the Seventh, weren't it?" said Hodshift and cracked a grin. "Not like it was one of the important ones."

Belphegor delved through the box. "You would still need a RS-232 serial data cable."

"I bet Ben's got one hidden somewhere," said Clovenhoof casually.

Hodshift looked at Belphegor with child-like hope, hopping from one foot to another. "What ya reckon, sir?"

Belphegor sighed. "It's the end of all things. What harm can it do? Go find your cable. And no lallygagging, imp!"

Once Hodshift had dashed off, Berith flung out an impatient hand. "If you have quite finished, can we now go see my armies?"

"Of course, dear Duke. Lead on," said Belphegor.

The armies of Hell were indeed an impressive sight. When Clovenhoof first glimpsed them, he didn't recognise them for what they were. In the gloomy half-light, he thought he was looking over a field of black wavering grass. Only when he focussed more closely did he realise he was looking down onto a massive valley of Hell which was populated, end to end, with pitchfork and spear-wielding demons.

"Satan's balls," whispered Clovenhoof. "How many soldiers have you got here?"

"Five hundred thousand, or thereabouts," said Berith.

"That's your basic grunts. Then there's the legion of Nephilim over there," he said, pointing at a contingent of armoured giants. "Plus we've got a herd of behemoth; and we've been training up the Leviathan."

Clovenhoof frowned. "Leviathan is a giant water demon. What good is an ocean-going demon going to be in a land battle?"

"Land, air and sea, we're prepared," said Berith.

This raised a question that had been skulking in Clovenhoof's brain. "The Final Battle. Where exactly is that happening?"

"*Revelations* says it will happen at Armageddon, otherwise known as Tel Megiddo," said Belphegor. "It's a hill in Israel."

"Oh. Anything special about it?"

Belphegor's grey whiskers twitched in his wrinkled face. "There's a kibbutz commune there, agricultural mostly."

"Won't they be surprised when all of Heaven and Hell's armed forces turn up on their doorstep?"

"Our forces will first meet in Limbo, sir," said Berith. "That's where we will initially face them. That's where you will strike the first blow against the arrogant angels of the Lord. Where it spills out to from there—" The red-faced warrior demon grinned. "Our war will consume the whole Earth, eventually."

Clovenhoof struggled with the scale of it – the size of the army, the fact that he was expected to lead them. "I didn't know we had so many demons."

"Been breeding them up for centuries," said Berith.

"Breeding?"

"Hardly breeding," said Belphegor. "We developed a technique to double the number of demons we had."

"Yes?"

"We chopped them in half."

"Right. I can see that would, er, numerically double them. But then you've just got two halves of a demon, haven't you?"

"Very resilient, your average demon," said Belphegor. "Nothing won't grow back, given time. Down there we have a corral for the bottom halves. They just bump around while we wait for them to grow a brain, maybe some fresh limbs."

"I see. And the top halves?"

"We send 'em straight back to work," said Berith.

"But they've got no legs."

"We tell them to grow a pair," said Berith simply.

"Of course." Clovenhoof saw a massive machine down in the valley floor. It was a fat barrel of a thing with a spiral nose cone. Its chuntering engines sent out clouds of black smoke. "What's that thing?"

"One of Belphegor's cute science experiments," said Berith with a condescending chuckle.

"It is as you say," said the inventor demon modestly. "Come, Satan. Let us inspect the troops and then get you to Lord Peter, eh?"

10

The doorbell rang as Nerys was towelling her hair. An afternoon spent trying to boost kindness in the local area by handing out umbrellas during a rainstorm had only elicited suspicious looks and a personal soaking.

She went downstairs and found Spartacus Wilson on the doorstep using his skateboard as a temporary shelter against the last of the day's rain.

"Mr C in?" he asked.

"I'm afraid not."

The teenager tutted. "That dead badger behind the Boldmere Oak isn't going to stay there forever you know. It's going to lose its badgeriness at some point."

She waved him in out of the rain. "I don't think we're going to see Jeremy for a while. He's—" She didn't know how to explain it, but it reminded her of the Apocalypse descending upon all the innocent people of the world. "Have you lived a good life?" she said.

He laughed. "Give me a chance. I've barely started. I did the thing."

"The thing?"

"The kindness exchange platform. You know. Honk if you're horny. All that."

"Helpful," she corrected him. "You've set it up."

"Piece of piss, really. I can show you." He had his laptop tucked under his arm.

Nerys led the way upstairs.

"He on his holidays then?" asked Spartacus.

"I don't think I'd call it that."

"Ah, prison." He saw that Clovenhoof's flat door was ajar and pushed it open. It swung wide on the quiet, unoccupied flat. "What's he inside for this time?"

"Er, the usual," said Nerys.

Spartacus frowned. "That's either painting rude graffiti or public nudity. Penis-based either way."

"Yes. Er, both," she lied. "Um, painting lewd pictures on walls using his own body as a stencil."

Both paused for a moment, trying to picture how that would work, then Spartacus walked in and opened his laptop on the table.

"Your kindness exchange is already live," he said. "It's a very straightforward interface."

Nerys looked at the website open on the screen. It was welcoming and clearly laid out, and didn't look like the kind of thing a teenager might knock up over a week.

"I can't believe how quickly you've done this," she said.

"My mates helped."

"But still..."

"You're going to want a way of filtering the requests that are coming through," Spartacus said.

"Really?" asked Nerys. "I'm sure nobody would—"

Spartacus flicked the screen to a back-end database thing so that she could read some of the early calls. People were already logging requests for lewd acts and sexual favours.

"Shame Mr C isn't here. He'd leap right in and help with some of these," said Spartacus.

"This was meant to be just so people could reach out and help each other. Sort of like Bob-a-Job."

"Bob-a...? That sounds rank."

"Bob-a-Job. You were in the cub scouts, weren't you?"

"Yeah. But we weren't into none of that. I'm not bobbing for anyone's jobbie. Now, we can search for keywords in the text to filter out the creepy stuff, but it might not be enough." Spartacus looked around meaningfully. "You know, I could work on this a bit more full time if I had a place to crash."

It took Nerys a moment to catch on. "Here? Why would you want to stay here?"

Spartacus shrugged. "Cos I don't like my mum's new boyfriend. He takes an interest in my hobbies and wants to know how I'm getting on at school, and keeps offering to take me and Bea out to the cinema and bowling and that."

"So, acting like a dad?"

"Yeah. It's not natural. I can't cope. Also, Bea is singing Ariana Grande songs at top volume twenty-four seven.

Besides, I'm sixteen now. It's time for me to move out and get my own crib."

Nerys was about to point out that Jeremy Clovenhoof was going to come back some time, before remembering that he probably wasn't.

"*Mi casa, su casa,*" she said.

"No thanks. I've already eaten."

As Spartacus looked round for somewhere to plug in his laptop, Nerys's phone rang. The caller ID was Tina.

She took a deep breath before answering. Nerys and Tina had known each other for many years, and their relationship teetered back and forth between deadly enemies and uneasy allies. Several people had suggested Nerys saw a mirror image of herself in Tina, and it was possibly the most infuriating allegation that could be flung at her; not least because it was true.

"Hi, Tina," said Nerys in a forcibly cheery voice which came out an octave higher than her normal voice.

"*Hi, Babe!*" came back Tina's voice, equally high and false. "*It's been too long!*"

"Uh-huh." Nerys was on high alert. Tina being pleasant was dangerous. "How's things?"

"*I've been very busy. Making good in the service industry.*"

"Servicing wealthy middle-aged men behind their wives' backs you mean?"

"*Nerys. Those days are behind me. Actually, I'm part of the hospitality team at the Luxor hotel at the Belfry. Very swanky.*"

"Oh, how lovely."

"*Anyway, I saw your new venture, Nerys.*"

"New venture?"

"Your helping each other website thing. I must say, it's adorable. I want to help."

"Oh. Right. You can sign up as a helper and get started right away."

"No, I don't want to help as a punter, I want to help you steer the ship."

"Does my ship need steering?"

"We make a great team Nerys. You can't deny it."

It was annoying but true, and Nerys was somewhat gratified by this development. Not only was this thing getting noticed, but if she'd stopped to think about the benchmark for appealing to those of a competitive nature, then Tina would surely have been her first thought. This meant she was on the right track.

"Actually, there might be a role for you," said Nerys. "The platform needs a moderator to make sure that inappropriate requests don't go live."

"Oh yes! I can do that! I'll be on the board or the committee or whatever it is too, right?"

"Sure," said Nerys. "Board." She knew Tina would fling herself into the endeavour if she was permitted to broadcast details of how very wholesome she was.

"Let me know when the next board meeting is. I will be there."

"What's this about Jeremy doing rude graffiti?" asked Ben, coming into the flat.

"Huh?" said Nerys.

Ben hitched a thumb at Spartacus. "Says he's doing nude Banksy paintings."

"Should call himself Wanksy," said Spartacus.

"Board meeting is in half an hour if you can get over here," said Nery and ended the call.

THE BOARD MEETING was held in Clovenhoof's abandoned flat. The four of them, Nerys, Spartacus, Ben and Tina, sat around the dented dining table. Nerys had chipped off the worst of the congealed stuff before Tina arrived.

"Nerys, what is this the board of, exactly?" Ben asked.

Nerys pointed at her chest. "*Honk if You're Helpful.* It's a social enterprise providing a platform for people to offer direct help to others who need it. We're like the Uber of helpfulness."

Ben's eyes swivelled from Nerys to Spartacus and Tina. "I'm still catching up here. When you say platform, is that like a software platform?"

Spartacus nodded. "Written by me."

"And moderated by me," said Tina.

"People ask for kindnesses and others deliver them. We facilitate the world becoming a better place!" said Nerys.

Ben nodded along. "So, what's my role?"

"We can figure that out as we go. We're adopting a 'test and learn' approach." Nerys was still revelling in her newfound knowledge that there were legitimate business terms for being haphazard and ignorant.

Tina tried to brush away flakes of dirt on the table, giving up when she realised they were stuck there.

"How many live requests do we have now?" asked Nerys.

Spartacus did something with his laptop and Nerys saw

Clovenhoof's horn-gouged television burst into life as a linked display.

"Here's the live dashboard," said Spartacus. "We have four hundred requests already logged."

"Fuck me," whispered Nerys.

"That's a surprisingly common request," grinned Spartacus. "I've implemented a workflow that sends all new requests to Tina for approval."

"I'm planning on putting a few people in the naughty corner," said Tina, with a prim smile.

"So, we've got around one hundred outstanding legitimate requests, with thirty already fulfilled."

"This is brilliant!" said Nerys.

"I'm working on a leader board," said Spartacus. "Oh yeah – you might need to order more t-shirts. We have quite a lot of investors for the crowdfunding."

"Ben, you can be in charge of t-shirt fulfilment," declared Nerys.

Ben gave a reluctant nod.

Nerys dipped into her handbag and pulled out the Shit-O-Meter device the demon had left her. She wanted to see if the platform's launch had impacted the reading, even by a tiny bit. She was disappointed to see that it was unchanged.

"Right, we need to set ourselves some challenging targets," she declared. "Each one of us can take on some requests, fulfil them in a big showy blaze of glory, and set the world of social media on fire with our hashtag. Man needs help with some tidying. I can do that."

Ben raised a hand. "I'm not sure there's anything here for me. I'm not really very hands-on."

Nerys rolled her eyes. "Spartacus?"

"Hm. Lady in Erdington needs help with her tax return," said Spartacus, reading from his laptop. "Or there's someone who wants help cataloguing a comic collection in Kingstanding."

Ben jumped out of his seat. "Oh! Oh, my God, I had no idea. Text me the address Spartacus!"

11

Nerys steered her car onto a track that looked as if it led to a farm and bounced along the muddy rutted surface. She pulled through a gate into a courtyard with a modest farmhouse at the one end and various outbuildings to the sides.

This was the address of the person who had requested some tidying. It was in an isolated yet possibly affluent area, and she was hoping it would be a wardrobe declutter, where she could take on the role of style mentor, which very much played to her strengths. A makeover where she turned someone from dowdy to stylish would be lots of fun.

The door was opened by a middle-aged man, dashing Nerys's brief fantasy.

"Here to help!" she declared, proudly pointing at her t-shirt.

He read it carefully. "What if I don't have anything to honk?"

"I'm the helpful one," she said.

"Are you going to honk something?" he said.

"Maybe later."

"That'll be nice. I'm Peregrine Thews. My friends call me Perry."

"Hi Perry. I'm Nerys. Why don't you show me what needs to be done?" said Nerys.

He led her to an outbuilding at the side of the house. It was like a large garage which could easily have accommodated two cars parked side by side, if it was empty. But it was not empty. It was piled high with boxes and entangled household detritus.

"Oh dear," said Nerys. "Which part did you need tidying?"

"All of it," said Perry. "It's got a bit out of hand."

"Let me look around for a moment, will you?" Nerys asked.

He left her and she wriggled through the mess. One thing was clear, she could spend a week of her time on this job, and at the end of it she would probably have one very grateful man, but it would not move the needle of the Shit-O-Meter. She considered backing away, but that was too much like giving up. She messaged Spartacus, asking if a job could be assigned to multiple people.

A few minutes later Nerys told Perry Thews, "Right, there will be six people coming along tomorrow morning to tackle this."

"Oh really?" His face lit up. Nerys realised that human contact was what he was really looking forward to.

"Yes. You will need to help them, though. Probably best if

you pull up a chair and tell them what needs to be kept, donated, or thrown away as they work."

She returned home to find a hum of activity coming from Clovenhoof's flat. Boxes of t-shirts were being opened, separated, and sent out again. Spartacus had set up a number of computers and widescreen monitors from which he could mastermind the logistics. Tina sat in the far corner, working on her laptop with an amused look on her face.

"Didn't fancy doing that tidying job yourself?" said Tina.

"I ... recognised more help was needed."

"Oh, so you're going to pick up something else and do that?" Tina glanced up at her. "Not going to let everyone else do all the hard work?"

Nerys ignored her and looked at the television, which was permanently set up as the live dashboard for the kindness exchange.

She could see the requests were coming in thick and fast, but not being serviced quickly enough to keep pace. She had asked Spartacus to work on some of the elements which would encourage competition, but in the meantime she thought there must be ways that a smart person could scale up their efforts. What was the opposite of Perry's garage? It needed to be an easy task that could satisfy several people at once. She paged through the requests looking for candidates. She spotted something almost immediately and dashed upstairs to her own flat.

"Twinkle, we have work to do!" she said.

Nerys could walk one dog, in fact she had a lot of experience walking Twinkle. What made sense for scaling up was to walk several at a time, which ought to be simple if each had a separate lead.

"Let's do some practice, Twinkle." Nerys swapped her usual right-handed walking style and led Twinkle back and forth across her lounge with her left hand. "Seems doable. So, I can double up. How many leads can I hold with one hand though?"

Nerys only had two dog leads, Twinkle's usual one and a spare, but she did have a comprehensive collection of sex toys and playful harnesses. She liked to think of it as an Ann Summers retrospective. She pulled out an open cup body harness with chains. It had straps that went round her neck, down her front and sides, while the chains dangled saucily below her boobs. Fond memories of wearing it made her smile, but she reckoned it had enough leatherette straps to simulate four dog leads. She tried it in her left hand and then her right hand. No problem.

Four leads in each hand for her and Spartacus. Sixteen dogs in one giant session of walkies.

She collected him as she went downstairs. "Come with me. We're off for a walk."

"Sure," said the lad, picking up his skateboard.

"You don't need that. We're going to have our hands full."

"We're going for a walk, yeah? Wheels make that easier. Physics says so."

Nerys had no easy answer for that, so she shrugged.

They collected the various dogs whose owners had requested walks, and by the time they reached Sutton Park they had the full complement of sixteen. Nerys had two collies, five cockapoos, labradoodles or some other thing that looked like a teddy bear, and her last dog was an Irish wolfhound. Spartacus had gravitated towards the scruffier dogs. Apart from a pair of elderly Jack Russells, Nerys didn't know what some of them were.

Nerys realised that lead tangling was going to be a major issue, so she walked slowly and spent a lot of time rearranging dogs. Spartacus kept speeding ahead as he rumbled along on his skateboard. As they entered the park, Nerys was struck with a thought.

"You go ahead, I'm just going to organise this lot."

Spartacus sped up slightly. Was his tiny entourage pulling him along?

There was a useful height differential between Nerys's dogs. She swapped leads around so that the five teddy bear dogs had their leads fastened to the collar of the Irish wolfhound. The collies she kept on a separate arm. She needed to take a picture of this! The smaller dogs milled around the big old wolfhound who lolloped along, seemingly without noticing them. She pulled her phone out and snapped some pictures, but at that moment a squirrel ran across the path.

The small teddy bear dogs all launched themselves forward as a single, but very uncoordinated unit, dragging the Irish wolfhound along for the ride. He was on a retractable lead, so the untidy scrum gambolled for a considerable distance before Nerys could apply the brake to the lead. The two collies both adopted the creeping stance that she had seen on sheepdog demonstrations. Did that mean that they were about to launch – yes it did.

"Shit!"

Nerys was swept off her feet as the collies ran towards the squirrel at top speed. Instead of getting in a tangled mess like the floofy teddy bear dogs did, this pair ran as a team, towing Nerys as an afterthought. As they approached the other group of dogs they simply jumped over them in pursuit of the squirrel, which meant Nerys was yanked off her feet and dumped on top of the first group of dogs. She still held both leads, determined not to lose the dogs, although she might have all her skin flayed off as she was towed around the park.

"What do you think you're doing?" she bellowed in the best dog-controlling voice she could muster from her position on the floor. She followed it with a bass, throaty rumble of general disapproval as she scrambled to her feet. Most of the dogs snapped out of their squirrel-based frenzy, especially as it had long since disappeared up a tree.

Nerys checked them all for any obvious signs of injury from her brief dog-surfing interlude, and organised them back into groups she could hold at either side. She kept the retractable lead at a shorter length to prevent the Irish wolfhound group from bolting, and reached into her pocket for a packet of treats. She would need to control the collies by keeping them very focussed on her.

Every one of the dogs recognised the crinkle of the packet. They all stopped walking and tried to be at the front of the queue. Which meant Nerys had dogs pawing at her legs from every side, threatening to sweep her off her feet again. She sighed in frustration and held one treat up in the air.

"Sit!" she tried.

Several of the dogs knew the word and plonked their

bottoms down. One of them was the Irish Wolfhound and he sat on top of some of the teddy bear dogs, setting off another chain reaction of milling and squirming. Eventually all the dogs fell under the spell and sat to attention.

Just for the briefest moment, Nerys smiled at the magic of having eight dogs being obedient and attentive. It all went to hell when she dispensed the first treat, as it sent the others into a disappointed frenzy. She gave each one a treat and they eventually set off walking again. Spartacus had looped around and was coming back towards them. Nerys hoped he hadn't noticed her own problems.

After an hour, Nerys was utterly exhausted. Picking up poo had brought its own logistical nightmare, but they had managed it, mainly by Spartacus pointing it out and Nerys picking it up. Now all they had to do was to back-track to all of the dogs' homes and drop them off with their owners. It became easier as the group grew smaller, and eventually they trouped home.

She checked the selfies she had tried to take with the dogs and saw they captured the exact moment she was swept off her feet. Her face was a rigid mask of terror as she was surrounded by a group of dogs having the time of their lives.

Spartacus leaned over. "I got some pictures of that too. I bet these will be popular."

So much for her indignity going unnoticed. They both uploaded pictures, and Nerys admitted they had a certain chaotic charm, even if the whole thing was a little embarrassing.

Nerys went home and put her feet up while she considered easier ways to scale the kindness that people could deliver, because dog walking seemed to have some in-built limits.

THE FOLLOWING MORNING, nursing an aching back and shoulders, Nerys watched some footage from the group that had tidied Perry Thews' garage. They were locals, and it seemed as though several of them knew Perry. It was a heartwarming sight as Perry regained his outbuilding space and the group sat around afterwards smiling and toasting each other with their mugs.

She called in on Ben to show him the photos.

"Look! It's lovely. How can we generate more of this lovely vibe?"

Ben pushed aside a box of *Honk if you're Helpful* t-shirts on the counter to look at the photos properly. "How nice! I got some pictures too!"

He pulled out his phone and showed Nerys a series of pictures. They had no people in them, but showed various nerd artifacts in cellophane bags with handwritten labels, standing upright in lidded cardboard boxes.

"Each one backed by acid-free cardboard and indexed for easy retrieval," sighed Ben. "Beautiful job, if I say so myself."

"You made one person very happy," said Nerys. "Does it help with the rest of the world, though? How do we make this into a viral sensation, Ben?"

Ben stared at Nerys. "Canderella isn't really coming soon at cinemas, is she?"

She caught his glance and sighed. "Okay, you got me."

"It's you and this odd new enthusiasm for helping people."

"What's odd about wanting to help people?"

"Nothing. *You* wanting to help people is odd. What happened? Are you dying? Were you visited by three Christmas ghosts?"

"I just want to make the world a better place, and I need to get other people to make it a better place too. Raise the general goodness in society."

"And is Jeremy really in prison? I've not seen any of these Wanksy paintings and if there'd been a trial, he'd have live-tweeted it or something."

She clicked her fingers in front of his face. "Focus, Kitchen! I need to get more people involved in kindness and community and all that crap?"

"Well, nothing brings people together like a disaster. You know how everyone in this country talks about the Blitz spirit when stuff goes pear shaped? It's always a disaster that makes people look out for each other."

Nerys stared at Ben. "Disaster. Yes, I can make one of those. I do believe you might be some sort of genius. That is exactly what we need. A disaster!"

"What? No! You can't make a disaster just to get people to behave how you want!"

"Just a small one. I need to make the world a better and fairer place."

"No, seriously! Getting the billionaires to pay tax would make the world fairer; definitely don't do whatever is in your head, for crying out loud."

"Thanks Ben, see you later."

Nerys climbed the stairs to her flat slowly, pondering the idea of a disaster, and whether she could either create a small, manageable one, or perhaps fake it. She had to keep her eye on the actual goal here though. When she got back to her flat she took the Shit-O-Meter out and checked the level. Still the same. If she set something on fire, or engineered something truly terrible then she might send it the wrong way, and she definitely didn't want to undo the good work she'd done so far.

"A fake disaster, Twinkle. It needs to be controllable though." Twinkle flopped over in his basket, unmoved by the idea.

She opened up the kindness exchange dashboard, thinking about the requests they had already carried out. The picture of her latest one with all of the dogs had proven very popular. She assumed everyone was simply enjoying her obvious discomfort, but no, it was something else. As she read through the comments she saw they weren't even about her, they were all focussed on the dogs and the obvious joy on their faces. People really loved dogs.

Yes. People *really* loved dogs!

"Let's do it Twinkle. I just need a name." Twinkle wasn't helping much. "How about Belinda Carlisle? I always wanted to be one of the Go-Gos."

Nerys created the request using her false identity. She found a really cute picture of one of those teddy bear dogs, reasoning that cockapoos and labradoodles were so thick on the ground in the local area that her fake dog could just be another.

I lost my beloved Fiona in Sutton Park this morning. She's such a timid little thing and she never strays far, but a larger dog spooked her and she ran off into the trees. I really need to find her today as she has medicine that she needs to take every few hours and I'm so scared about what might happen if she doesn't get her dose in time. If you can come and help me look, please do. If you can't look, then please just send me your best thoughts and prayers. #FindFiona

Was it too treacly? No. Nerys pressed submit and a few minutes later it was approved by Tina, who promised not only thoughts and prayers, but said that she would put a candle in her window until she heard that Fiona was found.

"Nothing brings people together like a disaster," Nerys nodded.

12

The Celestial City was a gleaming cube of a place, fifteen hundred miles to a side. The nearest gate, one of twelve in the massive edifice, was a beautiful and baroque thing of wrought gold, and decorated with intertwining vines and delicate leaves. Here, angels in robes of purest white that had never known the dirt of earthly existence, met the newly dead and guided them through to the city of eternal splendour.

With the returning saints and the archangels, Michael sidestepped the queue of new arrivals and made to go straight through.

He should have felt an intense joy at finally returning to his original home. He had been exiled on Earth for more than a decade, ten years of squalid existence as a man, with the tedium and degradation and unpleasant anatomy of a human being. He had spent ten years deep in the filth and the noise and the pettiness of mortal things, and he should have been nothing short of ecstatic regarding this return.

And yet the experience was leaving him emotionally indifferent. Certainly, the Celestial City was as glorious as it had ever been, and it suffered from none of the simple untidiness and routine that dictated life on Earth. Here there was no time, no messy changing of the seasons. Holy light permanently illuminated the city. There was no need for the sun or the stars or other randomly-rushing heavenly bodies. All was still and perfect and eternal. All was forever clean and ordered. And yet, right now, Michael realised he would have swapped it all to be back home in his Boldmere flat, preparing a dinner at the cooking island while Andy recounted his mundane news of the day over a glass of crisp white wine.

He would. He would swap Heaven for chopping vegetables and the clink of glasses and his love telling yet another story about how Gillian had messed up the gym membership database again.

"Excuse me, sir, you can't just walk in," said an angel with a clipboard at the gate, a hand raised to stop Michael.

"What? I—"

"There's a queue, sir. We will be with you soon enough."

Michael had allowed the others to get ahead of him. Raphael and Samael were blithely unaware they had left Michael at the gate.

"I'm with them," he said, pointing.

The angel with the clipboard looked to the disappearing archangels. "Are you, sir? Friends with the archangels, is it?

That's lovely. I'm sure you'll get to see them again real soon. Just join the queue."

"He can take my place," offered a softly spoken soul, near the front of the queue. "I am happy to queue again."

"That's very kind, madam, but we have to have rules," said the angel.

"I don't have to queue," said Michael. "I'm an angel too."

The angel looked at Michael, from his polished brogues to his product-sculpted hair. "You, sir?"

"Our brother is clearly distressed," said the soul. "I am happy to help him by—"

"No, madam. Rules is rules."

"But I'm the Archangel Michael," said Michael.

"I don't think so, sir. I'd have recognised the Archangel Michael. He doesn't … well, he doesn't dress like that, and for another thing, he's taller."

"Taller?" Michael huffed. "Listen – what's your name?"

"Myakos," said the angel.

"Listen, Myakos. I am the Archangel Michael. I'm with those guys. We're busy sorting out Armageddon which is apparently going to happen any time now. And then, once that happens, *this*—" he gestured irritably up and down at the queue "—all this will be over. Everyone dead and either here or in Hell. And then, dear Myakos, you will be out of a job. But for now, I need you to let me through."

"Look," said the softly spoken soul, "I'm going to the back of the queue already. Please, I give my space freely."

"Definitely not necessary, madam," said Myakos.

"No, it's not," said Michael and made to push past, but the angel put out a hand and held him in place.

"No one gate-crashes Heaven, sir."

"You have no idea who you're actually talking to, do you?"

Myakos looked at his clipboard. "Name?"

Michael stepped back and with an exertion of will he didn't want to make, his suit and clothes exploded into nothingness and were replaced by his white angelic robes. He grunted and wings, first one then the other, stretched out from his shoulder blades. His halo popped into existence above him like a mini spotlight.

"Michael. See?" he said, annoyed.

Myakos stared. "Sir. I had no idea—"

"Clearly not!" He violently brushed down his robes. "Made me ruin a perfectly decent Italian suit. 'Taller', indeed!" He stomped forward through the gates.

"Will we really all be out of job?" Myakos called after him.

"And not a day too soon!" Michael snapped back.

Michael hurried through the streets of the Celestial City, which were filled with the sounds of happy voices and the constant singing of praises. Legions of angels circled in the skies. There would have been a moment in his existence when he would have seen them and known they were fulfilling vital holy missions, in constant service of the Almighty. Now, they just looked like so many flocks of pigeons.

He eventually found the other archangels in a meeting room adjacent to the Empyrium, the location of the Throne of the Almighty. The three archangels, Gabriel, Samael and Raphael sat at a great table of cool marble. Raphael rolled his eyes at Michael's late arrival. At the head of the table,

Gabriel seemed to be struggling to get rid of St Francis of Assisi.

"But you see the pwoblem?" Francis was saying.

"No. I don't, Francis. Animals are not to be bodily lifted up to Heaven in the rapture. That's the fact."

"Well, yes, that is also a pwoblem, but more immediately, in the time of twibulation Earth is to endure after the Wapture, who will look after the lovely little pets of the enwaptured? If mummy or daddy are being whisked off to Heaven to avoid Armageddon then they will want to know their little fur babies are not going to be left in a state of distwess."

"We have more pressing matters to deal with right now," said Gabriel.

"Sorry. Did you just say 'fur babies'?" said Samael.

"A term of endearment," said Francis.

The angel of death, exhaled haughtily through his long nose. "Truly, all humanity deserves to die."

"We will try to address this issue as soon as possible," said Gabriel and stood to physically escort Francis to the door.

"Maybe if I dwaw up some plans and ideas...?" Francis suggested.

"Yes, yes, that sounds lovely," said Gabriel. "Make plans. Write a proposal. Include diagrams. Yes, yes."

He shut the door behind Francis with slightly more force than was necessary. The sound echoed hollowly around the vast white space.

"I swear the Celestial City was easier to run before humans got involved," he said.

"I'm sure our brother Lucifer said something similar," said Samael, drawing a scowl from Gabriel.

"I think it's a delight to have Michael back among us," said Raphael. "Couldn't wait to get back into the robes, eh?"

"I always thought I wore white better," said Gabriel.

Raphael's robes were a gentle sackcloth brown: monk robes. Samael's were an impenetrable light-sucking black. Michael had never asked but he suspected that Samael – with his shaggy ringlets and his world-weary body posture – had adopted a certain rock and roll aesthetic in recent decades.

Gabriel resumed his seat. "It is good that we four are together, at the end. And it is good that we alone lay out our plans for what is essentially our Final Battle against the forces of evil."

"As directed by the Almighty, of course," said Raphael.

"Of course," said Gabriel. "As that pointless meeting in Limbo has demonstrated, the addled forces of Hell have no idea how to organise a decent Apocalypse, so it's up to us to ensure everything runs smoothly."

"Can I just check," said Michael. "Are we absolutely, totally one hundred percent certain we are definitely going ahead with Armageddon?"

Samael produced an incredulous frown. "Why wouldn't we?"

"I mean is now really the time to bring it all to an end?"

"The signs are all there," said Raphael.

"I'm frankly surprised it hadn't happened sooner," said Gabriel. "Remember the first millennium?"

Raphael smiled and Samael's head shook with laughter.

"Midwinter in one thousand AD, ten thousand Christians looked up at the darkness, expecting the glory of Heaven to come bursting forth."

"Very disappointing," Gabriel agreed. "And again in the year two thousand. What was that bug which was supposed to wipe everyone out?"

"Y2K," said Michael automatically.

"And – *pfff* – nothing. A missed opportunity."

"But now?" said Michael.

"It has been decreed from on high. The sin and sickness of the Earth will be tolerated no more."

Samael gave Michael what was probably supposed to be a playful punch on the arm but the angel of death delivered it with such bony-knuckled sharpness that Michael couldn't help but wince.

"Are you worried that we're not going to win, Michael?"

"Me? Of course not. I have every confidence." Then doubt hit him. "I mean, we can't lose, can we?"

"As before, Hell's forces outnumber us by two to one at least," said Gabriel. "On paper, the forces of Hell are superior to those of Heaven."

"Oh. Oh, I see."

"But the boffins in the Research Centre for Scriptural Exegesis tell us that the signs are clear. Ninety percent clear."

"At least seventy percent clear," said Raphael.

"Yes, the signs are mostly clear," said Gabriel, "that we will win again."

"Mostly clear?" said Michael.

"Mostly," Gabriel nodded.

"We simply can't lose," Samael grinned rakishly.

"You sure?"

"We're the good guys, aren't we? The good guys always win."

Michael's phone buzzed and it took him a considerable time to find it within his new robes. Clovenhoof had sent him a message, although the Almighty alone knew what kind of data signal reached all the way across Limbo to the Celestial City.

"Something important?" asked Gabriel.

Michael grunted. "Stupid selfies of Jeremy and his pet."

13

Nerys stood at the bar of the Boldmere Oak twirling the stem of a glass of Chardonnay.

"Someone is looking particularly pleased with herself," said Animal Ed.

Animal Ed, local pet shop owner and specialist in illicit deals and unfortunate romantic entanglements, gave her a rakish look. Rakish was definitely a word that described Ed well. Not only was he shamelessly disreputable but he was also thin, and at his best when scraping around in the muck. Engaging Ed in conversation might open her up to an evening of tawdry pick-up lines from the man (and she'd fallen for them once before which was at least one time too many) but she was in a happy, devil-may-care mood.

"I am pleased with myself," she said. "I have launched a kindness exchange platform which enables people to more easily help each other out and improve the general level of goodness in society."

She didn't mention the fact that none of this had yet made the Shit-O-Meter shift any noticeable distance. She should take small victories where she found them.

"Oh, I saw that thing," said Ed. "The lost dog thing."

"That's right."

"Some woman wanted to put a sign in my shop window, said she'd read about it on some website." He clicked his fingers. "So, you're the 'honk if you're horny' woman."

"Helpful," said Nerys automatically.

He nodded approvingly and sidled up the bar. "So, what's your angle then?"

"My what?"

He gestured airily. "How are you monetising this?"

She frowned irritably. "I'm not... There's no angle. I just want to make the world a better place."

He laughed.

"I'm not being funny," she said.

"You think you can make the world a better place? I mean I applaud the notion but trying to just get people to do nice things for each other isn't going to make the world a better place."

"I'm sure there's a story that shows that every little action—"

"Yeah, yeah," he said wearily. "Nerys, my fine beautiful lady, you can't actually make the whole world a better place with tiny actions. This planet produces enough food to feed everyone, and the average income across the globe should be enough for anyone. And yet..."

"Well, of course it's not all fairly distributed," said Nerys, feeling annoyed for having to point out the obvious.

"Right. Your bloody super-rich hoard more money than they can ever need."

Ben had mentioned something similar, about the taxes billionaires failed to pay.

"I mean, I have nothing against wealth," said Ed. "You've got to have something to aspire too. Without the Gautam Adanis or Zhong Shanshans of this world, we wouldn't know what levels of wealth we can attain."

"Who?" said Nerys but she was already googling even as she said it.

"The biggest earners are more wealthy than whole countries," said Ed.

Nerys saw that despite their wealth, these billionaire types paid an estimated thirty per cent less tax than regular people. The billionaires who were bosses of big companies attracted lots of attention for the punishing pay and conditions that their employees often faced, which seemed particularly wrong when compared with their own wealth.

"That's crazy," she said.

"Right," said Ed. "So you promoting your kindness-swap programme or whatever it is – however lovely and cute it is – is a drop in the ocean. You're rattling your collection tin, trying to get scraps of money, of goodness, whatever, from passers-by when there are these whales just swimming by who have the power in their tiniest little finger to do far more than all the rest of us put together."

"Think you're mixing your metaphors there, Ed," she said.

"I've been drinking, what can I say?" He clicked his fingers at Florence who was working behind the bar and waggled his pint glass her. "Nerys, let me buy you a drink and we can discuss the state of the world a little more."

Nerys, distracted by what she was reading on the internet, automatically pushed her glass over for a refill.

"You clicking your fingers at me, man?" glowered Florence.

"I was just trying to get your attention."

"Man with only eight fingers is sure going to get a lot of attention," she said fiercely and snatched his glass from him.

Nerys read on. "Basically, the mere fact that billionaires exist is a sign of moral and economic failure."

"Woah, commie alert," said Ed.

Nerys sighed and slouched on her stool. "You know, when I was a kid, there was all this talk of factories being run by robots, and it would mean that everyone would get more leisure time."

"Yep. I remember that. Everyone going to be replaced by robots."

"Except us bar staff," said Florence, smoothly slipping a pint of lager and a glass of wine in front of them.

"Is that so?" said Ed, passing over a ten-pound note. Florence held it up to the light to check the watermark.

"It's our people skills," she said. "No robot can replace that."

"Oh, yeah," said Ed. "What would we do without your warmth and humanity?"

Florence dropped his change in a puddle of drink on the bar.

Ed sighed as he picked the coins out of the icky drink. "The idea of universal leisure time went the way of the flying car," he said. "Everyone's working several crappy jobs just to try and pay their bills. All that 'extra leisure time' has been converted into money—"

"And gone into the pockets of billionaires," said Nerys.

Ed shrugged.

"I wonder how I can get hold of a billionaire," she said.

"Why?"

"Just to chat to one."

She opened browser windows and cross-referenced rich lists with news articles and gossip magazines. Nerys knew where to go if she wanted to meet Aston Villa footballers, but she was looking at the tiny slice of society which was so very elite they could all stay in tax havens and on yachts for their entire lives if they wanted to.

"There's always the Belfry," suggested Florence.

"Sorry?" said Nerys.

"The golf club."

She was right. If there was anything that would bring the mega-rich to Sutton Coldfield it was the famous golf course down the road. There was a fancy hotel there too.

"Ooh, not a bad idea," said Nerys.

"I know the events manager at that Luxor hotel there," said Ed.

"Right," said Nerys, not really buying it.

Ed raised his chin with wounded pride. "You want to find out what billionaires might be visiting the finest hotel near the finest golf course for miles around…" He whipped out his phone and dialled while on speaker.

"Hello, Sophie."

"Ed? I thought I blocked you," came a woman's voice.

"Hi, yeah. I bet it's a surprise to hear from me, eh?"

"It is a bit. The last time I saw you, you were running down the road wearing only a pair of leopard print boxers."

Ed gave a small laugh. "Who knew your dad would have such old-fashioned values when it came to gentlemen staying over at his house?"

"You tried to steal his Asian dragon fish."

"I was only inspecting it."

"By taking it out of the tank and putting it in a plastic bag in the middle of the night."

"I love fish, what can I say. Anyway, I have a question for a friend who's researching for a magazine article."

"Uh-huh."

"So, the article is for the in-house magazine of a large hedge fund management company. The company is thinking of setting up an office in Birmingham, so they are trying to demonstrate why their people should take the relocation package."

"So far so very, very dull. What's your point?"

"One of the things that they are all obsessed with is the who's who of rich people hanging around the area. The mega rich, yacht-owning ones. I said someone might be able to drop her a couple of names, very much off the record."

"You want me to tell you who our guests are? Are you mad? I can't do that."

"She won't name them as such in the article, just hint at their identities."

"I'm definitely not doing that, Ed, it's very unethical and I would get in a lot of trouble."

"How about this then. You could give me a name and tell

me when they are expected and I could just happen by and get a quick picture. It's nothing to do with you then."

"You're not listening. I'm hanging up now—"

"I know where I can lay my hands on a Flowerhorn Cichlid at zero cost to him."

This gave Sophie cause to pause. Nerys had no idea what a Flowerhorn Cichlid was.

"Your daddy would love to add one of those to his aquarium, I'm sure," said Ed smoothly.

Sophie sighed. *"It is his birthday next month."*

"Ha!"

There was a momentary silence. *"This cannot come back to me. That is the rule. If you can't get your picture I don't care, right?"*

"Understood."

"Vanga Heddhop, the Swedish guy with all the hotel chains will be here in two weeks. He will helicopter in for the Thursday afternoon and leave in the evening. The whole place will be closed down tight though, because that's the way it works."

"That's wonderful. You are a star."

"Now, about the cichlid…"

"Yep, yep. Let me chat to my mate." He killed the call and spread his hands, pleased with himself. "Got you access to a billionaire, Nerys."

Nerys nodded, impressed. "And this fish you're going to get for – Sophie, was it?"

Ed tilted his head. "I know a bloke who works as a cleaner at the Sea Life Centre. All it takes is for a door to be left unlocked and one man to slip in with his little net."

"You are a scoundrel, Ed," she said.

"That I am," he leered. "Now, how about you show Ed a little gratitude…" His hands twitched on the bar.

"I'll buy you a drink and endure your company for an hour and, if you keep your hands to yourself, I won't feel compelled to stab you in the eye," she said.

"You used to be more fun," he tutted and downed his pint.

NERYS INVITED Tina over the next day to discuss her plan.

"I need your help in taking our venture to the next level," she said.

"I'm already doing a lot," said Tina. "I have been seeking political influence to further our cause."

Nerys narrowed her eyes. "Is this you telling us that you're back in the sack with Jacob Bloom, Tina?"

"I resent your tone, Nerys," said Tina. "Actually, Tessa Bloom and I have come to realise we have a lot in common."

"Apart from carnal knowledge of Mr Jacob Bloom?"

"Actually, our local member of parliament realises that I provide a much-needed service for Mr Bloom, allowing his wife to focus on loftier matters."

"My God," said Ben in faint horror, spilling tea from the pot as he tried to pour.

"Life is a rich tapestry indeed," said Nerys. "I'm not sure I want the Blooms and their like to be part of my kindness project."

"*Your* kindness project is it?" said Tina with an arched eyebrow. "Well, as it happens the Blooms *are* a part of this now, but very much under my stewardship. They recognise we are able to influence a large slice of the population, so they are keen to use those voices to maximum effect. They have been advising on how we can most effectively channel our efforts towards the law-making process."

"You mean, doing petitions and that?" asked Ben.

"It's that and so much more, Ben. I had no idea. Petitions are very much at the heart of it, but it's a multi-strand effort. For example, if we were able to add some educational content to the software platform it could really help."

"Like videos you mean?" said Ben. "Interesting."

"Then I'll get to work on some more material right away." Tina sat up straight and made some notes.

"But the thing I really wanted to ask you about was that job of yours. Did you tell me it was at the Luxor hotel near the Belfry." Nerys, in pursuing her first billionaire, had assumed she would be able to get work on the catering team for the event that Vanga Heddhop was attending. She had some experience at service work, but apparently there was an extended vetting process that would take at least a month.

"What about it?" said Tina. "The money's good and we get to dress up like a soft porn version of Downton Abbey. It made me think of you, actually. You should apply."

"I wouldn't mind giving it a go before I put myself forward. Can I sub one of your days? I'll do it for free."

Tina looked at her suspiciously. "You have an ulterior motive."

"An altruistic ulterior motive," said Nerys.

"You want to work my day, effectively be me…?"

"Yes."

"But I'll still get paid?"

"Yes."

Tina laughed. "Well, that sounds like delicious fun."

As simple as that, Nerys was going to be able to take Tina's place, instead of having to clonk her over the head or steal her ID card at knifepoint, she could simply borrow it. Part of Nerys was disappointed: she had quite wanted to clonk Tina over the head.

AFTER THE MEETING, Nerys went down to Clovenhoof's old flat to check in on Spartacus.

There were weird thumping and clattering noises coming from the flat. Such violent and mechanical noises made it almost sound as if Jeremy was back.

The clattering stopped for a moment. Spartacus opened the door, breathless. Behind stood three of his mates.

"Hi Jefri, PJ, Kenzie. What the heck's the noise?"

"We've set up an indoor skate park in here," said Spartacus, opening the door wider so she could enter to see. "See how the ironing board gives us a ramp off the sofa? We're using it to practise our kickflips."

Nerys stared at the scene before her. "Is it strange that the most disturbing part of what you just said is that Jeremy has an ironing board. What's that all about?"

"We found it down by the bins," said Spartacus.

"Fine," said Nerys. "Carry on then. It's definitely what he would have wanted. I came to ask if we can host some video content on the platform. Tina wants to upload some educational content."

There was a snicker of laughter from a couple of the lads.

"Someone might be following Tina on Instagram and Snapchat," said Spartacus.

Nerys recoiled. "You look at pictures and videos of *her*? She's old enough to be your grandma!"

"She's younger than you, isn't she?" said PJ.

"That's entirely beside the point," said Nerys, looking fixedly at Spartacus. "Videos. Yes or no?"

"Not a problem at all," he said. On a spinning hand, he produced his laptop, seemingly out of nowhere. "Also, we implemented a rating system recently." He brought up a display so that it showed a graph.

"What is that?" Nerys asked. "Is it the tasks that are most popular with volunteers?"

"More or less. Tina suggested different aspects that both volunteers and the recipients could give a value to after completion. Things like how satisfying it was to work on, whether they learned new skills, and whether it was a good social experience. The recipients grade the impact of the problem and stuff like that."

"Huh, that sounds good," said Nerys, impressed. "So can we draw any useful conclusions from this?"

"It seems as though people get more satisfaction when they are solving a severe problem. They also prefer the ones where they get to socialise with others." Spartacus shrugged and pulled a face.

"This is really useful stuff! Let's all put some thought into how we can use that to increase the impact of what we do," said Nerys.

14

A week later, Nerys put Operation Bully-a-Billionaire into action. She put on her tartiest make up to approximate Tina's look and dressed in her uniform.

Happily, they were near enough the same size, so Nerys could dress up in the housemaid outfit and fold her hair up into the tiny hat. High heels, a short skirt, a little frilly apron and she was set.

Nerys knew she could take on whatever task she was given on the day, even if it was the fancy one-handed serving thing, because she'd done waitressing many times. Of course, the task she really wanted was whichever one got her closest to the billionaire.

Nerys made herself invaluable during the morning setup, anticipating every need and making sure she did everything as quickly and efficiently as she could.

"Yes, sir. Right away, sir!" she curtseyed for the umpteenth time. She'd had enough practice being the submissive serving girl to play the part to perfection.

Her hard work paid off as she was told she would be waiting on the smallest of the private rooms once the guests arrived, which surely was where Heddhop would be.

"Positions everyone! Guests incoming!"

She smoothed her uniform. The staff lined up, because of course they lined up. Nerys kept her face calm and smooth, but wanted to roll her eyes at the whole thing. Curtseying was all well and good as a roleplay in the bedroom, but doing it for real grated on her nerves as much as the fake smile she had plastered onto her face.

The guests milled around in the reception room, sipping drinks and chatting before the meal was served. She needed to find a way to side-line Heddhop, which would be challenging – given her current role was very much to be seen and not heard. The manager circled, scrutinising each interaction and glaring at all of the staff so they knew he was watching.

Nerys approached the manager and discreetly whispered that she needed a bathroom break. He scowled and told her to be quick.

Nerys had managed to secrete her bag in a nearby room. A set of party clothes was tucked inside, and she changed into a slinky cocktail dress accessorised with a small hat and veil. It wasn't much of a disguise, but she hoped it would be enough to get past her colleagues without being recognised.

"Mr Heddhop, how nice to meet you." She eyed him from beneath her demure, lowered gaze, channelling the full

Disney princess effect. She had applied two layers of false eyelashes that morning for maximum impact.

"Oh hey. I cannot think that we have met. What shall I call you?"

"You can call me Nerys. Tell me something about the real Vanga Heddhop."

"You are very direct, I enjoy that. Something about me, let's think. I have a little dog called Soutache."

Nerys fixed him with huge eyes. "Oh, I love dogs so much. I can show you a very funny picture if you give me a moment." She found the picture of her topple-surfing across a pile of dogs during her dog walking session.

Heddhop guffawed with laughter. "You are most amusing. Perhaps you would sit with me for dinner?"

Nerys smiled. Oh, this was proving better than expected. She had cornered him, now all she had to do was convince him to give up a few of his billions to even up society.

"Your dog must be very special to you," she said as they ate a delicate layered terrine.

"Soutache means everything, yes."

"Everyone should know what that feels like, don't you think? Being happy, content, well-loved. You and Soutache know that feeling, how many other people in the world do you think know it?"

"What a generous thought. You are right of course. However, I am not sure there is a straightforward formula to ensure such happiness."

"Are you about to tell me you and Soutache could be

happy like that even if you didn't have all of your money?" Nerys asked.

"Aha, a verbal trap?" He wagged a finger at her. "Very good. I am not about to suggest that I don't require my own money; but it is true that Soutache would adore me in any case."

"No trap intended," lied Nerys. "It's more like there is a level of security that people need first. You might not be able to relax with Soutache if you relied on a foodbank, or if you were working three jobs to pay your energy bills."

He bridled at that. "I work very hard, you know. I am not a socialite!"

"But you are secure. You don't need to worry about food or a place to live." Nerys gave him another penetrating Disney princess stare. "Do you ever think about using some of your wealth to enable others to reach that same state? Soutache would be so proud."

"You make it sound easy to fix things," said Heddhop.

"I think if you are smart and creative it is possible. Not easy perhaps, but few things are." Nerys needed to pander to his ego a little. "So how about it then?"

"How about what?"

"You take a few of your billions and make the world a better place? It could be a lot of fun, helping others to find the happiness you and Soutache have found." Nerys gave a seductive smile.

Vanga gave a small nod. "I might have one or two ideas. Leave it with me."

"I look forward to being surprised," purred Nerys.

As she leaned at an angle to flash him her most charming

smile, she caught sight of her manager at the exact moment he recognised who she was. The transformation of his face would have been amusing, if the snarling rage that it contorted into had not been directed at her.

"Listen Vanga, I need to step away, but I really enjoyed chatting." She pressed a hand onto his arm and stood up from her chair. She calmly walked the few steps to the doorway, before breaking into a sprint as the manager scurried after her. Nerys grabbed her bag, hurriedly switched her shoes, and left through a fire escape. An alarm sounded as the door opened.

As she ran across a lawn Nerys was conscious of two things. She could hear the manager howling with rage above the siren, and as she glanced back at the hotel she saw Vanga Heddhop standing at a window, watching her flee and giving her a thumbs-up; along with a warm and amused smile.

THE NEXT MORNING, Nerys felt she was truly a master of multi-tasking as she ate her breakfast, threw a ball for Twinkle to fetch, and reviewed some of the latest material that had been uploaded to the software platform. Tina had added several videos to the new educational section so Nerys selected one to view. Everything was truly coming together.

Tessa Bloom was speaking directly to the camera, in a tidy looking street somewhere in the local vicinity. A former magistrate, Tessa Bloom had been the town's MP through ups and downs, over what seemed liked decades. Through pandemics, economic emergencies, and scandals at the highest levels of government, the good people of the Royal

Town of Sutton Coldfield had seen fit to return the same politician to parliament every time.

"*Today we will be asking some difficult questions.*" Tessa spoke in a clear, sharp voice, sharpened by a life of speaking down to criminals in the dock and MPs across the benches. "*This average street in nearby Erdington has been the location of a homeless shelter for three years now. Residents will tell us about the impact that it's had on their peace of mind. Proposals to place one of these shelters in Sutton Coldfield are now seeking comments from locals, so we want to make sure you have all of the information that you need.*"

The camera drew back slightly so that another person came into view. Tessa held up the microphone and looked earnestly into the face of a grey-haired man.

"*Archie, you live near the shelter. Can you tell us what your experience has been?*"

"*Aye. It's a nightmare,*" said the man. "*The door goes at all times of the day and night, people coming and going. You never know who's going to be there.*"

"*I see, so it's busy. What else can you tell us, Archie?*"

"*They have an extra bin, on account of all the rubbish they make. Nobody else can get an extra bin, can they? Cooking smells an' all come from there.*"

"*So, what would you say is your biggest concern overall, Archie?*"

"*My missus is afraid that the house prices have dropped down the whole road. They'll never go back up as long as we've got this here, will we?*"

"What the fuck?" whispered Nerys. She nearly choked on

her toast, and threw the ball so absentmindedly it hit Twinkle square on the nose.

"Thank you, Archie," said Tessa. "We'll have some more comments from concerned locals in a moment, but you can find a link below this video which will let you download a suggested letter to your local councillors with regard to a shelter like this in Sutton Coldfield. It's very important that we make our feelings known. Act now to prevent a homeless shelter driving down prices on your road."

Nerys paused the video and sent out a message to summon an emergency board meeting.

Tina had the furthest to come, given that she wasn't currently a resident in the building, but she was in Nerys's flat in fifteen minutes.

"I take everyone's seen it then?" said Spartacus, trying to squash down his unruly bed hair.

Ben popped a straw in a multi-vitamin box drink. "Seen what?"

Nerys played them a snippet of Tessa Bloom's video that *they* were now hosting.

"What on earth was that?" she said.

"Community outreach," said Tina. "Getting people involved and interested in what's going on locally."

"Sure, the effort to get people involved in decision-making is great," said Nerys. "But why on earth would you share the bigoted views of a grumpy neighbour and present it as information?"

"Woah, Nerys babe. Are you saying his views aren't valid?"

"They're stupid, is what they are."

"People don't like the homeless shelter being on their road," said Tina.

"For reasons that range from fear of strangers through to those who are convinced the water pressure had been reduced," said Ben, who had been taking notes.

"It's nothing but fearmongering and NIMBY outrage," said Nerys.

"Wimpy outrage?" said Tina in mock confusion.

"Pretty sure you heard me, Tina. Nimby as in 'Not In My Back Yard'. This is not educational content."

"Nerys, you need to think big picture, then you'll see that our goals align with the Blooms'."

"How can you say that? Our goal is kindness, and theirs is small-minded bigotry. They are opposites."

"Big picture, Nerys! Think of it like this. We know we're building the kindness movement by getting people to reach out to others nearby. Make a human connection, perform small acts of kindness and so on, yes?"

"Yes, that's right."

"Now the tricky part is how do we scale that? I know you've tried a couple of things, but you and I both know we can gain real traction if we get influential people on board. What the Blooms are doing is getting people to improve their own area by banding together. You might disagree with their methods, but they are effective in their own way."

Nerys searched for the right words. "We want to build a community, yes. The thing you're describing is more like tribalism. You're talking about building an elitist tribe based on them all hating something. How can it promote kindness if it's based upon excluding some people?"

"Maybe that's one of the decisions we need to make?" said Tina. "We should put it to the board."

"Er, guys," said Spartacus. "I thought we were going to talk about the other thing."

"What thing?" said Nerys.

"Your billionaire friend."

"She doesn't have any billionaire friends," said Ben.

Nerys raised her nose in a superior manner. "Ben, I took your advice about hassling billionaires to share their money more fairly. It's not so much of a quick win though. I tried with one. Vanga Heddhop."

"Right," said Spartacus. "And he was on the news today with some controversy about foodbanks."

"Er really?" said Nerys. She opened her phone to find the story, but Spartacus was already ahead of her.

"Billionaire bankrolls a new nationwide network of foodbanks, but is slammed for insisting that all claimants must also take a puppy," he read aloud.

"He did what now?" said Tina.

Nerys read on.

Vanga Heddhop stated: 'It's a question of short term pain for long term gain. Everyone should have a loving dog in their home and I am in a position to help with this as I have partnered each foodbank with a sizeable puppy farm. I have my friend Nerys Thomas to thank for suggesting this initiative. I know that people will be grateful once they have accommodated the necessary changes to their lifestyle. We also include a feeding tip sheet and a week's worth of puppy food.'

Animal welfare charities have condemned the move as irresponsible and harmful to dogs.

Ben peered over her shoulder to see. "You're named as part of this? Wow, Nerys, that is spectacular."

Tina leaned over. "He means spectacularly bad, Nerys, just in case you were wondering."

Spartacus was working on the laptop and updated the display. "We've got over a million registered users now. Not all of them are active, although I think a whole bunch of people joined just to get updates on Fiona the dog."

Everyone turned to look at Nerys.

"What? Yes. Okay, it went a bit wrong with the billionaire."

"And a simple reverse image search shows that the dog everyone is looking for is a prize-winning pooch from the US," said Spartacus.

"But it's bringing people together," insisted Nerys.

"Are you really sure your methods are better than mine?" asked Tina.

15

Clovenhoof was led to the Corporate Management Centre of Nameless Dread, which occupied a prime piece of infernal real estate. Clovenhoof had spent enough time on Earth to understand the look Peter had been aiming for. If this had been Earth, the Corporate Management Centre would have been a number of beautiful curving and asymmetrical buildings composed entirely of glass, set amongst a landscaped park of green lawns and artfully placed trees. Sadly, in Hell, grass and trees tended to burst into flames, and the overall effect here wasn't so much of something beautifully sculpted but of a strange lumpen and sand-blasted thing half buried in the volcanic landscape.

Peter's secretary, the damned Emperor Nero, escorted Clovenhoof into Peter's office suite. The misshapen alpaca Clovenhoof had created scuttled around them on unsteady hoofs. The office was a wide room with a commanding view over the torture pits of the ninth circle. There was a long meeting table covered in notes and, on a raised area, the captain's cabin to this galleon-sized room, was Peter's desk.

Peter signed off several sheets. "Satan. Had the grand tour?"

Clovenhoof looked around for a drinks cabinet. He could do with a glass of something strong. He turned to ask Nero to get him something but the odious man had gone.

"Hell seems much as I left it," Clovenhoof said.

"Changes can be subtle and not easy to spot," said Peter. "Preparations for Armageddon meet your approval?"

Clovenhoof shrugged. "Can't say I'm enthused by the whole thing."

"Course you aren't," Peter laughed. "You're going to lose again."

"I thought you were meant to be on my side."

Peter's expression was one of frank surprise. "What in Hell made you think that?"

Clovenhoof indicated everything around them. "You literally work in Hell. I'm the captain of your home team."

Peter's laugh was deeper now. Clovenhoof didn't like it.

"If I'm on any 'side', it is the side of prophecy. I am happy to oversee Hell, for there needs to be a Hell and it needs to be run properly. I am on the side of Armageddon because it is ordained by the Almighty. I am a true and faithful servant to the Divine Will and thus I want to see you ride out to meet the forces of Heaven, to fight to the very best of your underhanded abilities and then be thrown down and utterly destroyed by righteous angels."

"Oh, I see. Well, fuck you, Petey-boy. It seems like we're on opposite sides after all."

"Indeed. Doesn't mean we can't work togeth— What is that creature doing?"

Peter sneered at the alpaca which had leapt up onto some of the low comfy seats by the long window and was doing something energetic and vigorous to one of the cushions.

"Hmmm," said Clovenhoof. "I think he's either trying to scratch his back on it or impregnate it."

"Well, stop it at once. It's leaving stains! We have things to do and no time to mess about."

Peter looked for papers on his desk. Clovenhoof trotted over to the window and stroked his pet between the ears. "Who's a good boy, eh?" he whispered.

The daft creature shuddered happily and drool poured from its flappy mouth.

"Maybe you could do daddy a favour, eh?" said Clovenhoof. "Go and find me some Lambrini, yeah? Lambri-ni? Yeah? You can do that?"

The thing wriggled in what Clovenhoof took to be a very positive manner and scampered off and out the door. Clovenhoof inspected the soiled furnishings.

"Yes, I think he's impregnated your cushion."

"You can't impregnate an inanimate object," said Peter.

"Life always finds a way."

Peter spread out a number of files on the long meeting table. He had to push several large plans aside to make room.

"Working out how to reconfigure Hell for the final influx of the damned is a big enough problem, but it turns out it *is* also up to us to select an Antichrist."

Clovenhoof came round to look at the files. "So, if the Antichrist hasn't been picked yet, does that mean we've still got until the monstrous tyke grows up before the world is destroyed?" He looked at the cushion Moronic had soiled. "Do I have to get someone pregnant?"

"Oh, we're working to a tighter timescale than that. No one shall know the day or the hour, but we certainly haven't got years to waste in building an Antichrist from scratch. The Antichrist will come, claiming to be a humanitarian, offering peace and prosperity, while secretly seeking power and immorality. All we need to do is pick someone who meets those criteria and, essentially, offer them the job."

Clovenhoof looked at the offerings on the table. He tapped a finger on a photograph of a stern looking politician.

"I like this guy. He's got lots of nuclear weapons, talks a good talk about using them against the decadent West."

"I wonder if that's too on the nose," said Peter thoughtfully. "Like when we reveal he's actually the Antichrist, no one will be surprised. Who's this one?"

Clovenhoof looked. "He's that super rich tech guy who likes sending rockets into space. He's gone a bit mad recently, too."

"Ah, that's very much the kind of thing we're after," Peter picked up a third file. "And this man has hundreds of millions of followers on social media. Definitely sounds like Antichrist material."

"He's a footballer."

"A what?"

"A sportsman."

Peter dropped the file in disgust. "No, I don't think so. If we're picking an Antichrist we must have some standards. Oh – here's a late arrival," he said, producing a new file. "A woman, which could be a valuable option in this progressive age. Not quite to the same standards as the others, but she's stirred up some widespread hatred in record time. Supporting mad and offensive schemes involving foodbanks. Lying to the British public about lost dogs, which is apparently something they especially care about. Some really chaotic and disruptive behaviour."

Clovenhoof looked at the photo in the file. "I know her. That's Nerys Thomas."

"A personal connection with Satan himself! Capital! Oh, we'll put her at the top of the pile, then."

The office door swung open. It was not, as Clovenhoof had hoped, his alpaca returning with a cool bottle of urine coloured Lambrini in its mouth, but Nero.

"Sire," he said, "Lord Belphegor has come to prepare Satan for battle."

"Already?" said Clovenhoof.

"And there's also a delegation to see you, sire."

"A delegation? From where? There's nothing in my diary."

"They are representatives from the Union of Hellish Gatekeepers and Bum Pokers."

"The what? I've never heard of them."

"Freshly formed union, apparently. They want to speak to management about protecting their jobs after the end of the world. They've heard you're going to fire them all."

"Who told them that?"

"I don't know, sire."

Clovenhoof chose to say nothing.

"I simply do not have time to talk to union rabble

rousers," said Peter haughtily. "Get Infernal security to throw them out."

"Well, turns out the Gatekeepers and Bum Pokers have been chatting with some of the scrowfrog demons in security, and the scrowfrogs are now thinking about starting their own union."

"A union? The scrowfrogs have brains the size of gnat's eggs."

"Yes. The leader of the Gatekeepers – er, Pisskettle – told them you said that. Seems to have riled the scrowfrogs up a bit and made them all the keener to unionise."

"On today of all days!" Peter spat furiously. "Satan! Get yourself to Belphegor now while I deal with this petty insurrection!"

Peter stormed out and Clovenhoof, checking the room once more in case he'd overlooked a drinks trolley or a secret bottle of spirits, sauntered out after him.

16

Nerys, wallowing in recent failures, had declared it was time for an evening of drunkenness at the Boldmere Oak. Ben had said something about it not being the same without Clovenhoof, which was why Nerys got Spartacus to give her one of Jeremy's hideous smoking jackets. She stuffed a pillow inside to give it some form and sellotaped a paper plate to a wooden spoon to be his head. She took Stuffed Clovenhoof to the pub in a carrier bag and assembled it at their usual table.

When Ben arrived, Nerys had slurped down half a large glass of white wine and was feeling much mellower than she had been.

"This," Ben indicated Stuffed Clovenhoof, "is a cry for help, isn't it?"

Nerys patted the shoulder of the dummy and gave it a fond smile. "You were the one who said it wouldn't be the same without him. I quite like the way this one doesn't keep saying annoying things."

"And yet it retains something of the aroma," said Ben, giving the smoking jacket a small sniff. "Fine. At least he has a good reason for not buying a round."

"By an amazing coincidence, I found a tenner in the pocket of the smoking jacket," said Nerys. "So he can. Back in a moment."

Lennox busied himself making a cider and black for Ben. "So, the real one's inside for painting rude graffiti?" he asked, nodding over at Stuffed Clovenhoof.

"Yes. Yes, that's right."

"And you're missing him."

"Not in the traditional sense, although I do wish he would come back," said Nerys. She glanced around to be sure that nobody was listening. "He's actually back in you-know-where."

"Prison? I heard."

"No," she said. "The Other Place." She pointed downwards.

"In my cellar?"

"Christ, no. Deeper down, much deeper down."

Lennox frowned. "New Zealand."

"Hell, Lennox!" she hissed. "He's in Hell. I know you know. You saw his horns for what they were the first time you met him."

"A barman's got a special sixth sense," Lennox agreed, calmly. "What's he doing down there?"

"It's the end times."

Lennox grinned in his amiable way. "Tell me about it.

Who can afford to run a pub these days. Bills are sucking up all my profits—"

"No, the real end times. Armageddon."

"Our mate Jeremy's always got something going on. Well, he better be back before the Lambrini goes out of date, mind."

"It's not him doing this!" hissed Nerys. "They came and took him."

"Who?"

"The angels! He's supposed to fight in the war. Can you even imagine that?"

"No. I've seen him lose a fight with an unopened packet of crisps."

Nerys huffed miserably. "I don't know what to do, Lennox. How can we get people to stop being so crap? It's the only way to reset things."

Lennox shook his head. "Being crap is part of what people are. As a barman, I can guarantee that is an unchanging truth about human beings."

"Well yeah. But it's like we've made being crap into an artform where everyone's trying to outdo each other."

"Institutional crapness," nodded Lennox. "I see what happens in the world and I serve up beer so people can feel slightly better about it all for a few hours."

"Hurrah, for you."

"I'm sure I'll get my just reward in the hereafter," he said in the unfussed manner of one who could take or leave eternal rewards with equal humour.

Nerys carried their drinks back to the table after Lennox topped up her wine without even being asked.

"Ben, Tina is trying to bend the idea of kindness into something else."

"This the Tessa Bloom video thing?"

Nerys tried to explain her deeper concerns, tried to convey the danger in Tina's weasel-worded justification, but found herself substituting angry growls and gestures.

"So, Tina wants to persuade us all that forming communities based on selfishness will work faster than communities based on pure altruism?" said Ben. "That's your real problem?"

"Yes!" spat Nerys. "Are you really taking time to think about it?"

"I'm wondering if she might be correct in her thinking."

"What?"

"Even if it is a less ethical approach. Perhaps there is something to be said for building a community based on selfishness and then gently encouraging them to behave in a more altruistic way afterwards?"

"That is not what she's thinking," said Nerys. "Tina is up to something else. She always is. She's a shifty cow."

"Takes one to know one."

"What did you say?"

"Nothing, nothing," said Ben and supped his drink hurriedly.

AFTER A NIGHT of slightly drunken pondering, Nerys decided that her suspicions about Tina were worth pursuing. She asked Spartacus to find out where Tina had been most active in her work on the platform.

He came up to her flat a short while later. "You're probably not going to like this."

Nerys savoured the moment. Just for a few seconds she could revel in the fact that she'd been right: Tina *was* up to something. Her mood would obviously be spoiled when she found out what it actually was, so she gave herself a few more seconds of enjoyment. "Go on, tell me."

"You know how as the moderator she removes the requests that are weird and dodgy?"

"Yes," said Nerys, her mind already leaping ahead.

"Well. Turns out that instead of removing them completely, she puts them all into a private folder area."

"Tell me more."

"I can't tell what she's done with them after that, but the way she's organised them might give us some clues. She has a folder called Kinky Cleaners, a folder called Possible Future Services and a folder called Trash."

Nerys pulled out her phone.

"If you're about to google kinky cleaners in the Sutton Coldfield area I'm way ahead of you," said Spartacus. "This website here was set up a few weeks ago and offers a discreet and exclusive service to patrons." He tilted his laptop so Nerys could see.

"Unbelievable. I will talk to her about this. You probably want to clear down your browser history, Spartacus."

"No it's fine, I haven't finished checking out the gallery yet." Spartacus walked away, studying the screen intently.

. . .

NERYS EXAMINED Tina's kinky cleaners website. The offering was simple, a cleaner would come to your house wearing the firm's provocative uniform once you had filled in the form and entered your card details. They were not expected to clean when they got there, but offered a menu of sexual services that would be charged on a pay-as-you-go basis. The charges would show up on statements as dry cleaning, to avoid questions from anyone who saw your card statements. As a result, the menu had coy names like HAND FINISH, FLUFF AND FOLD and FULL SERVICE.

Nerys grunted in frustration. The entire thing was pure Tina, and she hadn't even made much of an effort to hide her involvement. Several of the gallery pictures featured Tina with a strategically held feather duster in otherwise nude poses. They were in much softer focus than some of the other pictures, but Tina obviously hadn't been able to help herself.

Nerys dialled the number on the website. It wasn't Tina's regular number, but when the phone was answered, it was Tina's voice.

"What is this, Tina?" asked Nerys.

"Are you calling to request some of our services, Nerys?" asked Tina. "I don't know if you looked at the FOR WOMEN part of the website, but I think you'll be impressed by some of the gentlemen on our books. I can offer you a free trial if you like."

"You know that's not why I'm calling," said Nerys. "You've been grabbing the blocked requests from HONK IF YOU'RE HELPFUL and using them as sales leads for your hookers!"

"I have indeed. More people with their needs met, isn't that what you want?"

"Tina, you're taking advantage of our movement!"

"We can arrange some compensation for you passing on the sales leads, Nerys. It's a simple matter of affiliate marketing. That makes it a win-win situation, wouldn't you say?"

"It does not!" thundered Nerys. "I can't believe you'd do this behind my back, I really can't."

"You're right Nerys," Tina said in a soothing, contrite voice. "It's been terrible keeping this from you, because I knew you'd be excited by it."

"No, I—"

"I'm so glad it's out in the open now. I can get your thoughts on some key parts of the operation. You will help improve it, I'm certain."

Nerys looked at her phone, as if she expected to see the bullshit oozing from it. She shook her head and huffed the thought to the back of her mind. It was time to focus on the practical. "So. What about this freebie then? You'd better fill me in. Pun absolutely intended."

To cleanse her soul of worries, Nerys joined the hunt for Fiona the lost dog she had faked under the alias of Belinda Carlisle. The search party was a task force made up of dozens of dog lovers and had been going for days. They had joined in small groups to begin with then, as word spread further, a support team sprang up co-ordinating the search. Someone had erected a tent near to the entrance of the park and sat at a folding table, with handwritten lists and a map.

This was goodness. This was decency. This was honest and loving human beings banding together to do something to help others.

"Hello, I want to help look for Fiona," Nerys said.

"Right," said the woman. "Have you got a torch?"

Nerys nodded.

"Good. I need you to head on down this path and then over to the sector marked as D on this map. Find someone down there wearing a hi-vis and they will show you where to search. Put your name down on this sheet and I'll need you to mark the time you arrived and make sure you sign out when you go. Hot drinks and snacks will be available from here if you need them."

Nerys saw a gas-powered water boiler behind them, and piles of boxes that looked as if they were from the local Indian takeaway.

All of this was also being documented in real time updates on *Belinda Carlisle*'s original request. Nerys felt a warm glow as she walked down the path and saw the concern on people's faces, listening to them worrying how scared and cold Fiona must be by now.

As she monitored the page, she saw that a local radio station had covered the event and even more searchers appeared. A small army of people were now tramping across the local area making whistling noises and gently calling for Fiona.

Nerys couldn't help herself when a TV crew turned up. She peeled away from the search and came forward as the tearful owner. On the one hand she was unable to resist being the star of this amazing show she had created, and on the other she was genuinely overwhelmed by the public response.

She briefly forgot that Fiona the dog didn't exist, and tears rolled down her cheeks. "Of course, while I am desperately sad about Fiona, there is something beautiful and uplifting about the way people are rallying in an effort to find her."

The presenter nodded. "So true. And what do you say to the allegations that you have faked the entire thing?"

"Sorry, what?" Nerys snapped to attention. "Me?"

"There have been rumours on social media that the picture you circulated is a stock image of a dog living in Wyoming."

"Oh my goodness, people can be so cruel," sniffed Nerys. "I can't imagine what would motivate anyone to say such a thing."

"And there are a number of people who have suggested that Belinda Carlisle might not be your real name."

Nerys held up a hand to block the camera. It had been a mistake to appear in public. "I need to distance myself from such toxicity. Thank you all for your support."

Nerys went home and posted an update to say that Fiona had returned home, very tired and frightened, and that Belinda Carlisle was withdrawing from her social feeds to give Fiona time to heal. She hoped that by doing so she would kill the story before the TV people broadcast anything.

She poured herself a nightcap measure of boxed wine, then took the Shit-O-Meter out of the cupboard to see if the reading had changed. It was such an infuriating piece of kit because it never changed.

Had any of her endeavours made the sinfulness of the world go down an inch? Had some of them made it rise a fraction? Did all the things she tried to do just cancel each other out?

Not for the first time, she wondered if the gauge on the device might be stuck. One of the cars she once owned had a petrol gauge that never went below halfway, even when the car had no fuel left. It had left her stranded so many times that she had secretly been grateful when Clovenhoof had put a tow rope on it and fastened it onto a petrol tanker for a bet. It had lasted half a mile before it smashed into the railway bridge by Chester Road station, writing it off completely.

She went down to Ben's flat.

"Hey Ben, do you have any WD-40?" she asked him when he opened the door.

"Have you seen the late news?"

"What?"

He ushered her into his lounge and she saw her own face on the TV screen.

"Oh bugger."

"*—thought to be a false name,*" said the reporter. "*The search has since been called off, but people are angry and have questions. Who is this woman and why did she mobilise a search* party of hundreds of people to look for a dog that she doesn't even own?"

Nerys saw the brief edited clip of her where her artful crying was made to look like snivelling theatrics.

"Well poo. That is annoying."

"Was this another part of trying to get people to be helpful?" said Ben. "I think you might have lost your way slightly."

"No!" said Nerys. "I took your idea and made it real. It brought people together in an amazing team, focused on a simple, unselfish goal. For a moment I came close to tapping into something really powerful. The sort of power that can heal the world."

Ben shrugged and pulled a face. Nerys obviously couldn't explain to him what was behind her recent behaviour, and Ben was clearly confused by it all. "The power of a few people chasing after a fictitious dog won't heal the world though, will it?"

"Fine! Maybe you're right, but I need solutions, not criticism."

Ben shook his head. "I wonder whether you're taking Jeremy's absence harder than you're prepared to admit. You've not been yourself at all, and you're indulging in the sort of nonsense he would normally be guilty of. Fixing the world by faking a lost dog is pure Jeremy."

Ben gave a sorrowful shake of his head and then produced an ancient and battered can from his cupboard. "WD-40. I don't do car repairs. If it's not fixed with this then I can't help. Show me where you want it spraying."

"I think I can handle the spraying myself," said Nerys.

Ben looked as if he wasn't certain. "There's a little straw so you can squirt it where you need. You can be very precise."

"I know. I saw where Jeremy used to squirt it. Hope you gave that a wipe."

Ben stared in horror and dropped the can. Nerys swooped in and picked it up, then retreated to her flat.

There were no obvious points on the Shit-O-Meter that looked as if they needed a helpful wiggle. She tried twisting the top, but it didn't budge. Nerys decided she would gently apply WD-40 to the whole thing. She squirted tiny amounts all up its length and then repeated the dose for good measure. After that she removed the straw and sprayed the length of the Shit-O-Meter liberally. It was now rather slippery, so she wiped it with a cloth.

"You know what it needs Twinkle? A quick tap to loosen it."

She wrapped it in the cloth and gave it an experimental tap with a rolling pin. She was being super gentle, so she did it again. Before long she had progressed to whacking it repeatedly with no effect whatsoever.

"Come on!"

She unwrapped the cloth and looked for any changes, even a scratch. She twisted and smacked it off the kitchen counter, but it remained unscathed, still showing the same reading of one point two. The little needle was behind some sort of protective cover, but she was unable to prise it open, even with the pointy end of a potato peeler.

"Right."

Nerys held it across the edge of the doorway to her flat

and shut the door, trapping it. She leaned on the door to hold it steady and tried to twist it.

"What?" she said to Twinkle who was now looking at her askance. "It definitely looks like it should rotate. In fact, it looks like something that should go round in circles and make a sound like *meep meep*."

She was unable to twist it, so she shoulder-barged the door in frustration. There was a loud snapping sound and the end of the Shit-O-Meter plinked onto the floor.

"Oh," she said, kneeling to retrieve it. With urgent and trembling hands, she grasped the broken end and tried to force it back on, but it was clearly broken. "Oh, hell!" she snapped, feeling tears of pity prick her eyes. "Will nothing go right for me?"

In answer, there came the sound of the doorbell.

It was night now, long after the socially acceptable time to be ringing people's doorbells. Nerys went down. Maybe it was a news team, come to doorstep her about her recent scandal. Maybe it was bitter and vengeful dog-owners, armed with handfuls of dog muck. Whatever, she was now in that frigid yet boiling emotional stillness where nothing seemed to matter anymore.

She opened the door.

There was a demon on the doorstep. The same demon, the one with all the ears.

"Speak of the devil and he shall appear..." she whispered.

"I mean technically not the devil 'isself," said the demon. "Name's Hodshift, yeah? Wonder if I can have a word."

"I didn't mean to break it," she said.

"Break what?"

She shook herself and looked up and down the street. "Yeah, sure. Come in."

Hodshift nodded and then pointed up at night sky. "What's up wiv the sun? Blown a fuse?"

"It's not in the sky at night."

"Really?" he said, interested. "Probably a glitch. Someone should look into that, shun't they?"

She waved him in.

17

Nerys had a demon in her flat. Short, yellow, covered in ears and very much in her flat. He sauntered into her kitchen and picked up the broken pieces of the Shit-O-Meter with a rueful expression.

"Yer've broken the peccadometer."

"It just sort of came apart in my hands," said Nerys.

He turned it over and rubbed a thumb across the display. "Them's potato peeler scratches."

"Are they?" she remarked innocently.

"We see them a lot in the fifth circle. Mostly on the faces of our clients, mind."

Nerys gave a tiny shrug by way of acknowledgement. "Can you fix it?"

Hodshift looked at her. "Fixing things is what I likes to do. Can't be doing wiv all that wishing things better, it takes away the fun." He looked around. "I bet you've got a whole load of broken things round here?"

"No, not really – oh wait, there is a clock belonging to my Aunt Molly that's not worked for ages."

"I'm an engineer and creative problem solver. Let me fix a few things for you and then maybe you can do something for me."

She narrowed her eyes. "What do you want from me? Is it my soul?"

He blew out his lips and scratched one of his ears. "Ten a penny, them. No, I wanted to lay my 'ands on some more of them cables. An RS-232 serial data cable to be precise."

"Oh. I see."

"Got a deal then?" He held out his hand.

Nerys reached to shake on it, but he batted her away. "Nah, the clock! Gis it 'ere."

When Nerys got up the next day, the demon was whistling to himself in the kitchen, the Shit-O-Meter was back together and Aunt Molly's clock was ticking loudly.

"Sleep well?" she asked automatically.

"Demons don't sleep," said Hodshift.

She knew this to be true because she hadn't slept a wink all night herself and had sat awake in her bed listening to him whistling and tinkering with God knew what.

"I upped the settings on your rack slack steam room," he said.

"My what?" she said.

He pointed at the dishwasher. "Had a go on it myself. The foamy steamy jets are good but I'd probably prefer the spikes in the bottom rack to be a bit sharper.

She realised his skin was a little bit more lemon-shiny and that he did now vaguely smell of clean crockery.

"Anything else you need fixing while I'm 'ere?" he asked.

"Not for the moment," she said and stepped out into the lounge, carefully closing the door after her. A demon in her kitchen. She'd met demons. Jeremy had been one, of sorts, hadn't he? But this? At a time when she was trying to uplift herself and the whole world morally and spiritually.

Throughout her life, Nerys had never truly feared for her mortal soul. Part of her hadn't really believed she had one. Part of her had very strongly believed that, if it was *her* mortal soul then it was nobody else's business what she did with it. If, after death, God was going to start lecturing her on what he, a man, thought she, a woman, should have doing with her life, then he was going to get a bloody earful on the subject of sexism, patriarchy and what must be the most abusive controlling relationship ever. Nerys, who had glimpsed Heaven and had heard first-hand accounts of Hell, had assumed she would rather go down than up, morally speaking.

But now, with the Apocalypse just around the corner, her inner feelings had taken on a slightly more ... pragmatic attitude, and she found she did indeed fear for her mortal soul. Sure, she was still ready to give the Almighty a lesson on power dynamics and his historic mistreatment of women, but she now selfishly felt she'd rather do that from behind the safe, cool, pain-free walls of the Celestial City.

She rang the Reverend Zack Purdey.

"Nerys! What a delight to hear from you."

"You have to say that. You're a vicar."

"Or maybe I'm a vicar because I'm always delighted to engage with parishioners."

"Can I ask you a question?"

"Ah, it's trivia time with Miss Nerys Thomas again," he said, chuckling to himself.

"Demons."

"Yes? Are you going to ask me if they're real?"

"No," she said, looking to the closed kitchen door and hearing the tuneless whistling from within. "No, I think I've got that covered. I was going to ask about what happens if people … engage with demons."

"Engage? As in … carnally?"

"No. God, ew, no. I mean as in just chit-chat. Cup of tea and a biscuit. Say you had a work colleague who was a demon."

"Ah. Fallen out with Tina again?"

"No," she said. "Well, yes, a bit. She perverts everything good I try to do, but no. I mean demons. Real demons. About yay-high, covered in ears, talks like a character off *Eastenders*."

"Hmmm. Not sure I'm familiar with that one. Padre Pio, Roman Catholic priest but an otherwise fine chap, he wrote about demons appearing to him in the form of black cats and naked women."

"Did he?"

"Mmmm. Recounted that they danced provocatively in front of him to tempt him. The girls, not the cats."

"Sounds like a young single man with an overactive imagination. And what did the cats do?"

"I think they were just ominous and evil."

"I'm more of a dog person myself," she conceded. "But demons, if you met one, is it okay to talk to it?"

"If a member of my congregation came to me with such questions I'd usually want to discuss their emotional state and maybe talk about accessing mental health services."

"I am as emotionally fine as I'm ever going to be, rev, and I'm stone cold sane, I assure you."

"Yes. I did always think you knew your own mind. So, hypothetically, if I met a demon... Gosh, I do like these exciting questions. There is nothing wrong with engaging with it. If a good Christian is afraid to face a servant of the enemy for fear of what they might say then I'd be concerned about the quality of their own faith. I mean it's fascinating isn't it, really? It's that old free will and good and evil thing."

"In what way?"

"We say that demons are evil but, more than any other creature, real or imaginary, they were made to be evil. They didn't get a choice. They're not like people – human beings I mean. They are intrinsically evil, but if they've always been that way then they've never chosen the path of evil. Morally, they're sort of outside the system."

"Er, okay," said Nerys, not quite following. "So, to recap, I don't lose brownie points for talking to demons."

"Unless they tempt you down the path of evil. Has this, um, demon tempted you down the path of evil?"

"He's mended a clock and had a ride in my dishwasher."

"I ... really don't know how to respond to that, Nerys. And can I just check? You've not taken any unusual drugs recently or perhaps used powerful cleaning products in an enclosed space?"

She laughed. "I am fine, Zack."

"Good, good," he said, uncertainly. "Now, when I said I was delighted to hear from you, that was also because I did want to speak to you on a certain matter."

"Oh?"

"And I'm glad we're not having the conversation in the church."

"Oh?" she said, uncertainly.

There was a click of a door on the line, the vaguest suggestion that he had stepped into a smaller, quieter space.

"I made some enquiries, based on our chat the other day," whispered Zack.

"Our chat?"

"It seemed like a reasonable challenge, and I wanted better answers to give you."

"Oh, right! You asked about the Church of England having a preparedness group or Armageddon plan?"

"I did. They told me that no such group exists."

"I see. Yet we're now having this clandestine conversation..."

He paused. "Nothing huge or concrete has happened. Nothing that makes me certain there's some grand conspiracy, but a few little things have made me wonder if I'm under scrutiny for asking."

Nerys blinked. "Do tell," she said, realising she was also whispering.

"I started to notice a man I'd not seen before," he said. "Nothing unusual in that, but he has turned up all over the place. I've seen him in the congregation, in the supermarket, and while I've been out in the community. I spotted him in a car once, and it was a massive thing with a chauffeur driving it. Again, nothing about any of that would matter ordinarily. People come to us from all walks of life. This man has been asking questions, though. It started off with a general interest in signs and portents, but got specific really fast. He even used the phrase 'unexplained trumpeting' which was so weird as you said the exact same thing."

"Yes, but I said it out of frustration," said Nerys. "What was the context when he used it?"

"He seems to be fishing, to see if we've had any unusual phenomena in the area. I don't think I'm the only person he's asked."

"And you think this was prompted by you asking questions?"

"I have no idea. Watch out for him though. A tall man with grey hair and big sideburns. Dressed in a plain suit. Has the most piercing eyes. Shhh!" His shush was violently loud. "I think someone's at the door," he whispered. "Gotta go."

Nerys stared at the phone after the call had ended. "Well, that was weird," she said. But at least he had been sort of clear about the business with the demon.

Nerys went to the kitchen. Hodshift had taken apart her tin opener and was scratching at the crud that mired the cog workings.

"How are we doing in here?" she said.

"Smashing," said Hodshift and then spat on the workings to lubricate them before twisting them.

"Can I ask you a simple question?" she said.

"Them's the best kind."

"Do you intend to tempt me down the path of evil?"

He turned and looked at her like she was mad. "I've got a

list of jobs to do as long as me arm. Why would I add Tempting Humans to that list?"

"But that's what demons do, isn't it?"

Hodshift chuckled throatily. "There used to be a huge Soul Enticement Centre in the Third Circle. Countless demons working to ensnare human souls and drag people to Hell. Then we had the flood."

"The flood?"

"Yeah, some monks broke into Hell, opened a door to the bottom of the sea..." He waved the whole thing away. "Bloody monks, coming down here on their jollies. Should be a law against in. Anyway, the Soul Enticement Centre was shut down for six month Earth-time and guess what?"

"The number of people tempted to evil didn't change?" Nerys guessed.

"Ex-acker-ly."

"Humans don't need tempting," she said. "There's something intrinsically ... crap about all of us."

"Ha. Tell me about it."

"In fact, getting them to just be a bit nicer is—" She threw her hands up in the air. "It's like herding cats. In fact I could probably use a bit of your technical help with this project I've got going on."

"Don't mind sharin' my expertise," said Hodshift, rolling his shoulders. "Now, about this serial cable you promised..."

"Yes, let's go talk to my friend, Spartacus."

They walked down to Clovenhoof's old flat.

Spartacus's friends were not around this early in the morning, although the skate park was still there. Had it grown? There were now scaffold boards turned into an elaborate series of ramps all around Clovenhoof's former living room.

Spartacus sat on one, tapping on his laptop and munching on a bag of Haribo.

"Spartacus, listen, there's someone I want you to meet; and some stuff I need to tell you about."

"Yeah?" he said, not looking up.

"It's related to Jeremy. You might find it a bit unbelievable."

"If it's about Mr C then I doubt I'd find it unbelievable. He is the man who invented sticky trousers so you can carry everything on the outside of your clothes without needing pockets."

"I'm pretty sure he just left them on his kitchen floor too long. And this thing is probably more unbelievable than sticky trousers, if I'm honest."

Spartacus shrugged.

She waved for Hodshift to come in. The demon obligingly stepped in off the landing.

"Now, don't scream, but this is Hodshift."

Spartacus looked up. "All right," he said in greeting.

"Mornin'," said Hodshift.

Spartacus either didn't notice that Hodshift was a yellow many-eared demon or...

"Hodshift here is a ... visitor," said Nerys. "He knew Jeremy of old."

"Well, he kicked me in the face once," said Hodshift.

"That's nice," said Spartacus.

Nerys frowned, and then sighed. The human mind was an amazing thing. It was the same as with Clovenhoof. No one seemed to notice that this bloke living among them was a red-skinned fiend with horns and hoofs. And now, Spartacus couldn't see that this creature in Clovenhoof's flat was some unholy horror. He had the wrong number of ears. It should have been unmissable, yet this salient fact washed over Spartacus like water off a duck's back.

"Hodshift is an engineer," said Nerys. "And here we have a device that measures the crapness in the world."

This made Spartacus look up. "A what?"

"A peccadometer!" said Hodshift, holding out the device.

"Basically a Shit-O-Meter," said Nerys, who preferred her name for it.

"Let's see what it's reading eh?" Hodshift studied it and pulled the face Nerys recognised from car repair shops and builders everywhere. "Oh deary me, still one point two gigapeccados a second."

"It measures how crap the world is?" said Spartacus.

"By measuring destabilisation in a sealed container of conductive morally neutral fluid," said Hodshift.

"Sounds like some Midi-chlorian level techno-bullshit," said Spartacus.

"I can't believe the overall level hasn't gone down at all," said Nerys.

Hodshift twiddled with something. "Well, there's been a local reduction since I was last here, just a small one, mind."

"Wait, there are more settings?" asked Nerys.

"Course there are! What use would it be otherwise?"

"Has it got an API?" asked Spartacus.

"A what?" said Nerys.

"Application Programming Interface," said Hodshift. "Oh

yes, lad. We'll have you connected in a jiffy." He shuffled over to Spartacus's laptop and the two of them leaned over it for a few minutes, before both settled back with smug grins on their faces.

"Come and look! It's on the dashboard," said Spartacus. "We called it 'background dissatisfaction rating' so that people know what we're on about."

Nerys looked at the semi-circle speedometer readout now on the top of the website page.

"That is tremendous," said Nerys. "Now, let's dig into those settings a bit more. I want to see what else this thing can do."

Hodshift cleared his throat. "Ahem. I believe you mentioned that this young 'un would be able to locate an RS-232 serial data cable."

"Never heard of 'em," said Spartacus, but before Hodshift could complain had googled it. "That's a cable from the sixties! That's like pre-history."

"Told you they were hard to find," said Hodshift.

"Nah, look. You can order them. Nerys, go get your credit card."

18

Michael hurried to one of the monorail stations which dotted the staggering huge Holy City and hopped on. It was seventy-two stops to the Research Centre for Scriptural Exegesis, which seemed like a lot. But time being an entirely metaphorical concept here, it really wasn't that long at all. He sat down with a struggle, because his wings just seemed to get in the way. He'd been without them for so long he'd forgotten how awkwardly cumbersome they were.

As the monorail set off, he wedged himself into a seat, side-saddle.

Four rows along the carriage he heard a couple of souls chatting. They spoke like an old married couple. Perhaps, between this life and the one before, they had been together for centuries.

"Well, Pedro in the next block over says we'll have to make room for the latecomers."

"Did he?"

"He did. Doomsday comes – crash, bang, wallop – you've suddenly got seven billion people knocking on Heaven's door."

"Ooh, not seven billion. Surely, most will be going ... you know..." said the other soul, pointing a cagy finger towards the floor.

"Even if it's nine tenths of them relocating there, that's still ... seven thousand... no, wait, seven hundred million people turning up here, suitcases in hand."

"I think Pedro's got it wrong."

"Do you?"

"I do. It's like Belinda Carlisle says, Heaven is a place on Earth. When all the dust has settled on Earth and Armageddon is over—"

"Ooh, I hope they don't leave the place a mess."

"Oh, I know. When it's done, there will be a new Heaven on Earth."

"Oh, that'll be nice."

"It will."

"You think it will be somewhere by the sea. Like Brighton."

"Could be. Could be. Or maybe somewhere exotic."

"Like Guernsey?"

"It is nice there."

The two souls realised Michael was watching them and stared.

"I was going to go on holiday to Mauritius," he said. "It's meant to be lovely."

The two souls silently contemplated this.

"Well, it takes all sorts," said one eventually.

Seventy-two stops later, Michael stepped off into a plaza with a large fountain at its centre. The Research Centre for Scriptural Exegesis inhabited a rounded building, topped with domes of green copper and glass. Michael strode up the steps.

Through the open doors, he entered a wide chamber filled with rows and columns of desks. Some were modern, with computer stations on them; others much older. Indeed there were still a great number of angled scribing stations whereon individuals worked with parchment, rather than paper or computers.

The hundreds of human souls were almost entirely absorbed in their work, and the air was filled with the hushed roar of a thousand clicking keyboards and a thousand scratching quills, and the intermittent *hiss-thunk* of the pneumatic tube system which carried communication cannisters around the building.

A woman at a nearby desk spotted the Archangel Michael and stepped up promptly to greet him. She took off her glasses and let them hang from a chain around her neck.

"Sir, we weren't expecting you today," she said in the powerful whisper of a zealous librarian.

"An impromptu visit," said Michael.

"I would have thought you'd have more important things to do, what with the coming Apocalypse and all that."

"Well, that's why I'm here," he said. "I'm very interested in what scripture has to say about the end of the world."

"Of course, sir. Of course. Very popular topic. Well, you've come to the right place."

Michael waved offhandedly at the woman's desk. "And this is where you do it? The exegesis? Working out what the holy scriptures actually mean?"

"Generally, yes," she said. "Specifically, no."

"Oh?"

"Actual commentary and interpretation of scripture takes place on the top floors. Saint Jerome and the scholarly elite. Very clever people there."

"So, this—?"

"Well, sir. Our best scholars interpret what the all the holy texts actually mean, but of course, their writing is itself open to interpretation. Language is such a tricksy thing."

"Ah, so you write the commentaries and exegesis on those commentaries?"

The woman giggled and her cheeks reddened. "Would that I could be so lucky, sir. No, that happens on floors eleven and twelve. Further down, top scholars work on interpreting the commentaries on the earlier commentaries."

"Really?"

She nodded, stepping to one side and turning her screen so Michael could see it. "Origen – he's on the fifteenth – he wrote *Contra Celsum* in two-four-eight AD, in which he beautifully rebuts Celsum's attack on Christianity. Now, Eusebius – thirteenth floor – makes important reference to *Contra Celsum* in his *Contra Hieroclem*. This in turn is both translated and commented upon by Tyrannius Rufinus – eleventh floor. You see where this is going?"

"I'm afraid I do," said Michael.

"Dominic Vallarsi wrote a wonderful overview of Rufinius's work in the eighteenth century. He didn't get to finish it during his earthly lifetime, but that's what Heaven's for, right?"

"Catching up on work you failed to do earlier?"

"Absolutely. So, now we come to the nineteen-thirteen edition of the Catholic Encyclopaedia and one of several entries written by Michael Ott. Benedictine from Germany. Lovely man. We're on the same bowling team. He wrote an entry on Vallarsi and has been expanding on it ever since he joined us in nineteen thirty-six. And *I* am currently writing a commentary on this little nugget."

On the screen was a scan of a typed manuscript and, in the margin, someone had written:

Collect laundry. Coffee. Carlo's deli – ½ pound pastrami.

"It's Ott's shopping list," said Michael.

"It is," said the woman. "It is – or indeed, is it?"

"It very much looks like it is."

"But why is it here? Why did he write it there? What theological revelation caused him to place this detail here?"

"And this is what you're working on? A commentary of a commentary of a commentary of— All the way back to something Origen wrote about someone else's attack on faith?"

"Yes!" she said. "It's really thrilling. The last big project I got to work on was a doodle of a cat in the back of John Paul II's diary. I wrote two volumes on that."

"Valuable work," Michael said politely.

"Thank you."

"So, if I wanted to find out what the Bible says – specifically what the Bible says – about the Apocalypse, who should I speak to?"

"You should go right to the top," said the woman, pointing at a lift door across the way. "Saint Jerome. I'm sure he'd be delighted to see you."

"Thank you." He paused before turning away. "If you and this Michael Ott are on the same bowling team, why don't you just go and ask him what that margin note means?"

The woman looked appalled. "That is not how scriptural exegesis works at all, sir! We can't just ask people what they think their words mean. We're scholars, not gossips. Once out there, the words exist all by themselves. The text is the text. The author's opinion is entirely irrelevant."

"I see," Michael said and backed away to the lift. Scholars and writers, he concluded, were all more than a little bit unhinged.

19

By mid-afternoon, Nerys wondered if she ought to be concerned at the amount of time Hodshift was spending with Spartacus. The two of them seemed to enjoy working together on the boy's laptop, puzzling over how to deploy the Shit-O-Meter more effectively.

By teatime, they announced they had something to show Nerys. She turned up in Clovenhoof's flat to find even more mess. Every flat surface was covered with electronic components.

"Where has all this stuff come from?" asked Nerys.

"I took Hodshift to the dump," said Spartacus.

"Waste like I've never seen in all my life," said Hodshift happily.

"Hodshift just jumps into the skips and takes the bits he wants," said Spartacus.

"We've enhanced the Pecca—"

"The Shit-O-Meter," said Nerys firmly.

"Hmmm, whatever. We've enhanced the directionality and added a broad spectrum diffuser so that we can sweep larger areas, looking for localised anomalies in the readout."

They pointed, and Nerys realised the Shit-O-Meter now sat in a cradle the size and shape of a suitcase. In fact it looked very much like the bottom half of an old suitcase. There was something like a satellite dish wired into a complex set of boxes. The whole thing fed a small display that Spartacus held out with pride.

"See? By putting this on the roof of your car and making a few circuits, we can map anything local that moves the needle either up or down. There's even a map on the display here, so we can tell you which way to drive."

Nerys looked at the size of the contraption. "You have seen the size of my car? You want me to drive round with this on the roof while you two tell me which way to go?"

"Yes. Exactly that."

Nerys had thoughts on how that was likely to go, but in the end she simply shrugged and agreed.

Soon, their suitcase was strapped in place, and they piled into the car.

"So, where to?"

They decided to tour the area in widening circles, so they could capture readings that covered an entire section of Sutton Coldfield and the surrounding area.

Every so often, Hodshift would insist on a small detour to capture more detail, but generally Nerys was able to dictate the route.

After three hours she declared she'd had enough driving for one day and they went back.

"You order the pizza, and we review the results," said Spartacus to Nerys.

"Pizza? But—"

"—Seriously, it's the correct food for a hackathon. We're not allowed anything with vitamins 'n' stuff."

Nerys sighed. Spartacus had always been wayward and stubborn, which was why he got on so well with Jeremy. She had to hand it to teen Spartacus though, he had found a focus that suited him well. Previous obsessions like his shopping trolley dance gang or whatever had been a little more difficult to understand, but this... She could see how a determined boy with an internet connection could take over the world one day.

Nerys went to the takeaway place at the end of the road to get four extortionately priced, greasy pizzas. On her way back, a man in a suit thrust a flyer at her.

"Look for the signs!" he declared.

"Signs?" said Nerys, turning the leaflet over in her free hand.

"*Then another sign appeared in heaven, a great red dragon with seven heads and ten horns and seven crowns on its heads!*"

"Right. That's quite a sign," she agreed.

"*When the dragon saw that he had been hurled to the earth, he pursued the woman!*"

"Got it. Dragon. Woman."

The leaflet pictured the Earth, alone in space and above it were the words Have you seen signs of the End Times? Call this number.

She frowned. "And, er, what if we do see signs of the End Times and we call this number?"

The man pulled himself to his full height, his grey sideburns bristling. "The church is always prepared. It's never too late to act."

"I see." A wild and dangerous part of her mind thought about pointing out there was a demon in her house who was in fact expecting to eat a quantity of the pizza she was carrying, but quashed the thought right down and hurried home.

Soon, they were all sitting in front of the television eating pizza out of boxes.

"You can see the readings overlaid as a colour on a map of the area," munched Hodshift.

"This is incredible," said Nerys, savouring the pizza as she gazed at the map. "You can see St Michael's church is a pale amber. Good old Reverend Zack is making a difference with his coffee mornings and his guitar."

Thoughts of Reverend Zack prompted a memory. He'd mentioned a tall, suited man with grey hair and sideburns. Nerys couldn't recall if the man handing out flyers had the piercing eyes that Zack had mentioned, but the other features matched.

Hodshift nodded. "Small stuff, but it's made an impact on that area. Mostly we're well into the red, though. Danger zone's what I like to call it, on account of it being dangerous."

Most of the map was a vivid scarlet colour. It was not a hopeful sight.

"So our best hope is a guitar-playing and biscuit-dealing

vicar?" asked Nerys. "I mean, seriously, is that the best we've got on here?"

"We picked up some readings right on the edge of our search that might be worth checking out," said Spartacus."

"The lad's right," said Hodshift. He pointed at the map. "We need to go and check out the north-eastern sector, extend our search slightly, although it's a bit more rural up there." The demon gave a small shudder.

"It's no good if you're going to tell me that cows are the answer," said Nerys with a huff. "We're stuck with people. We'll look in the morning.

NERYS DROVE SLIGHTLY AWAY from the housing estates of Falcon Lodge and Reddicap Heath and out into open countryside.

"Yeah, carry on. This is interesting," said Hodshift from the back of the car.

"If you see a left turn up ahead, go down it," said Spartacus.

"Here?" Nerys turned into a track and realised she had been here before.. One of those outbuildings was the garage that had been cleared by the volunteer task force she had arranged. "This is where Perry Thews lives."

"Who's Perry Thews?" said Spartacus.

"Peregrine Thews. Just an ordinary bloke with a messy garage."

"—And a stupid name."

"It was one of the first jobs we helped with."

"Would you take a look at that?" said Hodshift to Spartacus in wonder.

"It's totally green here," said Spartacus, stabbing the map display on his laptop. "Only green we've seen so far. It's mad! Just this place, it goes red again when you go outside."

Nerys walked towards the house, intending to ring the bell, but a voice sounded behind her before she reached it. It was a cheery welcoming voice.

"Good morning!"

Nerys turned to see Perry Thews carrying a spade. "Morning. Just a quick follow up on the job that we did here." Nerys needed to play for time. "Great spade!"

Perry waggled it briefly. "Just put a new handle on it for one of the Reddicap pensioners. No sense in wasting good tools."

"How interesting. Who are the Reddicap pensioners?" Nerys wondered if there was something here to unpick about how Perry was scoring so highly on the Shit-O-Meter.

"Pensioners who live at Reddicap Heath," explained Perry. There was no sarcasm there, just a straightforward wave of the hand in the direction of the edge of the town.

"So you're friends with pensioners?" asked Nerys.

"Never met 'em," said Perry. "But I've always said I'll do bits and pieces if I can. They drop their things off by the gate and pick them up again when I've fixed them."

Nerys watched as Perry walked over to the gate and put the spade next to a wheelbarrow outside the gate.

"Did you fix that as well?" Nerys had never seen a wheelbarrow with a patch before. Neat holes were drilled into the plastic and a series of cable ties held the patch like sutures. Nerys looked underneath and saw that it covered a large, jagged crack.

"I did. It's the only reason why the gate is open, so's I can put these out. People don't come in here much." It wasn't an accusation, just an observation.

"Yes. About that," said Nerys. "You're doing something really interesting here and I would love to learn more about it."

Perry continued to look at her, as if expecting her to finish. Nerys had dealt with lots of people who were socially awkward, but Perry didn't seem like someone who didn't know how to interact; more like someone who was simply happy with his own company and looked at Nerys as he might look at a bird on his fence.

"Perry," said Nerys after a long pause. "Could me and my friends have a chat with you. Would that be all right?"

Perry nodded obligingly.

The inside of the farmhouse was modest. Nerys started to build up a picture of Perry as someone who had practical skills and was basically self-sufficient on the land he had inherited. There was some sort of understanding with locals that he would fix broken things, and that he might also make eggs and vegetables available outside his gate. Was the key to human goodness as simple as that?

Perry didn't react to the fact he had a demon at his dining table. In fact he and Hodshift had an animated conversation about rivets and slot-headed screws.

"Collects 'em all I do. Becoming a rarity," said Hodshift.

"True enough."

Nerys persuaded Perry to show them around. With the

stable blocks and the outbuildings, there was quite a lot of space and Nerys started to form an idea.

"Your lifestyle, Perry, it's exemplary."

Perry gave a small shrug. "Don't know about that. Do I have a lifestyle?"

"Yes. Yes, you do. You have knowledge and a general outlook that is very valuable, and other people need to learn. Would you be willing to mentor some willing volunteers?"

"Like a teacher, you mean?"

Nerys tried to read his expression, to know how best to respond, but he had such a genial face that it was impossible to know if he was worried or excited by the idea.

"You could teach people if you want, but it would be more like a fully supported role model." The words came directly from the bullshit lobe of Nerys's brain, the part which knew how to wing it. "We build a small community, but you interact with it as much as you want to."

"I can teach people how to fix a spade, if that's what you mean," said Perry.

"Yes. Sure. That's exactly what I mean." Nerys knew it was a way in. Perry had accidentally become a monk of some sort. He would have no idea how to teach others to become monks, but he could teach them how to fix a spade. It was a good start.

Perry volunteered his stable block for accommodation and Spartacus took pictures for the brochure that Nerys told him they would need.

20

Nerys called an emergency board meeting. Tina and Ben eyed Hodshift as the five of them crowded together in Nerys's lounge.

"Won't you introduce us to the new person, Nerys?" asked Tina.

"Ah, this is Hodshift."

"Hod Shift?" said Tina. "Swedish?" she hazarded.

"Ish," agreed Hodshift happily.

"He's a consulting expert," said Nerys. "Hodshift's input has helped us refine some of our data feeds, and we're in a much better position to understand where our work has been most effective. So, I wanted to update you all on some fascinating insights. Not only do we have better data generally, we have, um, stumbled across the perfect place to scale some of our efforts and provide training opportunities for the general population."

She described Perry to the board and outlined the opportunity his farm offered.

Ben leaned in as Nerys finished. "So let me understand this correctly. We have a simple carpenter, living the quiet life, and you want to select a bunch of followers to go and live with him? You basically want to set up Jesus school?"

"What? No!" Nerys realised it did sound a bit like that.

"Ben's right," said Tina. "It would be a hard sell, and you'd get people coming along for all the wrong reasons. Instagrammers looking to video miracles, people bringing their sick relatives for a cure and all sorts."

"I'm pretty sure Perry can't do miracles," said Nerys.

"No, but that won't stop people putting two and two together and making five," said Tina. "What you want to do is appeal to the white saviours."

"What are white saviours?" said Spartacus. "Sounds like a racist baseball team."

"Close," said Tina. "You would make this idea work better if you got people to buy into the idea that they are going somewhere to build an orphanage or something."

"Who needs an orphanage in middle England?" said Nerys.

"Exactly," said Tina.

"People are weird," agreed Ben, "Tell them they are needed to help out with a community project on their doorstep, and people stay away in droves. Tell people they can go to Burundi or Haiti or somewhere and help the natives dig wells, and you get every Tarquin, Jocasta and Sebastian actually paying good money to go out there."

"Exactly," said Tina. "So, that's what you do."

Nerys opened her mouth to slam the ridiculousness of Tina's idea, then closed it again. It could work well as a way to select people who genuinely did want to do good things, even if they were muddle-headed in their motivation. "So..." she said tentatively. "These people would genuinely think they were going to some far flung destination to do manual work to help poor *foreign* people?"

"Yes," said Tina. "People will buy into that."

"You want to pretend a corner of the West Midlands is Harambe or somewhere?" said Spartacus.

"It could work," said Tina.

Nerys found herself agreeing despite herself. "We could maybe pull that off. Perry's farm is quite isolated."

"I am not comfortable with this," said Ben.

"You're not comfortable with anything new," said Nerys. "You still think *Snickers* should be called *Marathon*."

Spartacus looked thrilled at the idea of orchestrating a deception. "The website will need the right photos. I can add a filter, increase the light saturation. It will be great!"

"Tell me why we're doing this again?" Ben asked. "Deceiving people into joining a commune?"

"Perry represents the change we need in the world," said Nerys, really hoping nobody would ask for proof.

"Can you prove that though?" asked Ben.

"Sure can," said Hodshift. "Readings were off the scale on his farm. Every indicator was well in the green. We filtered out background interference, recalibrated all of our instruments and checked at different times of day. Scientifically undeniable mate."

Ben was poised to ask what instruments, but Nerys cut

him off. "It's our best chance to scale this, Ben. We have to try."

Spartacus edited some of the photographs to show crumbling walls against a sun-blasted landscape. Ben worked on the text, describing how volunteers would be provided with simple accommodation and food, and in return they would refurbish tools for the indigenous population and cultivate farmland to enable crops to be grown.

Tina appointed herself the role of recording videos, making heartfelt pleas to help the population of an unnamed place to recover their livelihoods and their dignity.

"That is really something, Tina," said Nerys, wiping away a tear as she reviewed the final video.

"Thank you. Mr Hodshift says he can make it into an advert for social media. He seems like some sort of expert on those."

"I bet he is," said Nerys.

Nerys was awoken by hammering at her door. Spartacus and Hodshift came inside, brushing aside her protests about it being too early or too late (she wasn't even sure which).

"You're charging people to volunteer for this thing?" asked Spartacus.

"It's to cover their air fare," said Nerys.

"I can get there on my bike in twenty minutes, they don't need to go in a plane! Anyway, I can't quite believe this, but you've already filled all forty places. They've all paid as well."

"Misery tourism," said Hodshift. "It sounds like a Hellish invention, but you lot did it all by yerselves."

"We must keep reminding ourselves that these people want to do good," said Nerys. "What's more they have committed to it – to the tune of five hundred pounds. That's the real reason for getting them to pay. We're depending on these people to help us reduce the Shit-O-Meter reading further afield once they are trained."

NERYS WAS at Perry's farm to greet the guests when they arrived.

Everything had been carefully phrased in their literature so that there were no actual lies, but it served up heavy hints that the destination was in a far flung destination. Nerys wore the sort of clothes she imagined she would wear if she was sent off to Africa or Central Asia. Khaki trousers, cotton layers, a wide brimmed hat and boots. The current drizzle spoiled the effect, but she hoped it would soon stop.

The guests would be travel weary and disoriented on arrival, so Nerys needed to get them settled in, fed and put to bed.

Perry seemed unfazed by all the preparations. Nerys had lined up a giant pile of broken tools for his workshops, and he was very happy at the prospect of mending them all. She had scoured rubbish tips and put adverts in the paper to flush them out. She hoped she wouldn't need to resort to actually breaking tools herself.

The plan was to get the tools fixed up, then to cultivate some of the unused pasture on Perry's farm. The group would erect a polytunnel, grow some crops and any surplus would be donated to a foodbank.

Hodshift had insisted the experiment needed to remain untainted, so it was essential that all guests remained on site for the duration of the experiment. Nerys had prepared notices about the dangers lurking beyond the boundary and displayed them all around the farm.

Landmines. Dangerous!
Take care of big cats
Poachers sometimes leave buried traps. Danger!

Did these posters constitute lies? Possibly. However, Nerys was prepared to argue that landmines were indeed dangerous, that one should always take care around big cats, and that poachers sometimes did leave buried traps.

Phones and other electronics had been banned for all guests. It was sold as part of the experience – that participants would go through a digital detox; but more than anything, Nerys didn't want them to consult a map that showed where they were.

Nerys heard the noise of a rough diesel engine and went outside to see a large, battered coach pull up. She had insisted the coach should be ancient, and a little uncomfortable, and this was perfect. Animal Ed had a mate who ran an old-fashioned travel agents, the kind that should by any rights have been killed off by the internet, but which somehow clung on by being the lowest of the low and the cheapest of the cheap. Said mate had provided the spluttering coach, and he'd arranged for the guests to be flown around on a chartered plane, circling the North sea, and landing back at a small airfield in nearby Staffordshire. While on the plane they had all been served with free booze, which made them drowsy enough not to notice they were travelling along roads which might otherwise have looked familiar.

"Welcome! Welcome!" Nerys herded the disoriented travellers into Perry's largest barn, which would be their mess hall. "We'll get you something to eat and then you'll probably want to turn in. It's been a helluva journey, eh?"

Spartacus and his friends had been given the role of local helpers. Jefri Rehemtulla and PJ McTigue were already unloading bags from the luggage hold of the coach and trotting into the mess hall, putting them into a corner.

Kenzie sidled over. "Do you reckon they might give us tips?" he asked.

Nerys shrugged. "If they do, then just give them a silent nod of thanks, yeah? We can't let them know that you speak English."

Kenzie practised his silent nod of thanks and rushed off to move bags. Nerys had promised to pay them, but she couldn't blame them for trying the tip angle.

21

The original Fortress of Nameless Dread had been mostly destroyed in a catastrophic flood and was now nothing more than a jagged stump. If it had ever been Satan's phallic 'fuck you' to the Celestial City above, said phallus had now been torn to shreds, as though ripped apart by a scornful lover. It was said that a whole ocean of sea creatures and aquatic demons now made their home in the flooded sub-basements and sub-sub-basements.

Between the ruined tower and the lightless seas, Belphegor still kept some of his workshops and storehouses in operation. Working out of a messy and hard to access lair had certain advantages, particularly for a duke of Hell who didn't appreciate other archdemons poking their noses and other appendages into his secret works. As he wobbled his way across temporary bridges and followed his escort through partially collapsed tunnels, Clovenhoof understood why James Bond's enemies and other supervillains decided to make their bases in hollowed out volcanoes and abandoned jungle temples. Presumably, he thought, there were estate agents out there who specialised in such things.

Belphegor met him in a large, cuboidal chamber. The iron-lined walls were marked with dents and scorch marks. Belphegor puttered over in his wheelchair.

"Nice place you got here, Belpho," said Clovenhoof.

"It serves, lord," said the demon.

Clovenhoof pointed at the largest sooty dent in the wall. "What happened there?"

Belphehor teased at one of the clumps of white hair sprouting from his face thoughtfully. "I believe his name was Sludgespoon. One of my more promising inventor demons, but had a problem with keeping track of decimal points."

"Yes?"

"Turns out that there is such a thing as 'too much dynamite'."

"Ah."

Belphegor made a short circuit around Clovenhoof, inspecting him closely.

"Got a problem there?" said Clovenhoof.

"You are aware that you are meant to be riding out to do battle with the Archangel Michael in a short period of time?"

"I hear that's what's meant to happen."

"Let yourself go a bit, haven't you?"

"What?"

Belphegor drew a pointy stick from some secret recess of his chair and poked Clovenhoof in the belly. "Fat!"

"More of me to love."

The stick slapped the backs of Clovenhoof's goaty legs. "Weak. Almost completely atrophied."

"Legs are over-rated."

The stick tapped the underside of Clovenhoof's jowly chin, then poked his upper arms. "Little more than a bag of piss and vinegar."

"Hey! You can talk! Fat and useless. As round as my testicles and twice as wrinkly."

Belphegor chuckled drily, entirely unoffended. "Lord Satan, I am the demon of sloth. My very role is to ensnare human souls with the offers of labour-saving technology and thus create even greater levels of laziness on Earth. I am meant to be fat and weak-limbed. You on the other hand—" he gave Clovenhoof one last savage poke with his stick "—are meant to be the glory of evil and rebellion; the poster child for non-conformity."

"I rock a certain look," said Clovenhoof, sniffily.

"Yes, the certain look of a man of advancing years who has lost the will to live."

"You're not getting the full benefit of it at the moment. Give me a pair of shades and an electric guitar and I cut a fine figure."

"Beauty is truly in the eye of the beholder," said Belphegor. "No. We need to do something about all ... this."

"Weightwatchers? Exercise?"

Belphegor gave a cough of amusement. "If only we had the time. Radical measures are called for. *Rutspud!*"

This last bellow brought a short demon scurrying from a side door. There was something about the demon's large ears and expressive eyes that spoke of an intelligence uncommon in demonkind. Intelligence was not always a positive survival trait among the demonic, but this chap had enough of the stuff to know to keep most of it hidden.

Rutspud threw a lazy salute at Clovenhoof.

"Our glorious leader is ready to begin his regimen of training and self-improvement," said Belphegor.

"Is he?" said Rutspud surprised. "Has he signed the dismemberment waiver?"

"No."

"But he is aware of the inherent dangers of what we're going to do?"

"No. I've not bothered to tell him."

"Er, what?" said Clovenhoof.

"If I told you, you'd probably refuse to agree," said Belphegor. "In this instance, ignorance is almost certainly preferable."

"Why? What are you going to do to me?"

"This way, Mr Clovenhoof, sir," said Rutspud, reaching up to take Clovenhoof's hand.

"I could refuse, you know," said Clovenhoof.

"The old Satan could have refused," said Belphegor. "The old Satan could flatten cities with a clap of his hands and steal a thousand souls with a single smile. Whereas you I can win over with the promise of a single glass of that fizzy piss you so admire."

Clovenhoof's ears perked up. "You have Lambrini?"

"Right this way, sir," said Rutspud and led him out of the chamber.

In a starkly lit laboratory, Clovenhoof was placed in a reclining dentist's chair.

There was a clattering in a cupboard. Belphegor looked sharply over.

"Hodshift? What are you doing here?"

The yellow demon straightened up in a sudden and guilty manner. "Er, nothing, my lord. Just getting—" He reached into the cupboard and pulled out a workman's tin box. "—Just getting my lunch."

Belphegor appraised him suspiciously but clearly had more important things to deal with. "Well, while you're over there, you can dig out the brain-map-a-ma-jig?"

Hodshift shifted about the contents of the cupboard. "Small, medium or large?"

Rutspud jumped onto Clovenhoof's lap and held out his fingers to measure while closing one eye. "Small," he judged.

"Hey," said Clovenhoof. "My brain's an extra-large at least."

The yellow demon bumbled over with a thing that look like a colander covered in sucker-tipped electrodes, and slapped it on Clovenhoof's head.

"I was promised Lambrini," said Clovenhoof.

"In a minute," said Rutspud. The demon began putting electrodes in place. "This one here and this one here. This one up your left nostril."

"That kind of stings," said Clovenhoof.

"Good. Means it's in the right place. Then this one here."

While wires and sticky pads were being put in uncomfortable places, Clovenhoof initially failed to notice other sly demonic hands tying down his wrists and ankles with fat leather straps.

"What the Hell?" he said.

"It's to stop you accidentally hurting yourself," said Rutspud.

"Is that likely?"

"There may be some flailing."

"Huh?"

Rutspud went over to a large panel of instruments that seemed to positively pulsate with electricity. His hands reached for a large brass-handled switch.

"Also, try to avoid biting your tongue," Rutspud advised.

"Huh?"

Rutspud used his entire body weight to pull down the lever.

At once, a tidal wave of noise and light and sheer nerve-shredding energy poured through Clovenhoof. It was like he was an electrical fuse; like he was a twanging guitar string; like he was a firework racing into the sky. It really fucking hurt. When Rutspud turned it off, Clovenhoof was left gasping and wide-eyed.

There was a strange, bitter smell in the air, like someone had set fire to a dog. Clovenhoof slowly realised that many of the hairs on his arms had singed away, while others were glowing like tiny candles. But that wasn't the important thing: that was what was going on inside his head. New information which hadn't been there before.

"I know Kung Fu," he whispered.

Rutspud pressed a button and a VHS cassette popped out of the electrical panel. "Series one *and* two," he said.

He reached for the next video cassette on a trolley. "Let's go with the Rocky films, one to four. And then maybe work up to some Bruce Lee."

"Lambrini?" suggested Clovenhoof weakly.

"Hodshift!" called Belphegor, but the yellow demon had vanished.

Rutspud presented a bottle to Clovenhoof's lips. Clovenhoof strained to put his mouth to the bottle neck and chugged.

"Actually, that stuff is just fermented monks' piss," said Rutspud. "I get it from a friend."

"Delicious," mumbled Clovenhoof as he drained the bottle.

"Right!" said Rutspud. "Stand clear everyone." He inserted the next video cassette.

AN INDETERMINABLE TIME LATER, Clovenhoof was lifted out of the chair and carried limply over to a table where life was massaged back into his frazzled body, and the last few fires in his body hair snuffed out. All the fighting knowledge that could be gained from a hundred low-brow action movies and a thousand hours of American adventure TV was coursing through his brain. He knew every karate move, every judo throw, and every cheesy comeback line a combatant could ever need.

While he struggled to assimilate and compartmentalise this vast array of information, Belphegor entered the room.

"How are we feeling, lord?"

"Ask me again when my brain is back in one piece. Got any more of that monk piss? It's tangy."

"In a while," said Belphegor. "Mental training is only half the job. We need to get you physically up to scratch."

Rutspud was waving a plastic nozzle nearby. "Liposuction."

"That's just a vacuum cleaner," said Clovenhoof.

"An *industrial* vacuum cleaner," Rutspud corrected. "I watched a ten minute YouTube tutorial. I'm fairly sure I know what I'm doing."

Clovenhoof tried to do a time-out gesture, but his brain was still struggling, and his hands missed each other. "Wait. Wait. I don't think that's necessary."

"And then we will begin the muscle grafts," said Belphegor.

For the first time Clovenhoof noticed a large trolley on which a big pile of wet somethings was covered with a white sheet. The sheet was damply stained with clear and pink seepage.

"Muscles donated by the burliest scowfrogs and warrior demons," said Belphegor.

"You're going to stick them on me?" said Clovenhoof. "Like ... won't that hurt?"

Rutspud and Belphegor looked at each other. The little demon couldn't hold back an amused smirk.

"This is Hell," said Belphegor. "We make plans. We devise schemes. At no point, lord, do we ever ask ourselves, is something going to hurt? In Hell, everything hurts."

"I mean, um, sure. I know that. Of course I know that and like, I say, pain? Huh! Bring it on!" Clovenhoof sat more upright on the slab, readying to run away. "What I mean is, is this plan of giving me fighting skills and stolen muscles going to work? Is this going to ensure I beat Michael?"

A thin smile crossed Belphegor's face. The inventor

demon had a nearly spherical head and such a smile was like a wound sliced from ear to ear. "Do you want to win the war with Heaven, lord?" he said.

It was an unexpected question, and Clovenhoof had to pause and think of an answer. "No," he said, and immediately felt the need to justify his answer. "I don't mean like St Peter, who thinks our defeat is some cosmic inevitability. And I don't mean I'm a coward either. I don't want to fight Heaven because it's bloody stupid. What's that thing they say about winning wars?"

"Never march on Moscow in winter?" suggested Rutspud.

"Not that."

"Fall to your knees then punch them in the ballsack?"

"No – although I do like the sentiment. It's something about picking your battles. Thing is, we're fighting this war because Heaven wants us to. They've called Armageddon when *they* want to."

"Actually, it's more to do with the level of evil rising above an unsustainable level," said Belphegor. "I sent one of my demons off with my peccadometer. I could show you..."

Clovenhoof shook his head. "No. Nothing happens unless the Big Guy Upstairs wants it to happen. They've picked this moment. They've picked this war. If everything I ever loved in the world above is destroyed..." He took a breath. "I've spent ten years slowly created an abstract mural on my bedroom wall composed only of my own snot. It's my sodding Sistine Chapel, I tell you. The fucking Almighty has chosen now to bring it all to a bloody end, and expects me to dance to his bloody tune. No. I don't want to fight, not on their terms."

Belphegor was nodding slowly. "I agree with you, mostly. Up in Heaven, they will have dusted off their battle strategies from the first War in Heaven. They will make the same plays as before. They will do this because they are arrogant. They will do this because they believe they are 'good'." He spat on the floor. "The angels are as unimaginative as the flock of chickens they so clearly resemble."

"Amen," said Clovenhoof.

"They expect you to walk out onto the field of battle, pumped up, unholy sword in hand, and prepared to do battle with Michael. And they expect you to lose."

"But I won't?"

"Oh, he'll tear you to shreds, lord. Even if we had longer to prepare and all the stolen muscles Hell could muster, in a straight fight, you will lose."

"Hey. You don't know that. I've got moves." From some recently reprogrammed part of his brain, Clovenhoof pulled out a karate kata and flung his arms about with expert timing, even if those moves were more Elvis Presley than Bruce Lee.

"You've got moves enough to distract them," Belphegor conceded.

"Distract?"

Belphegor nodded to Rutspud, and the short demon leapt up and pulled down a projector screen from the ceiling. From an unknown source, an image was projected onto the screen. It was a photo of something Clovenhoof had seen before.

"That's out on the plains with Berith's army," he said.

Belphegor's sharp stick pointed at the giant screw-nosed

machine in the picture. "The Rampant Tunneller. We first built those when we needed to dig fresh pits for the new wave of sinners."

"The Pit of Social Media Influencers, the Pit of Non-Fungible Token holders, the Pit of Face-Lift Addicts – who seemed permanently surprised to find themselves in Hell," said Rutspud. then made a downward drilling motion with his hands. "*Bzzzt! Bzzzt! Bzzzzt!* Instant pits."

"The Rampant Tunneller can chew through any substrate at a constant five miles an hour," said Belphegor.

"And?" said Clovenhoof, unclear about its relevance.

The image on the screen changed to a little pencil sketch animation. Hell and Heaven were represented by childish doodles with the plains of Limbo as a simple line between them.

"Heaven will ride out to start the War," said Belphegor. "You and Berith's army of monsters will ride out to meet them. Meanwhile the Rampant Tunneller will be making its way underneath Limbo—"

The little cartoon tunneller chugged along the screen.

"But there's nothing underneath Limbo," said Clovenhoof.

"Very easy to tunnel through then," said Rutspud.

"And it will come up inside the Celestial City with an elite force of my warriors following through the tunnel behind it," said Belphegor.

"All this while the majority of Heaven's forces have abandoned the city," said Clovenhoof, impressed.

"Most?" said Belphegor. "Can you think of a single angel who wouldn't want to be there to witness your defeat?"

"Take Heaven by stealth?"

"Operation Trojan Horse," grinned Rutspud. There was tinny rap at the door. He went off to answer it.

Clovenhoof slipped off the bed to look at the little animated plan closer. "It's so deviously underhanded."

"One of its main attractions," agreed Belphegor.

For the first time since he'd been hauled away from his home in Boldmere, Clovenhoof felt actual pleasure. It was just a mote of pleasure, a mere nugget, but the thought of being part of a plan that would surprise, annoy and even confound Heaven was very appealing indeed. "You need me to effectively put on a show?" he said.

"Give us as much time as possible to succeed," said Belphegor.

Clovenhoof mused noisily. "The one thing I can definitely do, Belphegor me old chum, is put on a show."

Rutspud came back through with a laminated card in one hand, a sheet of paper in the other, and a puzzled look on his face.

"Apparently, I've been pre-approved for membership of the CUGBPAWSD, the Combined Union of Gatekeepers, Bum Pokers, Ancillary Workers and Service Demons."

"What is that?" said Belphegor.

"That's a good question," said Rutspud. "But I've also been given a ballot paper for strike action."

He held up a piece of paper which was scorched around the edges, smeared with what might have been blood, and had the word BALUT written on it in charcoal with a tick box underneath.

22

Nerys addressed the group of camp volunteers as they ate their first breakfast, which looked like a slurry of porridge, or maybe lentils. Apparently, a long journey from England, round and round in circles and back again, had made them hungry.

"Good morning to you all. Your orientation will be brief, because I know that you all want to get on and make your own valuable contribution. Now, you will have questions about where we are exactly, but it's a politically sensitive area, so we will address things in a purely factual way. I'm sure you understand. This place is known as *Reddi Cap*." Nerys enunciated the two words as if they were very tricky. "That is *Reddi Cap*. You try it."

The crowd mumbled their way through the name.

"Excellent. We have arable land here, but recent turmoil has seen a downturn in productivity. Tools have become damaged and rusty with disuse, which is a crying shame. You are all here to turn that around, though. Are you up for the challenge?"

There were some enthusiastic noises, but Nerys pretended that she couldn't hear. "Sorry?"

"Yeah!" everyone shouted.

"You're going to be attending workshops with Perry, who is a veteran of this type of endeavour, and he knows exactly what needs doing. If you make a habit of paying close attention to Perry, then I guarantee we will have this site being super productive in no time."

There was a polite round of applause for Perry.

"We have some younger helpers as well. They are very smart, but largely non-verbal for their own reasons. I'm sure you will treat them with respect."

Slightly confused murmurs of agreement satisfied Nerys that Spartacus and his friends could get away without talking.

"Meals will be served in here. I hope I don't need to stress how important it is that you remain here on site. The risks if you leave here are considerable, so don't be tempted to stray beyond the boundary fences. You'll soon get used to the routine."

Nerys handed over to Perry who looked as if he couldn't wait to get them all rubbing down rusty tools with wire wool. They all trailed after him into a workshop space.

Spartacus, Kenzie, PJ and Jefri stayed quiet until the crowd had all gone. Kenzie opened his hand to show a crumpled fiver. "Got a tip," he said proudly.

. . .

NERYS DROPPED IN DAILY, bringing Spartacus and his mates on occasion. She drove to the farm in her car, but parked well away from the gates.

Some of the group had become very proficient at fixing up the tools, so Nerys had been out to collect some more, to stoke their passion. Metal that had been rusty and blunt was now super-shiny and sharpened. Perry had also overseen the construction of a cabinet where they could all be stored on neat racks.

Perry showed Nerys the group's progress while the team ate their food.

"It might have been a mistake to give them so many lawn edging tools," said Perry, pointing. "People have been asking what their purpose is in agriculture. I told them trimming bales is very important at the point of harvesting, but don't bring any more, eh? Lawns don't feature in agriculture."

"Right. Yes," said Nerys who had two more in her car. What was wrong with the gardeners of Sutton Coldfield that the tool most likely to be neglected was these stupid long-handled shears?

"Work on the polytunnel has started," said Perry, leading them all round to a wider space where large semi-circular hoops had been set into the ground like the skeleton of a giant beetle. "We'll get the cover on tomorrow, so we're planning a small celebration in the evening. Want to join us?"

Nerys nodded. It sounded like a good time to get some updated Shit-O-Meter readings.

. . .

NERYS RETURNED for the polytunnel celebration with Hodshift, Spartacus, Jefri, PJ and Kenzie. Kenzie had a large bag with him.

The celebration was modelled on the idea of a barn-raising party. Long tables were arrayed inside the polytunnel, and members of the group ferried food out from the farmhouse kitchen.

Nerys was surprised by the scale of the polytunnel now it was complete. When Perry had first described it she had pictured a budget greenhouse, but this was big enough to seat almost fifty people inside. There was a hen house next door, made from pallets, chicken wire, and the same spirit of optimism.

"What do you think?" asked Perry.

"It's enormous," said Nerys.

"We've drawn out the plans showing how we'll use it on the whiteboard over there."

Nerys drifted over to look. Random bits of carpentry supplemented the hoops that were the main support for the polytunnel. It seemed as though if a shape could be nailed together from old pallets then stapled with polythene sheeting, it had a place in the polytunnel. The entrance doors were constructed in this way, and a small office space had been created too. It featured a wooden bench backed with a whiteboard. A set of drawers that might have once been bedroom furniture sat underneath the bench.

The whiteboard showed a plan of the polytunnel, which was divided into sections, with titles like SEEDLING NURSERY and SALAD CROPS.

"Nettle beer?" asked a tall woman who had just entered

the polytunnel with a pair of bottles in her left hand and a stack of tumblers in her right. "It's our first batch and it's properly delish!"

Nerys hesitated before remembering she was essentially the patron of this group, so she needed to encourage them. "Sure," she said and took a glass. She had a small sip and discovered that it wasn't terrible. It was in the style of ginger beer, with a tang of composty botanicals. "Nice, I bet everyone will love that!" said Nerys.

"They will," said the woman with confidence. "It's been one of my affirmations. I say it lots of times and so it must come true. It was thrilling to discover that nettles grow out here." She continued down the long row of tables, pouring drinks for others.

Perry appeared at Nerys's side. "We'll be able to extend the natural season for salad crops if we grow them in here. We're building up towards a vegetable box scheme so people in the area can eat local vegetables. It's the sort of thing you had pictured for this group, isn't it?"

Nerys smiled at Perry. "I think it is. You're doing a terrific job." She nodded at the woman with the nettle beer. "Who's she?"

"That's Sandy. She brought some new ideas. They are not all fully in line with my own, but she's a hard worker, so I see no harm in letting her get creative."

The group was buzzing, and the noise levels moved steadily up. Sandy came bustling back down with refills of nettle beer several times.

"I say, who's the tubby fellow over there?" Sandy asked

Nerys, pointing to Hodshift. "I don't think I've seen him before."

"He's a consultant on the project," said Nerys. "He's here to do an interim assessment."

"He's got an unusual complexion. I might see if he wants some comfrey moisturiser for his skin. It'll tone down that ruddiness for him."

Nerys nodded, watching Hodshift walk around with the Shit-O-Meter, taking measurements.

"Those local lads have got the nicest artisanal jewellery," said Sandy.

"Eh?" Nerys snapped to attention.

Sandy pulled up her sleeve and showed Nerys a set of bangles. "We had to conduct the entire transaction in sign language, but from what I understand, there is a local custom of giving these as a wedding gift to a new bride. Aren't they adorable? They were happy to take English money as well, very enterprising."

"Yes, very," said Nerys with a glance over at Spartacus.

"Must get on," said Sandy. "I'll need to be serving up the dandelion coffee shortly."

"And by dandelion coffee you mean...?"

"Roasted dandelion root made into a coffee substitute. It's delicious in its own way. Remarkable to observe how much of the local flora is familiar."

"And yet there is no actual coffee?" Nerys asked.

Sandy made a *tsk* sound. "I can't ask Perry to go to that kind of expense when we have perfectly good alternatives."

"Well I *have* asked him," drawled a man sitting a little way down the table. "It's a basic human right as far as I'm concerned. If someone hadn't started roasting weeds then there would be no question of an alternative."

"Oh, Leif you must be decaffeinated by now," said Sandy with an indulgent smile. "You'll thank me for it in the long run!"

"Sure I will. We can all look to you as a role model and gain for ourselves the digestive system of a goat and the skin quality of a soviet era farmer's wife."

Sandy flushed red and hurried away with her empty bottles.

"That was a bit harsh," said Nerys.

Leif seemed amused. "She is annoying. I get cranky without coffee. What else am I supposed to do?"

Nerys rolled her eyes as she walked away. She wondered if Perry had any unpleasant jobs coming up. If so, she knew exactly the person to put forward.

NERYS DROVE THE GROUP HOME, and they shared their thoughts during the drive.

"Whole site is definitely still green as ya like," said Hodshift. "Stands out a mile against the background readings. So yer basic hypothesis that we can use it as a breeding ground ter send the green out to other places is going well, I reckon. Couple o' amber-looking ripples among that crowd in the polytunnel, but they'll probably straighten out as time goes by."

"Would dodgy sales of second hand jewellery from the charity shop cause those sorts of ripples?" asked Nerys. She caught a glimpse of Kenzie in the rear view mirror.

"I don't reckon so, no. A bit of a grey economy is more of yer spicy sprinkles than yer actual rot. Keeps up the levels of hope and cheer and suchlike."

"Grey economy, eh? Fine – but don't get too carried away!" said Nerys sternly to the mirror. "Although I recommend sneaking in a jar of Nescafe and flogging it to the man called Leif. Make him pay through the nose for it."

NERYS SPENT some time in the evening contemplating the things that moved the dial on the Shit-O-Meter. Her initial experiments with *Honk if you're Helpful* had seen a mild impact, but nothing compared with Perry's low-key efforts. Perhaps it was because Perry had been doing his thing longer term, but time simply wasn't on their side. She needed faster answers.

She went down to Clovenhoof's flat to question Hodshift. As she opened the door she saw the demon squatting on a skateboard as it flew across the room. He leaned into the curve of one of the ramps and jumped up, rotating the board with his hands underneath his lifted feet. He landed back on the moving board and skidded along the top of Clovenhoof's sofa.

"You're pretty good," said Spartacus.

"It's yer basic laws of propulsion," grunted Hodshift as he stood on the end and flipped the skateboard into his outstretched hand. "Wiv some applied mathematics. Nice to take it out of the lab."

"Hodshift, I wanted to ask you something," said Nerys.

"Earlier, when you mentioned the grey economy, you said that it added spice or something."

"Yeah, thassit."

"How did you know that?"

Hodshift shrugged. "It's one of yer basics in Peccadalchemy. Every demon who works in the labs knows that."

"Peccadalchemy, huh?"

"Yep."

"For crying out loud, tell me there's a manual or something!" said Nerys, grabbing the demon's shoulders.

Hodshift shook his head. "If there was one, it would be more like one of those old timey recipe books where they tell you to catch a good fat rat and make sure you do it in March while the moon is waning an' then—"

"Surely someone like Jamie Oliver could write it all down for you then?" seethed Nerys.

"He's not dead, is he?" said Spartacus.

"Well, no, but someone like—" Nerys tried and failed to name a dead celebrity chef. "There was a Fanny someone, wasn't there? Anyway, someone must be able to share this stuff with us?"

Hodshift regarded her with his unblinking stare. "Yes, me. I can share that stuff."

"So," Nerys needed to make sure she understood. "You know which things make the world better and which things make the world worse?"

The demon nodded. "Couldda sworn I mentioned that."

"Not in so many words, no," said Nerys through gritted teeth. "Shall we start again? If I get Tina and Ben over here, we can all hear it from you directly and make sure we only do the useful things."

"Sure." The demon cracked his knuckles. "You humans surprise me."

"In what way?"

"The sheer amount of effort you put into stuff. I know we demons work hard. We're famous for it, ain't we? But that's cos we got the feel of the lash on our backs. But you lot, you'll try to move mountains in pursuit of a dream."

"Oh, I'm a dreamer now, huh?"

"I'm just saying, if you ever got your 'ands on a labour-saving, wish-granting tool, who knows what you might achieve."

"Hodshift…" said Nerys. She thought about how the little demon tended to offer up only the most limited information. She was always left with the feeling that she just needed to ask the correct question. "Do you have a labour-saving, wish-granting tool?"

Hodshift was silent for a long moment. "Very fond of tools meself. The right tool in the right hands can do wonders. We've got a bloke called Steve Jobs who used to be very fond of saying that if you give people tools they'll do wonderful things with them."

"Used to?"

"Yeah, the Fourth Circle changed his mind on that one. It's amazing what demons can do there wiv just some simple tools."

"Hodshift, I can sense you are trying to duck this question." Nerys gave him a stern look. "Wish-granting? Is that a thing you can help me with?"

He sucked air in and made loud tutting noises as he shifted his weight from side to side. "It's just that there are some things people can get carried away wiv, and we wouldn't want—"

"Tell me!"

"It was a prototype, and quite honestly it was supposed to have been chucked in the lake of fire by now, because it's only ever caused trouble. It's called the Fulfilment Accelerated Actuator."

"What does it do?"

"It makes change happen. You tell it what you want, and it does it."

"It grants wishes?" Nerys asked.

"You could call it that, but I would suggest that such emotive language is fool—"

"—Whatever. We can call it the Wish-O-Matic. So, we can just tell it to make everyone be nice, yeah?"

"Ab-ser-lutely not! If you try to apply the Fulfilment Accelerated—"

"—Wish-O-Matic."

"If you try to apply it to the will of humans it will create a vortex of instability. Yer need to be smarter than that and use it to create conditions where everyone *wants* to be nice."

Nerys was about to ask what those conditions might be, but she realised she was wasting time. "Can you go and get it?"

"Nah," he said, "I still need that RS-232 serial data cable Spartacus ordered for me to get it up and running again. S'not arrived yet."

"Oh. Board meeting and hard work it is, then."

"Aye, right enough," said Hodshift.

THE IMPROMPTU BOARD meeting took place in Nerys's flat, and Ben dragged in a flipchart from somewhere.

"Thanks Ben, this is perfect. Um, can you lower the legs? Hodshift will be taking the lead."

Ben shortened the three tripod legs so that the flipchart was at Hodshift's height.

Nerys wasted no time. She had made a huge jug of sangria and she waved at it. "Grab a drink if you want one, but we need to listen carefully to Hodshift. He has a solid understanding of the things we need to do and those we should avoid."

She stooped in front of the flip chart and drew a line down the middle. "I made two columns. On the left we will list things that we should do, and on the right we will list things we should stop doing. Over to you, Hodshift."

"Right you are. I'll get cracking then." Hodshift picked up the pen and in a neat print added a list of words to the right hand column. "We'll start with the obvious. Murder, theft, and of course the coveting of oxen—"

"—Can I stop you there, Hodshift?" asked Nerys. "We probably know the basics. What we really need is some guidance on things which we here in this room can do to improve things generally."

"Right you are. I'll make some notes on the left then." His writing became a little scruffier as he scribbled words more rapidly. "We've got kindness, respect, generosity—"

"Hodshift!" shouted Nerys. "Seriously! Can we have the

useful stuff please? You know what things we've been doing. I need you to tell us if it's useful or not. You can do that, can't you? For example, you said a grey economy was something positive as it keeps people hopeful and cheery. Give us more of those things, now!"

Nerys looked around the room and regretted the slightly screechy tone she'd used. Hodshift looked fearful and hesitant and everyone else just looked appalled at her outburst.

Nerys plonked herself into a seat. In her peripheral vision she saw Tina give Ben a small nudge.

"Nerys, sweetie," said Tina, "you've been under such a lot of pressure. Ben's been telling me how much you miss Jeremy. I know you miss him dearly."

Nerys narrowed her eyes at Ben.

"It's fallen to you to do everything here, and it seems so unfair," Tina went on. "When was the last time you had a break, huh?"

Tina's false compassion had everyone staring earnestly, but Nerys wasn't fooled.

"I can't back away from this now, Tina. We're running out of time."

Tina held up her hands. "Nobody said anything about backing away, Nerys. You're our figurehead, no argument. I have a proposal that might just mean we can make better use of our resources. Hear me out. Why don't you take on a full time mentoring role at the Reddicap Heath project and we can keep everything else just ticking over for you?"

Nerys paused long enough to think about what that would mean. She had a hunch Perry's farm was the most important part of this puzzle. It was the greenest thing the Shit-O-Meter had detected, so perhaps it would be fruitful to commit more fully.

"Fine. I will do that. I don't want you making changes on this side without me knowing though."

"Oh no, no," said Tina with a dismissive wave of her hand. "We'll keep you in the loop at all times."

Nerys packed a bag to move to Reddicap Heath. She dropped Twinkle round at Ben's and thought hard about what she needed to take. If she was going full time then she definitely wanted to enter the programme herself. If she became one of Perry's disciples then she would automatically learn how to turn the tide on the Shit-O-Meter. It was her best hope.

She hesitated when it came to her electronic devices. She could sneak in her phone surely, as long as nobody there saw it?

What about all the other things that she enjoyed in life, like booze, make-up and revealing clothes? She had the feeling none of these things would be welcome at Reddicap Heath, but were they explicitly banned?

"Nerys, you fool. You actually wrote the rules."

And yet...

In the end she compromised. She packed only practical clothes, including some lip gloss and tinted moisturiser, and she dedicated a large suitcase to boxes of wine – discovering to her delight that she was able to fit eight in there.

23

Nerys left her car outside the gates and wheeled her suitcases in.

"Perry, I hope there's room for me. I'm joining full time," she told him.

"You're very welcome," said Perry. "Drop your stuff off and join today's lesson."

It turned out the lesson in question was inside the polytunnel. The space looked very different now it was cleared of tables and chairs. There was some sort of matting down the central walkway and exposed soil on the sides. Everyone was sitting cross-legged along the matting while Perry addressed them. Nerys sat on the floor and wrestled her legs into something like a cross-legged position. She hadn't sat like this since her schooldays. It was hard work, and more than a little indecent in the skirt that she was wearing.

"We need to talk about soil," said Perry. "If we're growing

crops it's the thing that we depend on, so we can't overlook how important its structure is. I want you each to take a handful and examine it. Tell me what you see."

Nerys wasn't sure she'd heard correctly. It sounded as though he wanted them all to put soil in their hands.

She put up a hand. "Isn't dirt a bit dirty to put in our hands?" she asked. "The clue's in the name."

"I'm not asking you to eat it, Nerys, but we need to be familiar with it, and we definitely shouldn't be afraid of it. Now, who wants to tell me what they can see and smell and feel?"

"I will," said Sandy. "It feels a bit gritty if I stir it with a fingertip, and a bit spongy if I squeeze it in my hand."

"Very good. The grit is tiny particles of stone. Very good for drainage. The spongy feel is organic matter, which helps to retain water. It's composed of plant and possibly animal matter in various stages of decomposition."

Nerys had just plucked up courage to pick up some soil and put it in her palm. Now she stared in dismay at the decomposing life forms. Did animal matter mean dead animals or animal poo? She wasn't sure which was worse.

"Oh hey, I got a wriggly thing!" shouted someone.

Nerys shook the dirt from her hands in horror.

Perry wandered over and identified the wriggly thing as a wireworm. "Anyone else got anything lively?"

Nerys pretended to study her palm, while carefully flicking away the last grains of soil. She breathed deeply. She had probably missed some essential orientation that would have prepared her for this. She glanced across at someone else's dirt while Perry went on to talk about microbes. Nerys wished for hand sanitiser and thought she had never looked forward to washing her hands more enthusiastically in her life. This even eclipsed Clovenhoof's well-worn 'mitten surprise' that he saved for cold days. At least she was generally at home on those occasions and had the luxury of washing her hands before delivering some violent revenge on the perpetrator.

"Are all the lessons like this?" she whispered to her neighbour, who was still poking at her dirt in awed fascination.

"Oh yes," said the young woman. "They are all *so* inspirational."

NERYS'S WISH for cleanliness was more than satisfied, as it turned out that the next scheduled session was laundry. Nerys had never seen the sort of equipment that Perry used before; she wondered if it belonged in a museum. Big tubs with arms and squishing sticks to stir the things around, and an honest-to-god mangle. There was a brief novelty in using a mangle, but she soon realised doing laundry manually was quite hard work. When everything was hung up on the washing line to dry, Nerys stared at her hands. They had never looked so pale and wrinkly.

"Perry, could I have a few minutes to talk to you?" she asked, steering him away from the group.

"Nerys, how can I help?"

Good question. "I feel as though I'm playing catch-up. The others are all settled into a routine and seem very happy. Do I need some extra tuition or something?"

Perry smiled. "No, Nerys. You just have to want to be a part of the group. Everyone here has a shared goal, and it makes even the most diverse set of individuals work together, as you've seen. They get excited about doing the tasks because they are focused on the goal."

Nerys huffed. "Yes, but the goal, I mean *their* goal, is not the same as mine."

"I think you'll find it might be," said Perry.

"Stop talking in weird monkish riddles!" she snapped. "It's me you're talking to. This whole thing was my idea. How can you tell me that I don't know what the goal is?"

"What is it, then?"

"The goal—" Nerys waved her hands, indicating the world at large. "Well, it's everything and everybody. It's to stop the world from being destroyed because we're all so crap."

Perry didn't look confused or overwhelmed, which annoyed Nerys a little bit since she had been confused and overwhelmed for many weeks.

"So we take care of ourselves, we take care of our community, and we take care of the world?" Perry's words were accompanied with gestures that made it look as though the two of them, the community, and the world were a neat set of Russian dolls sitting within each other.

"What? It's that simple is it? I force myself to be happy playing with soil, and the world will be fixed?"

Perry stared serenely at her. "You're an intelligent woman, Nerys. Obviously there will be challenges. This is all I know, so it's what I am teaching. I am sorry if it's not what you wanted."

Nerys flushed red with frustration, or maybe embarrassment. "It definitely looks as if you are doing a good job," she admitted. "The problem is mine, I'm sure."

NERYS WENT BACK out to the polytunnel on her own and stared at the soil. There was a lot of it, and she just needed to look at one small handful. She could do this.

She stooped and took up a handful. She had a multitude of teeming life forms in her hand, all invisible – oh not quite all— She tried not to shudder as something gently writhed in the middle.

"You are my minions and I command you not to freak me out!" she bellowed at her hand. She smiled. It was not quite the hippy trippy love-in that Perry had encouraged, but it was a start. "Nice meeting you minions, I look forward to picking you up again!"

Nerys brushed off the soil and walked away from the polytunnel, feeling that she had made one tiny step forward.

NERYS SLEPT BETTER than she'd expected. There was a dormitory for the women containing bunk beds. The only spare was a top bunk, and Nerys found it more challenging than she expected to get up the ridiculous ladder. There was probably a reason bunk beds were mainly reserved for children. She dreaded the day when she would have to change the sheets.

A few of the women were doing yoga, led by Sandy. Nerys wanted to become a part of the group, but she needed to build up to it. She wandered off in search of coffee.

The kitchen was a large communal space with picnic benches for seating, and a counter and a cooker off to the side.

"Is that coffee?" she asked someone with a mug.

"Herbal tisane," said the man with a shake of his head. "Made from some of the local plant life. You should try some."

"I was after coffee," said Nerys, not liking the needy tone she heard in her voice. She had been dismissive about the coffee complaints previously, but faced with the harsh reality of early morning she was dismayed at the prospect of not getting her daily caffeine boost. "What about the coffee substitute I heard about?"

She was pointed towards a cannister half-filled with hefty brown chunks. She gave it a sniff. It resembled the smell of coffee in the same way the burnt bits around her oven at home resembled food. She tipped some into a cup and poured on water from the kettle.

"You do know it's not granules, right? You will need to boil it then strain it."

"Of course I knew that. I happen to like it like this," said Nerys. She sipped the hot liquid and tried really hard to like it. It was hot water with a hint of something burnt. She forced it down, determined not to concede she might have preferred the tisane.

Leif entered the kitchen, followed by several others. He waggled a jar of Nescafé in his hand. "Who's for some of the good stuff then?"

Nerys almost choked in her haste to swallow the last of her burnt water. "Yes please," she said, raising her mug.

Leif made a small humming sound as he contemplated her request. In the meantime, one of the others had fetched him a spoon and a mug. Another put the kettle on to boil with fresh water.

"What's in it for me?" Leif asked. "All of these others have made it worth my while in some shape or form. What do you have to offer?"

"Um. The knowledge that you've helped your community?" Nerys tried.

"Oh per-lease! Save that for the earth mother herb freaks." Leif waved a hand at those sipping on their tisanes. "I'm all about sound economic decisions."

As he said these words, his small group all nodded along.

"Why are you here, then?" asked Nerys, puzzled. "The reasons for this project are purely altruistic."

"Such a narrow-minded view," said Leif. "Where there is human desire for a particular outcome, there is also an opportunity to make money. *That* is what I am here to explore. If altruism can be monetised then market forces make the good things happen. It takes a particular kind of genius to spot how to make that work." He tapped the side of his nose in a smug gesture that made Nerys want to tear him a new arsehole, but she wanted coffee more.

"Very interesting." She held out her mug. "For the price of a coffee I will lend you my undivided attention and you can tell me more about your theories."

Leif's smile faltered at the logical leap, but then he gave a small shrug. "Always happy to provide enlightenment."

Nerys savoured her cup of instant coffee in case she couldn't get another. Leif elaborated on the business model he favoured.

"So let me get this straight," said Nerys. "Shareholders now demand environmental, social and – what?"

"Governance. It's known as ESG for short."

"Shareholders demand companies do better at ESG things because everyone recognises the world is going to hell in a handcart. So you create a whole new business selling services to companies so they can claim they're good?"

"Yes, exactly," said Leif with a smile. "I am here to research the possibilities for a new stream of revenue."

Nerys could tell several others in the group also had a sniff of the idea there was revenue to be had. "So the value of Perry fixing a spade is not just the value of the spade?"

"Goodness me, no. It's the value we can claim in reduced carbon in the production and transport of a new spade, as well as the disposal of the old spade. It's the value of saying to the world that we made this happen and helped an indigenous population – accompanied by pictures of course. Smiles all round."

Nerys was stunned.

"It makes so much sense in a capitalist society, Nerys. If you want change to happen you need it to work with the system, not fight against it."

Nerys forced her face to remain neutral. "This is a lot to absorb, Leif. I will probably have more questions."

"No problem," smiled Leif. The smile dropped from his face as he added, "The next chat will not come with a free coffee, so work out what you have to trade."

24

The lift door pinged. Michael stepped out onto the top floor of the Research Centre for Scriptural Exegesis and into a world of paper. This floor was a single circular room where pneumatic communication tubes ran down from the domed ceiling and away into the floor. Every space in between was covered in paper. Every flat surface had a piece of paper or parchment pinned to it. There was even a little wheeled step ladder so paper could be pinned at higher levels. Across the centre of the room, tables, desks, and even the floor were covered in printed and written materials to a considerable depth. At the centre of this sea of paper there was a small raft, a red chaise longue upon which reclined a clean-shaven and robed man. He had his eyes closed and was slowly and repeatedly battering at his own forehead with a human skull.

Michael gazed at him for some time. The whole scene did not seem promising for an angel who had come looking for answers. He took a step forward. Papers rustled around his ankles.

"It's not ready yet!" the saint shouted, jerking upright.

"Um, isn't it?"

Saint Jerome blinked, seemed to take some time to get his pupils under control, blinked some more, then focused blearily on Michael. There was a red mark at the centre of his forehead from all the skull tapping he'd been giving himself.

"Have I come at a bad time?" said Michael.

"Time!" snapped Jerome. "What is time? There is no time. There is nothing but time."

"Oh, that's, er, good," said Michael and waded deeper into the seas of scriptural notation.

"I thought they banished you, Michael," said Jerome.

Michael spread his arms. "I'm sort of back. For the final, um, show."

"Ha!" Jerome laughed scornfully. "Michael, foremost of the angels. Do you know you barely get a mention in the Bible?"

"I know. Although the Book of Enoch—"

"Non-canonical!" Jerome yelled at unseemly volume. "Non-canonical! Second rate scripture! Why would a non-canonical second-rate archangel come knocking at my door when I'm clearly very busy?"

Michael wasn't sure if the patron saint of Bible scholars had gone insane, or just forgotten his manners over the millennia. He wondered how one would tell the difference. "I have come to ask some questions."

"You come seeking answers!"

"Yes. Yes, that. Across the Celestial City, the host of Heaven prepare for the final war, and I have been told that you – or this organisation at least – has confirmed the criteria of the End Times have been fully met and that the Apocalypse is, like, definitely on."

"Oh! Is that what you've been told? Is it? Is it?" The saint's fury and intensity seemed to be fixed at the highest level.

"Yes, it is." Michael was determined to be the voice of calm in the room.

Jerome propelled himself across the room towards Michael, with scant care for the sheafs of paper and volumes he kicked aside. "Nearly two thousand years has passed by on Earth. In that short time the Powers That Be expect me and my meagre staff to have completely analysed every morsel of divine scripture that exists?"

Michael wanted to point out that two thousand years seemed like a reasonably long time, but he suspected it would be absolutely the wrong thing to say at the moment.

"I just wanted to check if Armageddon is definitely 'on' and what we can expect."

"Definitely? He says definitely!" Jerome tittered in an unsettling manner. "Oh, you want *definitive* answers, do you?" He grabbed the edge of Michael's robe and hauled him over to a table where he tossed aside the surface papers. "Let's take a look at one piece of the picture, shall we? Hmm? Hmmm?"

"Er, okay."

"The so-called Horsemen of the Apocalypse. Here. Scripture. *'There before me was a white horse. Its rider held a bow, and he was given a crown'* blah, blah. *'Then another horse came out, a fiery red. Its rider was given'* yadda yadda. Then *'a black horse! Its rider was holding a pair of scales'*, et cetera, et cetera. Then *'there before me was a pale horse and its rider was named Death and Hell followed close behind.'* There!"

"Yes?" said Michael politely.

"How many Horsemen of the Apocalypse is that?" demanded Jerome.

Michael recounted carefully in case it was trick question. "Four. It's four."

"Ha! Fool! Fool! There are four *horses*, angel! Four horses! It doesn't say how many horsemen there are!"

"But it stands to reason—"

"Stands to reason? It's sloppy thinking like that which makes everyone think there were three wise men with gifts for the Son of God."

"Weren't there—?"

"Three gifts! Gifts! And an indeterminate number of wise men, you fool of an angel! It's sloppy thinking that led Dürer into making his cursed woodcut of four horsemen, and now everyone thinks there's four without bothering to read the divine scripture!" He dragged out a tattered printed sheet from the bottom of the pile showing the fifteenth century Dürer image of four riders, surrounded by dynamic billowing clouds. "If we can't trust how many horsemen there are, how can we be certain about anything?"

"Well, yes," said Michael. "That's exactly what I wanted to speak to you about."

"Oh, did you now?" said Jerome scathingly.

Michael could tell the saint wasn't really interested in meaningful discussion. He clearly had a lot to get off his chest and Michael both felt a charitable duty to hear him out, and also thought he might get some proper answers if he allowed the robed scholar to vent his frustrations first.

"Come help me solve this one, huh?" Jerome pushed papers aside. "Who are the Horsemen of the Apocalypse, eh?"

"I thought you said—"

"Yes, yes, but who are they?"

"War, Pestilence, Famine and Death?"

"Ha! Fool!" Jerome stabbed at a rider in Dürer's picture carrying a bow and wearing a jaunty Robin Hood hunting cap. "For over a thousand years, everyone knew the rider on the white horse was the Son of Man!"

"Jesus?"

"And then along comes Carl-Friedrich Zimpel with his idea that the white rider is the Antichrist."

"Carl who?"

"Well, exactly! An absolutely nutty nineteenth century homeopath. Old Zimpel thinks the Antichrist is Napoleon Bonaparte himself! Then everyone picks up on it and starts repeating the idea."

"I thought the horsemen were all just ... symbolic," said Michael, waving his hands airily.

"Oh, really? Symbolic of what?"

"Oh, you know. Just symbolically symbolic. Like, they're just an indicator of really heavy religious meaning."

Jerome screwed his face up so hard, Michael feared the man might dislocate his own nose. "So they just stand for ... stuff?!"

"Er, maybe."

"They are a metaphor for religious metaphor?" His voice had become strangled, rising in pitch.

"Perhaps?"

Jerome gave a little scream and tossed the papers from the table. "So everything is open to personal interpretation? It's all airy-fairy wishy-washy words that can mean what people want them to mean? All reality is subjective? Is that what you're saying? Is it? Is it?"

Michael didn't know what to say. He wanted to say whatever would make the unhinged saint stop.

"This is what's bloody wrong with the world below now!" Jerome spat furiously. "It's all, 'I can be what I want to be'. If I want to tell everyone I'm a tree then I can be a bloody tree now, and no one gets to say otherwise!"

"I don't think anyone seriously claims to be a tree and expects—" Michael began, but was interrupted by a saint in full furious slow.

"And woe betide anyone who tells the delusional tree people that they're not trees because that would be some sort of anti-tree prejudice! Even the lowliest peasant can re-dream their whole life and demand to be treated as they see fit!"

"I think people just want to be treated with kindness and the kind of respect that—"

"No!" Jerome bellowed. "Either things are what they are, or nothing is true and all is chaos! Do you want a world that makes sense, where there are answers to questions and those answers stay the same, even when you're not looking at them? Hmmm?"

"I did come here looking for answers, actually..."

"Good, because if you don't want cold hard truths then I don't even know why this building, or the notion of scriptural exegesis exists!"

"Right," said Michael gently. "So, if we could circle round to the Apocalypse, I have some simple questions. I just really wanted to know if the end of the world really *has* to happen, as in like *now*?"

"So," said Jerome with a bright zeal and no intention of listening to Michael, "you want things to be exactly what they should be?"

"Again, just a simple answer to what I hoped would be a simple question…"

"Come! Come! I've been debating over this one for some time. Look!" He whipped a covering cloth off a board on which were pinned numerous pieces of parchment. At the very centre was a crude sketch that Michael clearly recognised as one Mr Jeremy Clovenhoof in all his slouched and insouciant ugliness. Pieces of thread ran from the central picture to bits of scripture dotted around it.

"Who is this?" Jerome demanded.

"Is this another trick question?" said Michael.

"Come on! Who is it?"

"It's Clovenhoof. I mean, it's the Devil."

"Ha!"

"Wrong?"

"So wrong!" He slapped the board. "A distinct demonic entity called the Devil only gets properly mentioned in the Gospels when doing such things as trying to tempt the Son of God."

"N-no. He's in it from the beginning. Lucifer is—"

"Lucifer!" Jerome slapped the board in another place. "Barely a whisper of the light-bringing angel in all canonical scripture."

"Sure. He doesn't get a big mention, but he's there. He's Satan. He challenges the Almighty to make Job suffer—"

Another slap, hard enough to throw dust into the air. "Satan! The 'adversary'! *Book of Job* and some scattered references later. A challenger of God's rules!"

"And he tempted Adam and Eve in the Garden. I was there!"

"The Serpent, you mean? Yes. Definitely a snake. It literally says it in the book."

"He's all those things. Trust me. I know him. I shared a bloody house with him!"

"And the horns and the goat legs?" demanded Jerome. "Why would a snake or angel or a demon have those?"

Michael shrugged. "I don't know. Goats are just symbolically evil, aren't they? Kind of shifty looking. The Israelites used to spiritually place their sins on a goat and send it out into the desert to die."

"The Scapegoat!" snarled Jerome with a decidedly victorious tone. "The demon, the angel, the snake, the goat, even the Great Dragon. The Devil was never one single being!"

"Hang on. I know the man – I mean, the fiend – and he is definitely one person."

"Sloppy thinking! If we want things to be as they should be then we should sort it out!" Jerome ripped the sheets of the board and began to roll them into a tight scroll.

"What are you doing?" said Michael.

"What I should have done a long time ago. I was in two minds about it, but you've convinced me."

"I've done what now?" said Michael, feeling a rising panic.

Jerome carried the scroll of collected notes over to a pneumatic tube station.

"Wait," said Michael. "You can't make decisions on this now."

"It's not a decision!" said Jerome, ramming the notes into a container. "It's cold hard truth!"

"But I know Jeremy. I've known him since the dawn of the time. He is what he is!"

"He is what divine scripture says he will be!"

Michael, not knowing what he was fighting against but pretty sure he was too late, ran to stop Saint Jerome. Jerome placed the cannister into the receiving end of the tube, and with a *hiss-thunk*, it was gone.

CLOVENHOOF WAS ABOUT to ask for another restorative bottle of fermented monk's piss when a strange sensation come over him. It started as a rumble in his belly, but swiftly spread. He began to shiver, then the shivers seemed to subdivide – as though every inch of his skin wanted to act independently of every other inch.

"Er, guys, is this meant to happen?"

Belphegor wheeled his chair around. Rutspud's large intelligent eyes narrowed in wary curiosity.

The entire outer surface of Clovenhoof's body was like a turbulent sea, rippling and bucking. "Are these my new kung fu skills manifesting themselves?" he managed to say through gritted teeth.

"This is not normal," said Rutspud, taking a metal tray off a nearby surgical trolley and holding it protectively in front of himself.

"I think I'd like it to stop now—" said Clovenhoof, then he couldn't speak anymore.

There was a rip and an explosive pop. Clovenhoof had time to think no one should ever have to hear an explosive pop from inside themselves, then thought no more. Fine diabolical dust puffed up in the air. Rutspud ducked. Belphegor, speedy despite his decrepit appearance, had pressed a button on his chair and a clear plastic shield now surrounded him.

Slowly, Rutspud moved forward to inspect the space where Clovenhoof had once been.

"Er, boss? Mr Clovenhoof, sir?"

Shapes moved on the floor amongst the wreckage of the bed on which Clovenhoof had been lying only moments before. A hairy quadruped got to its feet. Something slithered. A hand pressed against the floor.

"Er, what's happened to him?" Rutspud whispered.

"Have we destroyed him?" said Belphegor, equally mystified.

A black-furred goat trotted out, vertical slitted eyes blinking in a daze. An emerald-green snake followed it. A white robed humanoid stood and turned, inspecting his smooth-skinned hands. He put the hands to his face and felt at the finely chiselled features, the perfect cheekbones, the high senatorial brow.

"Has it been so long?" he whispered in a voice that bore the gravitas of a god and the easy charm of a cinema matinee idol.

"Lord Lucifer?" said Belphegor astonished.

"Yes?" said the former angel, equally astonished.

The goat lifted a rear leg and pissed on the hem of the angel's robe. Lucifer looked sternly at him. The goat jerked a nervous head at the snake.

"He told me to do it," bleated the goat.

The snake smiled and said nothing.

"Have we really destroyed him?" said Rutspud.

"Broken him into his constituent parts?" suggested Belphegor.

Then, from behind the angel, came a small, red-skinned demon, as small and as wet and as naked as a new-born baby. It capered on stick-thin legs and waggled its over-sized penis in a jolly dance.

"Todger! Todger! Wang!" it sang.

"He always was a little demon on the inside," said Belphegor.

"I'm going to go out on a limb here and say this is not a good development," said Rutspud.

25

Nerys had been at the Reddicap Heath site for several days and was becoming slightly more accustomed to the routine of Perry's learning sessions and the community chores. There was some sort of discreet bartering system in place which meant some people bought their way out of chores, while others seemed to enjoy the extra labour. Sandy especially seemed to be constantly on the go, humming a song as she undertook some sort of manual labour. She was like one of those animals in a Disney cartoon.

"Hey Sandy, don't you get bored of floor mopping duty?" Nerys asked. The floor in the eating area got mopped three times a day because they trod so much dirt inside.

"No, I find a task like this is almost like a meditation. My body is occupied, and my mind can be still."

"But you're being exploited. Those wannabee merchant bankers are getting you to do their jobs!"

"They are paying me for the privilege," said Sandy with a wink. "And the joke's on them because these are all learning opportunities they are missing out on. Anyway, I think they might have found some interest at last, because they have more or less taken over in the polytunnel this afternoon."

"Oh have they indeed?" asked Nerys, immediately suspicious. "What are they doing in there?"

"Not sure," said Sandy. "But I heard them say a woman from the board is here with them, so it's bound to be important."

"Woman from the board?"

"She's come all the way over from England. Tina, is it?"

"Tina!" hissed Nerys. She stormed over to the polytunnel to find that her access was barred. There was a table across the entrance with a cash box on top. Tina sat alongside Leif, behind the table.

"Nerys! how lovely to see you. You'll know Leif of course," she said.

"Yes. I am interested to know how the two of you came to be acquainted," said Nerys.

Tina leaned forward and gave a conspiratorial wink. "I have you to thank for that, actually, Nerys!"

"Um, how?"

"You mentioned about a grey economy being a healthy thing. I decided I could help out with that, so I asked Spartacus who would be a good point of contact over here and – voila!" Tina pointed at Leif, who gave a tiny bow.

"By grey economy you mean—?" Nerys realised what was happening and a hand went to her mouth. "You've set up a knocking shop in the polytunnel!"

Tina shook her head. "Emotive language there, Nerys. We're offering a service, fulfilling a need. You should be proud we're expanding the world which you created."

Leif nodded, managing to look smug, proud and amused all at the same time.

"People don't need your help to have sex, Tina. It's something that can happen without money changing hands." Nerys recognised the flaw in what she was saying even as the words left her mouth.

"And yet here we are," said Tina, with a demonstrative wave of her hand. "We're fully booked for the next three hours."

Nerys avoided Leif and his attempts to exploit the group for a few days. Perry had said there would be challenges in adopting the correct mind set, so Nerys attempted to ask his advice when she passed him pegging out laundry.

"Perry, you know how you said we need to take care of ourselves, our community, and the world? I have been wondering how to do that better. What would I do if I thought there was something posing a threat to one of those things? What if it was this community for example?"

Perry gave a small nod. "This threat would be from something or somebody else who is not in your direct control, I guess?"

"Yes, it would," said Nerys.

"Do you remember when you first came here, and I would fix things for people and leave them outside?" asked Perry.

"Yes," said Nerys, forming a hunch about where his advice was heading.

"Well that is because I realised a long time ago that people and their drama, politics and gossip were beyond my influence. I cannot alter other people's actions, only my own. Which is why I chose to limit my exposure to them."

"So you would ignore it?" Nerys was incredulous. Perry was a good person, why would he be so passive?

Perry gestured with his hands. "You might have a different approach, Nerys. I'm telling you mine."

Nerys huffed with frustration and went to find Sandy, who was mopping the floor of the cooking area again. "Still mopping?"

"There is a routine, and it has a certain pleasing rhythm to it. I like to care for our community."

Nerys tried hard to imagine feeling that way about cleaning, but she just couldn't do it. "What if someone came and made it dirty on purpose, right after you'd cleaned it, because they wanted to annoy you?"

"I would probably clean it again," said Sandy.

"You'd get mad though, right?" Nerys said.

"If I wanted to practise self-care I would avoid doing that. I can't control their actions, but I can control the way I react."

Nerys stared at Sandy's face, looking for a glimpse of irony or any hint that annoyance loitered below the surface. "Seriously? I can't imagine being that controlled. I mean, I want to be a good person, but I don't think I could be good in ways like that. I would want to thump someone who did that to me."

Sandy smiled serenely at Nerys. "Acceptance of ourselves

is at the very heart of this. Do you love and accept yourself, Nerys?"

Nerys bit down on her first response, which was a sentence including the words 'new age bollocks' and composed a version that was less confrontational. "If I think I'm brilliant, does that count?"

Sandy gave her a smile that somehow *annoyingly* conveyed that she knew exactly what Nerys was thinking, but was fine with it. Nerys left Sandy and drifted outside.

She hadn't been in the polytunnel since Tina's visit. The task rotas had kept her in other locations, and now she stared at it, wondering if there was a reason for that.

Nerys peered in through the plastic sides and saw that Leif and his acolytes were hard at work inside. What could they be doing?

At the entrance to the polytunnel, Leif appeared and blocked her way. "Nerys, aren't you on laundry duty today?"

"Yes, I notice that I've been on laundry duty for a few days now. I reckon the rota could do with a shake up, don't you?"

Leif made an expansive gesture. "Perhaps it has been recognised that each of us has a specific expertise which can be harnessed for the maximum good, huh?"

"Maximum good for who though, Leif? Anyway, I am taking a break so I thought I would take a look in here, see how the salad crops are doing."

"I need to stop you right there, Nerys. We're doing some re-potting today and I can't have doors opening and closing. The draughts could damage the delicate roots of our plants. Come another day and we will see."

Nerys knew bullshit when she heard it, but she withdrew without an argument.

DURING THE EVENING MEAL, when everyone was eating in the communal area, Nerys slipped out of the door and went over to the polytunnel. She crept inside and walked down the central pathway. The plants had all grown a bit bigger, but everything seemed to be in order – until she reached the far end. A new bed of plants was growing, the shape of their leaves unmistakeable. There was a bed of cannabis plants growing in the polytunnel.

Nerys heard a noise and turned to see Leif walking down the centre pathway towards her.

"I see you have discovered another of my little ventures, Nerys. Fine sturdy plants, aren't they?"

"They are," said Nerys.

"Go on," said Leif. "You know you want to lecture me, tell me that I'm a bad person and I don't deserve to be here."

Nerys paused. She had no problem with the growing of cannabis, and she could empathise with Leif's constant searching for ways to make money. What was unforgiveable was the way he was putting all of the other members of the group in the firing line.

"You don't know about the punishments here for drug dealing do you?" she said quietly. "The local regime takes a very dim view of it. Very dim view." She mimed a knife going across her throat.

She didn't wait for a reaction, simply walked away.

Nerys had a half-formed plan, but she needed someone

dodgy to help. She sneaked off to her car and pulled her phone out from its hiding place. She made a promise to herself that she would not look at messages or social media before she powered it up, and almost stuck to it. Ten minutes of catching up were surprisingly disappointing, almost as if the world hadn't even noticed she had disappeared for several weeks.

She paged through her contacts and decided on Animal Ed. He was the most obvious choice for two reasons. One, he would do almost anything, no matter how illegal, for the right price, and two, she happened to know he enjoyed dressing up in a uniform with shiny buttons.

26

Nerys sent the go ahead signal to Animal Ed and knew all she had to do was wait for her plan to unfold. As they all sat for their meal, she heard the approaching vehicles.

Heads raised around the tables, as everyone knew the gate was kept locked. They stood as a group and went round to investigate, Perry in the lead.

There were three vehicles, but two hung back, their windscreens dark. The front was an open jeep and it contained four people. Animal Ed was dressed in the style that Nerys had advised, which was 'psychotic dictator'. He had embraced the over-embellished uniform, with its fringing, buttons and gold braid. He also wore a tall, peaked cap and aviator sunglasses.

His lieutenants were dressed in military camouflage and aviators, but they hung back. Nerys realised with a start that it was Spartacus and his mates, PJ and Kenzie.

"My name is Generalissimo Eduardo and I am 'ere to speak with the one called Leif!" screeched Ed with an accent that wandered across the globe, grabbing every growling, purring eccentricity Ed could squeeze in. "Breeng 'im to me!"

Perry was confused, but Nerys needed to let this play out. She craned to see where Leif might be, but he had melted backwards into the crowd.

Generalissimo Eduardo stalked through the crowd and continued his crazed monologue. "We tolerate this leetle place because it is the home of harmless foreign do-gooders, but eef zey brek our rules zen we will come down on them with the full might of our regime."

He pulled a small dagger from his belt and brandished it above his head. "When we need to make an example, we will take the perpetrator and I will personally use my ceremonial dagger, rather than turning them over to my death squads. Now, bring me the one called Leif, or you will all be packed off to be interviewed at the headquarters of my death squad."

He mimed air quotes around the word 'interviewed'.

It was only a few moments before Leif was propelled to the front of the crowd.

"You! You are the one known as Leif? You are the one peddling drugs to the sons and daughters of my land?"

"No!" Leif squeaked, relieved to see a way out. "No, I would never sell drugs. We are simply growing a small quantity for medicinal use amongst our group."

"All drugs are strictly forbidden here. The distribution of drugs is punishable by death! You would not undertake such a ridiculous enterprise unless you were prepared to die!" Ed raised his dagger high in the air. It was a virtuoso performance, and Nerys wondered whether Ed was a frustrated performer. It would explain some of his odd fashion choices.

"I didn't know, I swear!" pleaded Leif. "I can get rid of the crop. Please, sir! Be merciful!"

"If you are going to beg, then at least do it properly!" said Ed. "Down. Get down and grovel in the dirt."

Leif complied and grovelled at Ed's shiny boots.

"Very well. Please note that you are on your last chance, Leif." Ed spat the name. "My people will be inspecting these premises and seeing that you keep to your word. Ze arrogance of you people makes me sick to my stomach!"

Generalissimo Ed climbed back into the jeep and the small convoy left.

The crowd drifted back indoors, and it was noticeable that Leif's acolytes kept a considerable distance away from him, as if they were tainted by association.

Nerys resolved to bung Ed a bonus on top of the fee they had already agreed. He had overachieved on the goal of scaring Leif into scaling back his criminal activities.

She kept a watchful eye on Leif, but he spent several days sticking to the rules and staying quiet. If anything he was a bit too quiet. He seemed watchful.

"I've been observing some of the comings and goings, Nerys," he said to her when they were on cleaning duty together. "There are some things about this place that I simply don't understand. The climate and the alignment of the stars for one thing."

"The what?"

"I never paid that much attention in geography, but I see things." He used a finger to mime seeing.

Nerys snorted. "What is this?" She copied his mime. "Is that in case I don't understand what seeing is? You're not in a film, you know."

"I know it was you who snitched on me about the cannabis!" he hissed.

"Hey, I gave you the chance to talk your way out *before* you crossed the line into actual distribution, you idiot," she said. "Just imagine how different that conversation would have been if you were selling it to the locals."

He sniffed and moved away.

NERYS NOTICED that Leif was missing when it was time for the evening meal. Mealtimes were when the whole group was together, and even though Leif had been quieter since Animal Ed's intervention, he was always a noticeable presence.

"Anyone seen Leif?" asked Perry, also noticing that they were missing someone.

"Perhaps he is taking a nap?" suggested Sandy.

There was no chance to check up on that possibility, because Leif barrelled through the door at that point with a loud clatter.

"I've been outside," he said. "I climbed over the gate and walked into town. Guess where we are everybody?" He stared round at everyone in the group, leaving a long and challenging pause. "We are in England. Just outside Birmingham, to be precise."

Nerys opened her mouth to point out that Sutton Coldfield had always prided itself on being separate from Birmingham, but she closed it again. Now wasn't the time.

"No, that's not possible," shouted one person.

"We went on a plane!" shouted another.

"We can't be in England, we saw the crazy Generalissimo!"

After the first few protests, there was a brief silence and then people gave voice to the doubts they had been keeping to themselves.

"I wondered how they had the same milk bottles..."

"That's why the dandelions grow so well..."

"But ... but why?"

Lief shrugged. "Good question."

The rest of the group were all shouting out at the same time, so Lief silenced them by holding up both hands. "I don't think we need to speculate, we need to ask her." He pointed at Nerys. "Go on! Tell us why you did this. It was you, wasn't it? Why did you lie to us?"

Nerys glanced across at Perry, but he stood on the sidelines, an observer.

"Yes. This was me. I will answer your questions and you'll see that everything I've done has been for a good reason."

"A good reason. Hear that everyone? It's all been for a good reason. There you go." Leif was milking every word for maximum contempt, and he pulled a disgusted face to match. "You know what I think? I think that when we all reconnect with the world we will find that we have missed important messages, maybe we will have missed crucial life events. It turns out the reason for us being deprived of those connections with your loved ones was not for spiritual cleansing, or whatever bullshit they told us, it's so we didn't uncover the deception."

There was an angry roar.

"I apologise for the deception," said Nerys. She needed to shut Leif up. "Do you think I entered into this lightly? No. There is a lot at stake. The future of the world, in fact."

"Oh yeah? Tell us how come!" someone shouted.

Nerys hesitated. How could she give them anything concrete? "I have access to some data feeds. They indicate that the world is perilously close to collapse. Yes, really! But we found a pocket of hope here and we wanted to see if we could incubate a ... a task force. That was your role, to learn how to replicate what Perry is doing and spread that into the world." Nerys waved a hand at their surroundings.

"Bollocks! Mending spades and doing washing? It's not like it's superpowers or even fucking politics! How's it doing anything but turning us into your slaves? What a stupid scam!"

Nerys could not make herself heard over the shouts of abuse.

"I want my phone and my laptop."

As soon as one person asked, the others joined in. The sense of injustice, coupled with the realisation that they could now reconnect with their lives was a powerful cocktail and they advanced with as much menace as if they'd all been carrying pitchforks.

Nerys noticed Sandy step forward. If Sandy felt like being the voice of calm reason at this point it would really help. Her face remained serene as she reached into the wicker basket she carried. It was the basket which she took down to the hen house, and too late Nerys realised that Sandy had pulled out an egg. It sailed through the air and smashed right across Nerys's nose. Although it had smashed on impact, it was surprisingly painful. Nerys had no chance to recover from the first blow before the next egg arrived, and the next. How many eggs did Sandy have in her basket? Others joined in and Nerys was pelted from every side by handfuls of compost, food waste and something that really should have been flushed. She ran for cover, knowing she had to get out of there.

A few minutes later she had grabbed her bag and climbed into her car, but still the mob chased her. They only slowed down when she pulled onto the main road, and she saw them stop and stare in wonder at the road signs. The first touchstone they had with their real location distracted them long enough for Nerys to floor the accelerator and pull away.

Nerys went back to her flat, retrieving Twinkle on the way. Ben had questions, but she said she'd update him later. She wanted a shower.

Nerys couldn't get off the stench from the pelting she'd had. Even when she'd put all of her clothes into the wash and stood in the shower for twenty minutes, there was still a whiff of an eggy, shitty melange. It matched her mood. The commune idea had backfired in a way that could only make the Shit-O-Meter readings worse. She hadn't dared check yet.

She went out to grab some milk and bread, but she hadn't gone far before she realised something was very wrong. People were staring at her with open hostility.

"It's her, off that video."

She retreated back to her flat and grabbed her phone. There was a viral TikTok video where Sandy walked the viewers round Perry's farm and described how the group had been duped into thinking they were working abroad. She referred continually to 'people traffickers' and every time she said it, she put a picture of Nerys on the screen. The video ended with Nerys fleeing from the mob.

The various news outlets had picked up on the story and interviewed Sandy and Leif. The two of them were now apparently working together, and discussed the civil prosecution they were planning to bring against Nerys.

"Unbelievable," Nerys muttered.

There was also, on the local news, a clip of a tall man with sideburns and, yes, quite piercing eyes, telling the reporter about the 'evils' that she had perpetrated.

"*She is one of the signs foretold!*" he declared passionately. "'*You tolerate that woman Jezebel, who calls herself a prophet. By her teaching she misleads my servants into sexual immorality and the eating of food sacrificed to idols.*'"

"Jesus Christ," Nerys muttered. "I did nothing sexual to anyone."

Twinkle looked at her.

"Not recently. I've been kind of busy."

"*I tell you there will be further signs,*" the man went on, who was identified as a Deacon Armorer Phipps on the channel tickertape. '*The sun will turn black like sackcloth made of goat hair, the whole moon will turn blood red.*'"

"Thank you, Deacon Phipps," said the reporter, hastily steering away from him.

Nerys sent a message to the other board members.

You'll have seen what's happened. We need a crisis meeting.

Tina replied almost straightaway.

We already met, Nerys. We think it's best we create some distance between us. It's the only way we can keep the good stuff going, I'm sure you understand it's for the best.

Nerys phoned Tina's number. "It's not for the best, you grade A bitch!" she yelled. "What the hell do you think you're playing at?"

"Oh Nerys, sweetie," crooned Tina. *"It's damage limitation, pure and simple. It's for the greater good, and that's what we're all about, isn't it?"*

"Exactly. Greater good. We need to work out a plan!"

"That's right, babe. And the plan is for you to stay away from the rest of the project. You'll weather this storm, because you're tough as old boots, I know you. Then you'll bounce back and do something new and interesting, I'm sure."

Nerys felt the anger boiling up inside her. She wanted to hurl abuse at Tina until she was hoarse. "New and interesting"? Nerys had never heard such blatant code for "bat shit crazy" before. Nerys wanted to go round and wipe the smug smile off her face with a well-timed swing of a tyre iron. She wanted to howl with rage and frustration at the fact she was now the fall guy for the entire thing. She did none of those things, but she ended the call and kicked the edge of the sofa until she felt something crack.

"Twinkle, I'm on my own again," she sniffled, rubbing her now injured toes. "Apart from you I mean."

27

Michael all but fled from the Research Centre for Scriptural Exegesis. Saint Jerome had provided him with no answers at all but, perversely, had perhaps provided him with the only answer he needed.

He caught a Heavenly monorail back to the Empyrium. It took him a while to get to the station as there was a small but vocal band of angels handing out leaflets by the entrance gate.

"Show solidarity with your brethren," said one, thrusting a leaflet into Michael's hand.

"An eternity of service means an eternity," another called after him as he climbed the stairs.

Michael unfolded the leaflet. It was a hastily if colourfully illuminated scroll inviting him to attend a service at a nearby temple which would include *Singing of praises to the Holy Throne* and discussing *How the Apocalypse will threaten the God-given roles of many angels*. According to the little logo at the bottom, said service was being organised by the RESPECTFUL ALLIANCE OF GATE KEEPERS AND GREETERS. Michael had never heard of them, nor their motto: PROVIDING SECURITY AND SMILES SINCE THE BEGINNING OF TIME.

Michael went to stuff the leaflet into his pocket, before remembering robes didn't come with pockets. It was odd how he had once regarded simple robes as the perfect clothes to wear, how he had initially found modern human clothing tight and restrictive. Now he missed the tailored neatness and comfort of a decent suit, and the orderly supportiveness of modern underwear.

A sudden thought crossed his mind and he clutched himself through his robe. His penis was still there! The relief he felt was visceral and real – which was odd in its own way. Initially he'd not seen the point of human genitalia, and although he knew the Almighty's design plans were both ineffable and perfect, Michael had strongly felt that when it came to external male genitalia, the Almighty must have been having some sort of off day. Or at least had designed them to make a theological point which Michael had yet to grasp. Nonetheless, after ten years of being effectively human, and thus saddled with all the physical accoutrements that implied, Michael had grown attached to his penis. It was far from perfect, obviously. It had a propensity to sit awkwardly at times, to very occasionally get itself caught in zips, and it often had a mind of its own – particularly when he was sleeping, or when Michael's thoughts dwelled on certain beautiful bodies for more than a few moments. And yet, it was always there and demanded very little of him. It was sort of like having an ugly, brainless, low maintenance pet living in one's pants, and he was glad it was still with him.

A passenger glared at him holding onto his crotch through his robe. Michael let go immediately. "It's my penis," he explained. "I was just checking it was still there."

The passenger blinked.

"Angel with a penis," Michael went on. "I'm possibly the only one. I must ask."

The passenger very deliberately turned away. The monorail set off.

From the monorail's raised position, Michael could see a good distance across the city. In a city square larger than a football stadium, ten thousand warrior angels practised fighting moves in perfect synchronisation. Bronze swords flashed in the holy light of the city, waving back and forth like ears of golden corn in the wind. Viewed from a distance, those tiny figures seemed to move with a cheerful zeal.

"None of it needs to happen," he said to himself, a sentiment he repeated to the three other archangels when he re-entered the meeting room in the Empyrium.

"What's that?" said Gabriel.

"He says none of it needs to happen," said Raphael.

"I'd wondered where you'd got to," said Samael. "Thought you might have been trying to sneak your way back down to Earth."

"At our moment of triumph?" Gabriel seemed perplexed.

Michael looked at the items on the vast table. There was an unfurled scroll map of Limbo (which was pretty much a blank piece of paper) and little statuettes had been placed on it to represent the armed forces of Heaven and Hell. Heaven's forces were made from gold, Hell's constructed from rough grey stone. They were arranged in various wedges and box formations. It all looked very *military* and held absolutely no interest for Michael.

His eye was drawn more to the map of Earth further down the table. Colourful round-headed pins had been stuck in it in various places. Michael looked. Israel, Italy, New Zealand.

"What's this?" he said. "We fighting the Final Battle in New Zealand?"

"I should hope not," said Raphael. "We were picking out spots for the new Holy City on Earth."

Michael thought of the couple of souls discussing this very thing on his initial monorail journey. They would have been disappointed to see there was no pin in either Brighton or Guernsey.

"You're *picking* where to put the Holy City?" said Michael.

"It has to go somewhere," said Gabriel.

"That there will be a new kingdom on Earth is sort of a given," said Raphael.

"And you think New Zealand is a likely location?" said Michael.

"Have you seen it? Spectacular. It's got that sort of dreamy British greenness to it, but without all the horrible people spoiling the view."

"And it has volcanoes and earthquakes," said Samael with a grin.

"This is what I'm saying!" said Michael.

"You're giving your vote to New Zealand?" said Raphael hopefully.

Michael shook his head furiously. "You lot are saying that Armageddon is a religious inevitability; that it must happen."

"It must," said Gabriel. "The signs are all there."

"And yet I've just spent a disturbing half hour with Saint Jerome, the man in charge of determining what the holy scriptures actually say and he can't even work out how many Horsemen of the Apocalypse there should be, let alone the actual specifics of the Day of Judgement."

"Is that where you were?" said Samael, both bored and disappointed.

"And I come back here to find that instead of marching to the divine plan of the Almighty, you're literally sticking pins in a map to pick out the location of the Holy City, like you're planning a summer holiday! What happens when you've picked it? Are you going to spend the rest of your time arguing over what kind of Heaven on Earth the survivors of the Apocalypse are going to enjoy? I'm sure, if you ask three different believers what their new Heaven will be like, you'll probably get four different answers."

"Ah!" said Gabriel with a victorious raise of his index finger. "That's where my plan comes into its own." He spread his hands over the map. "Why have one Holy City when we can have several?" He pointed at the Middle East. "I think our more Zionist friends would relish a city in the Holy Land." The finger shifted to Africa. "If the Jehovah's Witnesses wish to believe that only a hundred and forty-four thousand souls get to go to Heaven, we can give them all isolationist Heaven's here, here, and frankly, wherever." The finger moved on to the United States. "And I don't think anyone but our Mormon friends has any interest in the State of Utah."

"This is bonkers," said Michael.

"I think it's very practical," Gabriel sniffed.

"All these details are utterly unclear, yet every bloody individual here seems to think that Armageddon absolutely needs to happen right now! There are thousands upon thousands of troops out there, doing drill practice in preparation for the big battle, utterly convinced that the Apocalypse is one hundred percent inevitable, rubber stamped, and signed in triplicate."

"Which it is," said Samael.

"What makes you so certain?"

The Archangel Gabriel took a deep breath and put his hands together, fingertips to fingertips. "You say there are thousands upon thousands of troops out there, preparing for war."

"There are!" said Michael.

"Why would they be preparing, if the war was *not* going to happen, Michael? Listen to yourself. Out in the streets, trumpets are being sounded, hymns are being sung. Why would that be happening if war was *not* going to happen?"

"But that's happening because you've told them it's happening."

"*I* didn't specifically tell them," said Gabriel innocently. "I've only been sharing what I've been told, and I have no reason to doubt what I've been hearing."

"I've certainly been hearing that Armageddon is happening," said Raphael. "And although I abhor violence, it is only prudent to prepare."

"Seems to me your questions are rather juvenile, Michael," said Samael. "Why, why, why. You might as well be asking why grass is green or why the sun is warm. You can ask, but that ignores the facts that grass is beautiful and it is good to feel the sun on one's face."

"Armageddon is a just and righteous culmination of the Almighty's plans," said Gabriel. "You should be celebrating, not questioning."

Michael screamed silently in the halls of his brain, but he could see there was little point venting out loud. These zealous fools seemed oblivious to reason.

There was a knock, the huge high door swung open, and the angel Eltiel walked in with a bundle of notes in his hands.

"Sirs," he said, spilling pink halo light all around him as he crossed the floor. "Sorry to disturb your vital planning session, but there is a delegation of workers outside who wish to speak to, and I quote, 'the management' about protecting their jobs in the new world to come. They are threatening industrial action."

"Industrial action?" said Raphael.

"Very much so." Eltiel shuffled his papers, dropping some in the process. "And I've had an unusual report of an angel alarming monorail passengers by making lewd boasts about his genitals."

"Genitals?" said Gabriel. "But angels—"

Eltiel made an effort to conceal his hand as he pointed surreptitiously at Michael.

"Oh, Michael..." sighed Gabriel.

28

The front door to Nerys's flat swung open and Hodshift bustled in and through to the kitchen.

"What the hell are you doing?" Nerys yelled.

"Gettin' a pair scissors," said Hodshift. "Gotta open this package." She could hear the sound of cupboard doors opening and closing.

His casual tone enraged Nerys. He had sauntered in through a door that she was certain had been locked. "How did you get through a locked door?"

"Oh, locked was it?" Hodshift pottered back to the door, went through to the other side, pulled it shut and knocked.

Nerys whipped it open. "Do you mean to tell me you can just wander through locked doors whenever you want?"

"Um, yes? Can I get those scissors please?" He held up a sealed plastic pack containing a coiled computer wire. "Your earth factories seal these things up tighter than a thousand chains."

"You do know they kicked me out, don't you?" said Nerys.

"Who did?"

"Tina and them."

"Tina? The one who's like your clone-sister?"

"She's not my clone-sister!"

"Or however you humans reckon it. I got bruvvers meself, cut from the same demon cookie cutter."

"We're not sisters!"

"Sure. Whatever. I'm not judging."

He found a pair of heavy scissors in her kitchen drawer and began working at the edges of the cable's packaging.

Nerys rolled her eyes and sighed. "So, did my efforts in the camp mess up the Shit-O-Meter readings?"

"It did take a bit of a plummet, yes."

She sighed even more deeply. "There's no fixing people, is there?"

"I don't reckon so. Not unless you've got a magic wand."

She frowned. "You mentioned you had a wish-granting gadget. That doo-hickey."

He shift his feet uncomfortably. "Dunno what you're talking about."

"The Wish-O-Matic."

"It's called a Fulfilment Accelerated Actuator, if you must know."

"Right. But it wasn't working. Not since it demolished the Second Circle of Hell."

"Seventh."

"Whatever." She realised something and looked at Hodshift's package. He realised too and immediately hid it behind his back.

"You needed an RJ45 or whatever to get it going again," she said.

"RS-232 serial data cable," he said, unable to resist correcting her. Reluctantly, he brought the new cable from behind his back to show her. "Wishes are dangerous things," he said.

"We need wishes to fix this problem now," she said. "Get your Wish-O-Matic and show me."

Hodshift looked very much as if he wanted to say no, but he sloped off. He was back in less than five minutes with something like a metal lunchbox.

"Is that it?" Nerys asked.

Hodshift put the lunchbox down on the kitchen counter and opened it up. There was a Gregg's pasty inside, which he lifted out with reverence. "Snack fer later. It's still warm." He then picked up a device that was in the bottom of the tin. It reminded Nerys of a vintage Dictaphone, with its clunky buttons. The new cable connected the tip to the base, with the excess wire wrapped around and held neatly in place with cable ties.

Hodshift pointed at the buttons. "There are three buttons. It was supposed to have erase and rewind, but it was too blummin' difficult, so the only one that does anything is the red one. You press it and talk into the microphone. You need to speak clearly."

Nerys grabbed it and turned it over in her hands. "Spell this out for me. Am I going to meet a smug genie that takes my well-intended words and turns them into a bad thing by being a grammar nerd?"

"Nah, nuffin' like that. When I said speak clearly I meant

like in a loud voice. The microphone is a Z800 and it's probably got bits of pasty in it."

Nerys turned it over in her hands. "I promise I will think carefully about how I use it."

"Make sure you do. Now I've got a pasty going cold and some light bulbs ter change."

"Are there any limits?" called Nerys as Hodshift ambled off.

"Limits?"

"Like only three wishes or will it run out of battery?"

Hodshift gave her a mournful look. "Most people don't get beyond three wishes, it's true, but that's not a hard limit. My advice to you is to take it very, very easy. If you have a list of things yer thinking of doing, do one then wait a week. Make sure you keep a careful lookout for unintended consequences."

"Yep, got it," said Nerys breezily.

WHEN SHE WAS ALONE she took the device back into her lounge and sat on the sofa, turning it over in her hands. Hodshift could not have been clearer about proceeding with caution, but then he was a worrier. She should probably start with something small. Or something smallish anyway.

"So, Twinkle," she said. "We're after a problem facing the world. We don't want to start with something controversial or divisive. There must be something that everyone agrees on."

Twinkle didn't offer any solid thoughts but licked her hand in encouragement.

The view from her window was limited to a small chunk

of the Chester Road, so she clipped on Twinkle's lead and went for a walk, determined to gather some low-level problems which might be candidates for fixing as a test run.

She paused for a moment by the pile of cans in the alley and the smattering of bees buzzing from one can to the next, looking for a sugar high or something.

"Bees are endangered, aren't they?" she said to Twinkle.

Twinkle snorted, then barked at nothing.

"We might have cracked our problem already."

Nobody would argue that the future of bees was important. Nerys was certain she had found the right thing with which to test the Wish-O-Matic.

"We're going to be super careful about this, Twinkle. We need to run the numbers."

Nerys quickly realised she had no idea how to run the numbers. As they walked to the park, she searched the internet for advice on how many bees the world needed. She wanted to be specific, but all of the articles she could find online described a world without bees or suggested how people could encourage bees in their garden.

"Who would know this stuff?"

Nerys came across the British Beekeepers Association. It would have been better if there was a worldwide equivalent, but she decided they would do. She found a phone number for a spokesperson who was quoted in an old article, so she dialled him immediately and her call went to voicemail.

"Daniel Boysenberry? I have a question and it's quite urgent. If I was able to get a load of extra bees for the world, what would be a good number? How many bees does the world need to ensure future pollination needs are met?"

There was a click, and the phone was answered. *"Hello? Can I just ask, is this the QI elves again?"*

Nerys hadn't thought to masquerade as a television researcher, but it was an idea she squirreled away for future reference. "Yes."

"Fine. Well I'm not sure this question has a straightforward answer. Obviously to meet future pollination needs the bees will need food, accommodation, and for us all to hold off on the pesticides."

"Uh huh." Nerys scribbled notes on the back of her hand.

"Also you wouldn't just want honeybees. There are many different bee species, so you would want a good spread of different ones."

"Yep, yep, how many?" Nerys had no time for caveats, she needed something actionable.

"Oh you people! I would love your job, I have to say. Always looking for something new and fascinating. How did you become an elf?"

Nerys was stumped for an answer. "Er, right place, right time, I guess," she said.

"Always the way, isn't it? Well, let's see. I might base my answer on the total estimated number of bees that are currently in the world. It's been suggested that there are at least two trillion. Two trillion bees, imagine!" He gave a small squeal. *"If we had another trillion, a population boost of fifty percent, then I think we'd have a much more secure footing, don't you?"*

"Trillion bees, got it. Thanks!" Nerys ended the call. "Well that was easy Twinkle, let's get to it."

She hurried back to the flat and positioned the Wish-O-

Matic on her lap and consulted her notes. She pressed the red button.

"I would like a trillion bees, please. They should be a good mixture of different bee species, and they should all have food, accommodation and no pesticides near them."

Nerys put the device back in the kitchen and smiled at herself at a job well done. "We did it, Twinkle! We were scientific and followed the advice of an expert. We totally rock!"

Twinkle staggered to his feet, looking less thrilled than Nerys expected at the success of their efforts. He whimpered and nudged her leg with his head, then lay down, quivering.

"What is it, boy?"

Then Nerys heard a noise. It was like a plane approaching, if the plane was something so massive that it filled the sky. Her entire body thrummed with the weird vibration. It was accompanied by a noticeable darkening of the room.

Nerys rushed to the window. "Oh shit."

She raced down the stairs and hammered on Ben's door. "Ben. Ben! How big is a trillion?"

Ben was distracted when he opened the door. "Can you hear that weird noise?"

"Yes, I might know what it is. How big is a trillion?" Nerys pushed inside.

"It's a million million, isn't it?" said Ben. "Although it's not easy to visualise such a huge number."

Nerys dragged him over to the window. "A trillion bees probably looks something like this."

"Bees? Nah, that's a freaky storm cloud or something."

"It looks a bit like a cloud, yes, but have you ever seen a cloud moving like that?" It moved with some sort of purpose. The shape was so massive that it completely blotted out the sun.

Nerys swallowed hard, recalling Deacon Phipps words. *"And the sun will turn black like sackcloth made of goat hair."*

"Pardon?" said Ben.

"And the whole moon will turn blood red."

"I don't know anything about blood red moons, but look there," said Ben. "Loads of beehives everywhere. It must be some sort of council thing."

Nerys dragged her eyes away from the mass of bees filling the skies and saw that Ben was right. Beehives filled the street, spaced out every few yards. Cars beeped their horns and screeched to a halt because beehives had appeared in the middle of the Chester Road.

"Is that where the bees are all going?" asked Nerys.

"Into the hives? Looks like it," said Ben.

There was a general downwards trend in the roiling cloud. Some of the streetlights had turned on because of the darkness their arrival had caused. When they got to street level, the bees split into swirling funnels as they filled the hives.

Nerys turned as she heard a movement behind. Hodshift ambled across the floor.

"Well I never," he said with a pointed look at Nerys. "It almost looks as though someone has introduced enough bees for the whole world and forgot ter spread them out a bit."

"What do you—?" Nerys faltered as she realised the truth

of Hodshift's words. Did they have a trillion bees just here in Boldmere?

"What would that look like, Hodshift?" she asked. "I mean, apart from the obvious view out of the window. Do you think there are none ten miles away?"

The little demon gave a small shrug. "If I had ter guess, yeah."

"What about their food?" said Nerys, as she remembered she had asked for that too.

"Look," said Ben. He pointed out of the window. As the cloud of bees thinned slightly, the rooftops were visible across the road. Every single one was ablaze with flowers.

"Oh." Nerys smiled. It was a lovely sight. She hadn't envisaged anything quite like this, but surely a roof full of flowers was a good thing?

"That one over there can't take the weight," said Ben.

Nerys looked where he was pointing and saw a flat kitchen extension that had bowed in the middle. Someone ran out of the door just as the roof caved in. Nerys couldn't tell if they were screaming at the damage to their house or because of the bees. The waving and swatting suggested it might be the bees.

"Does that mean they are on our roof as well?" asked Ben with a nervous glance at the ceiling. "Let's make sure all the windows are closed. Then I'm going to call the council. I feel sure something isn't right about this."

He disappeared off to check windows and Nerys looked at Hodshift. "Fine. Lesson learned. I guess I should have said that they needed to be spread around the world."

"Really? Isn't two thirds of the world covered with water?"

"The world's land mass then. Why do I have to be an expert in everything?"

"When it comes ter meddling, you need to know what yer meddling with."

Nerys wanted to argue, but she had nothing. He was right. "What can I say? It was a learning experience. I'm going outside to see what it's like out there."

She left Hodshift, and called goodbye to Ben, but he was too absorbed trying to keep bees out of the house.

29

When Nerys got out onto the street, it felt as if she had stepped into a strange new world where there were none of the usual sounds of cars, but still the pervasive buzzing of a trillion bees. Interspersed with the screams of people who had been in their path.

A woman stood immobilised on the pavement outside the house. Her eyes were screwed shut and her mouth was clamped tight. Her fists were balled, and she whimpered some sort of mantra that Nerys couldn't understand. Nerys tapped her on the shoulder and the woman screamed.

"Are you all right?" asked Nerys.

"Mn," said the woman with a shake of her head. "Meeph effywhere."

"Bees? There were quite a lot of them a few minutes ago, but you can open your eyes, they've mostly gone," lied Nerys.

The woman moaned and squinted open one eye, then

the other. She wailed as she saw that many bees still swirled through the air, drifting in and out of the hives, and zooming up to visit the flowers that Nerys could see hanging from the guttering of her own house.

"I hate bees!" she said. "Where have they all come from? I'm sure they're going to sting me!"

"Try to project some confidence," said Nerys. "They can smell the fear on you." She wasn't sure if she was getting mixed up with dogs, or bears, or maybe tigers.

It was disconcerting to walk in a cloud of bees. Nerys had the sense they were buzzing all around her, but not with any sense of menace. It was more as if she was in the way of them getting to and from the flowers. Some landed on her blouse. Initially she batted them away, then she couldn't be bothered, and walked along with a number of bee hitchhikers.

Some of the cars attempted to steer past the beehives, were even using their windscreen wipers to clear the screen of bees. Nerys saw one pushing past a beehive a little too roughly, tipping it over.

Nerys was amazed to hear the difference in bee sounds. She realised up to now the buzzing had been relaxed and peaceable, but the ones in the exposed hive became angry and agitated very quickly.

Spartacus appeared on his skateboard. "Check that out, you can see the honey leaking. How do you get it out?"

"No idea, why?"

"It's four quid a jar in the shops. Bea loves honey, there must be loads here."

Nerys thought the bees might be protective of the honey

from their overturned hive, but moments later Spartacus had leaned into the hive and pulled out a frame dripping with honey.

"Got it!" He sprinted back towards the house with a swarm of angry bees chasing him. Nerys thought that perhaps she had better go back inside. She didn't want to witness a mood change in the entire trillion bees.

Nerys was still at the front door when she heard Ben wailing. "Noo! You've brought them inside, get them out!"

Spartacus had disappeared into Clovenhoof's flat with his frame of honey, and a good many bees were now loose inside the house.

"Just open a window and let them out," said Nerys, trotting up the stairs.

"Are you mad? We'll end up with loads more inside if we do that," said Ben. "What on earth was Spartacus doing anyway?"

"It seems he was harvesting honey."

"I need to protect myself," said Ben, looking back inside his flat.

"What about Spartacus?" said Nerys. "He's the one they're chasing."

Ben wasn't listening. He went into his flat and left her alone on the landing.

She went over to Clovenhoof's door and tapped on it. "Spartacus, are you all right? Did you get stung?"

"No," he called. "*Ow!* Yes. I'm just catching honey in a saucepan."

Nerys wanted to help, but it sounded as though Spartacus was managing.

She turned when she heard odd scraping noises from Ben's door. It wasn't locked, so she pushed it open, to find Ben scrabbling uselessly at the other side.

"What the hell are you wearing?" Nerys said.

Ben's head was encased by a huge plastic bottle, the type that fitted a water dispenser. There were bits of soil across its inside surface.

"You planted an African violet in there. You called it your bottle garden!"

"Needs must." Ben's voice was weirdly distorted.

He had used tape to seal the join where it sat on his shoulders, although as he moved it shifted and buckled. He had also used tape to fasten fly swatters onto his upper arms.

Nerys picked up one of his hands. "Is this why you couldn't open the door?"

He nodded sheepishly. He'd taped sheepskin mittens to the ends of his sleeves, so his hands were useless flippers. "I didn't think I would need my hands, I just wanted to use the fly swatters."

"You can't kill bees, Ben. They are important pollinators."

He stared at her. "That's fine when things are normal, Nerys. This is not normal. It's like some sort of biblical plague."

Nerys stared in horror. What had she done? Ben was right, this bee invasion was straight from the *Book of Revelations*. And she had made it happen.

"Fine. I'm going upstairs. Try not to get stuck. Have you got a plan to get your hands out, if you need them?"

Ben's face suggested he didn't.

Nerys rolled her eyes. "I'll pop down in a bit."

Ben waved his fly swatter hands. Bees dodged his swipes with ease.

Nerys went up to her flat, knowing the only way she could fix this situation was to use the Wish-O-Matic. When she got there she found Hodshift looking even shiftier than usual.

"What are you doing?"

"I wanted to make sure you weren't thinking of using the Fulfilment—"

"—Wish-O-Matic. Why not? I need to fix this."

He nodded slowly. "See, that is the kind of knee-jerk reaction I tried to warn you about. I have put the device on a high shelf, and I would advise you not to touch it for at least another day. You need to think carefully about what you're doing with it."

Nerys narrowed her eyes. A high shelf by Hodshift's standards should be easily accessible when she searched for it. She would wait until he went away. "Fine, I was just going to watch the news anyway. For research and impact analysis."

She could tell he didn't believe her, but she put the television on anyway.

"Large areas of the West Midlands have ground to a halt today after a huge influx of bees descended upon the region. Disruption to transportation services has hit North Birmingham hardest, due to hundreds of beehives blocking railways and roads. The M6, the M42, and many of the city's major arterial routes remain closed. We have this from the British Beekeeper's Association's representative Daniel Boysenberry."

Nerys recognised the voice from her earlier phone

conversation. The clip sounded as though it had been heavily edited.

"—not easy to explain where all of these bees are from – leave hives alone where possible and volunteers will re-locate them – risk of stings is low if the bees are left alone."

The announcer came back. "Insurers have been inundated with calls from householders and businesses who claim that flowers have been planted on rooftops, causing damage and collapse in some instances. Later we will hear from our money saving expert about the best way to approach your insurer if you are a victim of guerrilla gardening."

Nerys turned off the television. All of the bees had turned up in the surrounding ten miles, by the sound of the reports. It was likely that Boldmere was ground zero, but hopefully nobody was about to pin it on her.

Where had Hodshift put the Wish-O-Matic? Nerys was about to go looking when she heard an anguished yelp from downstairs.

Nerys trotted down the stairs, expecting to find Ben trying to get back into his flat, but instead she found him swinging against the wall like a pendulum, his feet off the floor.

"How on earth have you done that?" she asked.

"I think the fly swatter got stuck on a nail or something," he said, the bottle on his head bumping against the wall as he struggled to release his arm.

Nerys thought he must have taken a running jump in order to get the swatter so high. "I'll fetch some scissors."

Once Nerys had chopped through enough tape to release his arm, Ben went into his flat. Nerys spent a few minutes ushering the remaining bees out onto the landing so Ben would calm down, then she closed the door.

"Can we get you out of your weird armour and have a conversation?" she asked.

Nerys unwound duct tape and pulled off the mittens. By that point Ben was able to release his bottle helmet on his own.

"Have they all gone, or just the ones in here?"

"Most of them seem to have settled down. We'll all probably laugh about it tomorrow."

Ben didn't look convinced. "Can you hear someone screaming?"

Nerys could hear something. She went to the window and peered down. "Nothing to worry about. You put the kettle on, I'll be back in a minute."

Down at street level she found Tina writhing and screaming.

Nerys was finding herself becoming accustomed to the bees. Their zooming around, a constant buzzing movement, was disconcerting, but they seemed too busy with their own bee-related business to bother her.

Tina was a different story. For some reason her hair was alive with insects. They crawled across every part of it.

"Tina! Did you know you have a bee on your head?" Nerys felt bad when Tina was too distraught to fire off a snappy comeback.

She approached Tina's hair. "Hold still, let me see if I can help. Did you use hair product that is sugar based, or something?"

Tina gave a tiny nod and a mournful sob.

Nerys found it difficult to picture a way of removing the bees. It wasn't like a hard surface where she could just knock them away.

She guided Tina up to her flat and sat her on a chair. Nerys had one of those afro combs somewhere from when she'd had an ill-advised perm. She found it in the back of a drawer and went to work, teasing and flicking to extract one bee at a time. The bees she released flew over to the window and buzzed back and forth, attempting to get out. When the last of them was done, she went over and opened the window, wafting them on their way with a hand.

"Go and rinse that stuff out of your hair while you have the chance," she said.

Tina emerged a few minutes later, patting her hair with a towel. "Thank you, Nerys." She wound the towel into a turban shape, and they stood together at the window watching the scene below. Another of the hives had been knocked down by a car trying to get past.

"What on earth has gone on?" Tina said. "They came out of nowhere. I was on my way over here for a meeting when the sky turned black."

"I saw it from the window," said Nerys.

Tina gave Nerys a shrewd look. "You are the only person I have come across who isn't totally freaking out."

"Oh, I don't know. Spartacus has been harvesting honey."

Tina flopped back on the sofa. "I could murder a gin and tonic. Steady my nerves."

Nerys rolled her eyes and resigned herself to the fact that she would have to wait for a while to use the Wish-O-Matic.

"Ice and lemon? I might join you."

. . .

NERYS WOKE up late the next day after enjoying quite a few gins.

"Do you want to know how drunk I was last night, Twinkle? I actually remember thinking that Tina wasn't so bad. Yeah, I know."

Tina lolled on the sofa, still fast asleep.

Nerys turned on the news, both as a way to rouse Tina and to get a feel for what was happening.

"*After the unexplained bee invasion that blighted travel in the West Midlands yesterday, we can report that most roads are now open. If you are aware of a beehive adversely affecting a public space, you can report it to your local council via their website. Councils are working closely with volunteer beekeeper task forces who are moving as many hives as they can to more rural locations.*"

Nerys moved to the window. Beehives had been shifted out of the roads onto pavements and things looked a lot more normal.

"*The widespread flower gardens that have sprung up have received a mixed reaction from those affected. Many people have hailed them as a much-needed greening-up of their neighbourhood, while others warn that they threaten the fabric of the buildings they are sited upon. Insurers are being asked to give a clear message to affected homeowners about when a claim might be justified.*"

"Is it safe out there?" said Tina sitting up.

"Definitely. A quick coffee and you can be on your way," said Nerys.

. . .

ONCE NERYS WAS RID of Tina, she went in search of the Wish-O-Matic. Hodshift had managed to get it up on top of the cooker hood, which must have looked like a secure hiding place from his point of view, but Nerys was quite a bit taller, and easily spotted it sticking out.

She thought carefully as she set it on the counter. She needed to avoid silly traps like forgetting to spread the bees around. She was certain that on balance, the extra bees would do good, but balance was key.

"Balance, Twinkle. It's all about balance."

Even saying the word out loud made her pull a face. Balance and moderation sounded like the essence of dullness. Nerys was more accustomed to seeking excess.

"How am I supposed to make sure something is balanced, though? It's not as if I'm a bee expert."

Twinkle responded by looking up at her with his soulful eyes and cute nose. He believed in her ability to do this.

She smiled at him. "You're right. I don't need to be a bee expert, I just need to tell the Wish-O-Matic what outcome I need."

What was she really asking for with the bee request? What was the vision? She closed her eyes and tried to picture earnest television presenters talking about wildlife, pollinators, hedgerows and the like.

"Blah, blah, biodiversity. Blah, blah, rich ecosystem." Nerys pulled a sad face and looked to camera where she was certain that they would be showing pictures of giant mechanised farm machinery chopping up all of the wildlife in its path.

She felt her way into the role. She was on afternoon television telling the nation's children how she was going to make sure everything would be fine.

"Time is running out for the much loved wildlife of the United Kingdom. We are a nation of animal lovers, so with this device here, we're going to secure the future of our flora and fauna forever." Nerys paused for a moment. Flora and fauna was plants and animals, wasn't it? Did it include fish? She sensed another trap. She tapped the Wish-O-Matic and spoke slowly and thoughtfully. "We want to see the entire ecosystem restored to a healthy state. There should be plenty of all native species – like rabbits, deer, alpacas and fish. There should be all of the other things that help it all to work, too. That means insects, I guess. And spiders. Bare minimum of spiders, mind, so we don't freak everyone out." She looked thoughtfully at Twinkle, while gently patting the head of the fictional deer that she'd have in the studio. "That's a good clear ask, isn't it? Now, we definitely want these things to be spread across the country nice and evenly. Everyone should have the chance to see – wait! When I said spread evenly, I meant in the appropriate places. Fish should only be in water, right?"

Relieved at having dodged a bullet, Nerys released the button. This was hard work! Attention to detail wasn't her strongest suit.

30

The four bits of what had once been Jeremy Clovenhoof sat around the meeting table in Belphegor's research laboratory. Actually, there had been five parts – the angel, the demon, the Scapegoat, the Serpent – and also a pile of steaming crud in the corner, looking like a smooth pile of manure that had been baked for ten hours in a hot oven. Belphegor waved at it indifferently, guessing it was probably just the excess crap the devil had attached to his psyche over the aeons. No one showed any interest in it, except for Clovenhoof's deformed hoofed creation, which snuggled up against it and dribbled all over it with its shapeless mouth.

Rutspud had sort of hoped that if the four ambulant parts of Clovenhoof were brought round a table together in a formal setting, things would seem somewhat less awful than they were. It hadn't really worked. The Scapegoat was mindlessly eating the arm of its chair. Lucifer was twirling a glass of dark red wine (Hell knew where he'd got that from!) and was staring into its depths. The miniature demon stood on its chair, vigorously slapping his manhood against the table edge, as though it was a fish, and he was trying to bash its brains out. The Serpent simply sat, coiled, and watched Rutspud coolly with eyes that seemed to have an inner light all of their own, which Rutspud – a demon who had seen all the horrors the diseased minds of creation could come up with – found a bit creepy and unnerving.

"Do you have any idea how this happened?" he whispered to Belphegor.

"Could be our accelerated training scheme interfered with his ontological morphic field?" said Belphegor as he fidgeted uneasily with his wheelchair controls.

Rutspud narrowed his eyes. "That sounded like almost convincing techno-gibberish."

Belphegor tutted loudly. "Fine! I have no idea, Mr Rutspud. Is that what you wanted to hear? I don't know what's behind this."

"It's not my fault," bleated the goat, around a mouthful of seat padding.

"Schlong!" shouted the demon in happy agreement.

"I think you should blame it on one of the other dukes of hell and use it as a pretext to usurp his authority," said the Serpent smoothly.

"Yes, thank you, Mr Serpent," said Rutspud and turned to Belphegor. "This is bad, right?"

Belphegor stroked his wrinkly chin with spindly fingers.

"On the surface, yes."

"And under the surface?" said Rutspud.

Belphegor's wide mouth pulled in a tight expression, that of an archdemon who didn't want to admit that the calamity in front of them was calamitous from crust to core.

"We need Satan because he is expected to fight Michael in the final battle," he said slowly. "And now we have four candidates instead of one."

"I think you should fight for me," the Serpent said to the Scapegoat, and the creature leapt onto the table at once.

"I *will* fight him!" the goat declared.

"With what?" said Rutspud, looking at the billy goat's little horns and, frankly, cutesy-wutesy hoofs.

"It's not my fault," said the goat miserably. "I was made this way."

"Wang!" yelled the red-faced demon with an emphatic wave of his willy.

"Okay, this field of contenders isn't looking so great," said Rutspud.

"Perhaps I could break out the Fulfilment Accelerated Actuator," said Belphegor. "Didn't Hodshift say he'd found the necessary components? I know it's dangerously powerful, but..."

There was a light scraping of a chair as the angelic Lucifer rose to his feet. Every pose between sitting and standing was worthy of a statue. This creature was beauty personified in every state. "Enough," he said. "Too long I have tarried here."

Rutspud made a noise in his throat and looked at the fallen angel suspiciously, and not only because he didn't trust anyone who used the word 'tarried' in everyday conversation.

"Volunteering to fight Michael for us?" he asked. "I mean, you do actually look the part."

Lucifer cast his goblet of wine aside. It smashed into the still-steaming pile of hardened crud in the corner. "I do not play Hell's games. I do not submit myself to the plots and machinations of demons."

"You are a demon, sir," said Belphegor, who was rummaging unsuccessfully in a cupboard as he looked for the Fulfilment Accelerated Actuator.

Lucifer flung out at hand at the other creatures. "These are demons, perhaps. I am the mightiest of all angels. I am His greatest creation."

"I mean technically," said Rutspud, "Man is his greatest creation. By which I mean men and women, although I've always struggled to tell the difference."

"On that point, He and I have always disagreed." Lucifer looked at his hands and arms. Rutspud could tell he was looking for chains and manacles that were no longer there. "I think I must make my case again."

"Case?"

"Not to plead like some supplicant subject, but to state lofty and great truths, brother to brother."

"Um, you're doing what now?" said Rutspud.

Lucifer fixed him with an imperious gaze. There was no actual fire but – by all that was infernal and hellish! – that gaze burned.

"I am going to Heaven, little demon."

"The name's Rutspud, sir. We've met. And when you say you are going to Heaven, you mean—?"

Lucifer was already striding out the door.

Belphegor, his raisin eyes as wide as they could go was gesturing vigorously. "Get after him, lad!"

"And then what?" said Rutspud. "I can't stop him!"

"Follow! I mean, getting him to go to Limbo and meet the Angelic Host was kind of the plan!"

Rutspud ran after the angel.

Belphegor sighed heartily. It was hard being a super-powerful demon with a mind like a steel trap when all around you was uncontrollable chaos.

And that was when he realised that it wasn't only Lucifer and Rutspud who had left the room. The Serpent and the Scapegoat had wandered off too. He looked under the table. He zipped around and checked behind each corner. But, no, the two creatures had run off, leaving him with a naked red imp of a demon, and Clovenhoof's unholy Limbo creation, which continued to lick the rapidly cooling mass of scaly rock.

Belphegor looked at the little red demon. He had started with a whole and complete Satan – a podgy and petty but nonetheless coherent Jeremy Clovenhoof – and, in no short order, was now left with a wang-wangling homunculus.

"Cocks!" declared the red demon.

"Quite," seethed Belphegor. He would clearly have to work out what to do before Lord Peter found out about this.

There was the sound of approaching footsteps – sandals on an iron floor – and the former Emperor Nero stepped in. Peter's PA wore a laurel wreath of bloody razors as part of his hellish penance, but the tubby Roman otherwise seemed to relish the modicum of power his role gave him.

"Lord Belphegor," he said, "Lord Peter wishes you to attend his offices immediately."

"Does he?" said Belphegor.

"Knob!" shouted the diddy demon.

Nero pulled back in disgust. "What is that?"

"Oh. Oh, an experiment. He's, um, called, er, Diddywang. I think I will have to destroy him soon enough."

Nero was disinterested. "And where is Satan?"

Belphegor smiled miserably. "He's ... here and there."

31

Nerys left the house, taking care to avoid Hodshift, who she thought was probably with Spartacus, as he so often was. She wanted to take a good look around at the effects of her wishes before the judgy little demon complained about her using the Wish-O-Matic again. She hid it in her knicker drawer before she left the flat so that he couldn't confiscate it.

Her second wish had been very simple. She had wanted a return to the improved biodiversity and natural abundance of the past. Nothing unnatural, nothing forced. She wanted to see clouds of starlings in the sky and hear the chirp-chirp of grasshoppers. She wanted balance restored.

She emerged onto the street and looked around. The traffic was still flowing, which seemed like a good sign. She could hear some distant screaming though. More insects than seemed normal buzzed through the air. A frog hopped across the path in front of her and she saw a hedgehog snuffling its way around the corner of the house. As she walked down the road she spotted larger animals. There were deer on the street in Boldmere. This was definitely not normal, but hopefully they would find their way into the countryside before they got hit by a car. Nerys wondered whether there would be venison available in the butchers in the coming days.

She had to find out what that screaming was though, so she made her way towards Chester Road station. She didn't have to go very far before she found the problem. It was an enormous dog.

"Whose dog is this?"

She looked all around, staring at passers-by. Most people were desperately trying to get away from it as it drooled and snarled aggressively. There was one woman who seemed especially distraught, and she was the source of the screaming. She held an empty dog lead.

"Is this your dog?" Nerys asked.

"It ate my Benji!" the woman wailed.

Nerys looked at the lead in her hand and guessed Benji must have been a much, much smaller dog. Had this brute of a dog really eaten it?

"Wait – is that a wolf?"

The beast turned on the spot and growled.

"I bet they used to be native to this country, didn't they?" said Nerys to herself. "I should have thought of that before bringing them back."

The woman stared at Nerys as if she was mad. "I don't care! It ate my Benji."

Nerys looked around in a mild panic, a small part of her brain wondering what other vicious predators used to be native. The immediate problem was the wolf. Nerys knew enough about dogs to recognise that this big scary one was having a bad day. Probably materialising out of thin air would mess up any canine's preferred routine.

"Yes. Good boy. Just stay calm and everything will be fine."

"Did you just call him a good boy?" shrieked the woman with the lead. "He ate my Benji!"

"I heard."

"He is not a good boy!"

The wolf's hackles rose and he continued to growl.

"Look lady, I'm sorry for your loss, but you need to be calmer otherwise—"

Nerys didn't have time to finish the sentence. The woman kicked the wolf viciously in the hindquarters as she howled with rage. It turned and faced her briefly, before jumping up at her shoulders and knocking her down. Nerys thought it was going to rip out her throat, but instead it just loped off along the Chester Road. If it had already eaten a small dog it probably just wanted a quiet place for a nap. Nerys sighed and helped the woman to her feet. She needed to get back and find out what other native species she might have resurrected.

"Ben!" she yelled as she burst into the house. "Ben!"

Ben emerged from his flat, a tiny paintbrush in his hand. "What is it now Nerys?"

"Back in the old days, what creatures roamed this country

that we don't have any more? Like wolves. We used to have wolves. What else?"

"You mean like hundreds of years ago?" Ben asked with a frown. "I guess we had bears too. And wild cats."

Nerys gave that a moment's thought. "What would it look like though if we had a good balance of native animals? Deer and alpacas and hedgehogs and everything else, there would be more of those than there would be bears and wolves, right?"

"First of all, I think you are talking about the ratio of apex predators to the things they would eat. So yes, there would be more deer than bears or wolves." Ben stared at the ceiling. "You lost me slightly was with the alpacas, though. Why did you include them in a list of native animals?"

Nerys frowned. "Alpacas. You know. Long necks. Goofy faces." She searched her mind for the reference she needed. "They have them at that country park we visited with Jeremy. Don't you remember?"

"Yes. But just because they can live in this country doesn't make them native. I think they come from South America."

"Oh. Poo." Nerys wasn't going to beat herself up about a small mistake like that. At least alpacas didn't go round eating people's dogs. Probably.

"Is this related to the weird bee invasion?" asked Ben. "Have we got a plague of wolves now?"

"I don't think there's quite that many," said Nerys. Truthfully, she had no idea how many wolves would make a plague.

"But there's more than zero? More than zero is too many

wolves to have on the streets of Boldmere. I'm having all of my food delivered until I know it's safe to go outside." Ben slammed his door shut, leaving Nerys standing out on the landing.

The door opposite opened and Spartacus and Hodshift appeared.

"Hey, guess what? I just saw a llama out of the window!" said Spartacus.

"It was probably an alpaca," said Nerys. "Although obviously that's just a guess. Did you know they're not native to this country?"

"You taking the piss? Of course they're not native to this country. Only an idiot would think that they might be. I'm going down to take a look." Spartacus ran down the stairs.

Hodshift gave Nerys a mournful look. "Someone's been messing wiv stuff again. Didn't I tell you—"

"—Yes, yes!" hissed Nerys. "This is better though, right? It's more balanced."

Hodshift said nothing, just giving her a pointed look before returning to Clovenhoof's flat. As he closed the door he peered round it. "If I ask you not to touch it again will you listen?"

"I am doing good work with it," insisted Nerys. "I am a good person doing good things."

"You really should stop it you know." Hodshift shut the door.

"What a buzzkill." Nerys decided to go and see whether Spartacus had found the alpaca.

Out on the street Nerys saw Spartacus had gathered

several of his friends and they had managed to manoeuvre the alpaca into the garden of the shared house. Its fuzzy head peered over the low privet hedge like a dopey cartoon creature. She could hear voices as the boys discussed what they were going to do.

"We could do rides with it," said Jefri. "Fifty pee a go."

"I don't think it's big enough to ride on," said Spartacus. "You never see alpaca rides on the beach do you? It would only be big enough for a baby."

"We'll need to get it a collar," said PJ. "Which bit would it go on? Its neck's quite long."

Nerys went onto the garden and saw them contemplating the anatomy of an alpaca.

"See, imagine if it wore a tie like the grammar school kids. Would it wear it up here, where its head is, or down there, where its body is?" PJ pointed earnestly at the possibilities, while the alpaca gazed placidly around the small garden.

"It might wear it in the middle as well!" PJ said.

They all looked up when they heard Nerys approach.

"It's ours, we found it!" said Jefri.

"Yeah, I know. It's possible there might be more of them out there," said Nerys. "Alpacas out on the streets."

She really didn't want the deaths of loads of cute alpacas on her conscience. They didn't seem like animals that would have a lot of road sense.

"Is there any chance you could perhaps ... round up as many as you could? To keep them safe?" she asked.

The boys might be hormone-fuelled gangly semi-adults,

but they were still very much boys at heart. The thought of being *asked* to go round up alpacas brought grins to half a dozen faces.

"You stay here with this one, PJ. The rest of us will look for any others," said Spartacus.

PJ seemed happy enough to play with the new pet in the garden, and the others headed to the gate.

"One moment!" shouted Nerys. "I have a quick question. Who would win in a fight between an alpaca and a wolf?"

"The wolf, dur," said Jefri. He realised how rude the 'dur' sounded and tried (too late) to turn it into a cough.

Nerys shook her head. "Take care to avoid anything that looks like a wolf, then. Or a bear."

They let themselves out of the gate. "Is she high?" whispered Jefri. He was immediately shushed by Spartacus.

Nerys pulled out her phone because she was curious about the collar arrangements for alpacas. "Here you go. They usually have a harness thing on their head."

PJ peered at the picture. "Where can we get one of those?"

"I have no id—" Nerys started, but then she remembered Animal Ed. She screen-grabbed the picture and texted it to Ed.

Can you get me a harness like this?

He replied moments later. *You too? What's going on? Let me send you a link I've been sending everyone.*

Nerys opened the link. It showed how to create an alpaca harness from rope.

As it happened, Nerys had some rope in her car. It was

surprising how many times it had come in handy, like the time Clovenhoof had accidentally thrown all of his clothes off a canal bridge and wanted to abseil down to get it. The rope had been useful for helping him out of the canal when he dropped from the bridge like a stone. She left PJ fashioning a harness and went to check out what the television news was saying about her latest set of improvements.

The newsreader sat against a background photograph that showed several deer outside the Bull Ring shopping centre in central Birmingham. A man in a beanie hat was caught in the moment of offering one a Five Guys bag, as if he expected the deer might like a burger.

"*A surprising influx of animals has confounded experts up and down the country. A great many native species have been found well away from their usual habitats. They have been turning up in urban and commercial areas with no indication as to how they got there. More worryingly, there have also been sightings of wolves and bears. The most unusual aspect of the events is that a good many alpacas have also been spotted. It was initially assumed they had been accidentally released from zoos or private collections, but nobody has reported any missing animals.*"

There was a live map showing reported sightings up and down the country, followed by some talking head experts who speculated on where the animals might have come from. Obviously none of them considered the possibility of them being conjured from nowhere using technology from Hell's R&D division.

Nerys turned off the television and went to the window when she heard a clattering sound outside. She couldn't quite see what was going on, so she went downstairs. There were now three alpacas in the garden, and PJ had succeeded in making a harness for the first. There was some sort of animated disagreement going on.

"Yeah but, how strong are they? You can't have them pulling a ruddy great cart. They're only tiny." Spartacus and Jefri had a shopping trolley between them and were yanking it back and forth.

"Do you think they can run fast? asked PJ. "We could have a race and take bets on them."

"We don't even know what they eat," said Jefri.

"I think we do," said PJ, pointing.

All three of the alpacas were enthusiastically cropping the lawn. At the rate they were eating it there was about an hour's worth of feed left, because it wasn't particularly lush at the best of times. The creatures' cuteness was undeniable, and Nerys swiftly took and posted a selfie of herself with them.

"We might need to get them something else to eat," said Spartacus with a frown.

At that moment a massive horse box pulled up outside. They all turned to look as the door slammed open and Animal Ed bounded over.

"You got three? Brilliant! I've managed to rent a secure field about 20 minutes away. I'll make it worth your while, lads, but we are going to make a killing out of this, just you see. Alpacas are pretty easy to care for, but we need to move fast. Load 'em up."

Nerys stepped forward. "Wait a minute, are you rounding up alpacas to sell them?"

"Absolutely! That's why they call me Animal Ed, Nerys. The market will be flooded for the next few days, but if I can get these beauties settled into a field their value will shoot right up in a month or so, you'll see."

"But I don't want you to take these ones!" shouted PJ. "They're ours!"

"Yeah!" shouted Spartacus. "We're going to do racing with them. Or something."

"There is the problem of food, mind." Jefri kicked at the scrawny turf beneath his feet.

"No. No way," said Spartacus. "If they get in that van, we'll never see them again. How do we even know you're not selling them to the kebab shop?"

Nerys could see the thought flitting across Ed's face as he processed it. He might have been Animal Ed, but if he thought he could get more for them as kebab meat he would totally do it.

"No lads, these are going to be the next big thing in pets around here. It's all about the marketing. You wait and see. Some posh bird on the telly will tell us how she's got one in her garden, that it's so easy to care for and she made it a funny hat." Ed acted out the fictional telly woman in a way that reminded Nerys of Ed's fondness for panto roleplay. They had only had the briefest of flings, but his bedroom version of Widow Twanky was a memorable experience. "Everyone will want one. Those who didn't get one this time round will be clamouring for one, and that's where I sweep in with a ready supply. I'll give you fifty quid for each one."

The three teens exchanged glances and went into a hurried discussion that was mostly conducted in whispers.

Spartacus emerged and faced Ed. "We can let you have one of them, but it's costing you a hundred."

"You're joking!" spat Ed. "I could have caught another one in the time I've stood here talking to you!"

"But you didn't did you. Seventy five."

"Done. In the back then." Ed went to the rear of the horse box and started to loosen the door bolts.

"Which one should he take?" Spartacus asked.

"I'm keeping this one," said PJ, who had a gingery brown one on a rope harness. "That one over there looks a bit squinty, let him have that one."

Everyone stared at the alpaca accused of looking squinty. Nerys couldn't see it, but her opinion wasn't important here.

"Fine." Spartacus and Jefri ushered the alpaca through the gate and up into the horse box. Ed handed over the cash and drove away.

Nerys saw at least another two in there. Still, Ed knew a little bit about animals, so hopefully they would be well looked after. She wondered if he knew about the wolves and bears.

The boys were left with two alpacas.

"They need names," said PJ. "I reckon this one's called Speedy. Did you see how he nearly ran away then? He would have done if I hadn't kept hold of him."

Nobody argued with PJ's fanciful assessment. As far as Nerys could tell it hadn't even twitched.

"What about this one then?" asked Spartacus.

They all looked at the remaining alpaca. It was a pale golden brown and had a serene expression.

"It's Aslan," blurted Nerys. "Like on the cover of *The Lion the Witch and the Wardrobe*."

She regretted the words almost as soon as she had spoken them, but the boys all shrugged.

"Aslan. Good name," said Spartacus. "We should see if there's any more to be had. Seventy five quid apiece, it's got to be worth a look."

32

Alpacas were everywhere. Why were there so many more alpacas than deer, for example? Maybe it was because Nerys had specifically asked for them; or maybe the Wish-O-Matic found them easier to make. Whatever the reason, there were a lot.

Ed's prediction that television personalities would hijack the alpaca invasion to raise their own profiles turned out to be eerily accurate. There were featured slots on all of the daily programmes about how to care for the alpaca that was suddenly in your life. There was advice on how to harvest, spin and knit the wool from their coats. Nerys had no idea alpacas were like comedy sheep, but apparently their fleece was much more valuable than regular wool. She felt as though she should have opinions on this as she was from Wales, home to so many sheep, but she found it hard to get excited about wool.

The most controversial television programmes were about eating alpaca meat. It was inevitable that some of the lovable gonks found their way into the food chain, and apparently were nutritious and low in calories, but the public was outraged at the idea.

On day three after the alpacalypse, Nerys managed to coax Ben out of his flat. She suggested they should go to the pub, but they eventually settled on drinks in her flat.

"Spartacus must have had a lot of friends over. I keep hearing them on the stairs," said Ben. "Noisy buggers."

Nerys nodded. "Don't worry about it. I expect they just want to be safe from wolves."

"Yes. Have they rounded up most of those now?"

"It's going pretty well I think." Nerys tried not to sound pleased with herself, but a few sips of wine had loosened her tongue.

"Well? I hardly think wolves roaming the streets could be described as good," said Ben.

"No, that part was annoying. But everyone loves the alpacas."

"Yeah, I know! Did you see there are a couple of premier league football clubs thinking of having a new team logo with an alpaca? Goes to show how it's suddenly everyone's favourite animal."

"Oh yes. I watched a thing on the news. There's a massive retirement complex over Erdington way. Apparently there's a big communal garden in the centre, and they now have a dozen alpacas living there. They have them in the lounge for the old folks to pet while they watch telly. What a time to be alive!" sighed Nerys. "There are so many more hedgehogs and badgers and everything too."

"Yeah, that won't last," said Ben. "It's just not sustainable to have that many. Most of them will just die."

"What? No. No! That can't happen." Nerys slammed down her drink in outrage. "Most of the alpacas have survived, haven't they?"

Ben shrugged. "The alpacas were a novelty. You don't see retirement homes opening their doors to hedgehogs, do you?"

"No, it can't just be the novelty of the alpacas. Even all the insects, you could see them all flying around. There were loads of them."

"You could, yes. On day one. I'd say the insects were probably the first to go. Where are they all now?"

"They've gone to the countryside," said Nerys. "That's what they were supposed to do."

Ben shrugged. "Sure. Maybe some of them did. But you know the decline in insects is one of the minor disasters underpinning a lot of other things, but people don't shout about it so much. You must remember your family going on a long drive when you were young and how you'd get loads of insects on the windscreen of the car?"

"Yes, that's true. It was really icky. We don't get that anymore."

"Exactly! That's why I am fairly confident all the insects from the other day will be dead."

Nerys was furious at Ben's calm acceptance of it all. "How dare you! It's like you don't even care about the world!"

"Whoa, cool it!" Ben said. "You know I care about the world, but I can't care deeply about every single episode of weirdness, otherwise I would lose my mind."

"It's not as if you've even been doing anything to help. You just shut the door, stay inside and hope for the best."

He shrugged. "What else am I supposed to do? I have no power."

"What if you did, though? If you could make loads of new animals appear, how would you make it so they didn't just die?"

Ben gave it some thought. "So I need to come up with a way to increase the wildlife without them all dying from a lack of space? Well, I guess I'd have to sequester a load of farmland or something."

"You can't just chuck all the farmers off their land," said Nerys. "There must be a better way."

"What, am I just making new land then? Am I making Atlantis or Doggerland rise up from the bottom of the sea to fit all these new animals on?" Ben flapped his hands in frustration at the idea.

"You're talking about making a massive new island for all this new wildlife?" mused Nerys. "If it was close by, then that could work."

Ben shrugged. "Doggerland, then. It's just off the east coast. Maybe we could have a bridge to it."

"It could definitely work."

"I'm not sure about that. It would be a huge engineering challenge," said Ben. "They reclaimed land in the Netherlands from the North Sea, but not as much as that."

"Engineering, right. How hard can it be?"

Ben finished his drink and cocked his head at a thumping sound. "I can hear those lads on the stairs again. I might give them a piece of my mind about the way they are stamping around."

"How about I do it?" said Nerys. "You pour us another drink, I'll be back in a moment."

Nerys trotted down the stairs and was not surprised to discover the noise Ben could hear was two alpacas on the stairs. "They are pretty clever creatures aren't they? Don't let Ben see you bringing them inside."

"We can't leave them out in the garden all night," said Spartacus. "It's not right, is it?"

Nerys didn't have an answer to that. There was so much about the current situation that wasn't right, she honestly had no view on where the alpacas should sleep. "Fine. Put them to bed. But be discreet."

The two alpacas trotted daintily up the remaining stairs and into Clovenhoof's room. Speedy and Aslan both had quite different characters. Speedy headed straight over to nibble the bale of hay that had appeared from somewhere, while Aslan surveyed the room and bobbed his head in approval. Nerys had the distinct impression that he thought he was in charge.

Nerys went back upstairs to her flat and picked up her drink. She held it up in salute to Ben. "I've told them not to make so much noise on the stairs. Should be fine now."

The following day Nerys drove out into the countryside. The reason for her journey was twofold. She wanted to double check on the amount of remaining wildlife. She had a sinking feeling that Ben was correct and the newly introduced insects had all died out. She had also brought the Wish-O-Matic with her, so if she decided to make a change, she was well out of reach of Hodshift.

She parked the car in a layby and looked at the windscreen. It was clean of squished insects. She left the car and walked up and down for a few minutes, looking at the ground and over the fence into a field of something that was planted in long green rows. No hedgehogs or any other visible forms of wildlife presented themselves.

She sighed at the thought that they hadn't survived. She knew enough about nature to understand if the small stuff dies then the large stuff would eventually follow. Everything except the alpacas was doomed.

She refused to become depressed about it, because she had a backup plan. She fetched the Wish-O-Matic and stared out at the horizon. It felt good to be stating her wishes out here where she could see further; it felt as though she was more directly connected with the places that she was affecting.

"Shit." Her face fell. The east coast was miles away. If she summoned Doggerland into existence she wouldn't be able to see what it all looked like. She needed to see it with her own eyes to properly evaluate whether it was successful or not.

She jumped back into the car and sped back home. She hammered on Ben's door.

"Road trip! Grab a bag."

Ben appeared at the door. "What?"

"I need you to come with me to the east coast. I want to look at Doggerland. Come on, I'm going now."

Ben rolled his eyes. "Nerys, there's nothing to look at. It's the North Sea. It would be a trip to, I don't know, Grimsby or Great Yarmouth, or somewhere to look out at the sea. If I wanted to leave the flat and waste my time, I'd at least open the shop and wait for customers."

"What if I told you I'd found an engineer willing to take on the project?" Nerys said. "I just need to, um, let them know what I want."

"Then I'd say you have found someone who is delusional!"

Nerys huffed for a moment. She wanted a buddy for the road trip, but more she wanted someone with Ben's general knowledge. "What would it take to get you to come with me?"

Ben looked taken aback. "Oh, well. Um." He thought for a moment. "How about I plot a route that takes in some interesting sites on the way?"

"Sure! Fine! Yes! We can do that. Get a bag ready, quickly."

Nerys ran upstairs to pack a bag herself. She was bending to retrieve a pair of pants which had fallen down the back of her bedroom radiator when she glanced through the window and saw a figure standing in the street outside their house.

The tall man was standing perfectly still and looking up at her. She recognised the sideburns and the clear blue eyes. Nerys pulled his name from her memory.

"Deacon Phipps."

As though he could hear her (which surely he couldn't) he raised a finger and pointed at her.

"Whore of Babylon!" he cried in a deep and penetrating voice.

Ben shouted from downstairs. "Nerys, I think one of your ex-boyfriends is outside."

33

As a demon, Rutspud was immortal, although in body only for he had no soul. He was proud to say that he was all hardware and no software. Many of his fellow demons took advantage of that immortality to upgrade their physical bodies from time to time. If a fellow demon's arm worked better than your own, there something to be gained from stealing it and using it to replace your own. Demon physical hardware was always compatible.

But Rutspud had never really indulged in such things. He was happy with the body he had been given. He had large, expressive and watchful eyes, and large and attentive ears. He had quick hands, faster than most eyes, ideal for snatching and concealing. And by effort or by chance, he had also been given a brain which, whilst not the pinnacle of intelligence, certainly scored highly on raw cunning. And if he was small demon then so what? Small meant easily overlooked, small meant good at hiding. Rutspud had forged a long and considerably successful career by knowing lots (including when to keep his mouth shut) and by keeping his head down.

What his body was not good for was running. Oh, he could scuttle with the best of them, but actual running was not his forte. When Lucifer had flown out of Hell's yawning cave entrance, scuttling-not-running Rutspud was soon left trailing in his wake. Rutspud had run out of Hell, past the mighty three-headed Cerberus and into Limbo, flailing his limbs and panting as though his very heart would explode (which it might, and he'd already eyed up some colleagues of approximately the right size and frame who he could steal one from if it did).

Soon, he was alone in Limbo. He wasn't fond of it. Like Earth, which he had cause to visit on numerous occasions, it lacked a proper ceiling, and that never sat well with him. And it lacked walls as well. In fact the only thing that could be said to be there was the ground, and he wasn't certain about that. To walk in Limbo was to walk on marshmallow clouds.

The dot which was Lucifer had long disappeared in the sky when Rutspud decided it was now pointless pursuing. He huffed and turned back towards Hell.

THE CELESTIAL CITY was now on a war footing. Where earthly cities might have been placing sandbags around important buildings or distributing gas masks to the civilian populace, the Celestial City's preparations for war were far more shiny and jingoistic. Angels marched in perfect columns through the wide boulevards, while others flew in tight formations high above. Bronze swords and polished lances were held at the ready, and plumed helmets of a classical design adorned every angelic head. There were songs in the street and banners unfurled from high windows. Michael was impressed by how these war-ready demonstrations seemed to imply both the unstoppable might of Heaven *and* a plucky underdog spirit.

But more than anything, Michael found these martial excesses depressing. Everyone seemed to be under the impression that this war *would* happen, without any real consideration of whether it *should* happen. The Archangels plotting proceedings in the Empyrium had now become entirely suckered into their little plans. Even Raphael, an angel of healing, seemed to be treating it as a sad inevitability and kept himself focused on the glories of Heaven certain to come afterwards.

Michael, unable to bear their naivety any longer, had come outside into the streets, only to be assaulted by these gaudy and bellicose parades. And the cheering! The people of Heaven were actually cheering this nonsense.

A hand gripped his elbow. He turned to find Eltiel suddenly beside him.

"Oh, Eltiel," said Michael and cleared his throat. "About earlier, the thing with the genitals. You see, when I was on Earth, I was cursed with a set of manly parts and I had somewhat become attached to them. Literally. And—"

"I am sure that if I was blessed with a male member," said Eltiel smoothly, "I would be just as keen to show it off to other people."

"I wasn't showing it off. That really isn't my thing."

Eltiel held up a gentle silencing hand. "I must talk to you about something else."

"Oh."

"There is a visitor at the gates of the city."

"What visitor?"

Eltiel looked uncomfortable. "The Adversary."

"Jeremy?"

"I ... suppose so," said the sparkly angel uncertainly. "It's best if you come."

Together, they hurried through the increasing crowds to one of the twelve gates of the Celestial City. The gate itself was oddly quiet, and Michael didn't see the reason why until they were through the grand arch and on the other side, in the fields of Limbo.

There were no more dead souls entering the Celestial City. A long and mostly patient line of souls stretched out into the mists of Limbo. The considerable team of angels who would otherwise have been greeting people, offering them a handy welcome pack in the language of their choice and keys to their initial accommodation within the city, were now marching back and forth with placards held high above them.

"This would be the Respectful Alliance of Gate Keepers and Greeters," said Michael, trying to read some of the placards as they passed. "*Job Security in a Post-Death World? No Work Without a Comprehensive Redundancy Package?*"

"I think the brush strokes on some of those is simply delightful," said Eltiel. "Say what you will about the liberal arts, but training in calligraphy and illumination is a skillset you will treasure for eternity."

"They've downed tools completely?" said Michael.

"It has been pointed out that once the world has been destroyed, there will be no call for any of these angels to retain their current role."

"Ah," said Michael, not sure if he'd been the one doing the pointing out. When a passing angel – Myakos, that was his name – gave a cheery wave and a thumbs up to him, Michael did his best to ignore him.

"No dead, no jobs," said Eltiel. "I'm sure they'll be reassigned, but people do get comfortable in their existing roles."

"Yes... And you'd like me to do what about this, exactly?"

"Oh, no," said Eltiel and pulled him on. "Your visitor is over there. Quick, before he actually gets here."

Some distance out, striding to the side of the ever-growing queue of the newly dead, was a figure. Michael stepped out to meet him, then hesitated. If that was Jeremy Clovenhoof he'd undergone a considerable transformation since he'd thrown in his lot with Hell's forces. He was dressed in a white angelic robe and— Had he grown taller? And more handsome?

"Lucifer?" Michael whispered. He realised he had come to a total stop; and further, if he was going to meet Lucifer, he'd rather do it as far from the walls of the Celestial City as possible. He hurried forward.

"Jeremy? Is that you?"

The two angels stopped a respectable distance from one another. This new Jeremy was indeed taller, taller than Michael in fact, and Michael found himself automatically straightening up to his own, slightly less impressive full height.

"Is it me?" said the fallen angel with a sneer. "Jeremy Clovenhoof was just an alias, a grubby disguise, a lecherous lothario with a paunch and a fungal infection in his hoofs. I underwent a radical transformation, detoxified of the petty demons and serpentine attributes that have been piled upon me."

"Ah," said Michael, understanding. "So, now you are just Lucifer."

"The bringer of light, first among the angels, the Almighty's greatest creation."

He held himself in a formal and heroic pose, as if he was taking publicity shots for the role of Superman. Michael couldn't help but notice that he wore a robe well. For such a shapeless garment, Lucifer always seemed to carry it like a perfectly tailored suit.

"I thought it best to come see what we might do to avoid this war," said Lucifer.

"Yes. Good," said Michael. "My chaps back there seem hellbent – well, heavenbent – on making sure this thing happens."

"As do the armies of Hell. They have been breeding up new troops in preparation. Their numbers are impressive."

"Breeding up demons?"

"Don't—" said Lucifer, a hand raised. "It is messy and

unseemly and I wouldn't want to taint your innocent mind with the images I have seen."

"This war doesn't need to happen at all," said Michael. "I've been to the Centre for Scriptural Exegesis to ask about the signs and wotnot required for Armageddon, and frankly, Holy Scripture gives us no hard and fast rules. If all Heaven's scholars cannot even agree on how many Horsemen there are, or even how many Wise Men visited the infant Son of God, then I don't see how anyone can be certain the Last Days are upon us at all."

"Interesting," said Lucifer.

"And clearly," said Michael with a wave, "if the scholars in charge wanted to declare that the Apocalypse is off, then they could do so. So it is writ, so will it be."

Lucifer stroked his handsome chin and arched a handsome eyebrow. "And what is 'clearly'?" he said, mirroring Michael's gesture.

"Pardon?"

"You know something."

Michael shuffled his feet. "I might be marginally responsible for – no, not responsible. I might have borne witness to the event that caused your recent transformation."

"Do tell."

"St Jerome is such an excitable figure, and I think he was only trying to make a point."

"Michael..."

"And I had no idea that it would have such a physical effect on you."

"Spit it out, brother!"

Michael sighed. "He sanctioned an interpretation of

scripture in which the Serpent and Satan and Lucifer were to be treated as distinct individuals."

"Sanctioned how?"

Michael shrugged. "Wrote it down, stuck it in one of his tubes."

"Tubes?"

"You know – *slurrrp-pop!* – one of those pneumatic tubes in the scriptorium."

"Interesting." Lucifer smiled. Oh, it was a handsome smile, but also a cruel one. Michael remembered it now and it sent a shiver down his spine.

"So," said Michael, trying to keep his tone bright and breezy, "it's up to us to stop this war."

"Indeed," said Lucifer. "And there seems to be an easy way to do that."

"Is there? Oh, good. Excellent."

Lucifer gestured past Michael to the Celestial City. "Lay down your arms, agree that my claims to the Throne of Heaven are legitimate, and there will be no need for any bloodshed."

The gears crunched and slipped in Michael's mind and, for a moment, he was speechless.

"B-b— What?"

"I am prepared to put the past aeons behind us," said Lucifer. "I am willing to be merciful. The last time we fought, I had one third of the angels on my side. Those angels still exist, in Hell, and they have grown powerful and resentful. And I have every demon brought into creation since then. Hell has grown. Heaven has not. You will lose the war."

"I thought we were trying to stop the war!" said Michael shrilly.

"Stop it before it starts, Michael. Make peace. Surrender. I will demand reparations for the wrongs I have suffered, but they will be small."

"No. No. This is not how this is supposed to go, Jeremy. We want no war, no change. We want to keep things as they are."

"Really?" sneered Lucifer. "Take a moment to look at the world your humans inhabit. Wars rage on several continents. Plagues sweep across the globe. Greed and venality create injustice and misery for man and beast alike. There is no goodness to be found in the world or in the hearts of men. The Creator made a mistake, and I have come to unmake that mistake."

There was suddenly a sword in Lucifer's hand. Its silvered blade gleamed so brightly it might have been composed of pure light. With a gentle press of his feet, Lucifer was aloft and his wings spread like a mighty gleaming eagle.

"If you fight me, Michael, you will lose," said Lucifer in a reverberating and amplified voice – the sort that would win a Sound Design film award. "And the Almighty will cower before me!"

A single flap of his wings and Lucifer shot up, rolled across the non-sky of Limbo and soared back towards Hell.

Michael watched him go, all the while trying to find the words that summed up his feelings about the current situation.

"Oh, fuck!" he muttered in bitter misery.

· · ·

Rutspud had barely made any progress back towards Hell when he saw the angel Lucifer returning. It was a white dot in a white sky and almost invisible but then, as it grew and grew, it gathered form and definition until it was quite clearly the angel Lucifer, the First of the Fallen, swooping back towards Hell.

"Mr Lucifer! Mr Lucifer, sir!" Rutspud yelled and waved his hands, but the angel ignored him completely and zoomed on.

"Typical," said Rutspud under his breath and staggered on.

His next step was to either find Lucifer wherever he now was in Hell, or go find Belphegor and tell him why it was never a good idea to send a stumpy-legged demon to pursue a winged angel. The cunningness of this step revolved around the correct wording to portray Rutspud's failure as a managerial failure on Belphegor's part.

It would have to wait though, for Rutspud could see a matter needing more urgent attention. One involving Cerberus and the Scapegoat.

The giant demon dog was chained up on a high ledge by the entrance, constantly straining at his bonds, snapping at the air, and generally being the poster boy for all Hell's infernal horrors. He was sort of like those posters of bikini-clad women that used to displayed outside strip clubs and lap-dancing parlours in years gone by: an entirely unrealistic and optimistic advertisement for the experiences one might enjoy inside.

Also up on that high ledge with the devil dog was a black

goat which was— Well, it could only be described as waving its arse provocatively in the dog's faces.

"Satan's balls!" yelled Rutspud, in anger more than surprise, and scrambled up the volcanic rock surface to get to the ledge.

Cerberus's jaws snapped. All three of them, like the click of monstrous castanets and the Scapegoat whisked its rear end away just in time and ran in circles bleating fearfully beyond the limit of the dog's chain.

"What in Hell's name are you doing?!" Rutspud screamed.

The Scapegoat spun round giddily and tried to focus on Rutspud.

"Are you drunk?" said Rutspud.

"He told me to do it," said the Scapegoat, waggling his bearded chin at the shadows by the wall, where Rutspud now saw the Serpent coiled, its tail wound about a half-drunk plastic bottle of what appeared to be very cheap cider.

"He told me to tease the dog," said the Scapegoat. "He said it would be fun."

"You should do it again," said the Serpent.

The Scapegoat looked at Rutspud. "Should I?"

"No!" said Rutspud. "Cerberus will eat you."

"I think you should do it," said the Serpent.

"You both make convincing arguments," said the goat.

"Here," said the Serpent and offered the bottle to the goat. "Drink while you think."

Rutspud dashed the bottle away. It spun off the ledge, splashes of cider sizzling on hot rocks. "I can't leave you two alone for a minute! I mean, apple cider? Ten out of ten for thematic consistency, Mr Serpent, but where did you even get that stuff?"

"I can tell you ... for a price," said the Serpent. "We're going to take up smoking next."

Conjured from nowhere, a zippo cigarette lighter danced in the grip of his tail.

"No drinking and no smoking!" said Rutspud.

The Scapegoat chewed and swallowed the roll-up cigarette that was already between its lips.

Rutspud growled in frustration. Above them, straining uselessly against his iron leash, Cerberus also growled, although with much more saliva.

"Oh, I agree with you," said Rutspud. "You! And you! With me!"

"And what if we refuse?" said the Serpent.

Rutspud lashed out and had the Serpent by what he guessed was its throat (although, he wasn't sure if the snake was all throat, or where that throat ended and the rest of Serpent began). Hissing, the Serpent wrapped its coils around Rutspud's arm and squeezed.

"Yeah, yeah," said Rutspud. "Try it, sunshine. I'm not one for threats but, to be clear, I am less frightened of you than I am of being held responsible for losing you. So, you either come with me as a live Serpent or as natty snakeskin belt."

"You would dare hurt me?" said the Serpent in a violent hiss.

Rutspud gave it some thought. "I would. I'd just blame goat legs here."

The Scapegoat opened its mouth to complain, then

gagged and turned its head to throw up an ill-advised lunch of cider and cigarettes.

"Right, this way," said Rutspud. With the Serpent in one hand and the goat's horn in the other, he led them in search of Belphegor and Lucifer.

34

Nerys and Ben had been on the road for what felt like hours, but that was partly down to it being a very boring drive. Now they were only a few miles away from the sea, Nerys felt as if she was going to explode with frustration at their break in the journey.

"Never thought I'd get to see it in real life!" breathed Ben, waving at the view. "Isn't it amazing?"

Nerys stared out at the lumpy field where they stood. It looked to her like countless other lumpy fields they had driven past on the way down the A14, but she wasn't about to burst Ben's bubble. Once he had soaked up all of the history he wanted, then they could move on.

"Sutton Hoo. It's such a famous site. The burial, the story, the ship!" Ben was giddy with excitement, turning on the spot, clearly seeing so much more in his mind's eye.

It took Nerys another half an hour to coax him gently

back into the car and get back on the road. They had decided that the small town of Southwold was a decent destination, because it faced the North Sea, and had a museum that Ben wanted to see.

Nerys found the car park had a view of the sea, if she looked in between the beach huts. That suited her fine, because the wind was brisk and chilly.

"You go and find your museum and we can meet up for a cup of tea over there in an hour or so, yeah?" said Nerys.

Ben shot off eagerly in search of automata, and Nerys retrieved the Wish-O-Matic.

"Right, let's begin. Now let me make it clear from the start that I want balance and sustainability to be achieved with what I am asking for here. I would like a big island to be created, on the site of what used to be called Doggerland. Don't you dare make it cause a tidal wave or anything bad like that! When the island is in place, it should have a rich and vibrant ecosystem, completely untainted. There should be a bridge for access, you can put it here in front of where I am, please, so that I can take a look. Now to be clear, it should have native species, no alpacas. Also, there should be no wolves and bears even if they are native." She thought for a moment. "One final thing, just to make the trip worthwhile for Ben, can we have a real life version of the Sutton Hoo ship out there too?"

Nerys sat back in the seat of her car and looked out at the grey horizon. She wanted to see the moment when the Wish-O-Matic made things happen. Then she realised she had somehow missed it. Instead of a grey horizon where sky met sea, there was land in its place. It extended much further to either side than she was able to see. She got out of the car and walked forwards. Sure enough there was a footbridge right in front of her.

She should wait for Ben. She suspected he wouldn't be long, but she stood at the entrance to the footbridge to make sure nobody else crossed it before she did. She spotted a cone in the car park. Just as she returned to the footbridge with the cone, Ben appeared wild eyed and running. "Did you see what happened?"

"I saw that we now have a big island, as we discussed." She waved at the footbridge. "Shall we go and have a look?"

"But there's a cone." Ben pointed.

"It's fine. We're allowed."

Ben looked incredibly confused, but he followed as Nerys led the way, placing the cone behind them as they stepped onto the footbridge. The power of the cone over the British public was well known. It would buy them some time.

It didn't take them long to cross over to the island, it was only a few hundred yards, but it was like entering a different world. The footbridge was the only man-made structure in sight. There were no paths, so for a few minutes they drifted around the shoreline, but then decided they needed to enter the forested area.

"If the island's new, how does it have mature trees growing on it?" asked Ben. "And that's not the only question I have. None of this makes any sense. How did it happen? Did you make it happen?"

"I sort of did make it happen," said Nerys. "I know some clever people, and they are helping me to improve the world.

Here we are with loads of lovely wildlife, in a place where it ought to survive. This is good, isn't it?"

"It's good for wildlife, sure. It's probably not quite so good for the Harwich ferry."

Nerys looked at him in horror. "A ferry?" She tried to remember exactly how she'd phrased the wish. She hadn't thought of ferries, but surely she had made it clear that no harm should be done? "There's a window in the front, where the driver can see out, surely? For crying out loud Ben, you could have mentioned that before!"

Ben gave her a look and walked on. "There are definitely more insects here," he said, wafting a big dragonfly from in front of his face.

"Excellent! Yes. I think it's a positive thing. Maybe we could make some more of these islands. They could be like breeding grounds for wildlife or something."

"I wonder if it will be like the alpacas all over again," said Ben thoughtfully. "There's the question of ownership. Everybody will want a piece of this."

"Well they can't have a piece of it, it's mine, I made it!" said Nerys.

"I suspect the law might view things differently. You don't have any kind of paper trail, do you?"

"I might have in a little while," said Nerys. She could get the Wish-O-Matic to conjure some up, surely?

"Ooh look, a hedgehog!" she said, crouching and pointing to the base of a tree where a mossy rock sat on the edge of a tiny stream. She stood up suddenly. "And a little lizardy thing too."

"I think that might be a newt," said Ben and then grinned. "Go on, say it's yours, like the island."

"Eh?"

"Just say it."

"It's my newt," said Nerys.

"It's not that small, it's just the right size," said Ben, mouth agape foolishly, waiting for her gales of laughter.

"Did you get that out of a cracker?" she sighed. "Anyway, I don't need to know what all these things are, I just need to know they're doing their job. Trees making fresh air and insects being food and doing their pollinating." Nerys dusted her hands together, confident she was making progress at last.

They turned to go back, but as they emerged from the treeline, Ben stopped in his tracks.

"No. Wait."

Nerys looked and saw that the Sutton Hoo ship was pulled up on the beach in front of them. It looked like a brand new construction, ready to take to the water. "Oh yeah, I thought you might get a kick out of this. Cool isn't it?"

"No. Oh my god. Do you understand what this means? We've gone back in time, Nerys. We're time travellers."

"What? No we haven't. Really." Nerys had not seen that coming.

"We've gone back to the times of the Anglo Saxon kings. This is so wrong! Time travel is fraught with difficulty! What if we meet ourselves?" Ben wailed.

"Ben, we all know how rubbish I am at history, but I am pretty sure you were not alive when it was Anglo Saxon king time. So how are you going to meet yourself?"

He went to the ship and touched the wood. "See, the oak is brand new! We must be in the eighth century."

"No, seriously. No time travel has happened. Look at me. Look at us. Do we look as if we belong in the eighth century? What about all of them, huh?"

She nodded towards the opposite shore, where the people of Southwold had lined up to stare at the shocking changes.

"I guess we probably spoiled their view a bit," said Nerys. "But look, the town is the same. Did they have beach huts and a pier in the eighth century?"

Ben looked. "No," he said in a small voice.

As Ben spent time admiring the ship Nerys began to fear it had been a mistake to ask for it. The distraction was too much.

"Come on. I need to get a feel for how big this island is. Any idea how we can tell?"

Ben reluctantly stepped away from the ship and looked thoughtful. "A bird's eye view would be handy. Someone local with a drone would probably— Ah, look!"

He pointed at a dot in the sky, rising from the end of the pier sticking out from the shoreline where the crowd was gathered.

"Ooh, somebody over there must be controlling it. Let's go and see what they can see."

They hurried back over the footbridge and found a crowd of people hovering just the other side of the cone.

"I must insist that you stay clear of this area!" said Nerys as she approached. "We have conducted an initial assessment, but further investigation is required. Do not, I repeat do not cross over this bridge!"

She swaggered past the crowd, trying to make bold assertive eye contact with as many of them as she could. It was inevitable that people would go to the new island, but she wanted to keep them away while she checked for unintended consequences.

They pushed through the crowds on the pier.

"Look there, that's the one with the drone!" Ben said.

There was a girl of about twelve operating the controls, while another stood alongside her with a tablet which showed the feed from the drone's camera.

"Can you see how big it is?" asked Nerys, leaning in.

"Back off lady, you'll get answers at the same time as everybody else," said the girl.

Nerys bit down on a retort, because she badly wanted the girl to co-operate. "Ben," she whispered. "How big is the area of Doggerland?"

Ben wrinkled his nose. "It was massive, I think. You could walk to most of Northern Europe thousands of years ago."

"So, how big? Bigger than the Isle of Wight?" Nerys waved her arms in a vague gesture. She had no real idea how big the Isle of Wight was, but she needed some sort of ball park.

"Loads bigger. I think it might have been bigger than England."

"Oh." She peered across to where the drone's camera was still pulling back and the new land continued to fill the screen.

"I'm at maximum height," announced the girl with the

drone. "We're at one hundred and twenty metres, and even if I turn the camera around I can't see the edges of that thing. Apart from this one here, where we are."

Nerys and Ben watched the tablet screen and saw that the lush green island extended way beyond what the drone was able to see. As the view swung round and displayed the town, it was clear this was quite an expansive view.

The crowd pressed forward, as everyone wanted to see, so Nerys backed away slightly. As she did, she briefly caught sight of someone through the sea of faces and frowned. A tall man with sideburns. She adjusted her position, trying to see him properly, but she lost sight of him in the crush.

"Come on Ben, let's get out of here."

They headed for a cafe and as they went inside there was the overhead swoosh of a low flying jet.

"Of course, the military will be assessing this," said Ben.

The television in the cafe was showing the news.

"*—reports of a gigantic new land mass off the coast of Britain. It appeared earlier today and appears to extend around most of the eastern counties. Remarkably, it appeared without causing any disturbance, and no significant seismic events have been detected. The government have issued no statements, but are believed to be assessing any threat to the UK.*"

They ordered a cup of tea and sat in silence for a short while.

"So, Nerys, what is the threat level?" asked Ben. "Whoever can make stuff like this happen is pretty threatening, if you ask me."

"Only if they had bad intentions," said Nerys. "I'm definitely getting the hang of it now."

Ben looked worried and confused. "We should head back to Birmingham soon," he said. "It seems as though it's got a little bit busy over here."

"No, I have unfinished business. I need to make sure the military don't do anything reckless with the island. I'd like to go back over there and check out a couple of things."

When they reached the footbridge, the crowd around it was very much larger than when they left it. There was a policeman guarding the entrance.

"Let us past please," said Nerys to the policeman. "Good job by the way, securing the bridge."

"I've been told not to let anybody across here," said the policeman. "It's been identified as a potential threat, so we need to isolate it."

"Do you know who I am?" said Nerys. "I am the owner. I am in charge. Let me past now!"

"Sorry, I have my orders." The policeman put his hand to his belt. It would have been a menacing gesture if he was the sort of cop who carried a gun, but as far as Nerys could tell he was threatening to use his radio.

Nerys strode off. "Come on Ben, we need to come up with a plan B."

"It looks like the only way over," said Ben.

Nerys pointed once she could see the sign she had spotted earlier. "There, look."

"A boating lake? You have got to be kidding me!" said Ben. "We're stealing a boat?"

"Yep. Let's go."

Once they got the boat into the sea, they each took an oar

and tried to work as a team, quickly abandoning that idea as they just kept going in circles.

"Let me," said Nerys, shuffling across the narrow bench seat. "You go over there."

Nerys took up the rowing and eventually found the correct rhythm. There were shouts from the shore as they were spotted, but Nerys ignored them. The boating lake had been pretty much abandoned as everyone gawked at the island, and all they'd done was borrow a boat.

35

"That looked awfully like the old Lucifer, didn't it?" said Eltiel to Michael, in the manner of one who was absolutely sure it was the old Lucifer, but wanted someone to tell him otherwise.

"I suppose it did," said Michael as they strode back through the city, unwilling to give Eltiel either the confirmation or denial he needed.

Michael was deeply troubled by this latest turn of events. In the more open arena of his conscious thoughts, he told himself he shouldn't be concerned. Michael had faced Lucifer before and had won. It had been Lucifer who had rebelled against the Almighty in the first place; Lucifer who had faced Michael in the first War in Heaven, and whom Michael had thrown down into Hell in the first place. However, in the more furtive niches of Michael's subconscious, he quietly admitted he had become very used to the more earthy persona of Satan: the one who had become Jeremy Clovenhoof. For all his faults, his many *many* personality flaws and uncontrolled passions, Clovenhoof was someone who could be reasoned with. Lucifer had firmly held beliefs and the utter conviction that he was right. Such people were almost impossible to deal with.

"You had no problem defeating the old Lucifer," said Eltiel, encouragingly.

"I was hoping not to have to fight him at all," said Michael.

"Really?"

"Still hoping."

Michael felt sure there was yet a way to bring all of this to a halt. If the Research Centre for Scriptural Exegesis held within itself the power to say what was and what was not, that same power could call off the Apocalypse. Failing that, Michael would find the holy Throne and plead to the Almighty Himself. Such a desperate ploy was unlikely to work. The Almighty might be a personal God, close to each and every one of his subjects, but he was aloof and inscrutable nonetheless.

Michael needed to convince his fellow archangels of the righteousness of his actions, assemble St Jerome and whichever scribes had the power to make changes. Something simple would be fine. A basic *"And lo, the signs of Armageddon were a false alarm and the Earth remained untroubled for another million years."* How hard could that be?

He practically ran up the steps to the Empyrium and into the vast meeting room, only to find the place vacated. The maps remained laid out on the long table, but the Archangels were gone.

"Bugger."

There was a flap of feet on white marble, and St Francis of Assisi came running into the room from an inner door.

"I told you they had gone, sir!" said the attendant angel following after him.

"But Michael is still here. He will be able to help me," said Francis, trying to keep hold of the scrolls that were gathered under his arms.

"Where have they gone?" Michael asked the attendant. "Gabriel, Samael, Raphael?"

"To the stadium, sir," said the angel. "To watch the dress rehearsal."

"Dress rehearsal. Right." He turned on his heel to leave.

"Wait! Wait!" cried St Francis. "I have to show you my plans."

"Do you?" said Michael, already walking.

Francis hurried to catch up and match pace with Michael. "The Wapture."

"The Wapture? I mean, the Rapture? What of it?"

"Gabwiel was vewy insistent that I dwaw up plans for how we would look after the pets of the saved when the Wapture occurs."

"Was he?" said Michael.

"At any moment, the blessed of Earth might be bodily lifted up in Heaven, but their poor cats and dogs and wabbits and guinea pigs... What is to become of them?"

"Ah, right. That," said Michael. "It's not at the top of my list of priorities right now, Francis."

There was more than one stadium in the vast Celestial City. The dead came to their final reward still clinging to their interests and hobbies, just like Francis with his unseemly and fervent passions for animal kind, and so the Celestial City maintained spaces for sports, ranging from Olympic athletics to horse racing to football. However, the biggest and grandest stadium was but a short walk from the Empyrium, and Michael headed towards it with some certainty.

"Gabwiel commanded I dwaw up plans and I have done so," insisted Francis. He thrust a scroll into Michael's hand. "I pwopose employing an organisation to act as emergency pet carer for all the animals. There are millions of pets to pwovide cover for, and in the time we have wemaining to us I simply don't think we can start wecwuiting pet-sitters one by one."

"Do you know how much time we have remaining?" said Michael.

St Francis forced a chuckle. "No one will know the day or the hour, Michael, but I stwongly get a sense things are accelewating."

Michael found himself irritated by the fact that Francis was right. The impending war and Heaven's military build-up were feeding into each other in a rapid and vicious circle.

They rounded a corner and the stadium was before them. It had a look of the Colosseum in Rome about it – or rather, a child's inflated dream of what the Colosseum looked like. Its arched walls were higher than any earthly masonry could stand. The pennants on the tops of the walls were little more than colourful pinpricks from way down here.

Michael hurried to the nearest entrance arch.

"So, I wanted to wun my plan past you," said Francis.

"Yeah, yeah, sure," said Michael disinterested.

Francis unfurled the scroll held between him and Michael. "There is this organisation, *Honk if you're Helpful*."

"Pardon?"

"I think it's something to do with geese. They wun this service on the internet. I am familiar with the internet, you know. And you can log a wequest for someone to help you with a task. It's fwee as well. Not a paid service. It's wun by this woman in England, and I can see she clearly loves animals. Look at her here, suwwounded by friendly alpacas."

"Right," said Michael, not really listening. He pressed on through the shady tunnel. There was much shouting and noise from ahead.

"So, all I need to do is to get a team of angels – I should say ten thousand – to log calls on this website—"

"Ten thousand?"

"Do you know how many pets there are on Earth. There are half a billion dogs alone."

"Really? You surprise me."

"And nearly as many cats."

"I see. Will even ten thousand angels logging calls be enough?"

"My thoughts exactly," said Francis. "But, with your say-so, I can get the team to log those initial wequests for help, and have a team of caring but damned individuals on stand-by to help the pets of those who have been whisked off to Heaven."

Michael thought of the massive and growing queue of people already waiting to get into Heaven. He struggled to comprehend what the sudden arrival of all the faithful of Earth would do to that queue.

Even if there were only a billion faithful on Earth (and there were certainly much more than that!) then such a queue would stretch for hundreds of thousands of miles, round and round the Celestial City many times over. Even if the newly dead were able to walk straight into the City without any congestion and delays, such a queue would take — He did a little mental calculation. Such a queue would take decades to filter through. Those protesting angels on the gates had little to worry about. They had job security for a long time to come yet.

"So, is it all wight if I do it?" said Francis.

"What? Yes. Sure. Go ahead," said Michael, letting go of his end of the scroll.

"Vewy good," said Francis and hurried away from the stadium.

Michael emerged from the tunnel into the stadium proper and stared up in horror at the skies above. Gone were the bright but sunless skies of Heaven, replaced now by towering and rolling clouds of black and steel blue. Red lightning crackled between the clouds. Far in the distance, great shapes moved above the horizon, mountains and islands ripped from the sea and tossed up to become an asteroid belt over his head. Over there, a squadron of angels, as dense as a swarm of flies, flew down in perfect formation, spears ready. And straight ahead, barrelling out of the tempestuous clouds, came four figures on horseback. They were spectral giants, as tall as the highest skyscrapers. The horse's hoofs pounded the earth like bomb blasts. The shaking of their reins was like thundercracks and the riders' weapons swung about as though each sweep would harvest a thousand souls.

Michael was pinned to the spot, awestruck.

"*Cut!*" yelled a voice and the massive spectacle froze and came apart. The clouds dissipated, the lightning ceased. The angelic horde dropped their attack pose and hovered in place, before breaking apart into chatty social groups. And the four horsemen became four mere horsemen, trotting along the oval race track of the stadium. Down by the centre, three archangels were gathered alongside a small army of human helpers.

A balding, broad-shouldered man in a loosely-buttoned white shirt put a loudspeaker to his mouth. "Famine, what do you call that?"

"Sorry, Mr DeMille?" said the man on the black horse, wheeling about.

"The thing with your scales!"

"I was swinging them about, threatening-like, sir!"

"It's a set of weighing scales, not a whip!"

"Yes, sir!"

"Right! From the top!"

Michael wandered over. "How's it going?" he asked.

Gabriel turned to him with a scowl on his face. "Actors!" he said witheringly.

The director looked Michael's way. His face, more controlled than Gabriel's, nonetheless revealed a man operating on the last shreds of his patience.

"I've directed Victor Mature and Charlton Heston. I have cast down the temple of the Philistines and brought forth the

Ten Plagues of Egypt. You would think it would be easier to tell a convincing story with the real deal."

"Our director is a perfectionist," said Raphael.

"I think there should be more death," said Samael.

"Oh, there will be more than enough of that when the time comes," said Michael wearily. "Listen, guys, I really need to—"

"This production sure needs something else," said the director. "You! Horsemen! One, two, three, four. Get over here!"

The horsemen of the Apocalypse, now reduced to a far more conventional size, clip-clopped over.

"There have been so many horse operas on the big screen that no horse is going to strike the fear of God into the hearts of sinners," said the director.

"You want us to be more … horsey?" suggested the rider with the sword.

"You want us to try something else?" said Gabriel.

"Motorbikes," said Samael. "I like motorbikes, especially when they don't wear protective gear."

"Pah!" spat the director.

"Look, maybe we don't need this at all," Michael tried to put in. "Guys, I know how we can stop this."

"Stop this?" said the director. "We are in production here, gentlemen."

"Exactly," said Gabriel with a caustic look for Michael. "Events in the world below are threatening to overtake us. Signs have been seen."

"Oh, there's always signs," said Michael witheringly.

"Plagues of insects," said Samael.

"Marauding herds of alpaca is what I heard," said Raphael.

"Alpaca," frowned Gabriel. "Not a traditional creature of the Apocalypse."

"I'm sure it would have appeared in scripture if there had been any in the Holy Land, back in the day."

"What are these alpaca things?" asked the director, putting his megaphone on his hip.

"A strange looking creature," said Raphael.

"Strange, you say."

"Hang on," said Michael and scrolled on his phone. "Jeremy's hideous pet formed from Limbo stuff has something of an alpaca-esque air about it. Here." He held up Clovenhoof's selfie for the director to see.

"Well, I'll be—" said the director, his brow going up in interested surprise.

36

In Jeremy Clovenhoof's old flat, Spartacus Wilson leaned back and ate a slice of cold leftover pizza. There was a special pleasure in day-old pizza. It wasn't as nice as fresh, greasy, cheese sticking to the top of the box pizza, but there was a unique minor pleasure in the congealed cheese of leftovers.

The mouthful he'd just torn off suddenly became a claggy mess in his mouth as one, then two, then dozens of warning messages popped up on his screen.

He swallowed hard and shouted. *"Hodshift!"*

Nerys's weird, squat helper friend came waddling in from the next room. He was a peculiar man, and not just in appearance. His attitude to the world, and his knowledge of it, was oddly lopsided. He seemed to know lots about some things and almost nothing about the most obvious facts of existence.

"So, let me get this straight," Hodshift said. "There are

business enterprises devoted to making paper to wipe your arses with, and they will spend a sizeable proportion of their wealth on televisual advertisements telling people why their arse paper is better than everyone else's?"

"What? Never mind that. Look at this?"

Hodshift peered over his shoulder. Onscreen, the *Honk if you're Helpful* website was being destroyed in real time.

"It's a distributed denial of service attack," said Hodshift.

"I know that!" said Spartacus. "But who is doing this to us?"

The website was being flooded with requests. In one corner of the screen, some of the requests popped up briefly before being pushed away.

"Noah Williams – cat sitter required. Maria Francisca – cat sitter. Yino Lee. Avigail Mayer. Felipe Gonzalez – in Argentina? – dog sitter required." Spartacus frowned. "They're from all over the world, and they're all requests to look after pets." He clicked on one and peered closer. "*To look after my dog after the Rapture.*" He turned to Hodshift. "What's the Rapture?"

Hodshift murmured unhappily. "I suspect this is Nerys's doing."

"Most things are."

Hodshift looked about. "Where is she, anyway?"

BEN AND NERYS dragged the boat onto the island and made their way into the forest.

"What do you need to do?" asked Ben. "You do know that it will be dark within an hour, don't you?"

"Yep. Totally knew that," lied Nerys. "Don't worry, you'll get to sleep in your own bed tonight. I just want to make sure this place is secure from interference."

"Uh huh." Ben sounded very much as if he didn't believe her.

Nerys had a more pressing need as well. She was convinced that weird priest vigilante was following her, so she needed to cut him off. Being on an isolated island seemed like a great idea, but it was short on amenities.

"You used to like watching Bear Grylls on the telly, Ben. How much do you remember?" Nerys asked.

"Only enough to know we would be really uncomfortable if we were stuck here after dark," said Ben. "We don't even know if there are predators here."

"Ah, wait! Yes we do," said Nerys. "There are no wolves or bears, so we should be fine. Doggerland wouldn't have any other kind of predator, would it?"

Ben gave a hollow laugh. "If you went back to when it was actually Doggerland you'd have sabre toothed tigers, but we should be safe from those."

Nerys kept her mouth clamped tightly shut.

"Nerys? I don't know what you know about all this, but tell me there's no chance we will meet a sabre toothed tiger."

Nerys was silent as she had no idea.

"If this island is as massive as I think it is, and if it's just been conjured into existence – which is completely mad, by the way – how do you suppose it's been designed?" asked Ben. "Do you think every part of this forest is unique, or if we walk around enough will we see repeating patterns, like a cookie cutter approach? Design a patch of forest and then copy and paste it until the island is filled?"

"Of all the questions I might have if I was in your position, Ben, I don't think that one would make the top thousand. Are you actually going to see whether you can spot any similarities?"

"I think I need to do something to stop myself going mad. I still don't really know why I'm here. I don't know why you're here either. What *are* we doing laying claim to a brand new island? If it's for nature, why don't we just go away and leave it to the wild things?"

"Because we can't trust people not to come and mess it all up. I'm just thinking about ways to protect it." Nerys needed a moment to herself. "Call of nature, I'll be behind that tree over there."

Ben looked unhappy about being left on his own, but Nerys knew just the thing to make him feel better. She brought the Wish-O-Matic out of her pocket and thought carefully about what she was asking for. "Right, I'd like our house to be here, please. Hereabouts will be great, although don't squash us underneath it obviously." Nerys thought about getting something to eat, she was pretty hungry. "My fridge needs some food in it, as if I've been for a big shop. Another thing I'd like is for the whole island to have some sort of force field, so that other people and their aeroplanes can't get here. Big force field, right?"

Nerys emerged from behind her tree and found Ben goggling at their house which was now directly in front of them.

"Nerys, I don't know how you're doing this stuff, but it's

freaky and I don't like it." Ben waved his arms manically. "Have I taken drugs? Look at this! Is there a gap in Boldmere where our house should be? Are there two of them now? How does this even work?"

"I have no idea," said Nerys.

"I've been in a car crash, haven't I? I've been in an accident and all this is a big dream I'm having."

Nerys looked up at the house. "At least now we have a base of operations. Come on, I need a glass of wine."

Nerys spread out food for them both after she checked her fridge was filled. There was something that looked like a whole ham studded with cloves taking up a lot of space. The Wish-O-Matic's idea of a 'big shop' was some sort of cartoon feast.

She was slightly sad to discover Twinkle wasn't in the flat, which Ben declared was proof that this house was a copy. At least it was a copy with snacks.

"Stilton, beef wellington, and prawn vol au vents to start. Shall we put on the telly?"

"The electricity is working," said Ben. "Water is coming out of the taps. How is any of this possible?"

Nerys shrugged and turned on the television. There was a map behind the newsreader showing the extent of the new island. It hugged most of the eastern coastline of England and stretched out towards Europe. There was a highlight showing the bridge at Southwold.

"Look at the size of this thing, it's enormous!" breathed Nerys.

"*—an unexplained barrier that prevents access.*"

There was a brief wobbly clip that showed someone in a

sea canoe glancing off an invisible barrier as they approached the shore.

"Did you hear that?" asked Ben. There was a muffled whump outside.

"I did."

They went to the window. Far above them in the sky was a fading corona of light.

"Did they just fire a missile over here?" Nerys said. It looked like something had exploded and bounced off the forcefield overhead. "They saw a protective shield and thought they'd test it?"

Ben took a hefty swig of advocaat. "I mean the technology for invisible force fields…" he muttered. "Science doesn't even know how to do that."

The front doorbell rang and they looked at each other.

"Just … what now?" Ben said. "I thought no one could get on the island."

"Local wildlife learning how to use doorbells?" suggested Nerys. "I'll see who's there."

She went downstairs and opened the door. It was now fully dark outside, but the light from the hallway illuminated a tall man with wispy grey sideburns. He held a weird shepherd's crook in his hand – weird in that it looked like it had been commissioned by a rapper with all the aesthetic taste of magpie. Gold filigree and diamond bling crowded its sparkly top.

"Deacon Phipps. How did you get here?"

"You cannot shake me demon," he said. "By hook or by crook or, indeed, by pedalo, I shall hunt you down." He shook his shepherd's crook as he spoke.

Nerys looked around for the pedalo, but guessed it was beached some distance away and had arrived before the forcefield had been put in place.

There was something about him standing at her front door that made Nerys feel as though she should offer him an olive branch. This man did not approve of her for whatever nutso reason, but she could be the bigger person. Probably.

"Would you like to come in?" she asked. There was a clamouring from elsewhere in her brain that insisted it would be a very bad idea, but she forced a smile onto her face and held the door for him.

His face contorted into a grimace of pure disgust. "Come inside this supernatural structure?" he roared. "It is conjured from Hell, is it not?"

Nerys gave a noncommittal shrug. "It came from the same place as the rest of the island that you're standing on."

"If I cross this threshold it will only be to set the entire place ablaze, so that your infernal voice can no longer be heard by the rest of the world."

"Or—" said Nerys carefully with a glance over his shoulder "—you might come in because there's a scary predator behind you. I think it's a sabre toothed tiger."

He gave her a withering look. "You attempt to distract me with tall tales? I am made of sterner stuff than that."

The tiger emerged fully from the tree cover at that point and snarled loudly. Phipps glanced over his shoulder and yelped with horror. He ran inside the door and Nerys slammed it shut.

"Join us in the top flat." She needed to keep an eye on him after his talk of arson. "You don't have to stay, but I might have something to help you to keep that thing at bay. Hey Ben, we have a visitor!"

Ben was on his feet at once, offering his hand. The man looked at it suspiciously and did not shake it.

Nerys poured a glass of advocaat, but Phipps batted it away with the back of his hand. It landed on the carpet, leaving a sticky mess.

"Rude," she said.

Phipps gave her a steely stare. "The tempter came to him and said, 'If you are the Son of God, tell these stones to become bread.' And Jesus answered, 'It is written: Man shall not live on bread alone.'"

"That was advocaat, not bread," said Nerys. "And remember, I just saved you from a sabre toothed tiger."

"What?" Ben yelled. "I knew it! This place is going to kill us all."

Nerys disappeared into the kitchen. She returned with a box. "Here you are, you can take some of this." She held up the box of *Kittee-Off* to show Deacon Phipps. "It's to repel cats. They keep away because they think that some other cat has claimed the territory. We use it to keep cats from getting in the garden and tormenting Twinkle."

"Yeah, we were never sure whether it worked because of the cat thing or because it smells so bad," said Ben. "It's worth a try, though. We should all fill our pockets." Ben dug into the foul-smelling cannister and held some out in his hand.

Phipps wrinkled his nose at the stench. "Hellish demon droppings, no doubt."

Ben checked the side of the cannister. "Apparently there

is lion dung included. Maybe we should rub it to activate the pheromones?" He rubbed it onto his arms, where it left brown streaks.

Phipps recoiled and Nerys groaned.

"What are you doing?" she said to Ben

"What? I don't want to be mauled by a sabre toothed tiger. Hopefully they are nocturnal and in the morning I can get back over the bridge. But in the meantime I'm taking no chances." He smeared more lion poo cat-repellent across his face.

"Ah yes, about the bridge. That might not work," said Nerys.

"She has trapped us here," said Phipps, his eyes narrowed and glittering. "The Antichrist prepares to lay waste to the rest of humanity and protects herself in this cage."

"Nerys?" Ben's voice was uncertain. "Were you planning to lay waste—?"

"—Don't be ridiculous! You know full well I am just trying to help. I could do with a little bit more support if I'm honest, rather than have you start believing the ramblings of the first nutter to rock up."

"Ben, my friend. Join me. We are not in a position to slay her, all we can do is slow down the corruption that she spreads."

With that, Phipps grabbed the television and dashed it to the floor, stomping on the screen to make sure it smashed.

"What are you doing? You absolute cock!" Nerys screamed. "How the hell am I supposed to be spreading corruption through the telly? That doesn't make any sense!"

Phipps looked around, breathing heavily. "We need to cut her off. It's the only way. Join me in the forest, Ben."

"Um, no," said Ben.

Nerys hoped Ben's prompt reply was down to their long-standing friendship, but she suspected the prospect of the scary forest at night played a bigger part.

Phipps turned to the door. He grabbed the poo cannister from Ben, streaking his cheeks and forehead with lion poo. He dashed into the kitchen and Nerys could hear him banging cupboard doors as he searched. He came back out with her laundry drying rack.

"That's my drying rack," said Nerys.

"A man needs a defensive shield!" Phipps declared.

They heard him clatter down the stairs and out of the front door.

"We should make sure the door's locked," said Ben.

They both stood at the front door watching as Phipps ran across towards the treeline. The sabre toothed tiger emerged, as if it had been waiting. Phipps held up the laundry rack and yelled "Back!" as he opened the rack, holding the top, its concertina-expanding legs directed at the beast.

It looked as though it caused more confusion than fear. Phipps opened and closed the rack a few more times, making the metal legs swing in and out. After a moment or two, faced with the rack and the bedazzled crook, the tiger padded away to find an easier meal.

"Huh," said Ben. "Clothes dryer fends off tigers. Useful to know."

37

Hell thrived on a certain form of chaos. It was part of its modus operandi. Its inhabitants occupied every conceivable shape. Its tortures were capricious and inventive beyond belief. Hell had an eternity to present its pains on its occupants and the worst thing it could be was boring and predictable.

However, the bubbling confusion around the gates where the recently damned were to be processed was more chaotic than Rutspud cared to deal with. The Combined Union of Gatekeepers, Bum Pokers, Ancillary Workers and Service Demons had downed tools, and the arrivals checkpoint for Hell was closed. The newly dead, infused with that innate desire to see their queue moving, whatever it was for, were grumbling and protesting at the long wait. It didn't seem to cross their mind what was awaiting on the other side; they were simply filled with that peculiarly human desire to 'just get it over with' even though, in Hell, there was no 'getting over' anything.

The Serpent in one hand and the Scapegoat in the other, Rutspud battled through the lines and up to the picketing workers. Demons were marching back and forth with grubby and singed homemade placards.

"We demand a reasonable and continuous influx of dead for the rest of eternity!" demanded one demon.

"And a thirty percent reduction in the size of bums!" shouted the demon, Pisskettle.

"Less bummage or bigger pitchforks!" shouted the demon, Lynchgill.

One of the thuggish Scrowfrogs added something in a wordless guttural gargle.

"You said it, brother!"

Rutspud wasn't entirely sure who these demands were being shouted to. Every checkpoint demon was on the picket line, and the only other audience were the dead souls. He said as much as he weaved his way through the line.

"Join us!" Lynchgill urged him.

Rutspud looked round. "Frankly, this all looks too much like hard work. And who exactly are you protesting to here?"

"Management!" declared Pisskettle, pointing upwards in an arbitrary direction. "They know we're here and they're hearing every word!"

"I doubt that very much," said Rutspud. "Listen, if you want to be heard, you have to take your grievances directly to them. In fact—" he added as the thought occurred him "—it's not like Lord Peter is even calling the shots on this Armageddon thing, is it?"

"Isn't it?" said Lynchgill.

"It's the goat's fault," said the Serpent.

"Is it?" said Lynchgill.

"Is it?" said the Scapegoat, intrigued and surprised.

"Course not," Rutspud tutted. "Peter runs Hell, but he's just responding to the situation that's arisen. You know who's really in charge?" He pointed toward the entrance to Hell, and figuratively to Limbo and the Celestial City beyond. "So, give it a rest. You're achieving nothing."

Irritated, he pushed on with jeers of "Boo! Scab!" following him.

"I think you should join them," hissed the Serpent.

"I'm too busy to go on strike," said Rutspud. "Who's going to do my work while I'm swanning about doing lofty political rallying?"

"No one," said the Serpent. "That's the point."

"And then who will get the blame when that work's not done, eh?"

"You could always blame me," said the Scapegoat. "It's my lot in life."

"Don't you get tired of being blamed for everything?"

"No," bleated the goat thoughtfully. "It's quite freeing. It's like fish have no word for water."

"Don't they? Has someone asked them?"

Rutspud spent the rest of the walk to Belphegor's R&D offices wondering if, on Earth, there was a marine biologist somewhere with a research grant for studying what words fish did and didn't know. It sounded like the kind of thing Earth scientists could get a grant for.

He met Belphegor just outside the entrance to the ruins

of the Fortress of Nameless Dread. The duke of Hell zipped over the rubble strewn landscape with ease in his powerful wheelchair, the tiny naked red demon riding shotgun on the arm of his chair.

Belphegor counted the fragments of Satan off. "One, two, three. Still lost the fourth?"

"I saw him come back this way, boss. A trip to Heaven and back."

"Sowing discord wherever he goes no doubt."

"How was Lord Peter?" asked Rutspud.

"I attempted to sell him Diddywang here as a potential Antichrist."

"Tallywacker!" declared the red demon happily.

"I take it Lord Peter was not sold on the idea," said Rutspud.

"He has made his choice. There is a woman on Earth using unknown infernal powers to build herself a new kingdom – an island rising out of the sea itself – and who sent a plague of animals and insects out across the world. You know Lord Peter's attitudes to women in positions of power."

"Oh, I do," said Rutspud. "Not a very modern man."

"And the whole 'Jezebel' and 'Whore of Babylon' allegory is one that appeals to him."

"So, a female Antichrist. Progressive."

"I suspect the day and the hour of the Apocalypse will very soon become known to us." Belphegor cast about. "We must find Lucifer and place him at the head of our armies at once."

"I am here," said Lucifer, like an actor hitting his cue

perfectly. The fallen angel touched down lightly on a high rock and folded his magnificent wings behind him.

"Ah, good," said Belphegor.

Rutspud couldn't be sure, but there seemed to be a tiny but noticeable note of fear in Belphegor's voice. It was true that Lucifer was a far more fearsome character than Jeremy Clovenhoof. Clovenhoof, for all his base desires and amoral machinations, was at least ... well, a very human individual. Lucifer acted and spoke with the cold, mad certainty of the most zealous believer.

"I was just saying to Rutspud here that it will soon be time for you to lead your armies into battle."

Lucifer tilted his head in thought. "I have plans."

"The plan is set ... Lord," said Belphegor. "You enter Limbo with the biggest infernal army ever seen at your back and slay the Archangel Michael."

"In time," said Lucifer. "Did you know, in the Celestial City, there is an edifice called the Research Centre for Scriptural Exegesis?"

"I may have heard of it," said Belphegor. "Is it relevant to our plans?"

"Entirely. It appears that a petulant slip of the pen by St Jerome has resulted in the partition of Satan into all these forms, an act which pleases me no end. If it is written then it comes to pass."

"Weenie!" shouted Diddywang in happy agreement.

"You have your Rampant Tunneller machine with which you intend to mount a sneak attack on the Holy City. I now present to you a target."

"Destroy the scriptorium?" said Belphegor.

"Do it, do it," hissed the Serpent.

Lucifer shook his head. "Use it. Whatever is written and processed there becomes religious truth. I believe the mechanism involves the pneumatic tube system."

Belphegor's eyes narrowed in sly amusement. "Rewrite the end of the holy books?"

"Grant Hell its victory," said Lucifer.

"Or stop the war before it happens," said Rutspud.

Lucifer shrugged magnanimously, as though either option was equally good, but Rutspud was not so stupid as to imagine Lucifer would accept anything less than complete revenge on those who had wronged him aeons ago.

Belphegor clicked his fingers at Rutspud. "I want you on the tunneller. Together, Lord Lucifer and I will craft a scroll that lays down a perfect final outcome for us. You will break into the building while Heaven's armies are diverted by Lord Lucifer here."

"I'm sure that, in the perfect world to come, a certain Duke of Hell might have a new position of power," said Lucifer. "We can write that into our scroll."

"I am satisfied with my own place and rank," said Belphegor firmly.

"We could get a new electron microscope for the laboratory though," suggested Rutspud. "And better Wi-Fi."

"*And it came to pass that Hell's R&D department had improved download speeds?*" said Belphegor. "It hardly has a scriptural feel to it."

"Just saying," said Rutspud.

38

Nerys and Ben didn't have the restful night's sleep they'd wanted, as the unseen bombardment of the forcefield continued at regular intervals, shaking the ground and rattling the windows.

Nerys also realised that Ben's mood was becoming increasingly fragile. Had that idiot with the sideburns put doubt into his mind? If only Nerys had a solid game plan then maybe she could defend her actions. She had wasted way too much time messing about, worrying that there might be unintended consequences. It was time to take the lead again.

"Breakfast, Ben!" she shouted. It seemed her big shop had included kippers, melon and peach juice.

His eyes were bloodshot. "If this is a coma dream, am I going to be stuck in it forever?"

"We're here for a reason," said Nerys, possibly overdoing the upbeat chirpiness.

"Really?"

Nerys cut up a kipper. "You play an important role here, Ben. I need your input to help me with my next move."

"Is there any chance your next move is back to Boldmere to make everything peaceful again?"

"No, this is definitely a situation where we need to keep moving forward. Retreat is not an option. So, assuming the forcefield can withstand the bombardment of whatever bombs and stuff they are throwing at us—"

"I can't believe how casually you're saying that," he fretted. "You're inciting war!"

"Assuming we're safe here, and that this new island is a positive move for the environment, then I want to tackle some of the other problems the world has."

"Really?"

"Really."

"Going to hide in your jungle lair and see how else you can fuck up the world?"

"*Help* the world, Ben."

Ben cut up a slice of melon and tried to compose himself. "Well, you already had a go at financial inequity with your billionaire project."

Nerys pulled a face. "That didn't go so well. I don't think I can rely on other people to do the right thing anymore. I need to sort things out myself."

"Right. You want to put everyone on a level playing field, like with a universal basic income? You'd need a lot of persuasion and policy changes to make that happen. It would take years."

"We don't have years," said Nerys. "I need to do the fast

version. So, if we looked at the money the billionaires all have – maybe leave them enough for a lifetime of fancy shopping and first class tickets – but we take the rest and share it out amongst the rest of the world, that would be a start. We can take all the other money that's stockpiled around the place too. Like in the films, where they have those gold bars piled up in banks."

"Do you mean the national reserves countries have to underpin their financial security?" Ben asked. "I'm not so sure that would be wise."

"If we take it from every country then surely it will even out?" said Nerys.

"This is entirely hypothetical, right?" he said warily. "You don't actually have the power to do this."

"Maybe I do. Anyway, we give everyone a one-off payment and demonstrate that the idea will work. The policy changes can come afterwards, yeah?"

Ben looked uncomfortable. "I'm not sure I'm the best person to advise on this, it's way out of my comfort zone. But even to me – me in a coma dream, that is – it sounds reckless."

"Why thank you," said Nerys with a bow.

"I don't think I know anybody else who would take that as a compliment," said Ben.

"Come on," said Nerys grabbing paper and pen, "we're on a roll. Everyone gets the money, so how can we be sure they know what is happening and that it's not just a bank error?"

Ben sighed, apparently surrendering to the plan "You need to tell them it's theirs to keep. Somehow you need to be plugged into the communications network." Ben gestured helplessly at their surroundings.

"We could do with having the old team back together again," said Nerys.

"What? The *Honk if you're Helpful* team?"

"Tina, Spartacus, Hodshift. On my terms this time, though."

"How will you do that?" asked Ben.

"I'll think of something."

After breakfast, Nerys privately retrieved the Wish-O-Matic.

"I have a bit of a list, so listen carefully," she said to it. "First of all, I need some of my people here. They might not be completely on board with this, so let's put them in a happy place. Er, let's put the Boldmere Oak next door, and they can all stay in there until they agree to do as I say. Bring Spartacus, Hodshift and Tina. Um, Animal Ed too. He's helpful. Uh, and Spartacus's friends, yeah? You know the ones. I suppose we'd better have Lennox the barman to pull pints." She drummed her fingers on the table wondering how to prevent the little demon from cramping her style. "I'll need security for the Wish-O-Matic, some sort of cabinet that can only be opened by me. I'll need a communications hub that lets me talk to everyone in the world, translating it all as I go. I need to see all of the news feeds. In fact, if I could have some sort of Tardis thing that lets me go and observe things anywhere in the world, that would be handy. The bar area will do nicely. Now, onto the big one. I want to confiscate all of the money that rich people have that exceeds what they could spend in a lifetime, and then share that money out between everyone else in the world."

Nerys paused, wondering if she had left any obvious gaps in what she wanted. No, she was happy with that.

"That's it," she told the demonic device.

She went downstairs, knocking on Ben's door as she passed. "We should have company!" she shouted and stepped outside.

She paused on the doorstep, looking at the Boldmere Oak directly opposite. It looked weird to see the somewhat rundown urban pub in this green and pleasant setting. Somehow the greenery and tranquillity leant the pub a rustic and cosy feel.

She pushed open the door and beamed round at all of the confused faces. Ben stepped in behind her and stopped.

"Nerys, what the hell is happening?" asked Tina. She was slightly under-dressed for the pub in a vinyl basque. Nerys wondered who she'd been with when she'd been whisked away.

"I was in bed," said young Jefri Rehemtualla who was indeed dressed in patterned pyjamas.

"I don't remember coming into the Boldmere Oak," said Ed. "Is this a kidnapping?"

"I'm getting the gang back together again," said Nerys. "Sorry for the lack of warning everyone."

There was an eruption of shouting. Only Lennox was silent, simply running a cloth across the bar and starting to polish glasses. Hodshift was also less vocal, simply fixing her with a knowing look.

Ed stepped forward and gave Nerys a long look. "Nerys,

can you perhaps tell us what just happened and why the view from the window is so unusual?"

"I can."

There was silence.

Nerys took a deep breath. "Many of you know I have been working on various initiatives to make the world a better place. Some of them have not worked out well, but I keep moving forward, because I'm nothing if not persistent."

"Stubborn," murmured Tina.

"Anyway, some new technology has been made available to me. Powerful technology. I cannot explain its workings or where I got it from, but it's enabled me to make some big changes." She swept an arm broadly behind her. "The pub has been moved to the new island of Doggerland, which is underneath a force field."

"The what?" said PJ.

"Where?" said Tina.

"There was a guy on YouTube who said it's aliens," said Jefri. "They are abducting humans and doing experiments on them. Are you working for the aliens?"

"What? No. There are no aliens, that's not what this is all about," said Nerys.

Jefri nodded to Spartacus. "That's exactly what you'd say if you were working for the aliens."

Nerys shook her head. "I wanted to bring you all in on this, because I believe you can help me nail this now. The island of Doggerland is a haven for wildlife and has given us a load more green space and diversity. Tick! Now my next move is to even out the financial situation in the world. Everybody has been given a fair share of the excess money that was being hoarded by financial institutions and billionaires."

"Sorry, what's happened?" said Ed.

"Don't worry," said Ben. "You're all in my coma dream. None of it's meant to make sense."

"It's real," said Nerys. "Everyone in the world has been given a fresh fair injection of cash."

"Including us?" asked Tina, pulling out her phone.

"Yes."

Tina tapped and gave a wide grin. "Ten thousand pounds! Excuse me for a few minutes, I have handbags to buy."

"Ah, right. No," said Nerys. "We must resist the base instinct to splurge it on designer goodies, and we need to convince everyone else in the world to do the same."

Spartacus spoke up. "How old do you have to be to qualify? Will us kids get the ten grand?"

Nerys wasn't totally sure. "I did say everybody, so I assume you will. Check your bank."

"And would, say, an electric scooter count as designer goodies?"

Tina was busily tapping at her phone. "Blast! Completely sold out. I think lots of other people are doing the same as me."

Nerys banged a hand on the nearest table. "Focus people! I need eyes and ears on the world, and I need to get to work on communications." She looked over to the bar. "Lennox, is there some fancy new equipment over there?"

Lennox nodded. "There's a button that reads *Press here to initiate comms hub*. Would that be it?"

"Yep. Now let's allocate roles, shall we?"

Animal Ed shot to his feet. "Whoa, whoa, whoa, Nerys! I'm not so sure I have a part to play here. If it's all the same to you, I'm going to make a move and see what all the talk of ten grand is about."

He walked to the door. Nerys and Ben moved aside and Ed stepped out. Except he didn't make it through the door: he bounced back inside the room.

"I'm sorry to do this to you, Ed, and everybody else, but now that I have you here, I need you to see this through with me. You're stuck in here until you get behind the mission."

Jefri tapped Spartacus's arm. "She's gone mad with power, hasn't she?"

Nerys couldn't help but notice Spartacus nodding.

Ed clambered up from the floor, dusting down his trousers and attempting to recapture his dignity. "Well there's bugger all outside, anyway,"

"There might be some things that would interest you, Ed. Have you ever seen a sabre-toothed tiger?"

"No, because they don't exist, that's why. They are from the old days."

Ben grabbed his arm. "I saw one last night. They are here! I think Nerys messed up when she said she wanted things that would be native to Doggerland."

"Hey!" said Nerys angrily.

"Actually, the sabre-toothed tiger lived in the Americas," said Ed. "I imagine what we have here is some other sabre-toothed predator, somehow revived through Jurassic Park-style technology."

"Nerys cloned sabre-toothed tigers?" said PJ.

"Sabre-toothed cat of some sort," said Ed, sagely.

"Another screw up," said Tina haughtily. "First the plague of alpacas and now this. Honestly, this sort of cock up is part of the reason we cut all ties with you. I don't know why we should change our minds now."

"Alpacas are in the cellar," said Lennox without looking up.

Everyone turned to stare.

"What?" he said looking up. "Don't shoot the messenger. I saw them there when I was checking the barrels. Your dog's in there as well Nerys."

"Twinkle!" Nerys shouted with glee. "Open up, Lennox."

Moments later there were two alpacas and a small excited Yorkshire terrier enjoying the freedom of the bar area.

Nerys picked Twinkle up. She hugged him tight and addressed the rest of the room. "You might not like the fact that you are here, but you have a unique opportunity to help me make a massive difference. If you choose to help I'll be really pleased. Now, I am off to address the people of the world."

"The what?" said Ed. "Can she do that?"

Nerys bustled over to find the button that Lennox had mentioned. "Initiating comms hub," she intoned, in a voice she realised she had borrowed from umpteen film supervillains as they prepared to launch their torpedoes. She coughed and altered her voice back to normal. "Pressing the button now."

The bar was transformed. Nobody moved, but the walls were now wrapped with television screens and workstations.

"Just a coma dream, just a coma dream…" Ben whispered to himself.

Right in front of Nerys was a podium with a microphone and camera pointing directly at her. She composed herself and pressed the button beneath a light that was helpfully labelled BROADCAST LIVE TO THE ENTIRE WORLD. It turned red.

"Greetings everybody. My name is Nerys Thomas and while you might be aware of some sudden and unexpected changes, I can assure you I am acting in good faith for the benefit of all humanity. I am taking steps to remove some of the problems existing in the world today. You will have seen that I have created a wildlife haven on an island in the area previously called Doggerland. I'd appreciate it if everyone could stop blasting missiles at it."

"It will stop the birds roosting," said Animal Ed from across the bar.

"It will stop the birds from roosting," repeated Nerys. "Nobody wants that, do they? Now my latest initiative is to trial a universal basic income. Everyone's been given a one-off payment so they can do something meaningful to help the world. I trust you all to do the right thing with the money, and prove to our leaders it's a sensible thing to do. I will be watching you, so use it wisely! Speak later."

Nerys pressed the button again and the light went out.

39

The occupants of the freshly transplanted Boldmere Oak spent the afternoon doing what most people would do if they found themselves magically transported to a pub in the middle of a prehistoric forest. This involved a lot of blank staring, a lot of confused chatter and, in several cases, a lot of drinking.

Spartacus, with Hodshift at his elbow, came over to Nerys. "I've collated the data feeds from all of the major payment aggregators to see where people are spending their money," he said.

Nerys wasn't about to ask how he had done that. "Cool. How's it looking?"

"Takings at luxury goods stores and high end holiday retailers are up by five thousand percent."

"Oh. Right. How about donations to charities and improvements to homes and communities?" she asked.

"Up by a small percentage, yeah," said Spartacus. His

tone suggested that the percentage was too small to name and that he was throwing her a bone.

"Well, that's a bit annoying. Maybe we should take this thing for a spin," said Nerys.

"What thing?" asked Ben.

"The bar should take us where we want to go. Anyone seen another button?"

Lennox pointed to the other end of the bar. "Over there."

Nerys moved towards the button, but Tina held up a hand. "Wait!"

Nerys stared at her. "Yes? What's the matter?"

"You said you wanted our help, yet you're still acting on your own. Where were you thinking of going, and what did you plan to do when you got there?"

"I thought we might go to somewhere like a Louis Vuitton store, where I'd talk to the people who were thinking of blowing their ten grand on fancy bags."

Tina coughed lightly and tucked her phone behind her back. "So you're going to take this whole building and land it in a crowded place? Was the plan to squash all the people so they can't spend their money?"

"What? No. I'm sure this thing must have an anti-squashing sensor." Nerys looked at the controls. It looked as though she would just need to activate the microphone and talk into it. "Fine, I'll take advice from the group. Where should we go?"

Tina shrugged lightly. "I suppose if we did go to Louis Vuitton, I could have a word with the sales staff. Maybe get them to close up the shop."

"Nice try, Tina," said Nerys. "That is just code for 'letting

Tina jump the queue to buy something fancy'. Can I just reiterate that we won't be leaving this bar? Put aside any ideas about jumping ship or buying things. Where to then?"

"How about some sort of transport hub?" said Ben. "A train station or an airport."

"Good idea," said Nerys. "A good cross section of people would be there. Let's go to New Street station in Birmingham."

"What? Am I understanding you right?" said Tina. "If you really do have the means to take us to any location in the world why would you choose a train station you could visit any day of the week by hopping on a bus?"

"Good point. Name a train station then. A big one."

"Why a train station? Let's go to the Champs-Élysées, or Rodeo Drive!"

Nerys sighed. She could totally understand Tina's enthusiasm for high end designer goods. "Fine, let's do that." She activated the microphone. "Take us to the Champs-Élysées in Paris, but we mustn't squash anyone or anything!"

A moment later the screens around the walls changed and showed the wide Parisian street.

"It's just on the telly," said Animal Ed scornfully.

"No," said Ben, looking through the door. "It's outside. You can see it through the windows as well."

They appeared to be hovering a few feet above the wide pavement.

"It's bedlam down there," said Jefri. "What shop is that?"

"Hermès," breathed Tina. She went over to the window and pressed herself against it. "Are we absolutely not allowed out? I could do a little bit of research, maybe?" She went round to the door and hissed with annoyance when she was unable to get out.

People were queuing outside Hermès and many other shops. They weren't particularly orderly queues, with lots of jostling and arguments. Traffic had come to a standstill, with cars pulled up directly outside several shops.

"Everyone gets some cash and immediately hits the shops," said Ben.

Nerys went to the comms hub. "Is there a tannoy to address the people outside?"

Lennox pointed at a button marked PUBLIC ADDRESS, which may or may not have been there before.

"Bonjour everybody on the Champs-Élysées!" said Nerys. "I know you're all keen to spend your money, but have you thought about how you might use it to benefit humanity?"

The people down on the street looked around in confusion.

"I think we might be invisible," said Spartacus. "There's a live webcam showing the street here and I can't see us on it."

"Don't be afraid, it's only me, Nerys Thomas."

"Your friendly mad dictator," Jefri whispered to PJ.

"Think of me as being something like your conscience," Nerys continued, "and, yes, also the leader that the world needs. Now step away from the scarves and handbags. Think about how you can make the world a better place with the money you've been given. I did that, by the way, I made that money come your way. I'm not saying you owe me anything. You don't have to adore me. You should at least listen to me, though. Take a moment, take a breath. Do you really need the fancy things you're queuing up for?"

They all watched the display as the crowd looked up at the sky, confused and thoughtful. Then there was movement. Some from the back began to elbow their way forward, and there was an eruption of outrage and barging. It seemed as if they were all doubling down on their attempts to get to the front of the queue.

Nerys sighed. "Maybe we should go to a different kind of place? Somewhere without the temptation of material goods?"

"Do we have to name a place, or can we just tell the thing what sort of place you want?" asked Spartacus. "What do you reckon, Hodshift?"

Hodshift had been silent up to now, but Spartacus looked at him as a fellow nerd, not realising he was behind the infernal technology.

"I reckon if you define it well enough the machine will manage," Hodshift said. There was a sullen tone to his voice, and every time he glanced at Nerys it was with a certain sadness.

"Why don't we take a look at a homeless community," said Ben. "They tend to be on the sharp end of things."

Nerys spoke into the microphone. "Take us to a homeless community. Is that a thing?"

"Of course it is."

"Again, no squashing people," Nerys reminded the unseen forces guiding the pub.

The display changed and they found themselves in an urban landscape. There was a large expanse of concrete that might have been the underside of a flyover. People wrapped in sleeping bags and cardboard huddled near to their shopping trolleys and bags.

"Where do you reckon we are?" Spartacus asked.

"I don't know where we are, but can you see what's going on?" Animal Ed said, pointing. "Look."

There was someone in motorbike leathers moving between the homeless people, pointing a machete and making obvious threats. He collected bags from each of them and piled them into a sports bag he was carrying.

"Oh no! These folks have cash. No bank accounts maybe. He's stealing it from them," said Ben.

"Well, do something, Nerys," said Tina.

Nerys activated the tannoy. "Hey, you! Yes, you! This is the voice of your granny in heaven. What do you think you're doing?"

The man with the sports bag dropped it in shock and looked around for the voice.

"What if I don't sound like his granny?" she whispered to the room, with the microphone off.

"Let's get the sound from outside sorted," said Spartacus, fiddling with one of the workstations.

"—*know who you are, but my granny's still alive and well and living in South Detroit!*" The villain turned in circles, brandishing the machete at the sky.

"Oh hey, we're in America!" said Ben. "His accent, did you hear it?"

Nerys activated the tannoy again. "I'm your granny's granny, cloth ears. Pay attention. I bet you didn't know she was from Britain, did you? Anyway, I want you to stop doing that. It's not what I wanted for my, um, great-great-grandson. You're better than this, do you hear me?"

The arm with the machete dipped and his body language became hesitant.

"Go on! Give the money back and get out of here!"

He dropped the sports bag and sprinted away, a single backwards glance showing a fixed and fearful grimace on his face.

Nerys wasn't done. "Right, the rest of you. I expect you to go to that bag and take what's yours and only what's yours. Now you will need to take care of it, so I expect you to band together and get it somewhere safe. Can you do that?"

There were hesitant nods, although one of the homeless people threw a remarkably well aimed beer bottle. It smashed on the wall of the pub.

"Let's get out of here, shall we?" said Nerys. "Back to Doggerland so we can have a bit of a debrief."

"What? And rate this appalling shitshow with marks out of ten?" said Tina.

40

Lucifer bent over a desk in Belphegor's laboratory, quill in hand. He looked at what he had written on the scroll, considered his choice of words and his phrasing, then nodded in appreciation of his own perfect intelligence. He rolled the scroll tightly and turned to his two lieutenants.

People failed to understand how difficult it was to be the single greatest creature in all Creation. Lucifer was will and power and divine strength personified, and he had no equal. All creatures were below him, way *way* below him. Even a human, forced to live among monkeys or ... *slugs* could not comprehend the true gulf separating Lucifer from all other things.

And yet, some gulfs were wider than others.

He regarded the two individuals he was compelled to rely on for this next portion of his plan. The Serpent, green scales shimmering iridescently, swayed. The Scapegoat, eyes paradoxically both cunning and vacant, chewed on a length of electric cable.

"Listen," said Lucifer. "Soon Belphegor's tunnelling machine will be setting off for the Celestial City, and I will be leading Hell's armies into battle. The tunnellers have plans to break into the Research Centre for Scriptural Exegesis. Belphegor has given Rutspud a scroll which is to be entered into the scriptorium's record and thus change the established divine truth. It is a bland work which might mention Hell's victory in the battle to come, but is essentially a maintenance of the status quo, and I for one do not— Are you listening?"

The Scapegoat had munched the electric wire all the way to the plug and was now rolling the three pin plug around in its lips like an oversized gobstopper. The goat looked guilty and spat it out.

"I do not want the status quo," said Lucifer. "I want something more."

"Is it devious? Is it perverse? Is it an act of pure rebellion?" asked the Serpent enthusiastically.

Lucifer raised the tightly rolled scroll. "It is nothing short of a total overhaul of all reality. No Heaven. No Hell. No humans running around liked spoilt and entitled brats, ruining a once perfect world. It is a rewind to that one moment when the Almighty made His two greatest mistakes: the creation of humankind and His refusal to listen to me."

"I like it," hissed the Serpent.

"Good," said Lucifer and presented the scroll to the two of them.

The Scapegoat craned its neck to take the scroll in its teeth.

"Do *not* eat it!" said Lucifer.

The Scapegoat hesitated, then grasped it tenderly.

"You will inveigle your way onto the digger," continued Lucifer, "secrete yourself in some corner for the journey and then, paying no mind to whatever Rutspud and his confederates are doing, lodge this in the records of the scriptorium. Any questions?"

The Serpent and the Scapegoat looked at each other and said nothing. There was a rhythmic slurpy crunchy sound from the corner of the room. Lucifer looked round sharply. It was the hideous creature he had made – well, not actually *him*, it had been concocted from Limbo stuff by one Jeremy Clovenhoof, a devil who was very much less than the sum of his parts. The Limbo creature was still licking and nibbling at the huge mound of congealed crud left over after the separation of Lucifer from Serpent from Scapegoat from tiny demon. Its boneless lips left slobber all over the mound.

Lucifer looked back to his minions, irritated by the interruption. "Go now. Be swift, be silent, complete the task."

"Will we get into trouble for this?" mumbled the Scapegoat around the scroll in its mouth.

"If you are successful then no one will ever know," said Lucifer.

The goat scuffed its hoofs in a desultory manner on the floor. "Don't see the point if no one's going to notice."

"Just go!" said Lucifer with an imperious wave of his hand.

The Serpent led the way, a flicker of green lightning across the floor. The Scapegoat trotted after. A second later, a double door swung open and the demon Rutspud entered.

"Ah, here you are, Lord," he said. "We're ready for you now."

"We?" said Lucifer, rising.

"Your armies. Berith, your chief general, has them arrayed in marching formation. All they are waiting for is you to lead them."

Lucifer sniffed haughtily. "An army is of no use to me. Without me, their cause is hopeless. With me at their head, they will have nothing to do but watch me seize victory single-handed."

"That's surprisingly uplifting, sir," said Rutspud. "I'm sure many of the lads will be delighted to know they won't need to fight. Maybe you could include that in your stirring battle speech, eh?"

Lucifer ignored the prattling fool and swept from the room.

"Right you are," said Rutspud, following swiftly behind.

Neither of them noticed that, as they left, a large eye opened in the pile of rough debris. It was orange and reptilian, and quite entirely malevolent.

41

The mood in the transplanted Boldmere Oak was critical at best.

"What do you want us to say, Nerys?" Tina asked. "Quite honestly, I don't think this experiment is going well."

"We only looked at a couple of places," said Nerys. "It's probably not like that everywhere."

Tina pointed at a screen behind Nerys. "Headlines from around the world suggest otherwise."

FINANCIAL STUNT DESTABILISES WORLD ECONOMIES AND CAUSES WIDESPREAD DISRUPTION.
BRITS ON SPENDING BENDER CAUSE HIGH STREET CARNAGE!
KIDDIE CARTEL BUYS AMUSEMENT ARCADE AT SEASIDE RESORT.

"Well there you go," said Nerys. "The media are part of the problem. People see that and assume it's the way everyone's behaving."

"Are you suggesting there will be a wave of copycat cartels?" Tina asked. "Kids up and down the country buying up amusement arcades?"

"Not that specifically, although who knows?" said Nerys, indicating the huddle where Spartacus, PJ and Jefri were exchanging urgent whispers.

"This is useful feedback," said Nerys, pacing the floor. "Controlling the media should take priority." There was a widespread chorus of dismayed noises, but she waved them down. "What else have we learned from the news, aside from those lurid headlines?"

"World leaders are blaming each other for what they are calling financial warcraft," said Ben. "They are now arguing about who should talk to who."

"Hm. World leaders. They definitely need to be tackled." Nerys scanned the screens, taking in the headlines, the news reports, and what was trending on social media. "Are there no good news stories at all?"

Spartacus, who seemed to be the only one who had bothered sitting himself at a workstation and figuring out how to control the screens, did some typing and changed a display. "There you go."

Animal shelters benefit from mystery donations. North Yorkshire fishermen report record catches as North Sea fish stocks are concentrated into reduced space.

NERYS IS THE NEW NUMBER ONE BABY NAME IN NORTH KOREA.

"Right." Nerys had no idea what to make of that. "Erm, listen. I need to pop over to the house for a short while. Get a round in and I'll be back in a few minutes."

"Don't let her go," said Hodshift.

There was silence as everyone turned to stare at the tiny demon.

"Whatever he's about to say, ignore him," said Nerys. She had an inkling of what he might be up to.

"Well I want to hear it," said Tina sweetly. "Do explain why we shouldn't let Nerys go."

"She's going to make more changes. She's gonna keep making changes and keep making things worse. If you arsk me, someone needs to stop her," said Hodshift. "This is Sodom and Gomorrah all over again."

"Let me get this straight." Tina counted off on her fingers. "Nerys is the only one of us who can get outside. If she gets outside, she can do more of her insane meddling. If we stop her getting outside, we can stop her meddling."

Hodshift gave a tiny nod in confirmation.

Nerys eyed the door. Tina eyed Nerys. Nobody moved – but several people weighed up where they were in relation to Nerys and the door.

Nerys feinted towards the main door, sending several people to block her exit. She jumped onto a table and swung a chair up with her. She stood on the table and brandished the chair at everyone.

"Right, let's make this clear. I can swing this chair and smash a window to get out. Even if you stop me doing this, I'll find some other way out. Don't forget though, there really are sabre toothed tigers here, so I'm not sure I'd want too many windows smashed if I was stuck in here. What's it gonna be, huh?"

"Grab her! We can tie her to a chair!" yelled Tina.

"Yeah, but she likes that," said Ed with a roll of his eyes, but his words were lost in the melee. Nerys swung for the window. Against all expectation the chair bounced off the glass and struck Ben in the face.

"Ow!" His nose gushed blood.

"Sorry Ben," said Nerys, even as she brought the chair around for another swing. The glass broke this time, but as she stepped forward to climb out, she was toppled from the table as someone pulled it out from under her feet. She lay below the broken window, the chair still in her hand, glaring up out at her team, who seemed determined to stop her.

"What? All right, let's take a deep breath and think about what we're doing, shall we? No good can come of us fighting. We should work together."

"Working together isn't going so well though, is it, Nerys?" said Tina. "As far as I can tell, what you mean by 'working together' is we should be your slaves while you make unilateral decisions without consulting us."

Nerys nodded. "I can see how it might look that way. Someone has to be in charge though."

"Spell it out for us, Nerys!" spat Tina. "What's the dynamic here? Do we get any kind of a say in how we all get out of this crisis – because look around you, this is a crisis —

or do you simply want a few extra bodies to push buttons and feed you information?"

Nerys took a beat too long to think about her answer. Tina growled with anger and moved to the controls. "Take us five miles away from here, deeper into the forest."

"No!" Nerys looked back out of the window and saw that they had moved. Away from their own home where the Wish-O-Matic was safe in its little cabinet. She was five miles away from being able to fix all of their problems. "Goddammit Tina!"

She launched herself at Tina and they wrestled briefly with each other, before Animal Ed stepped in and prised them apart. holding them both by an arm. "Pack it in you two. We need to come up with a better plan than just pissing Nerys off."

"Yeah, Tina! We definitely do!" said Nerys in triumph.

"And you need to stop acting like you're the only one round here who has a brain. Seriously."

Nerys pouted.

Spartacus stepped forward. "Are we like, in charge of the world now?" he asked.

"Kind of, I guess," said Nerys. "Sort of."

"I remember when Reverend Purdey and Michael took our scout group camping and they had us write a manifesto for how we wanted things to be run."

"Dead boring," said PJ.

"But maybe we should do that," said Spartacus.

"Kid's got a great point," said Ed, easing his hold on Nerys. "Let's do some brainstorming."

"Cool!" said Nerys. "I think this is the best idea I've heard so far. Did I see a dry-wipe board over there? We can use that. Bring it on everybody!"

"Well I have an idea," said Tina. "You'll love it. Basically, we completely re-jig the way people live their lives and get money. It's clear Nerys can make big changes happen with her magic wand or whatever, so why not try this? Everyone gets enough money to live on, and there's a system that monitors what they do. If they do good things they get more money, and if they do bad things they get less. Small things are only worth pennies, like taking your trolley back when you've used it at the supermarket. Bigger things like not flying to Thailand are worth more, obviously."

"That's stupid," said PJ. "Not flying to Thailand isn't such a big deal. I avoided flying there every single day of my life, and nobody ever paid me for it."

Tina gave a dismissive snort. "Details, details. We'll figure it out. Anyway it takes away the idea that you can get away with stuff if you're not observed. Everyone will be observed all of the time. The computers will decide what's good and what's bad."

"Not everyone will be a fan of that," said Ed. "Being observed all of the time sounds like a nightmare."

"Spoken like a person with something to hide," said Tina primly.

"Too damn right."

Nerys had been slowly working her way towards the door; now she reckoned she stood a decent chance of busting out. She barrelled her way past Tina to get to the door. Once through it she was out of everyone's reach.

She turned to address them. "Sorry. I really do want to

hear any more ideas you might have, but I can't be sitting on my hands in the meantime."

There was shouting from nearly everyone in the room, although Hodshift settled for a sorrowful shake of the head.

"See you all in a short while." Nerys set out into the forest, hoping she was going in the right direction.

She did not enjoy the walk back to the house. Five miles was way too long, even for a pleasant dog walk, but making her way through a forest with no paths when she wasn't even sure she was going in the right direction made it hellish and interminable. There was all of this excess nature too. She knew it was necessary for a healthy planet, but it was very inconvenient when it was tripping her up. And some of those extra pollinators were definitely biting her exposed flesh.

What made it worse, when she did find the house the pub was back there, right next door to it.

"Ha ha, very funny!" she shouted.

They must have moved it after she left. She would have done the same thing in their shoes.

She hurried upstairs to her flat to find the Wish-O-Matic. It was locked away in a cabinet that swooshed open when she put her hand onto the panel to unlock it. She was impressed with the slightly sinister coolness of it.

"Now then, Wish-O-Matic," she said. "We have much more work to do and I've had time to think about it. Let's deal with my team first of all, I want them here on the island because they are useful, but I can't have them overpowering me. Make it so that they can't get within a foot of me. That will mean I can move amongst them. Actually, it will mean I can take you around with me as well, which will be handy.

No more horrible hiking for me. Can you do blisters? Please make my feet better."

How could she fix the world if her feet hurt? It was reasonable to sort herself out, like putting the oxygen mask on yourself before you helped others.

"Let's give the team some powers so I can delegate some of the work. Everyone in the Boldmere Oak should be able to fly – that should speed things up. Now, let's deal with world leaders. Whoever is practically in charge in all of the countries of the world, I want them all here. Not right here, but somewhere they can talk to each other, and think about what they have done. Let's make them an amusement park next door. They can go on rides and eat junk food. They shouldn't be able to leave though, it's like their prison until I say so. No communications for them, either. Plenty for me though. I want camera coverage of everywhere around here."

Nerys thought about some of the other lessons from the last few hours.

"I need to tackle the media. I want good news stories only. They can only say nice things about me from now on, and encourage people to love me. Everything will go much more smoothly if people can see that I know what's best for them."

She tucked the Wish-O-Matic into a pocket and flexed her feet. They felt great, no blisters or pain.

"Let's go and see the team, we've got work to do."

She trotted downstairs and went into the Boldmere Oak.

42

"Roll cameras and... Action!" yelled the director.

The skies above the celestial stadium boiled and rolled. Billowing clouds of sickly hues spread across the landscape. By the light of a baleful sun, perfectly arrayed warrior angels coursed down toward the earth. In the distance, mountains and islands were flung high into the air, a world ripped apart.

"And ... cue horsemen!"

Across this sky came the harbingers of the world's end, four huge and terrible figures, taller than skyscrapers, riding upon the ghostly forms of woolly long-legged ruminants. Holy light glinted in their eyes beneath shaggy fringes.

"This?" said Michael aside to his fellow archangels. "We're going with this?"

"They are ... very striking," said Raphael politely.

"I like it," said Samael.

"Really?" said Michael. "I thought you at least would like

something a bit more—" He wanted to say 'a bit more like something off the cover of a heavy metal album' but didn't want to get drawn in that particular conversation. "—Something more iconic."

"I like the element of surprise," said Samael. "It's like a serial killer in a clown costume."

"Is it?"

"Or getting run over by an ice cream van. Sure, the Horsemen of the Apocalypse would strike terror in people's hearts, but it would be a comfortable sort of terror. It would make sense. Just imagine the looks on people's faces when they see the Alpacamen of the Apocalypse come tearing across the land! Terror *and* bewilderment! That's a more potent effect."

Michael looked up at the cuddly camelids. Armageddon was a single event, a spectacular one-night-only show, and it seemed a wild creative choice to switch the key apocalyptic animals at this stage. But this was perhaps symptomatic of Heaven's response to the whole situation. Angels of all ranks were being led by the fervent and wild belief that these things *should* happen because someone had insisted they *would* happen.

"You know, we shouldn't take prophecy as gospel truth," said Michael.

"Pardon?" said Raphael, wondering if he'd misheard over the clash and clang of the apocalyptic rehearsals.

"Listen to yourself," said Samael. "You've just said that prophecy, literally the predictions of the prophets, shouldn't be taken as holy truth. That's literally, *literally* what you've just said."

Michael shook himself. "No, Samael. Prophecy is never about the future."

"Someone's getting cold feet," said Raphael. "First night nerves."

Michael waved his hands at the sky. "When the prophet Isaiah wrote about the end of the world, he wasn't writing about the end of the world."

"You've lost me, mate," said Samael.

"He was writing at a time of exile, when things were looking grim for the people of Israel. The bitterness of his prophecy was projected fear for his current situation. When John wrote the *Book of Revelation* – which, for the record, definitely didn't contain alpacas – he wasn't really predicting the end of the world."

"Ahem," said Raphael, pointing up as though the big light and thunder spectacular overhead was a sufficient counterargument.

"He was writing during a time of Christian persecution," persisted Michael. "You know, Christians thrown to the lions and all that. *Revelation* isn't a step-by-step guidebook as to how the world will end. It's a declaration of anguish. It's bad poetry written by an angry teenager in their bedroom."

Samael gripped his arm tightly. "Listen, Michael, mate. You've picked a weird time to start questioning the entire basis of religious scripture."

"I've picked exactly the right time," Michael shot back. "This has to stop!"

Raphael held up calming hands. "We understand you're nervous. You have a big role to play. In fact..." He turned his head and shouted. "Omvial! Have you got Michael's armour!"

A lesser angel waved in acknowledgement and scurried off.

"There's no denying that the end times are here," said Samael.

"If you tell people there's no hope for the future then of course they'll believe there is no future. Self-fulfilling prophecy," said Michael.

"The best kind," said Samael.

"The signs are all coming to fruition on Earth," said Raphael. "Plagues. Lands rising out of the sea. Armies and navies gathering to fight."

"We just need to change our view of the holy books," said Michael, knowing his words were falling on deaf ears. "We just need to make some changes."

Samael's slap came hard and out of nowhere. Michael staggered, clutching his cheek.

"There are many things I never liked about you," spat Samael viciously, his black cloak billowing. "You were always vain and self-important. You were popular with the believers on Earth. You played up to your warrior angel image, even though we all knew the sun was in Satan's eyes that day and you were lucky to get in the critical stab with your lance. You've been an insufferable prig for thousands of years, but you were never a coward."

"Samael..." cautioned Raphael softly.

"No, he needs to hear it!" said the angel of death in a voice like cold iron. "You have a major role to play in the tribulations to come, Michael, and you will play it. Even if I have to force you into that armour myself and drag you out onto the battlefield."

The angel, Omvial, came scurrying back carrying a gleaming bronze breastplate and an equally shiny Roman helmet.

"Now, suit up!" said Samael. "And face the end of the world like a man!"

43

Tina looked at Nerys's flushed face as she came back into the bar. "Wow, Nerys, you took your time walking back. We went on a world tour while you were gone."

Nerys wasn't sure whether Tina was joking. "Did you? What did you see?"

"Mostly we saw more of the same. But we brought you a present." Tina strode over to Nerys and thrust out a hand. She slammed up against the invisible force field twelve inches from Nerys. "I see you're taking extra precautions. Can't say I blame you. Here you are." She put a pen on a nearby table.

Nerys picked it up. "The White House? Wait – I have questions. I get that you could have navigated to there, but how did you get outside? You're trapped in here."

Tina smiled. "You set the rules Nerys. You said we couldn't go outside until we got behind the mission."

"Oh I see!" Nerys beamed with delight. "If you're all behind the mission then. That's great."

The smile dropped from Tina's face. "Not all of us, no. In fact, it seems Spartacus is the only one who can leave."

Nerys turned to the boy, who shrugged. "What can I say? It all makes a lot of sense to me, plus I get to play with these neat computers." His eyes flicked between Nerys and Tina. "I'm sort of glad you're back, if I'm honest."

Nerys whirled to face Tina. "I don't believe it! You tried to get Spartacus to go and buy your wretched handbag, didn't you?"

"What? We had to navigate past there anyway, it seemed harmless enough to call in," said Tina, fluttering her eyelashes. "I am keen to support artisanal makers. They are an important part of the economy."

Nerys tried to keep her cool. She took a deep breath. "While I was away, did you do any of the brainstorming manifesto thing?"

"Why don't you go first?" said Hodshift, stepping forward. "Walk us through the changes you made since you left."

"Well, yes. I did alter a couple of things. They shouldn't come as a huge shock, we kind of talked about them." Nerys looked around the room, trying to gauge the mood. "So, we have a summit of world leaders here on the island..."

Ben's face creased in confusion. "A summit of world leaders? Here? Like now?"

"That can only be a good thing, right? I also put some restrictions on the media, so they give everyone a more positive view of things."

"Hang on," said Tina. "You've got all the world leaders here? Where?"

"Somewhere nice," said Nerys.

"I can get you some visuals," said Spartacus. "We've got motion sensors covering the area all around here." He rattled the keyboard, typing fast. The image changed on one of the displays – it showed a split screen view from a theme park.

"Um," said Ed.

"Er," said Jefri.

"Is that the Prime Minister on the teacups?" asked PJ.

"It is," said Tina. "But most of them are wandering around looking angry and confused. Did you just throw them in there, Nerys?"

"Yes I did. We can work out what we want to do with them next."

"Won't it look to the rest of the world as though they've all been abducted? Because they kind of have been," said Ed.

"Well, luckily for us, the media's on our side," said Nerys, chirpily. "Shall we take a look?"

They all studied different news displays for a few moments.

"There's more amusing cat stories than I'd normally expect from the BBC," said Spartacus. "I quite like it actually."

"Apparently someone's measured a reduction in harmful CO_2 since Doggerland appeared," said Ed.

"What about our ideas?" said Tina. "We did have a few things we thought would make a positive difference."

"Cool, yeah. What have you got?"

Ed spoke up. "Well, personally I think we need some

actual experts in the room. People who know about economics and politics. People who know how international trade and spin doctoring works. It's great that you invited all of us here, but we don't know how to do those things."

"Ah yes. I'm glad you brought that up," said Nerys. "I wanted to do things differently, you see. I could relocate the people from the Houses of Parliament and the civil service here, but then all I've done is recreate the old model, and we all know that's broken. The whole point of making these bigger changes is to overturn the usual way of thinking. I firmly believe I can do this. I can mend the world by treating people well."

Ben caught her eye, and Nerys instantly felt a blast of guilt from the many times she had been mean to people in the past.

"Mostly I strive to treat people well. I'll make mistakes, but I will fix them as I go."

"How will you know?" asked Hodshift, shuffling closer.

"Sorry?"

"How will you know you've made mistakes when you've silenced your critics, and nobody can oppose you?"

"Yes, well." Nerys thought quickly. Hodshift was a bit too sneaky and perceptive for her liking. "I have a good team here to give me feedback. We have data feeds in real time. We will be results-driven because we're adopting a test-and-learn approach." The bullshit phrases from her crash course in loan applications came flooding back and she grinned in triumph.

"We'll only hear about results that are good news wiv the

changes you made, won't we? What about if something bad's brewing? How will we hear?"

"Hm. That is a good point. Has anybody got ideas of where we might get that information?"

"Wonder if we can get some sort of feed from the US? Like the stuff that the CIA have maybe?" Spartacus said with a shrug.

Everyone stared at him.

"I don't think they share that stuff," said Ed.

Spartacus was not deterred. He went over to a workstation and started typing. Hodshift sidled over to help. A few minutes later, there were multiple screens filled with live feeds and bullet-pointed analyses of world situations.

"I need an access code," said Spartacus. "I'm just going to pop over and see if I can get it from the US President." He left the pub while everyone stared at the screens.

There was a long silence.

"What's martial law?" asked Jefri.

"It's when the military take over things," said Ben.

"A lot of countries have declared martial law," said Tina quietly. "Missing leaders, financial markets suspended, and rioting in the streets." She sighed wistfully. "I bet looting is happening now. I wish I could have got a Hermès handbag when we were right by the store."

Nerys held up her hand to shut Tina up. "Right, there's one more thing I need to tell you. It's important it doesn't go to your heads. We have a lot to sort out, right? Well, I gave you all a little boost so we're well placed to achieve it—"

Nerys broke off as a thumping sound came from elsewhere in the pub.

"What's that?" She went over to the cellar door and could see it shaking. She yanked the door open.

Two alpacas hovered in mid-air, bumping up against the door in their bid for freedom. It was like a pair of very ungainly bees trying to find their way out of a room by butting the window.

"Oh yuck!" Tina exclaimed. "Why are they doing that? It's horrible! Don't let them wee on me!"

"You see flying animals and your very first thought is that they want to wee on you?" asked Nerys.

"Yes. It would be awful."

"So, this is one of the new things," said Nerys. "Although I didn't intend to give it to the animals, I must admit." She needed to find out how it worked. She gave a small jump and flapped her hands. "Ooh, yeah! So, we can fly now." She hovered a foot off the ground and worked out how leaning one way then another would steer her in different directions.

Moments later, they were all airborne.

"Well. I was hoping it would be a bit speedier, if I'm honest," said Nerys. "Like, we could fly over to do talks in the Middle East, then fly back for teatime."

"Might be too late for talks by the looks of these feeds," said Ed. His head blocked the screen as he hovered in front of it.

"Get out of the way," muttered Nerys. She gasped when she saw the unmistakable sight of enormous weapons emerging from underground siloes and being readied for deployment. "Someone tell me we got our wires crossed and this is from a film. Are those nukes?"

There was silence.

"How do we tell where this feed is coming from? Where's Spartacus?"

"Still with the president I suppose," said Jefri. "I hope he brings doughnuts back."

Nerys went to the door. "Please don't say the world leaders have gone feral and taken him prisoner." She looked outside. "Oh no."

Spartacus was being hauled bodily along by Deacon Phipps.

44

Nerys had blocked Phipps from her mind, hoping that he'd just decided to leave her alone, but apparently not.

"Surprised to see me, huh?" he said, teenager in one hand and blinged up shepherd's crook in the other. "Now this is a friend of yours, I assume?"

"Never seen him before in my life. I expect he came over from the mainland. You might just as well let him go."

Phipps shook Spartacus. "I don't think so! See, I've been watching that amusement park over there. You have some highly distinguished guests."

"Good old Camp Lookalike, you mean? Those people will be such a hit on the cabaret circuit, once we've perfected their acts."

"Your young friend is some sort of spy operating on your behalf. Obviously you need help when it comes to engineering Armageddon."

"No. Nope." Nerys pulled the door closed behind her, in case he caught sight of flying people and alpacas. "And that's no to the Armageddon part, as well as the help part. I do have some quite urgent business to attend to though, so please just let him go and bugger off."

Spartacus shoved at his captor. "You're a dodgy old paedo. Maybe I just want to talk to famous people. You never thought of that did you? Anyway, she's not the boss of me."

Phipps tightened his grip on Spartacus, and with an extended *sccchhhting*! pulled the head off his crook. "You both need to listen to me very carefully. I have trained all of my life for this role. Nothing will prevent me from interceding. Nothing. The entire future of humanity is at stake, so if I must take a life to further my aims then I will not hesitate to do so."

"What? Are you mad, you daft twat?" spat Spartacus. "I'm a kid, you need to get your hands off me."

"I take no pleasure in this young man, but your leader needs to have her wings clipped. If I need to use my ceremonial crosier to let your blood, then I will live with that stain on my soul."

"No, you really don't need to," urged Spartacus.

Phipps held the top of his crook threateningly. The top was all sparkly bling and curly gold twirls, but the bottom part was a dagger blade, thin and sharp.

"We can talk about th—" Nerys began, but the sound of smashing glass made them all look up.

An alpaca soared through the air and dive bombed Phipps. A well-aimed kick sent his crozier spinning into the distance, then the alpaca landed with a gentle clip clop sound and nuzzled Spartacus.

"Aslan! Good boy, nice work," said Spartacus, scrambling to his feet. He had been knocked to his feet by Aslan's intervention, but was unharmed.

Phipps reclined on the ground, cradling an arm that might have been broken. "This is not over."

Nerys ushered Spartacus and Aslan back inside. She was tempted to leave Phipps lying on the floor as a handy snack for the sabre toothed tiger, but instead helped him to his feet. "Go on, scram, you're embarrassing yourself," she hissed and went back inside the pub building.

"Everything's fine," she said to the querying looks. "I mean, we're running out of windows to smash, but on the plus side, we do have some sort of action hero alpaca in our midst."

"He can fly now," said Spartacus. "He's very smart."

"Flying. Yeah we can talk about that in a minute," said Nerys. "But there are some very alarming images on the feed, Spartacus. Where are they coming from?"

"That's why I went to see the president. The metadata feed, or labels if you like, is separately encrypted. I should be able to get access to it now."

"He just gave it to you?" asked Ed.

"Once I got the rollercoaster working for him, yeah."

A few moments later the screens changed, they all had a detailed caption at the bottom. There were a lot of acronyms that Nerys didn't understand, but the location at least was clearly labelled.

"Coulport, Scotland," she said. "Those are our nukes."

"There are more," said Spartacus. "All over the place."

There was near silence for a few moments as they realised almost every country with a nuclear capability was heading towards launch.

"Well, shit," said Nerys.

Everyone burst out talking at the same time. There were exclamations, ideas and sheer terror in the clamour, and Nerys couldn't make sense of anything. She put her hands over her ears.

"Stop! Shut up!" she screamed.

Everyone was quiet. They all stared at her. Everyone expected her to do something.

"It's fine. It will all be fine. We can fix this," she said. She put a hand to her pocket to pull out the Wish-O-Matic. She'd avoided using it in front of others up to now, but this was no time to be coy. Her hand closed in the empty pocket. She patted herself down, a sick feeling making her sway with the enormity of what had happened. "No. The Wish-O-Matic. It's gone!"

There was only one person who knew about the device.

"Hodshift! Did you do this? Where is it? We need it!"

"Wusn't me," said the demon with a small shake of his head. "Yer know my feelings on the matter. Leave well alone, I say."

"I can't leave this alone!" howled Nerys, waving a manic hand at the screens. "It's a catastrophe! I need to fix it! I need the Wish-O-Matic!"

She mentally walked through her actions since she last had it. "Phipps. It must have fallen out when I helped him up." She ran outside and searched the ground, scuffling through leaves and dirt, but there was nothing there. She looked up and tried to see where he'd gone. "Phipps! Phipps! Come back here, we need to talk!"

There was no sound from the forest, apart from the background twittering and rustling of the nature Nerys had created.

She slumped and went back inside. "The device I've been using to fix things, it's gone. We need to find Phipps, I think he's got it."

"Hold on, hold on!" Ed had a hand up. "We want someone to call off the nukes, yeah? Well, there must be a less, erm, woo-woo way to do that. Haven't you got all the world leaders penned up over the road? Surely you can make them fix things? It's their actual job, isn't it?"

Nerys nodded, her mind a whirl. "We should try that. We should try all of the things. I don't know how much time we have—"

"—Less than an hour," said Spartacus. "That's my best guess."

"Less than an hour, right. We need to divide and conquer."

Tina gave Nerys a penetrating look. "Nerys, dearest, have you brought about the end of the world?"

"No," she said. "Definitely trying to stop it. Um, definitely."

45

As Michael's hands touched the helmet offered to him, there came a sudden blast of trumpet sounds. High and pure, low and blaring, they seemed to come from both near and far. And there was something about them, a quality that defied description, which told Michael they were not part of the massive Hollywood effects-laden practice run going on around them. These trumpets were *for real*.

The theatrical tempest overhead stuttered and dissipated. The riders of the Apocalypse astride their massive alpaca mounts came to an uneasy halt, and every face was raised to this new sign.

"Is it time?" said Gabriel, uncertainty catching in his throat for a moment. He raised his voice. "It is time!"

"Time?" said Michael.

Samael grinned and slapped him on the shoulder. "It's time, brother. Armageddon. The Almighty has spoken."

"Are we...? Are we sure?"

Samael fixed him with a look, then snatched the helmet from Michael's hands and wedged it onto his head. "The warheads of the human arsenal are flying. And so shall we."

He grabbed the breastplate from Omvial and thrust it against Michael, ordering Omvial to help him with the straps.

Across the gulf of Limbo, Lucifer heard the clarion trumpets of the Heavenly City the second they sounded. It brought an involuntary smile to his lips and joy to his heart. "My moment," he whispered.

As he stepped out across the fire-blasted landscape of Hell, it was clear others had heard. Hell's own discordant trumpets sounded. War drums took up a thudding doom-laden beat.

Duke Belphegor came scooting over in his all-terrain chair, the demon Rutspud tripping and stumbling in his wake. "Your armies await!" the duke shouted above the din. "This way!"

He set off at a pace. Lucifer watched him go. Then, with a gentle springing jump, took to the air, spread his wings, and soared.

Below, the uncountable masses of Hell's minions flowed across the inconceivably vast caverns of Hell. The damned human souls were left abandoned, in their pits, on their racks. Some of the more institutionalised were either demanding to know where their torturers were going or simply got on with the business of torturing themselves.

The army of Hell's soldiers, the ones who had been bred for war, gathered in a massive valley. Various captains and sergeant majors, or whatever the infernal equivalent might be, were haranguing and whipping the foot soldiers into line. The demon Berith was at the head of the valley on a steed which looked like the unlikely result of a night of passion between a giant centipede and a suit of armour. His mount bucked and rippled, and Berith grinned like a child who'd been given a flamethrower for Christmas.

Lord Peter stood on a rocky outcrop close by, flicking back and forth through a clipboard of notes.

"Right, right," he said, obviously flustered. "The first wave, composed of imps, gnarlies and gargoyles will line up at the gates of Hell at— What time?"

"Oh-six hundred, sire," said Nero, next to him.

"Right, right. And when's that?" asked Peter, since time in Hell was an entirely arbitrary construct.

"Now?" suggested Nero.

"Berith," said Peter. "I want you to—"

What he wanted was entirely ignored. Berith presented a silencing hand to Peter.

"Lord. This is the business of war, now. My army is following my orders."

"*My* army," said Lucifer, touching down.

Berith twisted in his spikey saddle, wrestling with the reins of his impatient steed. He tried to stare down the newcomer.

Lucifer laughed. "Are you ready to ride?"

Berith acquiesced, but only a fraction, enough to give a begrudging nod.

Belphegor skidded to a halt, throwing up black dust from the ground. "Remember! You need to put on a show!"

"A show?" scoffed Peter.

"Yes!" With a flick of his hand Belphegor encouraged Rutspud to run on towards the awaiting Rampant Tunneller. "We will win this war with cunning, not brute numbers."

"Might makes right," said Berith.

"*I* will win this war," said Lucifer. "We go now! Berith!"

Lucifer shot up again and turned towards the entrance to Hell. He flew on, fast and high, not knowing or caring if Berith's demonic army kept up with him.

As he soared over the entryway to Hell he saw there was already a huge, massed group there. They didn't quite look like soldiers. Many were waving placards. He heard the sound of chanting voices. Perhaps, he thought, these were the bannermen and singers of brave battle songs.

"Onward!" Lucifer called down in an amplified voice that none could deny. "Onward to victory!"

"Lord Lucifer is joining our cause," he heard one voice shout out of the hubbub below.

Lucifer swept his arm round and pointed onward. He swooped low at the great cave entrance and flew out into Limbo.

THE GATES to Heaven were many and massive, yet there were bottlenecks as hundreds of thousands of angels attempted to get through at once. Michael found himself pushing through sign-waving members of the angelic workers' union.

"It's Michael, isn't it?" said a cheery angel as they were pressed together in the gateway.

"Er, yes," he said, surprised that anyone could recognise him with the noseguard of this helmet covering half his face.

"It's me, Myakos," said the angel, tapping his chest. "We met at the gate earlier. I thought you were a human, jumping the queue. You told me you were an archangel. I didn't believe you. How we laughed."

"Um. If you say so."

The angel rummaged around in his robes for a leaflet. "I was wondering if you'd consider joining the Respectful Alliance of Gate Keepers and Greeters."

"I'm not a gate keeper or greeter."

"Oh, we're already branching out," said Myakos. "There are so many sectors where angelic workers are being undervalued and their voices going unheard."

"I'm sorry," said Michael. "I've really got to go. You see, there's this war I have to fight."

"Well, exactly. Now is precisely the time to be thinking about your own job security and benefits. How are your employers looking out for you?"

Michael frowned. "My employers?"

"What happens if you're struck down on the field of combat?"

"I'll be dead, won't I?"

"Exactly! Or even if you're not and you're victorious, what then? Will they throw a parade for you and clap and cheer?"

"Possibly."

"But what does that mean? I don't think clapping and

cheering are sufficient recompense for your services. Front line fighters deserve proper rewards."

There was a tangible release of pressure, a sudden freedom of movement, as they came through the gateway and into the fields of Limbo.

"I really have to go," said Michael politely, leaping upwards to join the angelic forces falling into formation in the sky. At his back he felt golden light and warmth. There was no sun in the afterlife, no need for it. This was the light and the warmth of the Almighty himself. God had come to bear witness to the final battle.

46

Rutspud ran up the steps in the side of the Rampant Tunneller. The vehicle was as big as an earthly train carriage and sat upon two squat sets of caterpillar tracks set just behind its sharp screw nose. If someone had pointed out to Rutspud that it looked awfully like one of the vehicles from the *Thunderbirds* TV show, he would have shrugged, pointing out a great inventor is never frightened to steal ideas.

"Lickspear, Fire up the engines! Wyrmstool, start shovelling coal!" he instructed as he entered.

The interior was cylindrical, half-filled with seating, half-empty for storage. A furnace and engine sat at the rear. An elevated steering area stood at the front, Lickspear sitting at the many levers on the control panel. Rutspud ran to the front and pulled down the periscope. He looked about, glancing momentarily at the columns of Berith's army as they moved off.

"Angle down forty degrees, make straight for Limbo."

He turned to a navigation table and the draughtsman's rulers fixed to its side he would use to draw out their intended journey. The engines rumbled and rattled, then the floor tilted as the nose of the craft dipped.

Behind Rutspud, a team of half a dozen demons sat strapped into their seats. They were all worker-level demons like Rutspud; honest lads who didn't have ideas above their station and had never bought into Hell's propaganda. Rutspud looked back at Codmince, Pigcrack, Rimpurge and—

He blinked. Side by side, sitting politely with their seatbelts on among the other demons were the Serpent and the Scapegoat. The goat paused in its chewing for a moment to give Rutspud a tiny goaty smile.

"Satan's balls! What are you two doing here?" said Rutspud.

"Just along for the ride," said the Serpent smoothly.

Rutspud made a doubtful noise. Given the option he'd have opened the door and kicked the pair of them out, but the vehicle was now crunching through strata of heavy volcanic rock, and he didn't have time to back up to the surface to eject stowaways.

"I don't want any trouble from you two," Rutspud said firmly.

"We'll be good," said the Serpent. "Trust me."

Rutspud made a deeper, even more doubtful noise.

Soon, Rutspud felt the tone of the tunneller's engine change. It became smoother, softer. There was a gloopiness to the running of the vehicle, as though it was spinning its tracks in mud. He looked out through the periscope. The view of the way ahead was obviously limited, given they were digging headfirst, but Rutspud could see white swathes of stuff flowing past his viewfinder.

"Limbo," he said. "We're tunnelling under Limbo itself."

"Engine's running super easy," said Lickspear.

"It's like there's nothing really there," said Rutspud. "It's like... It's like that really soft stuff humans stick in their ears."

"Brains!" shouted Codmince.

"Knitting needles!" shouted Rimpurge.

"Cotton wool," said Rutspud, remembering. "Cotton wool, or candyfloss."

"You should go out and taste what it's like," the Serpent said to Codmince.

"Should I, sir?" said Codmince, already getting up.

"No! Of course not, no," said Rutspud. "And *you*! Don't you dare take your seatbelt off!"

This last was to the Scapegoat, who looked as if it would be delighted to go out and chomp on the local rock. "That's Limbo stuff," said Rutspud. "It's probably dangerous."

"Is it?" said Rimpurge.

"I dunno," shrugged Rutspud. "But it's raw and undefined nothingness."

"Nothing don't sound that dangerous," said Pigcrack.

Pigcrack had lost three arms in the last decade to three surprisingly similar industrial accidents. He'd lost the third one pointing into the machinery, to where his second arm was still lodged. Pigcrack's grasp of what was dangerous was more than a little suspect.

"Limbo is what everything was before it was something,"

said Rutspud. "It's just raw potential. In the right hands, anything can be made from Limbo stuff. Look at that creature- thing Lord Satan made when he was just passing through. He—" Rutspud glanced around the cabin as though, against all probability, it might be there with them. "Where did that creature get to?"

HELL WAS ALMOST EMPTY. Hell was quiet.

The demons had all gone. Gone were the warriors, strikers, spectators, those who thought it would be nice to take a wander into Limbo (and maybe later Earth itself was the rumour). Gone were the demons, devils, imps, shades, ghouls, gargoyles, fallen angels and weird beasts conjured from the minds of bored medieval monks. All of them gone, leaving behind the millions of damned souls who were the main purpose of Hell's existence.

This came as relief to many, and generally they treated it as unexpected holiday, or a snow day when school is closed, and the teachers are nowhere to be seen. Many kicked back and relaxed. In several places, barbecues were lit. Some of the damned, with a bit of free time on their hands, set about decorating their pits and having a general tidy up. Because some people are like that.

In the ruined cellars of the Fortress of Nameless Dread, the Research and Development laboratories of Lord Belphegor were also quiet – apart from a crunchy, slurping sound.

Chomp chomp chomp sl-sl-sl-sl.

The long-necked, long-legged, but not really alpaca-like

creature Clovenhoof had created from Limbo stuff chewed and slobbered merrily over the massive mound in the corner of the laboratory. The creature had been in existence for no more than a few days. It hadn't been given much in the way of purpose, or biological urges. It didn't have any drive or direction. It had been fussed over and loved. It had done something messy to one of Lord Peter's cushions. And now it was enjoying the textural sensation of running its mouth over this big lump. The surface, beneath the outer crud layer, was equally rough. It was pitted and ridged and scaly.

A small hole flared in the surface. The creature ran its mouth over it and waggled its lips around the rim. The hole gave a blast of hot air and the Limbo creature skittered back. A second hole appeared next to it. Nostrils.

The Limbo beast took a step forward. The mound quaked and a head reared. The Limbo alpaca didn't have any cultural reference points, so did not consider the head to be at least the size of a large family car. Which it was. Dust cascaded as a mouth opened in that head. The mouth was huge and crocodilian. The lower jaw stretched, and hundreds of sharp teeth could be seen, each one a curving black dagger.

The Limbo creature, in its short existence, had not known danger. It had not known fear. With nothing but curiosity (and a desire to lick this gargantuan creature some more), it stepped forward to inspect the jaws more closely.

NERYS GAVE URGENT COMMANDS, as elsewhere in the world nuclear missiles prepared to wreak havoc.

"Some of us search for Phipps, and some of us get the various presidents to call off the missile strikes," she said.

"Aren't you forgetting something?" asked Tina, a caustic edge to her voice. "You made us all prisoners of this building. We can't do any of those things."

"Oh yeah, well I can fix— Oh, no, I can't." Nerys clenched her fists.

"Only you and Spartacus can go outside, and Spartacus is doing a great job in here," said Tina.

"Spartacus fixed it for himself though, didn't he?" said Nerys. "He got behind the mission. Why can't the rest of you do that?" She stared at them, challenge blazing from her eyes. "Come on!"

Spartacus nudged PJ who was standing next to him. "Give it a go."

PJ and Jefri were either startled by the sudden attention or just cresting a sugar high from all of the doughnuts Spartacus had brought. It wasn't clear.

"Eh?" said PJ. "What should we do?"

"You want to stop the world being obliterated by nuclear missiles?" asked Nerys.

"Sure."

"Step outside then."

The two of them went to the door and stepped outside.

"Oh cool!" said PJ. "We can go and see if there's candyfloss—"

"Wait there!" commanded Nerys. "Now, who's next?"

Ben and Ed were able to cross the threshold, so they joined PJ and Jefri.

"Hodshift, you too," said Nerys.

"Not sure as I can get behind the mission, I'm afraid," said Hodshift, shuffling from foot to foot.

"What? Surely you don't want to see an end to all life on earth?" Nerys's arms were getting tired from all of the wild gesturing at the ominous scenes displayed on the screens, but she did it anyway. "Look! Destruction and death to all living things. Who wants to see that?"

"It's not that so much as the meddlin', see? I'm more of a one fer lettin' nature take its course. I warned yer early doors about unintended consequences. It's Sodom and Gomorrah all over again."

"Gah!" Nerys wanted to wring his stupid yellow demon neck, but he was consistent. She had to give him that.

Lennox had drifted out of sight. Maybe it was best to leave someone who could furnish people with drinks. That left Tina.

"You coming, Tina?" Nerys asked.

Tina went to the door, but as she tried to leave, she was repelled backwards. "Um."

"Come on Tina!" roared Nerys. "You do not want to see the world burn. Get behind this!"

Tina tried again, taking a little run-up, but she was flung backwards and stumbled to the floor. "This is really annoying! Seriously Nerys, could this be any worse? I could have done a much better job of this than you have."

And there it was. Nerys rolled her eyes. "Tina, you halfwit! Are you seriously saying you're not on board because you're annoyed with my management style? Get over yourself. In fact, here's a thought. If there is any kind of tomorrow, then Future Tina can take a free swing at Future

Nerys and Future Nerys will just suck it up. How about that?"

Tina stood up and gave a nod of acknowledgement. "I might be motivated by that mental image. Let me have another go." She gave the door a hard stare, then charged at it with a roar. She rushed through, barrelling into the group waiting outside.

"Hooray!" The group applauded spontaneously.

"Two groups then. Ed, seems as if you might like to try your hand at international diplomacy. Take Jefri and PJ as back up, and see if you can get those presidents and leaders to talk to each other. Then liaise with Spartacus to see how we can get the message out to their countries. The rest of you spread out from here, see if you can find Phipps. He can't have gone far. I'll monitor from inside. Maybe our phones will work, but I doubt it. Everybody, signal with a fist to the sky if you find Phipps or have something significant to report. Don't forget you can fly!"

Nerys watched as the group took to the skies.

47

In the Rampant Tunneller, Rutspud consulted his charts. "I think we've got to be close," he said.

"You don't know?" said the Serpent witheringly.

"It really is hard to tell," said Rutspud. "We are, you might have noticed, underground. In Hell, we could judge distances by cutting times but here..."

The engine abruptly rose in pitch and volume and the craft jolted.

"Stone!" shouted Lickspear.

Rutspud grabbed the periscope and looked. "La-di-dah white marble! We're under the Celestial City." He went back to his charts. "Assuming marble and volcanic basalt are ... well, not the same..." He scribbled on his chart and made swift calculations. "Ten degrees up bubble, Lickspear." He'd always wanted to say that, for some reason. "More coal, Wyrmstool!"

They started to rise. Rutspud turned to face his

colleagues and, unconsciously, he put his hands behind his back in the manner of commanding officers everywhere when addressing the troops.

"Very soon, we will be in the Celestial City," he said. "If we are lucky, the Research Centre for Scriptural Exegesis will be close by. It's a big building with domes on the top. I don't know how many of those there can be in Heaven. For all of us, it's our first time inside the Celestial City and for most of you, it's your first time outside the realm of Hell. So, the first thing you're going to notice is that it's going to be very bright."

Codmince's hand shot up. "Is it true there's no ceiling?"

"As you know full well from our briefing. So, under your chair, in your emergency case, next to your sunglasses, there is your own portable ceiling."

Pigcrack already had his out so he put it on. It was effectively a sun visor on a stretchy headback, albeit one that stretched out a foot in front of Pigcrack's temple and came round in a semi-circle.

"Cool," he said.

"I would advise everyone against looking up," said Rutspud. "If you are overcome by nausea and existential terror, I am not carrying you back to Hell. Our sole goal is to get this—" he held up the scroll Belphegor had given him "— into the records of the scriptorium. By the power of the Big Guy Upstairs, this will dictate our own victory."

Codmince's hand shot up again. "If the Celestial City is all holy, won't we be blasted into nothingness the moment we set foot on it?"

"That is also a possibility," said Rutspud. "Which is why

you will also find in your emergency case a pair of rubber Crocs to act as an insulator between you and the holy ground of Heaven. May I suggest you put them on now."

THE PLAINS of Limbo were vast. Actually, they were infinite. Limbo was nothing. Limbo contained nothing. To give it borders was to give it *something*. And yet, from high above, it seemed to Michael that the mass of Heaven's armies filled Limbo from end to end.

There were angels and principalities and thrones. There were powers and dominions and virtues. There were the mighty cherubim who looked nothing like the little baby angel cherubs featuring in Earthly art. They threw back their lion heads and roared their defiance. Several savagely pawed at the air. And then there were the seraphim, most powerful of all angels. Many-winged and, in some cases, bristling with eyes, the mightiest angels hovered over all like warships, ready to rain down destruction on their enemy.

"Gosh, the gang's all here, aren't they?" said Michael weakly, but no one seemed to hear him.

And from across the plains came the forces of Hell. They were, in comparison to Heaven's army, an undifferentiated and shapeless mass. From a distance they were nothing but a tide of brown and black and red and sickly yellow. Certain distinct creature types could be seen. The incubi and succubi (who looked like they were dressed for a suburban swingers party rather than the final battle). Drudes marched in ordered lines. Behemoth and the impossibly huge Ziz bird moved through the back lines, probably crushing hundreds of their allied troops with every footstep.

A band of what Michael took to be Heaven's angelic foot soldiers was streaming ahead of the main force.

Gabriel swooped into position beside Michael. He grinned. "They are filled with righteous desire for victory, wouldn't you say?"

Michael screwed up his eyes and squinted. "No. If I'm not mistaken, those are the protesting angels."

"What?"

Michael peered harder. "Yep. I recognise the ones at the front. The Respectful Alliance of Gate Keepers and Greeters. They're just marching to demand job security in the world to come."

Gabriel laughed in disbelief. "Then that front row of demons is going to make mincemeat of them all."

Michael squinted even harder at the ranks of demons who were way out in front of Hell's army lines.

"Er, no. They appear to be striking workers as well. If I could just see— Goodness, their penmanship is atrocious. The, er, Combined Union of Gatekeepers, Bum Pokers, Ancillary Workers and Service Demons."

"You're making that up," said Gabriel.

"Yes, I'm not sure about the bum poking bit. Maybe I'm misreading it. But it appears there's equal worker discontent among Hell's forces."

"Then let them make mincemeat of each other!"

"Is this really what the end of all things looks like?" said Michael, both horrified and disappointed. "I would have expected something a bit more organised."

Gabriel's hand shot forward and he pointed. "There! It is the adversary!"

A speck in the sky was resolving, becoming the winged form of Lucifer.

Michael felt a moment of sickening déjà vu, except it wasn't déjà vu because they really had been here before. Angels and fallen angels would be pitted against each other in the sight of the Almighty and, despite what individuals on either side might say, the outcome was not fixed.

"You can beat him, Michael," said Gabriel and slapped him on the back.

As Michael swooped down to meet Lucifer, Gabriel produced his horn from beneath his robes and began to toot the order to advance.

Hesitant though he was, Michael flew as swiftly as possible to meet Lucifer. It would be far better to meet him in the unoccupied territories of Limbo, as far from others as possible, a chance to try to talk some sense into what remained of Jeremy Clovenhoof.

Lucifer sped to meet him, and they drew up, ten yards apart, high above the closing lines.

"We don't have to do this," said Michael.

Lucifer looked amused. A dark curl of hair fell perfectly over his perfect brow. Lucifer didn't wear any armour. Michael guessed it would obscure his good looks, and the Proud One, the great betrayer, couldn't bear to have his cruel beauty hidden.

"But we want to do this, don't we?" said the Fallen One.

"The world will be destroyed," said Michael.

Lucifer shrugged.

"You liked the world," Michael reminded him. "Lambrini. Findus crispy pancakes. *Love Island.* Heavy metal music. Internet porn. Roadkill. Shouting out the answers at pub quizzes. You love all of that."

"A part of me did," said Lucifer. "But that part of me has gone." He cast his eyes about as though he might see the purged part of himself. "Down there, possibly. Slapping itself in the face with its oversized member."

"You..." Michael frowned. "You sacrificed your penis?"

Lucifer laughed. "A pure and simple example of the Almighty's flawed human design. Seriously. A little flappy sausage tube right there on show? Lunacy. An embarrassment. Glad to be rid of it."

Michael was perturbed. "I can see why you're angry, now. I'd be angry if they took mine."

"I'm not angry!"

"I mean, I thought it was stupid when I was first sent to earth and given all the human ... accoutrements. I didn't even want to touch mine."

"Exactly!"

"And women! Oh, they don't get off lightly either, let me tell you. Sure, their genitals might look like they're all neatly tucked away, but seriously, that's a plumbing disaster down there. No wonder women need a whole gynaecological department in hospitals. Ugh! Rubbish!"

"And God placed those creatures above us!" Lucifer snorted.

"I know!" said Michael. "I really struggled to see it at first."

Lucifer hesitated. "At first?" he said.

Michael waved his hands at their two armies. "Look at us. Going to war with swords and pitchforks. Our minds are trapped in the bronze age. But humans are ingenious and inventive."

"They keep finding better and better ways to kill themselves, you mean."

Michael shook his head. "They keep finding better and better ways to do *everything*. I've met people on Earth who preached nothing but the end of the world. They speak of Armageddon as the dawning of a bright new era. Those people have minds as closed as yours and mine. They see no future, and they have given up their fight to control it. But there are the others – the millions of others."

"Destroying the world with their cars and factories," Lucifer sneered. "Breeding like rabbits until only war and plague and starvation can halt their numbers. You admire that?"

Michael shrugged. "Sure, they've screwed up a few times. On an hourly basis, really. And they've got a mountain to climb to fix some of their problems. But humans on Earth have never been this ... *connected* before. If there is injustice and suffering, they know what it is and they have the tools to tackle it. They can feed the hungry and treat the sick. They can educate the young and care for the old."

"Someone hasn't been watching the news," said Lucifer.

"I didn't say they were always good at fixing those problems. But we need to give them time. They've got some rather urgent deadlines of their own, to be frank. But we need to give them time and encouragement. They don't need gods and angels and the promise of a gleaming afterlife.

Heaven should be a place on Earth. And humans should build it."

There was a rising roar, from ten thousand indistinguishable mouths, as the front lines of the unionised angels and the striking demons met below them.

"The war is here," said Lucifer. "It's unstoppable."

"Nothing is unstoppable," said Michael.

Lucifer flicked his wrist and a sword that gleamed like a strip of sunlight was suddenly in his hand. "You are a naïve and optimistic fool, Michael."

"I'd rather just think of myself as human," said Michael.

He held out his hand and there was now a long bronze lance in it.

Lucifer's face was filled with a terrible joy. "Come then, brother! Let's see how well naïve human optimism fares against my blade."

Michael leaped forward. Lucifer side-stepped and swiped with his sword. Metal rang against metal.

Spartacus appeared at the door of the pub, frowning. "What's going on, can *everybody* fly now?"

"We all can," said Nerys. "Now, let's think about how we can patch our presidents through to their mission control chums if Ed can talk them round."

"Really fly? Me too?"

"Yes, yes. Amazing, I know. Now, I really, really need you to—"

Spartacus wasn't listening. Grinning, he launched himself upwards with a loud whoop.

"—Wait!"

Spartacus shot to the ceiling and hit his head on a protruding beam with a loud crack. He fell to the floor, limp.

"No! Spartacus!" Nerys rushed to his side. "Lennox, he's out cold. What do we do?"

"I'm getting a cloth," said Lennox.

"He's our only hope of getting peace out there to the warmongers and you want to polish the bar?"

"Cool damp cloth on the bump, bring down the swelling," said the barman, now crouching by the teenager.

"Oh. Right, yeah." Nerys applied the cloth to the boy's head. "Shit. What am I even doing, Lennox?"

"With that cloth, or in general?" he asked.

"Generally."

"You're doing your best, I reckon. Not very well, but you're trying. Now why don't I take over here, and you can keep an eye on your team."

He gently took the cloth from Nerys. She stood up to look at the screens, which continued to show the movements of everyone in the area.

"Oh fuck!"

Ed, Jefri, PJ and Tina all had their fists in the air. Tina had Phipps in what looked like a pair of handcuffs. Nerys shouldn't have been surprised that Tina had handcuffs.

"Without Spartacus, we can't get their message out, can we?" Nerys nodded at the world leaders in the amusement park. "They have no comms, and we can't release them from the park without the Wish-O-Matic."

"Correct."

"You actually understand the situation?"

Lennox shrugged. "Sure. Old Clovenhoof is off somewhere else. You've teamed up with that yellow demon over there, and some wish-granting device—"

"Wait, you know Hodshift is a demon?"

Lennox grinned. "A barman sees everything."

At the end of the bar, Hodshift raised a martini glass in cheers.

"You should be more surprised the others don't realise it," said Lennox. "I mean, the little feller's got a hundred ears. But, yeah, I get it. You're trying to fix the world with magic and—" He looked around and sighed. "Without your magic wishing stick the world is doomed."

"Sodom and Gomorrah," said Hodshift. "Guvnor, you wouldn't mind putting another one of your fizzy piss drinks in here, would you?"

48

Lucifer stabbed and twisted, but Michael was too close for him to make effective use of his blade. Michael fell closer against him, entwined his legs around Lucifer's, and with the flat of his lance, pinned back one of Lucifer's wings.

They fell. Lucifer yelled. He screamed to Michael to break apart, but Michael held him in a powerful hug.

At least the ground of Limbo was not that hard. They slammed down and rolled apart. Great clods of white nothingness flew out from their impact. Lucifer rolled away and leapt to his feet before Michael could reaffirm his grip on him.

There were angels and demons about them. A hurried space had been created where the two angels had fallen, but beyond that immediate circle, the creatures of Heaven and Hell were tightly packed.

And they were all staring at Lucifer. Lucifer looked from

the angels to the demons and then back to the angels. They were just standing there, watching.

"Why aren't you fighting?" he shouted. "Don't just stand there!"

Michael staggered to his feet and looked about. Panting, he waved at the placards and signs. A pair of enterprising demons were carrying a sort of embroidered banner which read THE NOBLE AND HISTORIC ORDER OF BUM POKERS. It had a big pair of stylised human buttocks on it. Lucifer had no idea where in Hell demons might possibly get the materials and thread for the sewing of such a thing. The needles he could understand but everything else…

"Strikers," said Michael.

"It's management!" yelled an angel.

As one, angels and demons waved their signs in well-mannered annoyance.

"We want guaranteed job security until the end of time!" shouted an angel.

"Longer!" shouted a demon.

"And paid holidays!" shouted another.

"Plus a recognised training and accreditation scheme!"

"Plus medical and dental!"

"What's that?" another queried.

"I don't know, but it's a thing!"

"We want that too!" shouted a demon.

"And we want whatever they're getting!" shouted an angel.

"Equal pay for equal work!" agreed a demon.

"What is happening here?" Lucifer demanded.

"They are … uniting…?" said Michael.

The idea didn't seem to have occurred to the striking workers until that moment. The angel Myakos stared in incomprehension for just a moment, then randomly grabbed the hand of the nearest demon and thrust it into the air.

"Fair work and job security for angels and demons alike!"

"Aye!" shouted the demon. "We want what they've got! And vice versa! But even more so!"

"No war until disputes are settled!" yelled another voice.

"No Armageddon until I'm a-geddin' decent working conditions!" bellowed another.

A cheer went up.

Lucifer glared at Michael. There was actual fire in those eyes now. "This is your doing!"

"Nothing of the sort," said Michael. "I swear."

Lucifer swung round at the closing crowd. "This isn't how it ends! This ends with my victory!"

"Maybe we should call the whole thing off until we've got this straightened out," suggested Michael, lightly.

Lucifer sprung up in the air, flourished his sword, and prepared to come down on Michael with a killer blow. Michael leapt up, wings folded behind him like a jet plane, lance aimed straight up. Weapons clashed and the strikers flooded into the gap where they had just stood.

"You can't win!" Lucifer laughed. "My victory is already written."

THE RAMPANT TUNNELLER came up into the Celestial City, great chunks of broken flagstone cascading off its spiral nose cone. The vehicle came down from its elevated angle and onto its caterpillar tracks with a loud and jolting thump.

Rutspud, clinging to an overhead strap, addressed his demon colleagues.

"We have arrived, and by luck or judgement, I'd say the big domed building to our left is the Research Centre for Scriptural Exegesis. I've got the scroll which will ensure our boys on the battlefield win the day – or at least get to come home in as few pieces as possible."

Rutspud turned the wheel handle on the bulkhead door and pushed it open. Yellow, loving light flooded the vehicle.

Pigcrack recoiled and hissed.

"Sunglasses, everyone," Rutspud reminded them and leapt out. The demon squad followed.

The Serpent and the Scapegoat, still in their seats, looked at each other. The Scapegoat had nibbled through its seatbelt on the journey here.

"And you still have *our* scroll, don't you?" said the Serpent.

The Scapegoat reached behind itself and pulled out the smaller and more tightly rolled scroll: Lucifer's much more specific and selfish plan. The uncreation of the human world and the installation of Lucifer as Lord over all.

"Good." The Serpent wriggled from its own seatbelt with ease and out into the Celestial City.

The demons were a short distance ahead. With sunglasses and sun visors on, and big plastic slippers to protect them from the holy ground of Heaven, the demons looked like a band of elderly holidaymakers on a sunshine vacation.

The stragglers were talking amongst themselves.

"Where's the pits then?" said the demon Codmince. "I don't see no pits."

"There's no pits," said the demon Wyrmstool. "They've just got these posh buildings."

"Then where do they do the torturin' if they've got no pits?" said Lickspear.

"They don't do no torturing," said Wyrmstool.

"What?" said Pigcrack.

"They don't do no torturing. Least that's what I heard."

"Nah, you've got that wrong," said Codmince. "Torturing is what the afterlife is for. What do they do here if they're not torturing?"

"Other stuff," said Wyrmstool, with the vague air of someone who really wasn't sure what that other stuff might be.

"Scourging?" suggested Pigcrack.

"That's just torture."

"But it's a different kind of torture."

"Different to what?"

"Different to the torture they don't do here."

"But they don't do torture here," said Wyrmstool.

"What about gouging? They must do some gouging."

Codmince looked down at the Serpent as it overtook the bickering demons.

"And why ain't he bursting into flames or nothing? We got to wear these stupid shoes and he's just wriggling along on his belly."

"I'm not a demon," said the Serpent. "'*The Serpent was*

craftier than any of the wild animals the Lord God had made'," he quoted.

"And I'm just a goat," said the Scapegoat, skipping alongside.

"But you should test it," the Serpent said to Codmince. "Take off your shoes."

Codmince had his foot out of his shoe and was holding it fearfully above the ground when Rutspud shouted from up ahead. "Don't you bloody dare! Do not listen to the Serpent! I can't believe you need to be told that!"

"I was just testing," whined Codmince.

"Shoes on! Inside!"

The Research Centre for Scriptural Exegesis was the tallest and most ornate of the buildings in the local vicinity, although that was like saying something was the wettest puddle, or the hottest fire. Everything here was grand, elegant and ornate, to the point where words lost meaning.

The Serpent was not interested in architecture. It was however interested to note that Lucifer had been correct. This building, indeed this entire city, appeared to be empty. No-one, human or angel, had come running out to complain about the tunnelling machine which had come up in the middle of their previously pristine plaza. Everyone had gone out to either participate in or observe the final battle.

It slithered up the steps to the entrance and was over the threshold a moment after Rutspud.

"Split up!" Rutspud commanded his crew once they were in the vast desk-filled ground floor. "We need to find the pneumatic tubes that will send the scroll into the official records. Find the tube then find me. Go!"

The idiot demons ran off in all directions.

"This way," the Serpent hissed to the Scapegoat and led it down a side corridor that none of the others had taken.

"You know where to go?" said the Scapegoat.

It's not easy for a snake to shrug but the Serpent gave it a go. "I'm sure they're everywhere. We just need to do this out of the sight of the others."

It looked up and saw a tube of glass and concertina rubber descending from a great height to behind a desk.

"There!"

The Serpent wrapped and wriggled its way up a chair leg and onto the desk where a mountain of books and scrolls stood.

"It's behind here somewhere," it said and nudged the nearest scroll off the table.

The Scapegoat reared and butted the table violently with its horns. The unstable mound of scrolls wobbled and fell and, as they rolled away, an opening to the pneumatic tube system was revealed.

"Ah-ha!" said the Serpent. And in front of it, oh so conveniently, was a lozenge-shaped cylinder for carrying items through the tubes. With its lower jaw, the Serpent flipped open the little door. "Pass me the scroll."

The Scapegoat raised its head and spat the little scroll onto the desk.

"Excellent," said the Serpent and slid it inside. "Ta da!" Once posted into the system, all reality would be rewritten, with Lucifer as master overall.

"This would make an enormous cigarette," said the

Scapegoat. It held a large scroll by one end in its mouth and swung it from side to side.

"You should definitely smoke that," suggested the Serpent automatically.

"I should," agreed the Scapegoat, looking around for a light.

The Serpent produced a zippo lighter. It had no pockets, but a creature born to tempt and debase had to have access to certain instruments of temptation and debasement. Forbidden fruit didn't just grow on trees. The goat poked the scroll in the snake's direction and the Serpent lit the end. The dried and ancient scroll quickly caught light.

The Scapegoat took a mighty inhalation and coughed out thick grey smoke. The Serpent laughed at the foolish Scapegoat. The Scapegoat laughed to see that he was being entertaining and paraded back and forth, swinging his massive roll-up. And the more he coughed and spluttered, the more the pair of them laughed.

The Scapegoat brushed carelessly against a number of desks and shelves, shedding smouldering ash across the floor. Here and there new fires sprang up among books and scrolls, but the Serpent didn't care. Fire was chaos. The Serpent loved chaos.

"You look so cool," it said as the idiot goat hacked and coughed and cavorted about for the Serpent's amusement.

49

Michael stabbed. Lucifer blocked and tried to riposte, but Michael stabbed again. That simple lance was relentless. The bloody angel, the bloody effete Archangel Michael, was driving him back!

"It! Shouldn't! Be! Like! This!" Lucifer panted, fending off blow after blow.

The stupid Serpent and the goat should have put the scroll in the scriptorium by now. This should all have been undone. No war, no hell, no petty politics, and certainly no Earth to fight over. Had his minions been so pathetic they couldn't complete one simple task?

Below them a war was not exactly raging. Hell's and Heaven's respective armies hadn't yet managed to reach each other. Directly beneath the fighting angels a great mass of discontented workers had formed two lines and were spreading out, each haranguing their own side. Angels waved placards in the faces of spear-wielding angels.

Demons thrust their signs at their demon brethren. The Final Battle had turned into a protest march and both powers were failing to police it.

Lucifer desperately swung with his sword and swooped back to create some distance between him and Michael. He just needed a breather. He just needed to personally regroup, find his strength and...

"You won't win!" he shouted at Michael. Unfortunately he could hear the self-pity in his voice.

Michael, equally breathless but still somehow less worn down, rolled his shoulders. "You know what's funny?" he said.

"What?" snapped Lucifer.

"I remember it being harder last time."

From across the plains of Limbo there came a massive boom. It was one of those sounds that rolled around: a huge edgeless wall of noise which nonetheless carried, in its heart, the notion that something catastrophic had happened. Hundreds of thousands of heads turned.

A vast shape approached through the air. It spread its wings further. It grew. It didn't just grow by getting nearer. It was getting nearer, *and* it was growing. It was red and had seven heads, each on a sinewy and sinuous neck as fat as a skyscraper.

"Oh," said Michael softly.

"The Great Dragon," said Lucifer.

Memory was strange. Religious truth was strange. Lucifer clearly recalled that it was he, the angel Lucifer, who had rebelled against God. It was he who had been cruelly and unfairly defeated in the War in Heaven by Michael and thrown down to Hell. And yet he also recalled, just as clearly, that Michael's fight, both then and now, was with the Great Dragon. The part of Lucifer that recalled his sordid and earthly existence as Jeremy Clovenhoof remembered the large banner hanging at the rear of St Michael's Church in Boldmere, in which the Archangel Michael was poised, lance held high, to run through the serpentine Great Dragon. In truth, the image did not do this creature any justice. The dragon on the wall hanging was barely bigger than a horse, a sad-faced horror brought low. This Great Dragon – *the* Great Dragon – was a slathering and fuming physical embodiment of hatred and chaos. Its scales shone with slick poison. Its talons were yellow and brown, dyed to their roots with blood. And as for size, it was bigger than— Well, it was rapidly defying scale. Bigger than an aircraft carrier, bigger than a mountain. Soon enough, one would have to start using only geographically-based similes. It was currently bigger than Liechtenstein and any moment would be bigger than Barbados or Luxembourg.

What Lucifer didn't recall about the Great Dragon's past appearances was any mention of a small white and very ugly creature riding on it. Again, his own specifically Luciferous memories of it were vague, but yes, riding upon the brow of one of the dragon's seven heads was the creature Jeremy Clovenhoof had made from Limbo-stuff.

Michael turned the lance in his hands and Lucifer could see that those hands were trembling.

"Am I expected to fight both of you?" he said, almost laughing with disbelief.

On wings big enough to cover the Vatican on one side and

San Marino on the other, the Great Dragon soared low, opened its mighty jaws, and vomited fire onto the armies below. Demons and angels, it did not distinguish. Huge rolling rivers of napalm death flooded out, cutting through ranks of warriors and burning through the very fabric of Limbo itself. Forces scattered, the roars of battle became screams of panic.

"Was this your plan?" Michael shouted at Lucifer. "This carnage?"

"No plan of mine," Lucifer replied.

The Great Dragon twisted in the air. The Limbo creature on its head, grinning moronically, tilted into the wind as though it was riding a surfboard. More fire belched forth and down below the ground was sinking, melting away. Until suddenly, there was nothing below. A great sinkhole, a chasm, had opened up like a break in the clouds.

Lucifer looked down and saw the world under it all. It was the Almighty's creation, Earth. Willing and unwilling, leaping, flying and falling, demons and angels poured through the chasm and towards the Earth.

THUNDER RUMBLED overhead as Nerys flew out to meet Tina. Dark grey clouds rumbled ahead. Typical, thought Nerys. Gain the magical ability to fly just before it starts to tip down with rain. And also on the day when the Earth might be engulfed in a nuclear war.

She dropped down beside Tina who had the crazy Deacon Phipps in handcuffs (accessorised with pink faux fur).

"Nice work, Tina," she said. "Now, we just need Phipps to hand over the device he picked up."

"No idea what you're talking about," said Phipps. "You might as well let me go now."

"No chance," said Nerys. "You're Tina's plaything now. I'd be afraid, if I were you."

"Did it look like a little Dictaphone thing?" asked Tina. "I found him smashing it up with a rock."

"Evil work of the devil," spat Phipps.

A cold wave of horror washed over Nerys. "No. That can't be. You can't have broken it."

"He did," said Tina. "Lots of little pieces."

"But Spartacus is out cold, and we needed him to make the comms work and if we can't—" She couldn't wrap her head around what would happen if they couldn't get the message out.

From nearby, Ben, Ed, Jefri and PJ descended. Ed's flying was encumbered by the weight of the man he was carrying who, if Nerys wasn't very much mistaken, was the American President. Ed let the old man down gently, then tried to rub the feeling back into strained arms.

"Here we are!" he said. "The woman who will sort it all out for us. Now Nerys, let me introduce you to my very good friend—"

Nerys shook her head. "It's over, Ed."

"What?"

"Spartacus is out cold, so we can't do the comms. And the device is broken."

"No," Ed gave a small laugh, as if he was embarrassed in

front of his new VIP friend. "No, that can't be right. It can't be over."

Nerys pummelled her forehead with her fingertips. "We've trapped the leaders of every country here. The armed forces of the world have responded with the worst kind of knee-jerk reaction."

"And the sky's gone weird," said PJ.

"Not at the top of my list," Nerys seethed.

"No, really weird," said Ben, his face raised to the sky. There was something sufficiently ghostly and awestruck in his voice that forced Nerys to look up.

'Weird' did not begin to cover the sheer astonishing imagery of what was going on in the sky overhead. Nerys's only points of reference were some of the church ceilings she and Clovenhoof had seen on their 'honeymoon' tour of Italy a few years back; those ones where the dome was surrounded by a circle of painted clouds and the great and the good of Heaven were shown as looking down, robes flowing, halos gleaming.

Except this was no oil painting, not in any sense. Directly above, the amassed clouds had pulled back into a wide circle and ... things were pouring through it. Yes, there was a bright white and holy sky above, and yes, some of those things flying down were definitely angels. But there were other things beside. Demons, hoofed, spindly-legged, bloated, horned, many-limbed, were tumbling down like a succession of skydivers. The shower of angels and demons tumbled and mixed and fought as they fell.

"I think if this is a coma dream," said Ben, "I'll just take death now, please."

. . .

CHAOS AND CARNAGE ruled over the battlefield in Limbo. If the end of the world was meant to be a showcase of the horrors of war then that job had been achieved. Angelic and demonic forces were locked in close and bloody battle. Limbs were hacked, bodies were skewered, and the ground flowed with the grue of the dismembered. It was impossible to distinguish which of the figures were loyal combatants, and which were engaged in the difficult and seemingly bloody business of fighting for workers' rights. Not that it mattered. Chaos and carnage were the order of the day.

Yet the bloodshed was but a decorative border to the main event unfolding in the widening rift between the afterlife and the mortal world. From his vantage point above, Michael could see down onto the Earth.

The Book of Revelation did indeed read like a step-by-step guide to the Apocalypse. It was a list. This happened, then this, then this. It made the end of the world sound neat and orderly. The reality, Michael could see, was nothing of the sort. Whether it was fire or blood or darkness or bitter waters, everything was being thrown at the Earth at once. And the Great Dragon – the physical representation of Hell's hatred, the sum total of the bitter moodiness of every teenager who had been sent to their bedroom and who had stomped on every stair, slammed every door and screamed they hadn't asked to be born – the Great Dragon was pouring out its hatred onto the poor and mostly innocent people of the world.

And what was most galling, at least to Michael's eyes, was

that Heaven's forces seemed only focused on their own petty victory over Hell.

There was the blast of discordant horns. Michael could see Hell's forces in Limbo suddenly swell and lead a charge against Heaven's lines. Where this fresh energy – and fresh numbers? – had come from, he couldn't tell. It was almost as if someone had suddenly and magically decreed that Hell should win the fight.

"This is not good," he muttered to himself.

"It is glorious!" yelled Lucifer ecstatically, barrelling across the sky towards him.

The fallen one was spattered with the blood of the slain, and a fresh wildness filled his eyes. He swung at Michael as he sped by, and Michael parried his blade away.

"I don't want to fight you," said Michael.

"No choice," said Lucifer.

"We will win," said Michael.

As if in agreement, there was fresh trumpeting from the direction of the Celestial City, a hundred horns, harmonious and insistent. Then, across the plains (perhaps as a little mortal film director with a megaphone shouted "Action!") there came the mighty Horsemen of the Apocalypse: taller than worlds and intent on spreading righteous justice.

Except they weren't *horse*men. The last minute artistic direction had been kept.

Lucifer was so surprised he forgot he was meant to be attacking Michael. "Are they … are they llamas?"

"Alpaca, actually," said Michael.

"You decided that the Four Horsemen of the Apocalypse should be—"

"Please. Please, don't. It's not my decision. I'm embarrassed for everyone involved, I can assure you."

"It's so stupid," said Lucifer.

Michael sighed. "I know. I know."

And while Lucifer was momentarily distracted by the approach of the alpacas of the Apocalypse, Michael tucked his wings behind him and plummeted like a diving falcon through the rift in Limbo and into the skies of Earth. He brought his lance forward and aimed towards the Great Dragon. Above and behind him, Lucifer gave a shout of annoyance and followed.

50

On the forested island of Doggerland, beneath an increasingly reddening sky, a handful of Boldmere residents (and the President of the United States) looked up at the enormous entity coming down through the clouds.

"It's a dragon," whispered Jefri.

"Did you wish for a dragon, Nerys?" said Tina, suspiciously.

Nerys could only shake her head. If she had wished for a dragon, Nerys would certainly have wished for one more pleasing to the eye than this one. This was no sleek and majestic fantasy creature. It was a seven-headed beast, as cute and cuddly as a famished crocodile.

"*A great red dragon with seven heads and ten horns and seven crowns on its heads...*" she heard herself quoting.

At the end of a huge snaking neck a mouth gaped and

liquid fire spewed forth, falling like molten rain upon the forests.

"It's coming for us!" yelled Ed.

"Why us?" said PJ.

Nerys saw the suspicious look Tina gave her.

"Not *everything* is about me!" Nerys tutted.

"Oh! Now she realises!" Tina sniffed. "You messed this up, Nerys!"

"Me? I was trying to fix it. Fix this shitty world with its shitty selfish people."

"By what? Starting wars? Magicking alpacas out of the air?"

"I was aiming for a ... a low key kindness!"

"What?"

"You know, like on Perry's farm! People just doing little things to help each other!"

"You missed, you absolute knobhead!" Tina fumed. "Oh, God, you missed by a mile!"

Above, the huge creature was diving straight down. If there had been any sun, the monster would have blocked it out with its mind-boggling bulk.

"Excuse me, miss," said the President of the United States, pointing up with a quaking finger. "Is that—?"

"Yes! It's a dragon!" Nerys spat. "Obviously, it's a big dragon, come to eat us all!"

"I meant behind it, miss. My eyes aren't what they once were, but those riders coming behind. Are they on alpacas?"

He was right. The president was absolutely correct. Far behind and high above, four mighty riders were descending through the maelstrom, swords whirling, crowns gleaming.

"The alpacas of the Apocalypse," said Nerys faintly.

"I thought so," said the president, seemingly more satisfied than horrified.

Across this new landscape, trees exploded into flame. Tremors shook the ground. The dragon, impossibly huge now, mouth agape and claws outstretched, continued its descent.

"We've got to get out of here," said Jefri and took to the sky, PJ hot on his heels.

As if to accentuate the urgency, something pinwheeled end over end from above and clonked Deacon Phipps on the noggin, laying him out cold on the muddy ground. The offensive object in question appeared to be a wood and cardboard placard which read: S*maller* B*ums or* B*igger* P*itchforks!*

"I think I've gone mad," said Ed, bewildered.

"It's probably for the best," said Ben in solid agreement.

"This way, Mr President," said Tina, pulling the older gentleman away into the relative safety of the trees.

Safety! Nerys scoffed at the ridiculousness of the notion. Gigantic dragons, nukes already possibly in the air, fire raining down from the heavens. Armageddon was upon them, and deep down, Nerys couldn't help but see her part in it.

She looked at Ben and Ed and, even though neither of them said a word, felt compelled to say, "This isn't my fault! Really, it isn't!"

The silent looks they returned went through a succession of emotions that sort of went *"What?"* then *"We didn't say it was!"* then a sort of *"But why would you say that if it wasn't your fault?"* then a firmer yet surprised *"Oh, my God, it is your fault!"* ending with a final, weary and sad rather than angry *"Bloody hell, Nerys, you did this, you complete muppet!"*

"We have to run," she said, stumbling back. She kicked off and took to the air while Heaven and Hell and all the other horrors came plummeting down towards them.

RUTSPUD SEARCHED through the Research Centre for Scriptural Exegesis. Though the pneumatic tube delivery system was clearly visible on the walls and in the junctions on the ceiling overhead, finding an actual interface amid all the clutter had taken a little longer than he'd anticipated.

It wasn't that the Celestial workforce here was untidy. Far from it, they were obsessed with order, but Rutspud was staggered by how much stuff there was. Scrolls, tomes, ring binders, microfiche, floppy disks, desktop computers. These Biblical navel gazers had created far more material than any holy book surely warranted. Was there much to say about holy scripture apart from the obvious: The Almighty made the world then got angry when humans started acting all human. Then it was anger, forgiveness, anger, forgiveness for several thousand years, then, depending upon your own personal flavour of faith, the Almighty did or didn't send some sort of human proxy to Earth to offer well-meaning but not very practical teachings before promising He'd sort it all out at the end of time. Bish bash bosh. Rutspud could wrap it all up in a couple of sentences. Didn't need a whole warehouse full of reflection and interpretation.

He located an access point on a mezzanine gantry between two computer stations. "Found one!" he shouted.

He picked up a nearby cannister and inserted Belphegor's well-considered scroll. He didn't stop to check if Belphegor's rewriting of Armageddon included improved Wi-Fi in the R&D department. It would nice if it did. On reflection, Rutspud wondered if they should have asked for one of those coffee machines too, the ones that needlessly used wasteful non-recyclable plastic pods. Never mind.

He put the scroll inside, put the cannister in the tube, and with an oddly satisfying *hiss-thunk* it was carried away.

He watched the cannister vanish into the system. Codmince came clomping along the metal gantry in his heavy rubber shoes.

"When does the magic happen?" he asked.

"Who knows. It's all down to the will of the Almighty."

"He wants this to happen?"

"No. But He's a big believer in fixed rules. If you do X then Y happens. We've done the X, so…"

"It's always X and Y, isn't it?" said Codmince, almost wistfully.

"What?"

"When letters get up to stuff, it's always X and Y. Okay, it's sometimes A and B, maybe with C getting a look in if it's three of them. But generally it's X and Y. You never hear of J and K getting up to mischief, do you?"

"No. No. X and Y aren't actually doing anything. It's—"

Rutspud's nose wrinkled. His nose wasn't as sensitive as his ears or as insightful as his eyes, but he couldn't definitely smell something.

"Can you smell smoke?"

Codmince sniffed loudly. "Yeah." He looked round, whipped off his sunglasses and pointed.

Down below, on the other side of the great hall, there was fire. It was not a big one, but it was getting bigger. A whole set of shelves filled with books was merrily ablaze and burning with that strong yellow flame which suggested they had no intention of burning out any time soon. In front of the flames, the Scapegoat and the Serpent were leaping and swaying about. It was hard to tell if it was in delight or growing panic.

"Satan's balls!" spat Rutspud.

THE AIRSPACE over Doggerland was as crowded and as chaotic as the land. Not only were there swarms of angels and demons (those demons who could fly, at least) there were also the jet fighters of those nations whose naval ships crowded round this new land. And there were alpacas too! Not just the four alpacas of the Apocalypse, but the earthly team of Aslan and Speedy from the pub cellar. And it was raining fire. And there was a dragon. 'Crowded' was perhaps an insufficient word at this point.

Screams and explosions rang across red skies. Lightning and gunfire and fiery hail were as one.

Nerys flew as fast as her fear and will would allow. Something spun past her ear, screaming. Off to her left a forest blossomed into towers of flame. Something small and hairy came shooting up and hit her in the chest. She rolled, about the push away from it, when she realised it was a terrified little Yorkshire Terrier.

"Twinkle!" she cried and would have burst into tears if she'd had the energy or breath.

There was a roar from above like a passing jumbo jet. The big, horrible dragon had come out of its dive and was passing over Doggerland, a stormfront in reptilian form.

Nerys swallowed, not wanting to entertain the thought that it did indeed seem to be following her.

She pivoted and turned, and the great beast turned with her. A claw came round, talons open.

"I'm not the Antichrist! I'm not the Antichrist!" she shouted into the wind.

As the claw filled her vision, Nerys saw a tiny movement to the side. A pale gold hoof took aim and stamped on the thin scaly flesh stretching between the enormous talons. There was a bellow of distress from the dragon, a bass rumble that hit Nerys with a fetid blast of the beast's stinking breath.

Aslan's cheerful face swept past as the alpaca turned for another attack. If it had found a tender spot on the dragon Nerys was all for it.

"Good boy Aslan!"

Speedy was there too. The two alpacas went higher and rained down more blows on the thinnest parts of the dragon's claw. Their hoofs were tiny in comparison, but pain was definitely affecting the dragon. Nerys saw it withdraw. She sighed in considerable relief. Then the talon swept down and sharply up again with an impossibly fast backflip, sending the brave alpacas spinning away high into the sky.

The claw closed in on her once more. Whatever mystical muscles propelled Nerys in flight, they had all run out of juice. As the grip closed about her, she pushed Twinkle away from her with a final savage thrust.

"Run, Twinkle!"

She saw her precious bundle of fluff spinning away in the hurricane, then she was caught, pinned on all sides, held roughly but not crushed, only her neck and shoulders poking above the topmost claw.

A dragon head curled to face her. It might have been her imagination, but there seemed to be a wicked smile on those lips. Hot dry breath washed over her. Her eyeballs prickled in the heat, but she couldn't tear her gaze away.

And then something flashed past, white and bronze, and the massive head reared. A spear was embedded in one eye socket, and gooey juices flooded down the mountainside of its face.

Six other heads wheeled around, tracking the speeding angel.

Was that Michael? It *was* Michael!

Nerys would have said she wasn't one to resort to lazy stereotypes, but the Michael she had come to know over the last decade seemed to play up to the archetype of urban gay man. He always seemed mannered and image conscious, and not above slyly throwing shade at others. He was not averse to being a little pretentious, and was undoubtedly far from earthy.

She barely recognised this dirty, sweaty superhero swooping round on powerful wings, dodging the dragon's snapping heads.

"Michael!" she yelled and would have waved if she could move her arms.

Michael shot up, through the nest of overlapping necks, wrenched his spear from the dragon's eye, and powered onward towards the rip in the Heavens. The dragon, enraged, thrust upwards in pursuit.

As the G forces pressed Nerys down, she saw another angel, just as bright, just as dynamic, braking against the wind to chase Michael and the dragon back up.

51

Michael flew low, barely a spear's length above the panic-stricken armies of Heaven and Hell in Limbo. The Great Dragon was hot on his heels. Michael could literally feel its hot and fiery breath licking at the soles of his sandals. He could also hear, from within the Great Dragon's claw, the sounds of Nerys Thomas yelling and shrieking. It was hard to tell if they were in terror or fury. It was highly likely to be both.

Competing with those cries was the bleating/yodelling coming from Clovenhoof's Limbo-made nightmare. It had somehow managed to stay atop the dragon's head throughout all its aerial manoeuvres.

Michael willed himself to move faster, but there was no denying that the Great Dragon (and it truly was great now – quite possibly the size of a Slovenia or a Wales at the very least) – could clamp its jaws around Michael any moment now.

"This is my victory! My victory!" screamed Lucifer from on high.

Michael looked up, sweat streaming into his eyes and saw the Fallen One barrelling towards him, all composure lost, soot on his face, a mad hatred in his eyes, and a blood-stained sword in his hand.

Michael couldn't swerve, not without losing the race with the dragon. He had no strength to rise and barely any ground clearance to dive. What hope did he have but to wait for the last moment, to drop to one side, hope that between dragon and angel and the blades of the horde he might just survive for another few moments.

Lucifer's bitter war cry at least heralded the mad angel's descent. All Michael could hear was screaming.

FIRE SWEPT through the Research Centre for Scriptural Exegesis. Rutspud stood at the foot of the stairs and counted his demon colleagues out as they ran for the exit.

"Rimpurge, Pigcrack. Codmince, why are you bringing a chair with you?"

"It's a souvenir, innit?" said the demon happily.

"What?"

"Gotta bring back a souvenir from your holibobs."

Rutspud scowled. "Call it holibobs again and I'll shove you back in the fire."

Codmince gave him a look that said he wouldn't care either way. And on the surface, why would it? A raging inferno was a more pleasant environment for these devils than the clean marble streets of the Celestial City, but

Rutspud wasn't taking any chances. Surely holy fire was bad for demons, and what could be holier than a million religious scrolls going up in flames. Who knew? Maybe the thick grey smoke pouring off these crackling tomes was purifying and sanctifying Rutspud's lungs every moment he remained here. Rutspud closed his mouth and held his nose.

Last out was Wyrmstool. Rutspud grabbed him by the rolls of skin round his neck and dragged him out into the street.

The Serpent and the Scapegoat were dancing around each other in the most jolly fashion, like kids on Christmas morning. Very very pleased with themselves.

The demons looked up at the high building. Flames poured out of many windows. Up top, glass domes exploded under heat and pressure, and a great mushrooming cloud of black smoke was released.

"Mission accomplished?" said Lickspear.

"Hardly!" said Rutspud.

"Dun't matter if we burned things in there, does it?" said Pigcrack.

"We were trying to add something to the accumulated wisdom and interpretation of holy scripture," Rutspud reminded them. "Not burn it all to the ground." He reserved a special glare for the Serpent and the Scapegoat. "This is your doing!"

"We have done our work," said the Serpent. "My goat friend put our scroll in the magic tube system, and we have also spread a little—"

"Wait, wait," said the Scapegoat, immediately ceasing its merry prancing. "I didn't put the scroll in the tube."

"Of course you did," said the Serpent.

"No. You were the one who found the tube."

"And you were the one who had the scroll."

"But then you started waving that big fat cigar scroll around!"

"Which *you* set fire to!"

The Serpent frowned, which was a neat trick without eyebrows, sticking its tongue out to say something biting. Then, in a puff of glimmering embers, it vanished into nothing. Gone. The Serpent had disappeared.

The Scapegoat blinked.

Rutspud looked up at the building. "Interpretations of holy scripture are being destroyed. New truths are being undone."

The Scapegoat blinked again, then finally understood. "No! No!" it bleated. "It's not fair! It's not my fault! He told me to do it. *He* told me—!"

The indignant and panicking goat disappeared in a sprinkling of light with a sound no louder than that of crumbling ash.

CAUGHT in the air between a dragon and an angel, Michael twisted and rolled but knew, in the act, he was too slow, too late.

There was a sound, no louder than the sound of a candle being blown out, yet still oddly audible above the din. And suddenly there was empty space about him. No Great Dragon. No Lucifer. Only Nerys, the Limbo creature, Michael and one other figure, tumbling through the air amid fading golden sparkles.

Michael fell and hit the ground hard. Fortunately, this being Limbo and composed mostly of nothing, it wasn't that hard.

THE DEMONS outside the heavenly scriptorium were silent, staring at the spot where the Serpent and Scapegoat had just stood. There was the creaking, crunching sound of wooden floors giving way inside the burning scriptorium.

"So was that a good thing or a bad thing?" said Rimpurge carefully.

"What should we do, boss?" said Codmince.

Rutspud turned to the Rampant Tunneller, parked by the hole in the centre of the plaza.

"Lads, I'm a big believer that when you don't know what to do, running away is not the worst option. Come on! Everyone back inside! Home we go! And, yes, Codmince, I suppose you can bring the chair."

NERYS LAY among white spongey stuff and stared upwards for a long moment, before giving a heartfelt and well-considered, *"Ow!"*

She sat up. She was surrounded by whiteness. Weird white ground and an unnervingly blank white sky.

She saw Michael getting to his feet. He was dressed in the kind of angelic robes she had assumed he owned but never saw him in.

"Am I dead?" she said. "Is this Heaven?"

"Close," said Jeremy Clovenhoof, getting to his feet and stretching his back with an audible crack. "Heaven's a mile or two that way!"

"Jeremy!" cried Michael, with a surprise and joy the angel never expressed towards the old devil. The hug he gave Clovenhoof was doubly surprising. "I never thought I'd say I'd be glad to see you back."

Clovenhoof patted himself all over, checking his horns, his pot belly and his groin. "I've been a bit out of sorts," he admitted.

"Yeah, yeah. It's lovely we're all here," said Nerys sarcastically. "Where'd that dragon go?"

"In here somewhere," said Clovenhoof rubbing his belly again.

That made no sense, but a lot of what Clovenhoof said made no sense.

"So what the fuck's going on and what do we do about it?" she said. She spun around and realised they were surrounded on all sides by bedraggled masses of creatures; things out of children's illustrated Bibles, things out of nightmares. "And who the fuck are they?"

Clovenhoof and Michael pointed in opposite directions.

"Heaven," said one.

"Hell," said the other.

She wrinkled her nose. "Despite what you said, this does look *a bit* like *Lord of the Rings*."

"And what's this about you being the Antichrist, eh?" said Michael.

"I've been trying to *fix* things," she said with a firm tone. "In my own way."

Clovenhoof put his hands on his hips, surveyed the chaos about him and farted contemplatively. "Have you, though?"

She looked about for something to throw at him, picked up a clod of the white Play-Doh ground and lobbed it at his chest.

"I'm sure Nerys was trying her best," said Michael, in a deeply unconvincing tone.

Nerys flung her arms out at the crowding armies, and the horror show visible through a rift in the ground. "So, this is Armageddon, is it?"

"Evidently," said Michael.

"Can't say I'm impressed."

"Trust a human to be unimpressed by the end of the world," said Clovenhoof. "There's angels and demons, until a short while ago I was a world-devouring dragon. The nukes are flying. Streets running with blood."

"I know," said Nerys and pulled a face. "But this... This has more of the air of a badly organised music festival. Slapdash. I'm not going out like this. We have to stop it." She looked at her neighbours, the devil and the angel. "How do we stop it?"

"Stop it?" said Michael. "It's happened."

She was shaking her head before he'd said two words. "Nah. I'm not having that. God can do anything. And if He wants to, He can undo this. I'm going to talk to Him. Where is He?"

"Well, God is everywhere," began Michael. "He is in all

things. He is both within the world and beyond it. Transcendent and—"

"The big glowy thing in the sky," said Clovenhoof, pointing.

Nerys looked up at what she had automatically assumed was the sun. But now she was looking at it, she saw it was something far deeper, far more complex. It was blinding, sure, but within that blinding light was a myriad of shifting colours, a kaleidoscope, one of those trippy fractal things that went on forever. The light above contained literally everything.

"God, huh?" she whispered.

"The one, the constant, the eternal," said Michael.

"Personally, I think He's put on a bit of weight," said Clovenhoof, "but don't tell Him I said that. So, your plan is just to go complain to God."

"Yes," said Nerys.

"And if He doesn't do what you want, demand to speak to His manager?"

"Does God have a manager?"

"No. I'm just astounded you're going to try to save the world by being a complete Karen."

She shot him a hard look. "The idea of the 'Karen' is a sexist cliché that paints women as stupid and entitled when they demonstrate any kind of assertiveness."

"But that's the plan?" said Clovenhoof.

"Basically," she said.

Although the seething hordes around her were very much in motion, there was also a stillness to them, as though they were waiting and watching. Perhaps they were surprised the Archangel Michael and Satan weren't duking it out according to the script. Perhaps they were waiting to see what she did.

Nerys took a step forward. "Oi! God!"

The blizzard of light seemed to shift slightly. If this was a cheap *Lord of the Rings* knock-off, then this big ball of light was the all-seeing eye of evil whatsisface. She didn't know the names of the stupid creatures in *Lord of the Rings*. She was prepared to bet Ben did. She glanced at the boiling inferno which was all she could see of Earth. Ben was probably dead down there and, though he was more of an irritating feature of her life than anything else, the thought of him dead gave her energy and leant volume to her voice.

"Oi! Sunshine! I need a word with you!"

God's light seemed to turn entirely upon her, and Nerys suddenly felt very small, like a microbe looking up through a microscope.

The ground beneath them shook, and from the hole in the world a bright light shone through, an unpleasantly piercing and cleansing light. Nerys realised there was nothing holy about it, but the first of the nuclear missiles exploding on the surface of Doggerland.

"I want you to stop this," she said to God. "I want you to undo it. Rewind. Start over."

Waves of light, purple, green and pink, yet all brilliantly white at the same time, rippled above her. It was speech, it was meaning, and to her surprise Nerys realised she could comprehend it.

"I don't think we deserve Armageddon. I don't think it's fair," she said. "You didn't give us a chance."

The Almighty pulsed and shone in dazzling patterns.

Clovenhoof stepped forward, chuckling. "No, mate, you can't bring up that whole *forbidden fruit in Eden* thing. You and I were both there, and we both know it was your plan all along. You can't fall back on rules when you know they're going to be broken."

The light flared angrily with a hot intensity that would have given any human instant sunburn. But Clovenhoof was already an angry sunburnt red, so he merely sizzled gently.

"I mean, what's the point of any of it, if you don't get to see where the human race can take itself?" he continued. "What's the point of building this crazy beautiful world – and it is beautiful. They've got these things called dirty burgers now. Like, swimming in grease. You're meant to eat them with your hands, but you can't. And chilli cheese fries. It's like they're trying to make the eating experience deliberately disgusting. It's fantastic. If it's dirty burgers and chilli cheese fries today, what will they come up with tomorrow?"

"You need to give us a chance," said Nerys, trying to wrest the discussion away from fast food if possible. "We need to show we can fix things, that we can be good."

There was another reality-shaking rumble. Another nuclear detonation.

Michael stepped up beside her and addressed the majesty of the Almighty. "Lord, I have been both an angel and a human, and I know which I prefer—"

The Almighty pulsed questioningly.

"No, it's not just the penis thing. I really don't know what some people have been telling you. But, since you mention it, yes, that's a good example. It looks like a design flaw.

Humans are flawed, horribly flawed. They're weak and selfish and so, so gullible. Like the dirty burger thing. I mean, it's just stupid."

"Could you stop talking about dirty burgers?" hissed Nerys.

"He started it," Michael hissed back, then cleared his throat and addressed God again. "The point is, Lord, humans are your greatest creation, and it is their flaws which allow them to ascend to greatness. The joy in human existence is seeing what we can achieve together, despite our individual flaws."

Lights spun.

"Okay, okay," said Nerys, feeling the burn of accusation. "I've had a rough few days. You can't tell a girl the world's going to end and then expect her to act rationally about it. Especially when you put a Wish-O-Matic within her easy reach."

Clovenhoof shook his head at the wavering starshine that followed. "You can't blame Hell. Or our devices. And you can't blame me. I mean, *you* made me, right? If you're going to blame me for every little thing I did, squire, then really you can only blame yourself."

Across the battlefield a creature came bounding and bouncing on four mismatched legs. Nerys thought it was quite the most horrifically pathetic thing she had ever seen. It was a bit like an alpaca, a bit like a child's crayon drawing of a sheep. It was a bleating, boneless thing, the same colour as the weird land that surrounded them.

The Almighty's glow recoiled from it momentarily.

"I made it," Clovenhoof explained, grinning. "Turns out

this making things malarkey is tougher than it looks." He frowned. "But you knew that. You know everything."

Nerys remembered something: a memory of Ben which made her both wistful and angry at the same time. "Ben said that... We were in the pub, the Boldmere Oak, back when it was still in Boldmere. He said that God – you – knows what we're going to do before we do it. People talk about life being a test." She made a grand gesture to the hole in reality and the burning fires within. "A test I spectacularly failed, I know. Really, I know. But you don't need to test us."

"Omnictopus," nodded Clovenhoof wisely.

"If you need to inflict all this suffering on us, just to see who is good and who is bad," she continued, "then you're either not as all-knowing as you make out, or you're just being a bit of a dick."

She had called God a dick. God, the Almighty, Our Father who Art in Heaven. She'd called him a dick. She wondered if she'd get blasted with lightning or turned into a pillar of salt. Or maybe both.

The sound of nuclear Armageddon was now a rattling tattoo of booms and a mounting crescendo of light that Nerys thought would never cease.

"She's right," said Michael. He took Nerys's hand with his left. He took Clovenhoof's with his right. "Basically, Lord, are you going to admit you're fallible and human like the rest of us?" He pressed his lips tight. "Or are you going to be a dick your entire life?"

The light of Armageddon flooded around them until Nerys could see nothing at all. But she held onto Michael's hand with all her might.

52

Michael was surprised to find himself walking through the Celestial City.

One moment, he was on the fields of Limbo, prepared to find himself or his friends obliterated by the Almighty's holy wrath, and the next he was walking on cool stone, through a street lined with olive trees and buildings with graceful marble arcades.

He was surprised, but not alarmed. He'd run out of the capacity to be alarmed some time ago, probably at the point at which he thought the Great Dragon was about to eat him.

Michael recognised this part of the city. There was a beautiful open plan feel to the place. The light and the trees made him think some holy architect had been aiming for a Roman feel when they made this place. They had got it mostly right.

Ahead was a plaza where something curious was

occurring. Curious, but not alarming. There was a big hole in the middle of the plaza, as though a giant's fist had punched its way up from underneath and scattered the flagstones all around. Now, very much in the manner of a film running backwards, stones were rolling back into place and earth was flowing back to the centre. In a second, the hole had healed itself.

There was a crumpling creak and the exact sound of glass unshattering. Michael looked up to see the windowpanes of the Research Centre for Scriptural Exegesis come back together and the crazed glass become whole, as though the cracks were simply wiped away.

Michael was the only one to see it, for he was the only one currently here. There would be a reason for that, he thought, and climbed the steps to the scriptorium's double doors.

All was quiet within. The place was actually nice when it wasn't full of scholars dissecting and re-dissecting what passed for holy truth. It was calm and beautiful, and Michael wondered, if it wasn't for the existence of his small but perfectly formed boyfriend back on Earth, he could enjoy the life of a monastic scribe.

He shuffled over to a desk, glanced about to see if anyone was looking, and sat down. There was a quill and there was ink, and there was a fresh sheet of cream parchment. Michael dipped his quill in the ink and, pausing only for a moment to consider what divine truth he might write into existence, put quill to parchment and wrote.

. . .

JEREMY CLOVENHOOF SAT BACK in his deck chair and sipped his Lambrini.

THAT WAS A GOOD START. A world turned back to normal would start with Jeremy Clovenhoof and a glass of Lambrini. It wasn't necessarily an ideal world, but it was a normal one. Michael continued writing.

BEN KITCHEN SAT NEXT to Jeremy, a book open in his lap. It was a good book, but the warm day threatened to send Ben to sleep.

JEREMY CLOVENHOOF APPROVED HEARTILY of Perry's farm. It was like going on holiday, but without all the annoying travelling to get there. A few minutes outside of the city and he, Ben and Nerys could be in an isolated rural idyll. What's more, the weather was always perfect inside the polytunnel. Sat side by side with Ben, drink in hand, he could close his eyes and imagine he was in the warm sun at some expensive spa resort—

"*JEREMY!*"

The shout made him sit up, almost but not quite spilling his drink in the process. Ben snorted awake and looked round, startled.

"I wasn't asleep," said Ben defensively, then, "What was that?"

"I believe it was Nerys shouting at us from somewhere."

The hanging flap of door on the polytunnel shifted and Twinkle ran in, did a few laps, yapping in the way of all irritating miniature dogs, and ran out again.

"What do you think she wants?" said Ben, struggling out of his chair.

"World peace, an end to hunger, a hot man between the sheets," Clovenhoof grumbled. "Who knows?"

They wandered outside. A sea of furry faces jostled at a nearby fence. Perry's farm was home to a great many alpacas. No one could say how or why there were so very many alpacas here, but thankfully no one was asking.

Clovenhoof pointed. "I think I could rock the hairdo, what do you reckon?" he asked Ben.

"Yeah, do it," said Ben.

"Seriously?"

"It would be hilarious. You do realise it's basically a mullet?"

"No! It's much more punk, but with longer bits..." Clovenhoof paused. "It's a mullet."

"*JEREMY!*"

The shout was coming from the barn. This time it had been Tina. Above the barn door was a new company logo. It featured a T and an N intertwined. It looked like the two letters were fighting each other to be the biggest, the most prominent. Which was probably the case. The words EXCLUSIVE HANDBAG DESIGN were almost pushed out of frame by the squabbling letters.

Inside the artisanal workshop (Jeremy understood 'artisanal' to mean 'can't afford modern equipment or proper chairs') Nerys and Tina were bent over a table covered in handbag designs. Spartacus Wilson sat on a nearby stool, a laptop perched on his knee.

"Jeremy, help us settle a debate," said Tina. "If someone buys a luxury handbag featuring textiles woven from the fleece of an alpaca, is it cute or weird if you tell them the name of the particular alpaca it came from?"

"It's cute and weird," said Clovenhoof. "Obviously that means you should do it."

"It means we'll have to track the provenance of each fleece and track it through for each bag," said Spartacus. "A bit of a rejig of the database design, but that's fine."

Nerys smiled at Tina as she sashayed forward. "Cute and weird sounds very on-brand to me. Listen, I just got off the phone, and guess what? I've got a meeting with a buyer for Selfridges." She posed with a pair of handbags on her outstretched arms.

"Really?" Tina gasped.

"Well, I have good information from Animal Ed on where she walks her dog," said Nerys. "Which is enough to work with."

"It certainly is." Tina frowned. "Speaking of contacts, I appear to have the American president's phone number in my contacts now. Is that ... odd?"

Nerys shrugged innocently.

There were several other people in the barn, working on handbags at various stages of construction. Ben had a particular fascination for the small hand tools used to shape and emboss leather. He had discovered that tiny scraps of thick leather made excellent stands for the models which he painted at home, so he stopped by to collect up a few offcuts.

"Can you check these new website images, Tina?" said Spartacus, waving her over. PJ McTigue rolled by on a skateboard and dropped off a steaming foamy cup next to Spartacus.

Nerys and Clovenhoof stood together, gazing round at the shiny new reality.

"Of course, the world is still a horrible shitty place with selfish people all around us," said Nerys.

"Always has been," said Clovenhoof.

"But this... This is not bad. It's got that low key kindness thing going on."

"Right," Clovenhoof mused. "Does this mean you're giving all your profits to charity."

"'A fixed portion of profits goes to local and global charities,'" Nerys quoted from her own literature.

"You know," said Clovenhoof, scuffing his hoof on the floor. "Neither of us can do low key, of course."

"Nope," said Nerys. "Which is probably why I trampled all over the actual solution while I was looking for answers. I mean, how can low key kindness take over the world? Low key doesn't travel far. How do we stop sin from bubbling up and taking over the world again?"

Clovenhoof grinned. "What do you know about sin?"

She gave it some thought. "Brad Pitt taught me everything I need to know about the seven deadly sins."

Clovenhoof could see her mentally reconstructing the list of sins from the murders in the film *Se7en*. "He doesn't get the recognition he deserves from the Research Centre for Scriptural Exegesis, it's true. That list of sins. They were just invented by someone. Off the top of their head."

"Really?"

Clovenhoof tried to think. "Evagrius Ponticus, I think."

"You just made that name up," she smiled. "If you don't know something, you can just admit it."

"There's a list of seven virtues too."

"I bet it reads like a guide on how to be a nun."

Clovenhoof nodded. "It does, yeah."

"Not much hope for us, then."

"Probably not. But it's all just words made up by some desert dudes with too much time on their hands. The important thing, I reckon, is that recent events have been a learning experience."

"Are you mad?" she said. "We're the only ones who remember anything! How can it be a learning experience?"

"For us it's a learning experience. We have a brand new, exciting challenge to face, don't we?"

"And what's that?" asked Nerys, her eyes narrowed in suspicion.

"How to combine low key kindness with being fun-loving knobheads? It's a tough line to tread, and I am more than prepared to admit I will repeatedly fail. But it should be fun."

"Yeah, I see your point." Nerys thought for a moment. "In my case, it's how to combine low key kindness with having nice outfits, and making sure this banging body doesn't go to waste on chastity." She glanced at Clovenhoof. "I bet that's on the sin list, isn't it?"

"Banging bodies?" Clovenhoof shrugged. "Probably. Who cares?"

"Yeah. Cos if the list also mentions drinking alcohol, then I'm screwed." Nerys had a faraway look of utter horror.

Clovenhoof took her arm. "No more lists. Low key kindness will do for now. Now, where did I put my drink?"

ALSO BY HEIDE GOODY AND IAIN GRANT

HankyPanky

There's life in the old dog yet...

When Jeremy Clovenhoof realises that he's become too fond of his creature comforts, he signs on as a roadie for a Danish heavy metal band and goes on tour.

A whirlwind adventure of sex, drugs and rock and roll awaits this horny devil. However, things take a turn for the ridiculous when they pick up a band of Morris dancers on their way to a grudge match competition in the North of England. Will the world ever be ready for the unholy fusion of rock music and folk dancing, especially when it's Clovenhoof centre stage?

The ninth book in the Clovenhoof series is a madcap romp featuring talking dogs, disco-dancing angels, vintage erotica, flamethrower guitars and a conga dance into the gates of Hell.

Hankpanky

Oddjobs

Unstoppable horrors from beyond are poised to invade and literally create Hell on Earth.

It's the end of the world as we know it, but someone still needs to do the paperwork.

Morag Murray works for the secret government organisation responsible for making sure the apocalypse goes as smoothly and as quietly as possible.

Trouble is, Morag's got a temper problem and, after angering the wrong alien god, she's been sent to another city where she won't cause so much trouble.

But Morag's got her work cut out for her. She has to deal with a man-eating starfish, solve a supernatural murder and, if she's got time, prevent her own inevitable death.

If you like The Laundry Files, The Chronicles of St Mary's or Men in Black, you'll love the Oddjobs series."If Jodi Taylor wrote a Laundry Files novel set it in Birmingham... A hilarious dose of bleak existential despair. With added tentacles! And bureaucracy!"
– Charles Stross, author of The Laundry Files series.

Oddjobs

Sealfinger

Meet Sam Applewhite, security consultant for DefCon4's east coast office. .

She's clever, inventive and adaptable. In her job she has to be.

Now, she's facing an impossible mystery.

A client has gone missing and no one else seems to care.

Who would want to kill an old and lonely woman whose only sins are having a sharp tongue and a belief in ghosts? Could her death be linked to the new building project out on the dunes?

Can Sam find out the truth, even if it puts her friends' and family's lives at risk?

Sealfinger

ABOUT THE AUTHORS

Heide and Iain are married but not to each other. Heide lives in North Warwickshire, Iain lives in South Birmingham and they each share their houses with pets and children

Printed in Dunstable, United Kingdom